# Demon's Sanctuary
## Requiem of Stone Book Three

Julie Boglisch

# Dedication

Hey Mom, Dad, if you are reading this, know it's because of you that this book is even a thing. I could not have done it without the both of you. To my editor, Kathie, thanks for being there in every-way possible, from the editing to when I was grousing about the fact that I could only send you ten pages at a time when I usually send twenty. Your friendship and help pushed me to finish this piece. Finally, to all of my fans, to all the people who have read my previous works. You all mean the world to me. I might not always show it, but trust me when I say, I appreciate every single one of you. Your enthusiasm and delight makes my little creative heart happy and I hope to be able to provide more in the future and I know I will with this new book. So, with that, my dedication is done. Go ahead and read!

# Chapter One

Milos stared at the Demon before him that flew over the waters and landed on the deck of their ship without a care in the world. The blackened wings dissipated to reveal a slender woman remarkably similar-looking to Alex, to the young man he followed all the way to this Demonic Sanctuary, a place that he rightfully knew could be his end.

It was a thought, a realization, that all of them put off for so long. He was an Alertian. A hunter of Demons; yet with everything that happened as of late, of fleeing the capital and crossing the dangerous stretch of ocean now behind them, it ended up being pushed to the side as an afterthought.

Now, as he stared at this incredibly powerful Demon, it was finally in his face and he had no idea what to do.

Milos knew it should have been easy. His goal, his very life, had always been to kill Demons. Alex, the young man he came to see as a friend, didn't count. He was too gentle.

The woman before him was different. Yet, his hand remained glued to his sword, his fingers curling and uncurling around the metal hilt as he watched the woman step forward and pull Alex into a deep hug, filled with a foreign warmth which Milos never saw before. The gleam of her signifiers, thick metal chains around her wrists, clanked and shone in the light of the day stones. It wasn't hard to take note of the scars around her neck, similar to Ari's.

It was strange to think about. His plan since the very beginning was to kill a Demon, a spawn of Satan. It was the reason he descended into the Underlands, where they were now. He hunted this very Demon's scent, only to come upon two strangers.

Alex, the young man before him, had no idea he was a Demon when they first met. It seemed he learned about it around the same time Milos did.

Rita, the woman who seemed to stick to Alex like glue, was a witch, a healer, and a good friend.

She was also part of the reason he wasn't lunging forward as she gripped his upper arm tightly, a pointed look on her face.

"Not now." Her voice was quiet. "I thought we would have more time before we encountered any more Demons." She shook her head, clearly peering past the two family members and to the distant island piercing up from the waters and curling all the way up toward the distant walls of the edge of the Overlands. "I thought we would have more time to plan."

Milos had nothing to say to that. He felt some condolence in her acknowledging that they hadn't thought this fully through. Their main goal, for the past couple weeks after their escapades in Raynout, had been to journey northward to find the last Demon refuge and, in particular, Alex's mother.

It was more than a little perilous and, Milos had to admit, he had no idea the Underlands held such a large underground ocean, or that it was populated with all sorts of strange creatures, from enormous eel-like fish to beings like Suzuhah, a creature called a Vulfulas, that seemed to like to maintain the form of either a young man or a little girl.

Suzuhah hated water Demons and Alex was part water Demon. The last island they arrived on almost resulted in Alex's death and the two groups being separated.

Milos had been able to lead them to Alex, but he was unable to protect the group when the resident self-proclaimed Demon king chased after them, seemingly obsessed with having Alex for himself.

Actually, that was part of the reason Milos found himself so on edge, even as Alex's mother pulled back from her hug, gently checking her son over. It was clear, however, that she was uncertain. The way her fingers hesitated, her eyes glanced nervously, her posture just that slightest bit tense, it all pointed to her being nervous about the situation, even though she belied it all with a smile.

It was a stain, to both Milos' ego, and to his goal that she wasn't even paying him much mind. The Demon king from before barely acknowledged him as being dangerous.

He'd gotten so weak over the past few months. He was taking too long. He was an Alertian, a weapon to fight Demons, and he had two right in front of him. There was a whole island before him.

If only he could just do it…if only it wasn't Alex and someone so close to Alex, his mother.

Alex, his black hair curling around his face as he turned to them, smiled. "Hey, Mom, I want to introduce you to everyone."

The woman turned, following Alex's gestured arm, her gaze locking with Milos, only to start.

For a brief moment, Milos felt the air twist and he could have sworn claws formed over the woman's fingers before she settled herself back down. A reaction he very much expected and knew would occur even more now that he was here, in a place he thought was all but a fable.

"Oh? It's a pleasure to meet you."

She turned her attention to the others, the smile back in place, though a little more strained. Her black hair hung long and it was easy to tell the two were mother and son with how remarkably similar they appeared. "I'm sorry, my name is Valencia. I'm Alex's mother." She bowed her head, her gaze flicking to Milos briefly before she continued, "May I ask yours?"

"Ah! Right." Alex chuckled before pointing to each person. Before he could say anything, Rita stepped forward and, caught off-guard, Milos was pulled after her. He stumbled forward before wrenching his arm from her grasp.

She briefly smirked back at him, the smirk flitting away before she turned back to Valencia. "Hello, my name is Rita. I've heard a lot about you from Alex."

"Oh?" Valencia glanced side-long toward Alex, who shrugged sheepishly.

"She's not wrong!" Suzuhah spoke up from where he was steering the ship closer to the piers Milos could acknowledge were quickly approaching. "By the way, the name's Suzuhah. It's a pleasure."

"The pleasure is mine." Valencia bowed her head politely before turning to the rest of them.

Milos refrained from clicking his tongue, feeling his muscles tense upon noting the harsh gaze on him. There was a feeling of power that irked Milos and made his blood almost itch to lunge forward, sword drawn. Only part of him held steady, resisting the urge, but that part was slowly crumbling.

3

"This brute is Milos. Don't mind him." Rita stepped forward, stepping slightly between the two of them, a gentle hand placed on Milos' arm, not grasping, but firm. "Those two beside him are Ari and Leon, slaves Milos rescued."

Milos admitted, he almost forgot about the two in question, his thoughts in such turmoil as it was.

Ari, the young slave he received upon arriving in the Underlands, bowed her head, the barest hint of a smile crossing her normally stoic lips. Leon nodded, shifting his body slightly to hide the fact he was missing his arm due to a fight with a creature of the Underlands called a Drega, or, well, more because Milos didn't want to lose anybody and cut his arm off as he was being lifted away, but that point was now moot.

"I see." Valencia's voice, almost melodic in tone, shifted slightly. Milos turned his attention fully back onto her, once more locking gazes. "It is rare to find an Alertian so far north. I hope you know what you are doing."

"Mother," Alex cut in, his expression annoyed. "Milos helped me get here. He's the reason I'm even here to begin with and, anyway, we all have our reasons…or at least, I hope we do."

The words were very much pointed, and it wasn't hard for Milos to guess what he meant. After all, Valencia did hold the truth about Alex's heritage from him and ran away to the north, not even searching for him.

Reminding himself of that thought made Milos' blood cool, and it was all he could do not to turn his expression icy, though he might have failed when he met Alex's worried gaze.

"Pleasure." He spoke up, keeping his words clipped. "But I will be below. We do have things to gather for our arrival."

He turned and, without another word, attempted to head into the ship. Rita didn't stop him this time, and he was grateful as he slammed the door behind him, almost shattering the doorframe on either side. He made it all the way to the room he shared with Alex and Leon before his sword was out of its sheath and embedded itself deeply into the floorboards. A mix of emotions rammed through his thoughts as he tried to straighten them. He was so close to a goal he wasn't even sure he wanted, but did it even have to do with want at this point? Honestly? He was more likely to die than accomplish his goal, a feeling that was growing more accurate the closer they got to the sanctuary, practically brimming with magic, energy and life, more so than he ever felt in the Underlands or Overlands before. It was overwhelming and somewhat terrifying in equal measure.

He called himself a weapon yet, as he stood in front of such a powerful being, he hesitated. As he approached a place spoken of in whispers from the rest of his people, he found himself unnerved and worried.

He pushed his forehead into the pommel of the sword, wanting to scream. He was supposed to be an Alertian. He had to be…He didn't have a choice.

That Demon, That woman, had been right there. She was distracted, an easy target and yet he did nothing. All because he didn't want to hurt Alex. In fact, even worse, he made himself known. That Demon knew right away what he was and he doubted it was just because of his signifier.

The red chain trailed over his shoulder, a vivid reminder. The long blond hair caught his attention and caused him to screw his eyes shut to push it away. He couldn't fail. He was there for one reason and one reason only: to fulfill his duty as an Alertian, as a Demon hunter.

It wasn't because he liked Rita and Alex, nor because he wanted to stay with them, it wasn't even because it was the most fun he had in years.

His fingers clenched around the metal as his thoughts screeched to a halt. He really couldn't lie to himself.

Why couldn't he get the calm thought process from before? It was so easy to push his thoughts and emotions away; to just become a weapon. So why were those very emotions coming back?

He heard the sound of running water and then a quiet soft splash. He didn't pull his head away as a familiar figure stepped to his side, dipping down slightly to peer up at him.

The Aqua Wraith, the ghost of a dead naiad or nyx, who had been their guide on these open waters, stared up at him. Her watery figure swirled gently before him, long hair curling in and out as she watched him with a quiet pain.

"Young one. Don't fight. Thou emotions art there for a reason."

Milos pursed his lips, pulling back, but keeping his grip on the hilt.

The Aqua Wraith swirled upward, legs drifting a few inches off the floor as she examined him. "Thou hast nothing to fear here. You are not a weapon, you are only a man." She pulled herself forward, fingers reaching toward him. He didn't pull back as she stopped inches from his cheeks. "Thou knowest the reason why thou art here…and we both know it hast nothing to do with heritage. Remember that…" She pulled back, a faint, tired smile curling over her face. "The ship will dock soon. Thou may be an Alertian…but we hast both seen there is more to it. Trust thy companions, they will not steer thou wrong and be wary. Thou has a good heart, but thou goest into a den of fear for Alertians and the past. I knowest thy hadn't the time to decide what to do, but I believest all will be well in the end. Stay safe, Milos, and fair thee well in the coming trials."

With those words, she dove below the floorboards, her form disappearing as if she was never there to begin with.

Milos stared down at the place she was before slowly pulling the sword from the floorboard.

"Sorry…" he apologized quietly before sheathing the sword.

Unfortunately, he wouldn't have much time to think over her words. As he peered through the window pointing northward over the water, he could see they were rapidly approaching the pier. The wooden beams and rails were stark against the stone that covered most of this land. A couple figures stood on the pier, holding what Milos could tell were ropes, and other forms of tethering.

It seemed they officially arrived at the last Demon refuge.

He did not miss the irony.

# Chapter Two

Alex felt a mix of elation and dread as the ship slowly bumped up against the pier. Mother stepped forward toward the edge of the ship, signaling someone who must have been on the pier itself.

"You know, I think that's the first time I've actually heard her name." Rita's voice caused him to jump.

He turned to her as she grinned, hand on her hip. "So, what do you think? We finally made it."

"Yeah, it seems a bit surreal," he admitted, as he stared back at his mother, who was gesticulating toward the people below. "Oh, how is Milos?" He glanced around, noting that the man disappeared, probably below.

Rita winced before shrugging. "I honestly don't know how he's feeling, but I have no doubt the REASON behind how he's feeling." Her gaze flicked to Valencia before turning back to Alex. "I think both of us hoped this wouldn't happen."

Alex sighed, unable to argue.

"Plus, he was more than a little tense during that whole exchange, but that's no surprise." She waved toward Mother. "I mean, come on, your mother appeared before us as a freaking speeding winged Demon…no offense."

She winced.

"Well, it is an apt description," Alex conceded before letting out a breath. "I'm going to go che—"

"Nope!" Rita cut in, stopping Alex in his tracks. "Stay with your mother, I'll go check on him." Alex couldn't help but give her a deadpan expression. "Oh, come on. I know we argue a lot, but…" She let out a breath. "As much as I hate to say this, I'm worried about him as well, plus, there are already enough people up here. Let me check on him, alright?"

Alex watched her for a moment, unsure, before letting out a huffed breath. Even if he argued, she would do it anyway. "Alright. Let me know if…"

"I'll let you know if anything major is wrong." She grinned before spinning toward the doorway. "We'll be out soon, don't worry!" She disappeared inside, her footsteps descending down into the ship.

Alex watched her go before turning back toward his mother, who just pulled away from the side of the ship with a sigh.

"Seems like things are settling in. You'll have to wait here for a bit, but I don't think there will be too much of an issue getting onto land." Her gaze flickered down below as she walked over. "Alex, sweetie, are you sure about your companions?" She spoke softly as she watched him, a worried expression flickering over her features. "I mean–"

"Mother," Alex cut in. "I trust them. They've been with me, well, ever since you disappeared that day."

Mother winced, her fingers flitting to her stomach before she quickly pulled away. "Yes, I'm sorry. I never got a chance to explain."

"No. You didn't." Alex couldn't stop the hurt from slipping into his voice. " We'll talk once we're on the island."

He didn't want to talk here. He had a feeling it was a fairly long conversation and, to be frank, he wanted Rita and Milos nearby for it. "Anyway, why is it going to take a while? Our ship is connected to the pier, right?"

"Precautions." Mother peered over the water for a moment. "You know this is the last refuge for Demons like us. We need to vet anyone arriving just to make sure nothing terrible happens. You can understand, right?"

"I suppose." Alex wasn't sure how he felt, but he supposed it made sense to be cautious. He thought, with having his mother aboard, it wouldn't be an issue. Seemed that wasn't the case.

That was fine, though, it gave Rita and the others more of a chance to settle into the fact that they were here. Though, he glanced over to Suzuhah, who was chilling near the railing, arms crossed as he leaned against it, delight on his face. It seemed Suzuhah wasn't too worried. Made sense, if Alex recalled correctly, the Vulfulas had been here before with his previous mistress. This probably wasn't as nerve-wracking for him.

He almost felt a little envious about that, but pushed it off. There were other things to think about. For now, he might as well settle in to wait. He wasn't sure how long it would be, but he figured he might as well get comfortable. He took a seat on the deck, his mother joining him without a word.

While his thoughts ran a mile a minute, not a word came from his mouth.

In some ways, he wondered if he actually wanted to know.

~ * ~

Rita quickly descended the stairs, heading straight for the men's room. She had no doubt where he was even as her mind whirled with curses. Why hadn't they thought of the implications of MILOS of all people arriving at a Demon sanctuary? Okay, sure, she thought about it, but never more than how he was helping lead them. The implications were now smacking her in the face and she dearly wished they actually thought through what to do to keep Milos safe. She stopped as quiet words filtered through the doorway, a conversation? The only person she could think of who wasn't still above deck was Milos and the Aqua Wraith. She hesitated for only a moment before pressing her ear to the door. It was hard to hear what was being said, but she faintly caught the Aqua Wraith's archaic tongue and, pressing a little harder, caught the tail end of what must have been the conversation. "The ship will dock soon. Thou may be an Alertian…but we hast both seen there is more to it. Trust thy companions, they will not steer thou wrong and be wary. Thou has a good heart, but thou goest into a den of fear for Alertians and the past. I knowest thy hadn't the time to decide what to do, but I believest all will be well in the end. Stay safe, Milos, and fair thy well in the coming trials."

Rita frowned as the sound of water disappeared and Milos let out a quiet muttered apology…wait, an apology? Did she hear that right? She quickly filed that away for later use as she heard a strange 'shink' sound from the other side.

She pulled back from the door before, instead of knocking, she just walked right in.

Milos' gaze flicked to her, but he didn't react much beside that, hand on the hilt of his sword and watching as the boat gently lapped against the side of the pier.

Rita stepped up beside him without saying a word. She followed his gaze for a bit before finally turning her head just enough to stare at him. "Do you want to talk?"

A faint snort echoed from Milos, but he didn't refute the question. He stared for a moment before pulling his attention away. "Why are you down here, Rita? Alex is upstairs."

"Yes, and you are down here." She pointed, letting her unamused tone slip into her voice. "I thought it was just my imagination earlier, when we were going upstairs to finally see this place, but now I know it wasn't." She pushed her finger into his chest. Milos raised an eyebrow, but didn't react beyond that, which only annoyed her even more. "You're not yourself. I know you try to pull this stoic BS, but Alex and I also know you do care." She didn't miss the faint wince that he tried and failed to hide. "There is something wrong and I can only guess at the reason why…" She pulled back letting out a long breath. "Okay, I know ONE of the reasons why, but I also doubt that is the main one. Contrary to what you might think, we do…" She trailed off, pursing her lips. "Well, you know." She paused once more before throwing her hands up. "Okay, look, I'll only say this once, because I know something is wrong, but we actually do care about you, you know that."

Milos seemed startled for a moment and, while Rita prepared for a scoffing reaction, or even a raised eyebrow, all she got was an expression of mixed emotions that completely threw her. "Heh…I never thought–" He cut himself off, shaking his head. "I'm fine. I just had a lot on my mind." A smile crested his lips as he loosened the grip on the hilt of his blade. "I didn't mean to worry any of you. I am just not sure how they will take having an Alertian in their home."

"Ah…yeah. That MIGHT be a bit of a problem," Rita conceded, wincing. "That's what I meant by ONE concern…"

She knew they pushed the thought off but part of her just hoped they would accept him like she and Alex did. Though, she supposed their group was probably a unique case. She couldn't ever think of a time when an Alertian, a witch and a Demon walked alongside each other, along with two slaves and a Vulfulas... She let out a huff. "Okay, point." She crossed her arms over her chest. "What do you think we should do? You can't exactly stay on the boat and you KNOW Alex is going to want you to come with us. I know we should have discussed this earlier, but we BOTH know that wasn't possible."

Milos' expression twisted into one of apprehension and hesitation, a rare sight. Rita would normally catalogue that away, but right now, she could tell there was something very wrong and while part of her had a feeling she knew, it didn't change the fact that she didn't like it. Milos quickly schooled his features and shrugged. "I'll figure something out. The residents here have probably not met an Alertian in many years." He winced and Rita wondered what he meant by that before he continued, "I'll stick close."

Rita smirked and curved her arm into his, catching his elbow. He almost jumped, hair whipping to the side as he stared at her, startled. She grinned up at him as she dragged him toward the stairwell. "Well, if you are going to stick close, might as well come up to join the rest of us. Don't worry. I'll hold onto you the WHOLE time."

He pursed his lips, the familiar and welcome annoyance flashing over his face. "That is not necessary."

"Oh, it TOTALLY is."

She stuck out her tongue, adjusting her hat with her free hand before continuing up the stairwell. He didn't resist as much as she thought he would, but he did seem more than a little unamused by the whole circumstance. Whatever, he needed a little cheering up and, as much as she might deny it, she was truly worried about her friend. Her grip tightened on his arm at the thought of just how much danger he might be in, only to force herself to loosen the grip. He seemed to notice, but didn't say a word.

It wasn't long before they were once more on the main deck. Ari and Leon were not visible, she guessed they were probably gathering supplies. She hadn't thought to grab her bag, except her normal satchel which she always had on her. Her gaze shifted as she heard pattering footsteps, to meet Suzuha's blue gaze, a broad smile on her face. At some point when Rita was downstairs, Suzuha must have changed into his younger form. The little girl spotted the two of them, chuckled at the sight and then said, "Good you guys came back up!"

"You switched forms." Milos spoke up, narrowing his gaze.

"Yep!" She popped the p and tilted her head, hands behind her back. "Honestly, it's easier this way, no one will question me like this."

Rita couldn't deny that. Suzuha's younger form, a little girl that appeared to be around the age of ten or so, was a tiny little thing that seemed unable to hurt a fly. It was as if Suzuha picked out the most innocent features to use for her female form.

It didn't stop Rita from grinning, reaching forward, and rustling her hair.

Suzuha let out a squawk of protest before glaring. "Really?"

A quiet snort echoed from behind her and Rita was grateful she got any reaction from Milos. Suzuha let out a sigh and turned away. Rita followed her gaze to see Alex and his mother, Valencia, talking quietly off to one side. She couldn't make out their conversation, but from the light air around both of them, it was probably something simple. After all, it was a few months since either saw the other. She wondered if Alex was hesitating on talking more in depth with his mother, or if they had the conversation when she was down below. She had a feeling it was the former rather than the later.

"So that's Alex's mother." Suzuha's voice was soft, a strange sadness slipping into the words. "She seems…"

Rita winced, but it was Milos who spoke. "Does she remind you of your mistress?"

"Somewhat." Suzuha turned to them. "At least, the air about her. My mistress had the same doting air that she does with Alex."

Rita blinked, thinking over what she knew of Suzuha's mistress. It wasn't much, unfortunately, but she knew the woman was a heavily accomplished Seer. She was strong enough to create Suzuha, a Vulfulas, and, from the sounds of it, instead of using Suzuha as a 'slave' like many Seers did with Vulfulas, she instead treated her as a daughter or son. It wasn't a surprise that when they finally met Alex's mother, Suzuha would think of the one she lost.

Honestly, it was taking everything in her not to think of her own lost family. She gripped tightly onto Milos once more and felt him twitch, but he surprisingly didn't pull away.

Suzuha shook her head, and placed her hands behind her head, rocking from side to side, exaggerating the movement of the boat. "Well, enough about that, how long do you think it'll be before we can actually get on the island? I swear, I don't remember it being this complicated when Mistress and I traveled here. Though I suppose it makes sense." She paused, finger to her lips. "They knew Mistress and we did fly here instead of going by boat, so... I mean, there aren't many who can fly, it's kind of rare and all that, so I guess it makes sense we weren't held up like this."

She turned to Milos, tilting her head up toward him. "Speaking of, Alertian, what are your plans?"

Milos stiffened and Suzuha's smile widened. "Don't worry! We'll protect you." She chuckled quietly, shifting to his other side. "Seriously though, sarcasm aside, I highly doubt Alex or your friend Rita would let them even get close to you if they could avoid it."

"You're right." Rita cut in, making sure her smile was genuine, catching Milos' strange expression. He seemed more than a little conflicted, emotions flying a mile a minute, before eventually, a very faint smile flickered onto his lips.

Rita knew she wasn't the only one who saw it, because Suzuha's expression grew more genuine as well. Guess she wasn't the only one who noticed Milos' obvious reaction to this situation.

She heard some quiet footsteps and glanced over to see Alex walking over, gaze flicking to Milos for a moment before his posture relaxed slightly. At his side was Valencia, keeping surprisingly close to her son.

Rita furrowed her brow slightly. If she was that close and that worried, then why didn't she come for him? Why didn't she even try to find him?

Rita held no doubts that Alex was wondering the same from the way his gaze flicked to his mother briefly before he smiled softly at the group.

"I was talking to Mom," he spoke up. "It shouldn't be long before we're let on to the island. I heard we're just waiting for..."

His words were cut off by Milos stiffening and turning toward the pier.

Rita followed his gaze, along with the others, to see an older man. His hair was a shock of white that was cropped short with a bushy beard kept neatly trimmed. However, he moved with an odd grace, his footsteps clicking softly on the dock. The workers finished up during their conversation and were now bowing as he passed toward the boat. At the same time, Rita heard a shuddering sound and glanced over in time to see the gangplank slap down onto the pier, the Aqua Wraith having come up from below.

"Who is that?" Rita asked, keeping her voice low.

It was Suzuha who answered, "That's the second-hand of the chief, and is usually busy with the council. His name is Ludwig Verion. I've only seen him in passing, I've never met him myself."

Rita nodded as the man, who appeared to definitely be in his upper sixties, moved up the gangplank and stopped at the edge to observe the ship.

Rita felt her back straighten as she held onto Milos with a tight grasp.

Milos himself seemed to be almost twitching, lips pursed so tight to be almost white and the furrow to his brow was deep enough to be made permanent.

"I'm guessing he's also a Demon?"

No one answered her question, but she felt it wasn't necessary.

Ludwig's stern gaze drifted over the group, stopping briefly on Suzuha, who waved, before continuing onto Milos.

The air seemed to catch for a moment as they locked eyes before a thin wiry smile trailed over the man's lips. However, as soon as it occurred, it passed as he finally settled on Alex and his mother. "Valencia, I assume this is your son? Alex?"

"Yes." Valencia nodded, gently reaching over to ruffle Alex's hair.

Alex quickly batted her hand away, an awkward expression on his face that almost indicated discomfort.

Valencia winced, pulling back. "He just arrived, along with his companions. You felt it when they arrived as well."

"Indeed I did." The man turned, his gaze once more alighting on

Milos. "It has been many years since I've seen an Alertian in the flesh, many many years." He stepped off the plank and onto the deck itself. Milos's posture, while stiff in her arms, appeared relaxed. She couldn't deny, he was unfortunately quite decent at hiding his emotions.

The man's gaze flitted to Suzuha briefly and he nodded. "I have heard tell of your loss, young Suzuha, my condolences."

Suzuha bowed her head down for a moment before nodding. "It's fine." She finally spoke, the words stilted at best.

Rita knew that was a bold-faced lie, but she supposed Suzuha was doing slightly better than when they found her.

The man nodded, before turning his attention to Alex. "Where are my manners?" He gave a short bow, expression neutral showing about as much emotion as Milos when he was completely closed off. "My name is Ludwig Verion. I am the second in command of this village. We all felt this ship's arrival. It would be hard to miss with such powerful entities on board."

Alex tilted his head slightly, confusion flickering on his features briefly before he nodded.

Rita could tell Alex wanted to ask something, but was hesitating. She couldn't blame him, even though he hadn't said anything untoward, the man was somewhat intimidating in his presence. "So, are we allowed onto the island yet? I'm kind of getting sick of being on a ship." She finally spoke up, noticing that no one else seemed to be saying anything.

The man turned to her, observing her quietly before he nodded. "This is all of you, correct?"

Rita glanced around, spotting the two slaves coming up from below, bags in hand and watching in silence. "Yes."

"We will allow you onto the island, but first…" Once more his attention drifted to Milos. "Alertian, what is your intention on this island?"

Silence filled the space and Rita could almost feel a heavy weight press onto her. It was almost a little nerve-wracking, until she realized that it wasn't even directed toward her, and she wondered what Milos was feeling.

Milos cringed, a strange expression flashing briefly over his features before they smoothed out. "I am here to help guide Alex, nothing more." His words came out clipped and, only because she knew him at this point, very slightly nervous.

Milos…nervous? She felt herself tense up at the thought. She couldn't even pretend to joke about it.

The man watched him closely before his attention drifted back to Alex. "Do you trust him?"

The words were spoken quietly, but Rita could feel the weight behind them as she tightened her grip on Milos's arm.

"Yes." Alex spoke without hesitation. His expression shifted to one Rita wasn't used to seeing, hints of annoyance slipping into his voice. "I trust everyone here, everyone that came with me, with my life. Now, can we go?" His words came out surprisingly clipped and Rita didn't miss the change in wording as his gaze flicked to his mother briefly before turning back to the man.

Valencia shifted away slightly, holding her arm close, but not saying a word.

Ludwig seemed a little startled for a moment, but he bowed his head and the pressure seemed to lift. "Of course, it is only customary to ask and it is a strange sight to have an Alertian mingling with a Demon such as yourself." He turned to Valencia. "I will go and let the chief know of their acceptance."

"Of course." She spoke up with a faint smile. "I'll keep an eye on them."

"I'm certain you will."

With those parting words, he stepped down the gangplank, nodding toward the crew before he headed back toward the village.

"Well, that was fun." Suzuha's voice came out slightly choked as she chuckled weakly. "No wonder my mistress avoided him."

"He is a good man if a little abrasive." Valencia spoke up, turning to Alex with a furrowed brow. "He is only intending for the well-being of these people. Alex…"

"He was annoying me." Alex spoke up, startling all of them.

Annoying? Alex actually got annoyed with someone?

"You can get annoyed?" Suzuha spoke up, confused. "I didn't even manage that, or imagine that it was possible, for that matter."

Alex blinked, glancing toward the group before rolling his eyes. "Of course I can." He sounded a little put out at the assumption. "Milos, are you alright?"

"I'm..." His words came out hoarse for a moment and Rita suddenly wondered if she missed something with the earlier exchange. Had that man done something? "I will be alright." He finished, voice soft.

Alex hesitated before he nodded and turned to his mother. "So, can we go now?"

Valencia, who seemed to have been observing them closely, turned to him and nodded, a faint smile on her lips. "Yes, we should let the Aqua Wraith return home."

"So you do know of her." Suzuha spoke up as the group headed toward the gangplank. Ari and Leon stepped down, making sure it was securely on the pier before turning to them.

"Of course," Valencia said. "She has come here once or twice before, or at least, from the stories I've heard, she has. I've never met her myself."

She turned, glancing around. Her attention drifted to one side of the gangplank, where the Aqua Wraith was waiting. Her watery form swirled gently in the air as she smiled, glancing over the group. Her gaze drifted to Valencia as she bowed slightly.

Valencia's expression shifted to a warm smile. "Thank you for taking care of them."

"Of course, my lady." The Aqua Wraith tilted her head back up, leaning backward slightly. "'Tis quite troublesome, but they art good and honest people."

Valenica said nothing to that, but bowed her head before heading down the plank. Suzuha bowed toward the Aqua Wraith before hurrying after her.

That just left Alex, Rita and Milos on the deck, facing the woman.

"Thank you." Alex spoke up, stepping quietly up to Milos and Rita, who stopped just across from her.

"Young one, tis no need." She smiled brightly. "Twas my pleasure." Her gaze drifted toward Rita and Milos. "Thou journey hast ended, however, I worry there is still much to fear in the days ahead. I have never felt such hatred on my ship before. I knowest it would come to pass, but not in such powerful waves and so soon." She shook her head, water dripping onto the ground before fading. "Tis the beginning of another difficult journey, I am afraid. Be safe and watch thy backs as much as thy allies."

Hatred? Was that the pressure she was feeling earlier? Usually she could tell those things, but if that man was as old as she thought he was, it wouldn't be surprising that he would be able to hide certain emotions.

"So that was what I felt." Alex spoke up quietly, gaze flicking toward Milos. "Thank you for the warning and hopefully it won't be as bad as you say, but we will."

The Aqua Wraith shook her head. "Tis not much I can give." She turned to the gangplank, gesturing. "Thou family ist waiting. I shalt return home. Be safe."

With that, she dove into the planks, disappearing below.

"You too!" Rita shouted after her. She heard a faint chime of a tune and huffed, chuckling slightly.

She turned to Alex, who stepped to Milos' other side, grinned, and looped his arm into Milos'.

The man jumped, turning to him with what Rita could only assume was a glare. Alex chuckled and pulled, leading them in a chain toward the gangplank.

Rita laughed. It was probably the most awkward way of descending the gangplank that they could think of, but neither Alex nor she let go of Milos, and Milos didn't seem to be pulling away either.

It was both comforting and making her incredibly nervous. At least she wasn't alone in the feeling.

Either way, though, she certainly didn't like it.

~ * ~

Milos couldn't deny he was grateful for Alex and Rita's grip. As incredibly annoying and awkward as it was to arrive on the pier, upon meeting the gazes of the workers, he couldn't help but grip back just as tightly, if not more so.

He wasn't sure whether it was instinct, or something else, but part of him wanted to bolt. He never truly felt that way before, but it seemed he wasn't alone in that feeling, which made him feel slightly better.

He could do without Alex and Rita hanging onto him, but he was only partially lying to himself about that. Having them nearby was very much helping his nerves and he would deny it, but he did find himself clinging to both a little more than he should. As soon as he noticed, he quickly pulled back. Rita glanced at him with a raised eyebrow, only the faintest hint of amusement on her features, but Alex didn't seem to notice as they arrived on the island itself.

Milos peered around. He could hear the ocean beating softly against the stone and sand. A path weaved up from the pier that seemed to have been chiseled out. There were stone steps in areas of stone. Wood was set in places where there seemed to be patches of sand and dirt. He could just see bits of vegetation poking out along the side. A faint breeze indicated that this place was near a vent. A large one, from the feel of things. Ari and Leon followed behind them as Suzuha moved to the front, almost skipping ahead without a care...well, almost.

Milos could see the way the girl kept glancing over the surroundings as they ascended, her attention occasionally drifting back toward them before she would continue forward.

Rita and Alex finally let go, but stayed at his side. Milos, surreptitiously, shook out his arms. They almost fell asleep in their tight grasps. At the head of their little pack was Valencia.

His senses were still trying to make sense of what he was feeling. While the man from before was powerful, almost excruciatingly so, Valencia felt more suppressed and yet...

His gaze flicked to Alex, who was watching their surroundings with a hint of awe. Was it being suppressed on purpose, unlike with Ludwig? He supposed that was very likely, but he couldn't much wonder about it as the waves of Demonic energy hit him.

He was unable to stop himself from cringing at the sudden influx. On the boat, it was powerful, now it was almost excruciating.

There were a lot of Demons here and they were doing nothing to hide their presence.

Alex seemed to be rubbing his temples, sparing a glance his way occasionally.

Milos admitted, it was taking all of his willpower not to stop and puke. While he felt a lot of Demonic energy when he was within the Martinet guild, it was nothing compared to what he was feeling now. He underestimated the overwhelming sensation while he was still on the boat. Now he found himself inundated so much his head spun and his stomach twisted into knots of nausea. He wondered if he would be able to get used to it.

"This place is probably incredibly poignant to an Alertian." Valencia spoke up, tilting her head to glance back at him, a hint of something he didn't expect flashing over her features, almost worry, though it was probably his imagination. "You are Alex's companion, while I have no reason to trust you, I can understand that this is probably overwhelming for you. Some Demon's have an inherent connection with magic. I have heard that Alertians used to be one of the beings that held that connection and enhanced it, to a negative degree, unfortunately, for our kind."

Milos stared at her for a moment before, giving her the faintest of nods. She wasn't wrong.

Her expression softened as she turned fully to them, a few steps above. "Alex, you are probably feeling it too?"

Alex didn't hesitate in his nod, pressing his palm on his forehead with a grimace.

She descended a few steps, stopping in front of the three of them. Rita seemed to be watching her closely, but no one else seemed to be paying them much mind.

Thankfully, it was only their small group and Valencia, everyone else seemed to be staying at the pier for now.

She reached over to Alex, both hands holding his head loosely. "I'm sorry, my little angel, I forgot what it was like first arriving here."

Alex grimaced, but didn't say anything and Milos had a feeling it was probably to stop himself from puking. Milos tried to control his breathing, half-listening to Valencia's words. "Your senses have gotten much stronger now. As you might have realized, Demons can sense other Demons, it's not as prevalent in slave Demons, but those who are free have no reason to hide their presence. What you are feeling is their essence, their very raw magic."

Her words were soft, but Milos couldn't help but agree. It made sense. He wondered why the feeling was so faint, even in the capital. Sure, it was powerful, but considering how many Demons were there, it wasn't anything extraordinary, but this? It was noticeable before, at the boat, but now it was positively thrumming in his skull.

"For now, let yourself feel their magic, their presence. It will dull with time."

"How are you feeling?" Rita glanced toward him, probably noticing as well. He wasn't necessarily hiding it.

"It is…" He wasn't sure what to say, but he tried to better sense the energy swirling around him.

"I forgot how much LIFE there was here." Suzuha spoke up quietly, catching his attention.

Ah, right, this magic was filled with life and energy, it vibrated through his body. His chest ached, but as he concentrated, his mind slowly quieted. He let out a breath, finally adjusting to the waves and turned to Alex. Alex seemed to be struggling a bit, but it was no surprise. Milos was used to his senses and how to control them, Alex was not.

His gaze flicked briefly to Valencia, who was holding Alex with gentle hands, worry clear in her posture. He hesitated for only a moment before lightly placing his hand on the back of Alex's neck. The boy glanced at him briefly as Valencia startled, pulling back just slightly. Milos wasn't surprised, she tried to avoid staying close to him. "Alex, remember when you first turned into a Demon?"

Alex blinked up at him in confusion before letting out a huff. "Of course, I do."

He kept his hand steady, Alex relaxing slightly with the touch. "Then you remember how you felt. You were able to control it then, the sudden burst of senses." Alex mentioned it once before, during their travels.

Milos never thought he would bring it up, but it seemed to have caught Alex's attention.

Alex paused for a moment, seeming to think back. He let out a light breathy chuckle. "Right, I forgot about that."

He breathed in and slowly breathed out, relaxing his shoulders. The tension in his neck slipped steadily away.

Valencia caught Milos' gaze, a bit startled, but saying nothing. Milos pulled away and Alex nodded, a faint smile on his lips. "Thanks."

Milos shrugged. He didn't necessarily do much, he simply reminded the boy.

Rita leaned over, peering up at him with a faint grin. "You know, you're not very good at the whole comfort thing, what even was that?"

"Shut it, I have no doubts you're even worse."

"Takes one to know one." She grinned, but pulled back anyway.

Milos just shook his head as Alex chuckled faintly.

After a moment, Valencia seemed to catch herself and turned. "Are we ready to move on?"

Milos nodded sharply as Alex said, "Yes."

They ascended the stairs in silence. The air itself seemed to shift, lightening in some places, thickening in others, wave after wave of not just energy, but air. The sweet air of the surface. He should have guessed that there would be a large vent here for air. His attention drifted to the large overhanging archway that was above them, steadily growing closer as they moved upward.

It was elaborate in its detail, runes of the ancient tongue with interweaving flowers and vines decorated the marble like pillars. It was, however, when they reached the top that he found his breath taken away.

The sight before him was something out of a fairy tale. Beautiful two story homes with carefully placed paths weaved into a central plaza where a fountain sat directly in the middle. Off to either side, curling up low hills and cliffs were other homes, more beautiful than even those here. Up stairs in the center, hard to see where he was standing, was a set of buildings around a single beautiful one, gleaming white in the day stones' light. He could barely see a few beyond, as the ceiling descended to meet the ground far above. He could see people moving about and hear in the distance the shout of tellers. It was a bustling city.

It was filled to the brim with every type of Demon imaginable and, to his surprise, quite a few humans as well.

"Alertian." Valencia spoke up, getting Milos' attention. "You should wear something to cover your signifiers. While some might be able to sense you, most will not, so it would be best if we don't catch more attention than necessary." Valencia paused, peering up the steps to the giant building far in the distance. "I'm not fond of you here, but as long as my son is okay with you, I will handle it. After all, the sovereign made it allowed that anyone may come here if they are seeking a place to stay."

Milos barely heard her, the words settling through his mind as he felt his fingers twitch, almost hearing a quiet hum in his mind. The Demons…there were so many and so powerful. He heard shuffling before he felt something settle around his shoulders. He jerked, turning to see Alex pull back with a faint smile. The thick layers of the boy's cloak lay over Milos' shoulders as Alex reached up, tugging the hood up, startling Milos. "Mom said it might be better if you hide. Let's do that, okay?"

Milos stared for a moment, fingers twitching before he shoved the feelings down, managing to pull back on that faint hum of strange emotions.

He let out a breath as Rita took a few steps forward, glancing at him briefly before peering around.

"There are humans here?" Rita asked, awe coloring her voice.

"Of course." Valencia's voice held a hint of a smile. "This is a refuge. Sure, most people believe it's for Demons, but as I said earlier, the Sovereign has allowed it for all manner of slaves who escape this way."

Milos' gaze flicked to her as she shook her head.

"Come, it has been a long journey. Let's get you all someplace to rest, then we will speak in the morning."

Alex seemed hesitant, as if he wanted to say something, only to let out a breath and nod. They followed Valencia through the town, staying near the edges, Milos noted. Though, he wondered for whose sake that was. Even with trying to stay out of the main thoroughfare, their little group garnered a lot of attention, much of it Milos could have done without. He felt a few glares directed his way and found himself unsurprised. Though, thankfully, the majority seemed to not be able to notice. The few who did, hurried away, heading up the stairs toward the main building far above.

Still, he could rightfully admit, this place was beautiful. Unlike much of the Underlands, it was clean and gentle. The air was fresh with a breeze ruffling hair and clothes alike. The homes were made of stone, like elsewhere, but it was colored in dyes and flowers, some of which he never saw before. He could see Rita flit away for a moment, before pulling herself back. Her gaze snapped from flower to herb to whatever else seemed to grab her attention. He thought he heard her mumbling a few words under her breath about names, the uses in potions and questions. He left it alone, staying beside Alex who held a gentle smile as he peered around.

Valencia stopped to one side, telling the group to wait a moment before returning, handing each person a bag. Inside was some a mix of fruits and breads with a few thin slices of cheese. "We always try to give refugees food when they arrive, so there are many stalls here that will help with said tasks." She glanced over all of them, hesitant. "Eat while we walk. I'll lead you to the inn since I do not believe they will allow me to bring you to the place where I am currently staying." Her expression softened as her attention flicked to Alex. "I'll make sure you can join me soon. Alright? I just need to get confirmation first, but I don't think that will be a problem." She smiled before peering ahead. "We should be almost there."

Alex seemed a bit hesitant, gaze shifting from person to person before landing on Milos. Alex paused, catching his gaze and worry clouded his features. "Milos? Are you alright?"

Milos went to respond, went to say something along the lines of 'of course', but no words left his tongue. His throat felt tight and he promptly cleared it. "I'll be fine," he finally managed to get out.

Alex furrowed his brow, probably unsure how to respond. He seemed about to say something when Valencia cut in and said, "We're here."

Milos and Alex jerked, turning toward where Valencia stopped. She gestured toward a humble two story building that, to be frank, reminded Milos a lot of the Overland homes near his residence. Even though it was humble, it seemed to stretch to either side, the first floor deceptively large. It was actually made of a strange wood that Milos only saw occasionally while down in the Underlands. Intricate carvings decorated the side of the double wide doorway as they drew to a stop beside Valencia, who opened the door to reveal a large hall interior. There was a fireplace on one side, lit with a few fire stones and, on the other, was a desk.

"This is one of our base inns. We usually have someone stay here until we can find them a place to live." Valencia's gaze drifted to Milos. "Or have them banished."

Milos stared back, getting a quirked lip from Valencia who turned back around, stepping into the entrance hall and toward the table. A young woman with thicker features and a warm smile glanced up and said, "Hello, I didn't know we were having new travelers. Welcome." She bowed her head. "Valencia, it's good to see you again."

"You too, Catherine." Valencia nodded, her tone surprisingly warm as she gestured to the group. "Mind giving our guests a room for the night? They have only just arrived."

"Of course." Catherine, the more portly woman, stood, picking up some keys as she moved around the desk toward their group. "Just the four of you, correct?"

Milos shook his head. "There are two more." He glanced back, noting that Ari and Leon stayed back, seeming nervous.

The woman peered around him before her expression softened. "Ah, I see." She hurried around the group and walked up to the two. "Hello, you two. Come, come. This place is for you as well."

She held out a hand to each of them and waited. Ari stared, hesitant, while Leon glanced toward Milos. Milos nodded, receiving a smile in return. The two took the woman's hand, allowing her to lead them into the room and toward the opposite door. "Come, come. I'll lead you all to your rooms. Valencia, would you be a dear and grab the keys for rooms 406 and 407?"

Valencia nodded, hurrying around the counter as the group followed after Catherine. She let go of Ari and Leon, but stayed even with them. "You two seem healthy. These people been treating you well?"

Ari nodded as Leon smiled slightly.

Catherine glanced toward his arm, and seemed to start. "Oh dear, I noticed this earlier, but may I ask what happened?"

"Master Milos saved me." Leon kept his voice light and Milos didn't miss the way Catherine seemed to shift at the words, specifically at 'master'.

Her gaze flicked around the group, stopping on Milos and Alex before returning to Leon.

"Master, eh?"

"Yes." Leon bowed his head, voice stern. "He deserves it."

"Master Milos saved us." Ari's voice was soft, even softer than usual, but there was a sense of strength to the words Milos didn't miss.

"I see. I am glad you two have found someone like that. Ah, here we go." She stopped in front of one of the doorways spaced evenly down the long hallway. They had taken a few turns and Milos could hear quiet chatter from some of the doors.

Catherine gestured to six rooms around them. "Here." She handed four of the keys she grabbed to Milos, Rita, Alex and Suzuhah before taking the final two from Valencia and handing them to Leon and Ari. "The bathroom is down the hall. There are multiple stalls if you need to bathe or shower that will firmly lock for privacy and it seems you already have the food so you are well there. Do not worry. You do not need to pay for the rooms. It is all reimbursed by others. Rest easy tonight. It must have been a long journey."

Ari and Leon took the keys and, sparing a glance at Milos, who smiled at their brief spout of enthusiasm, watched as they hurried to their rooms, peering inside before walking in. They were clutching their food bags strongly, clearly excited to eat as well.

"Separate rooms, huh? It's been a while." Rita spoke up as she nodded good-bye to Catherine and Valencia before stepping toward one of them. "It's gonna feel weird."

Milos shrugged, picking a room. He peered back, noting as Catherine and Valencia left, talking quietly to each other, too faint for him to hear. He wasn't surprised. Demons were known to have stronger hearing, so those around would have to be careful of their volume and distance when whispering. Still, it was strange. The woman wasn't a Demon. She didn't even feel like a half-Demon like Alex. He found himself baffled to think that there were both humans and Demons here, even though he clearly saw it. He wondered if he would get used to something like that.

"Earth to Milos, are you going to see your room or not?" Rita's voice snapped Milos out of his thoughts, causing him to notice she was leaning out of her room, staring straight at him in worry. Alex was near his doorway, having paused as well to peer back.

"Just keeping track of some things, unlike some people I know."

Rita huffed, closing her door with a slight bang. Milos let out a weak chuckle before heading into his room.

It was nothing fantastic, but it was warm and comfortable. A single bed with a window and a few dressers. There was no bathroom, but he supposed that made sense, considering the one at the end of the hall. He peered over, debating before grabbing some things and slipping down the hall, keeping the hood up. There were two doorways and he quickly slipped into the proper one before finding a stall. Being somewhere later in the day, it was relatively quiet. He peered up, letting out a faint breath of relief. He smiled as he realized there was both a water and heat stone. He wondered how they got so many before shaking it off and settling into a quick shower.

The water pounded over his shoulders and through his matted hair as he worked to get the dirt, grime and sweat loose. He could hear footsteps and familiar humming before another door opened and shut nearby. It wasn't hard to guess who that was.

Milos closed his eyes, letting the warm water sink into his skin as he tried to calm himself. He wasn't sure whether he was more worried about the Demons out there...or himself. He made sure to leave swiftly, not wanting to meet up with the other boy. He got back to his room without issue, eating a few pieces of cheese and fruit, saving the rest for the morning. A heavy tiredness fell over him as he closed and locked the door. He didn't belong here. That thought sat heavy as he tried to slip off into a restless sleep.

# Chapter Three

Alex settled the towel over his waist as he headed back to his room, gaze flicking briefly to Milos' room. He felt a bit worried, but the feeling soon passed as he wondered about his mother, glancing down the hallway at the long departed figure as he slipped into his room. She left so quickly, without saying anything. He knew she wanted to talk with him tomorrow, but the way she avoided him, when they could talk now... He shook himself from the thought, quickly changing into comfortable clothes and devouring what food there was. It was strange. He was relieved to know she was alright, but it felt so awkward, uncomfortable. Did she not want to be near him? Did he do something? The thoughts spun through his head, a headache forming in his skull.

He let out a huff and took a seat on the bed. It was comfortable, wide windows and wood dressers lined the room, pulling him from his thoughts as he tried and failed to wrap his head around everything that was happening. He was happy to see Mother again, but at the same time, he wasn't sure how to feel about the fact she kept pushing off the conversation. Sure, he was a little tired, but not so much that he couldn't talk with her. He let himself fall backward, bouncing slightly on the soft bed. The ceiling caught his attention with the wood swirls. So much wood, where did they get it? He didn't see any trees around like on the last island, so...

He shook his head, pulling from the thought. He was grateful the surge of Demonic energy he felt earlier had subsided, either that or he finally got used to it. Knowing Milos was around at the time helped. Though he certainly felt bad for Milos, this whole place just seemed like a trap for him. Alex rolled onto his side, frowning slightly. He was grateful to get his own room, but he worried about the others. This place was beautiful, his mom was here, so it would be safe, right?

He wasn't sure. Especially with all the hatred directed their way, just by walking through town with Milos' signifier hidden away as it was.

He knew Milos could sense Demons, but how did some of those Demons know who Milos was?

Alex sighed. His mind was just going in circles at this point and it wasn't getting him anywhere. He sat up, peering out the low window that showcased part of the sanctuary. It was surprisingly well lit with light stones decorating the streets like little lamps. The day stones shone brightly above, casting shadows over the homes that felt more calming than eerie. He could see they were starting to dim, shifting to the traditional night stones. Flowers, not just the white ones Alex was disinclined towards, were on almost every corner, or at least, from what he could tell. He could hear hustle and bustle from the street itself, along with faint incomprehensible chatter. Still, he wasn't quite sure what to do. Part of him was tired after the long and exhausting journey, but part of him was energized, excited to see something new, be somewhere safe.

He slumped back on the bed, curling up on his side and, after some thought, closed his eyes and began to hum softly. Sure, it was still early, but he was tired from the long few days and it was almost night anyway. He felt relaxed. The melody, sweet to his ears, slowly lulled him into a gentle sleep.

~ * ~

When he awoke, it was to a light knocking on his door. He blearily sat up, rubbing his face to wake himself up. "It's time to get up." Mom's voice echoed through the door and Alex sighed. He pushed himself to his feet, noting he had fallen asleep, again, in his normal clothes, which were now ruffled and untidy. He opened the door, peering up toward his mother, who blinked and chuckled. "Come now, my little angel, get yourself cleaned up."

Alex shifted uncomfortably, but nodded, doing what he could to make himself more presentable with what little he had. At least he was able to take a shower the night before. Mom seemed to accept it and continued knocking on the other doors, waking everyone else.

The others woke and stepped out, almost all of them just as groggy as Alex. Rita seemed to be mumbling under her breath in distaste. The only one who seemed somewhat put together, to no one's surprise, was Milos as he lifted the hood over his head once more, blue eyes watching with a strange guardedness that made Alex wince. Ari and Leon were quiet, but surprisingly or maybe unsurprisingly considering who they were, they were also clearly ready for the day.

Suzuha herself just rolled her eyes and skipped up to Mom with a nod and a wave.

Mom squatted down slightly, smiling. "Hello there, you are a young one." She paused. "In appearance, it seems."

Suzuha grinned. "You're more observant than your son." Alex crossed his arms over his chest, but couldn't argue. "Yes, I'm a Vulfulas."

"Ah, I see." Mom nodded. "The first one I've seen. Are you this one's…?" Her gaze skipped to Rita, who seemed startled.

Suzuha shook her head, a flash of sadness morphing her expression. "No, mine died a long time ago."

"Oh, I'm so sorry." Mom actually seemed apologetic as she swept Suzuha up into a hug. "Well, I meant to say this yesterday, but thank you for helping my son get here." She let go, peering up at everyone except Milos. "That goes for all of you."

"Mom, they get it," Alex cut in, feeling a little embarrassed.

Mom just chuckled and stood, Suzuha seemed a little out of it. Though, Alex supposed, she was probably unsure how to react to being hugged suddenly like that.

Mom was an affectionate person, usually, so yesterday was strange, to say the least.

"Mom? Are you going to tell us today?"

Mom sighed and Alex realized, with disappointment, that she was trying to push it off by means of conversation. She nodded, gesturing. "Come, follow me, all of you. We will meet within the commune area to talk." She didn't say anything else, just led them away from the little hotel. The woman at the reception from the night before waved cheerily before getting back to work.

Alex glanced toward his mother, who was walking with purposeful strides, not glancing his way once. Was she trying to avoid him? It actually kind of hurt to think about, so, instead, he focused on watching his surroundings. It was different than watching through a window. There was a general sense of calm, which was soon disrupted as their little group passed by. Alex couldn't deny that, even without Milos, their group was a bit eclectic. With Milos? Yeah, no wonder they were getting stares. Though, it seemed they got more than usual, considering the man was once more hidden under Alex's cloak.

"Valencia," a powerful, feminine voice called as a woman, a very tall one with snake-like scales coating her arms and a tail that she used to slither over to the group, stopped before them. She actually stood a good head over Mom. "What is this I hear about you accepting an Alertian into our midst?" The S's were very clearly hissed as the woman peered over the group. Her gaze settled on Alex. "Ah, is this your little one?"

"Yes, Sechrondes. He's my son, Alex." Mom stepped forward, nodding her head. "The companions he is with brought him here. You know the rules of the sanctuary. I was hesitant at first as well but I got confirmation from the Sovereign that it would be fine."

Sechrondes raised her head, before she smiled, a fang shining in the light. "Yes, quite. Good to hear." Her gaze traveled over the group once more, hovering on Milos and Leon briefly with an amused, strange air. Her gaze settled on Milos and a faint frown crossed her lips before she turned back to Mom. "I take it you are bringing them to the Sovereign?"

"Yes, we were on our way there. Now, I understand you wish to discuss some things, but we really must be going." Mom gestured before lightly putting a hand on Alex's shoulder, startling him.

"Why, yes, of course." Sechrondes slithered aside, hand to her chest which Alex was trying NOT to look at. It was quite exposed. "I would not wish to intrude on your affairs."

"That's fine, Sechrondes." Mom waved, chuckling, though it sounded strange. "I will speak with you later, and no touching the males, especially my son."

Sechrondes actually seemed to pout at that. She bowed and slithered away.

Alex let out a breath he had been holding for way too long as he glanced toward Mom. "Who was that?"

Mom sighed, finally dropping her grip on his shoulder. "One of the matron Demons of the sanctuary. She's an odd one, but many of them are much like the Sovereign's second in command." She paused, peering over the group. "It would be best to stay away from them while you are here. Especially you, Alertian." She actually turned to Milos for that.

"I can tell." Milos' voice sounded a little off. "I am not dismissive of the strength I can feel from them."

Mom quirked her lip up in amusement before turning and continuing on her way. They came across other Demons and humans, but none stepped up to speak with them like Sechrondes had, though many clearly recognized Mom. They all seemed welcoming of her at least, which Alex was grateful for. "Well, enough of that, let's continue. We need to meet with the Sovereign."

Alex furrowed his brow, confused. What did meeting with the Sovereign have anything to do with Mom telling them…him the situation? If anything, it just made him feel more uncomfortable. Staring quietly at his mom, he almost stiffened. He had been ignoring it earlier, but now he noticed that her hands were behind her back.

She was in that mode she got into when she was playing a slave. Though, now, after meeting Ari and Leon and seeing the other slaves, he wondered if it was actually playing or if she was in that mode.

Was that why she was not looking at him? Why? Why was she acting like a slave here? How long had she been here? Alex felt another surge of the magic he was trying to ignore and felt a little sick. He thought he would enjoy this place, it was a sanctuary, but while it was beautiful, he couldn't help but feel like he wanted to leave already.

Finally, they stopped near a large white stone building which gleamed in the morning light of the day stones. It was a strange structure with arched doorways and tall pillar-like holdings.

"A relic of the Overlands?" Milos whispered, startled. "I did not expect to see something like this down here."

"Astute." Mom nodded. "Yes, from what we know, this building was made in collaboration between humans and Demons. Well, the few humans who were aware of us, that is, before the Demon-Human war." She sighed. "Come, let's get inside before we meet any more of the nobles. They tend to converge around here, for obvious reasons." She moved up the staircase, feet clacking with each step. Alex followed, glancing over it curiously.

"It's marble." Rita spoke up, catching up to him. "I've never seen it used in such expanded and ridiculous opulence." She shrugged. "It's not the most common mineral out there, after all, or at least, not the most common to produce."

Alex nodded as the doors, wooden ones, opened inward, revealing a tall arched ceiling. Light stones were set next to pillars that reached upward. A painting of Demons flying, swimming and walking through the Underlands decorated above in a beautiful array of colors. Alex found himself enamored. It was so rare to see such artwork, or anything like this since he left his grandfather's home. It stretched across the ceiling, sometimes even curling around pillars. Parts of it sparkled with light from what was probably embedded stones.

It also, sadly, made him feel a little homesick for a place he knew he could never go back to.

So, when he heard a faint chuckle and footsteps, he jerked, startled. He pulled his attention away from the ceiling, glancing down from the high arches and froze, barely missing the smile on Mother's face. "Hello, Alex, it's been a while." A warm deep voice caught his attention.

"Riviera?" Alex took a step forward, shock running through him. "But, how? Why? What?" The man was just like Alex remembered, darker skin, chopped brown hair. What shook him slightly was the clothing he wore, finer than Mom's, and the signifiers he wore…

They were not the ankle and wrist chains he recalled Riviera wearing. Instead, from his ears, dangled twin earrings of brilliant green curled in the shape of birds.

"You know this guy?" Rita leaned forward, catching his attention.

"Yeah, he was a slave with my mom and me when we were still at the Grand Duke's place. He helped take care of me. What are you doing here?" Alex gestured, feeling more than a little confused.

"That's a bit of a story." He chuckled, glancing toward Mom before turning toward the doorway. "I was heading to see the Sovereign myself. I heard you were coming, so I had to see if that was actually the case." He peered over his shoulder. "Good to see you are alive and well, Alex."

"You too?" Alex blinked before turning back to Mom. "You are going to explain, right?"

She chuckled and reached out, ruffling his hair. He found himself taking a step back. She froze at that before a familiar fake smile fluttered onto her face.

He never felt it directed toward him before and he found himself shocked to the core. So, his mom had been pretending. He frowned as she followed after Riviera. "Yes, he's a big reason for why some things happened that made the situation as it is." Her expression faltered and she didn't say anything else.

The others stayed silent behind him, the only sound being their footsteps clacking loudly on the marble flooring and the very quiet conversation coming from nearby rooms.

Soon enough, the group arrived at another door with two guards set to either side. One bowed and opened it, gesturing inside.

Alex felt a little unsettled about all this pretense. He also didn't miss how stiff Milos seemed. It could have been his imagination, but he could have sworn he saw a flash of uncertainty on the man's face as they passed into the room.

It was a decent-sized chamber with windows set to either side of the back walls, a clear sparkling glass that caught Alex's eye as much as the scenery outside. From where he stood, they were overlooking what appeared to be makeshift parks, if the way the stone was sculpted and flowers set was any indication. The room itself was comfortable, a fire stone flickering to one side, shedding a gentle warmth into the room. Mom bowed her head while Riviera did a big sweeping bow.

Milos definitely stiffened at that, narrowing his eyes. Had he realized something Alex didn't? He wouldn't be surprised.

At the other end of the room, seated in a plush chair with a desk of wood in front of her, was a younger woman, to Alex's surprise. She had long cascading dark caramel brown hair that almost seemed to hit the floor and was dressed very cleanly, if plainly. She almost seemed to glow with health, her skin surprisingly dark for an Underlander, a warm brown, similar to Milos. It was something Alex rarely saw, though he wasn't surprised.

There were probably more darker-skinned people like herself and Milos in the Overlands.

She smiled, sweeping to her feet in an exceedingly graceful movement. Her gaze flicked to Milos and she stilled for a moment before shaking her head, gesturing towards the seats. "Welcome, travelers, Valencia, Riviera." The woman slightly tilted her head down, voice melodious. "To those of you who have just arrived, my name is Lillianna Ren, Sovereign of the Sanctuary. I hear we have much to discuss." She gestured to a few seats around the room. "You may sit or stand, as you please." Her gaze drifted to Milos once more and, this time, Alex recognized it. There was no hatred in her gaze, just curiosity and a few other emotions Alex couldn't pinpoint. She met Milos' gaze, seeming lost for a moment before turning to the rest of the party.

Milos stayed back, leaning against the door frame, arms crossed, hesitant. Rita and Suzuha plopped themselves into nearby chairs as Ari and Leon took seats on the floor near the fire. Alex, unsure what to do, ended up sitting on a couch next to his mother, Riviera on the other side of her.

The woman, Lillianna, bowed and smiled faintly. "I sense there is much confusion, and that is understandable."

"I'm sorry, but I have to ask. Are you a Demon?" Rita hesitantly brought up, staring at her as she lightly held a hand to her bag.

"She is." Milos's voice was quiet. "A powerful one."

The woman smiled and nodded. "Quite astute of you, though I suppose it is not surprising." She let out a breath. "Your Alertian friend is correct." She placed a hand to her chest. "I have been the Sovereign of this sanctuary for a long time, ever since the disappearance of my sister, near the end of the Demon-Human war."

Alex perked up, shocked as Rita gasped, Milos just narrowed his eyes.

"Wait, can Demons live that long?" Rita muttered.

The woman chuckled at that. "You met a friend of mine, the Nyx who ferries travelers here. Is it that surprising?"

"I mean, she is a ghost." Rita blushed, seeming uncomfortable. "And you clearly aren't."

Lillianna gave a faint smile as Mom sighed, shaking her head.

Riviera just seemed amused.

Alex wasn't sure how to feel. Lillianna gave off a relaxing aura, but… "If you've lived that long, then wouldn't you hate Alertians?" Alex asked carefully, keeping half an eye on Milos. "You were there for…"

She slashed her hand outward, a movement that seemed to silence the room instantly. A moment later, she let out a tired sigh. "Young one, I can understand why you might believe that, but no…I cannot hate their lineage." Her gaze flicked to Milos and her expression softened. "No matter what some might say, I know the truth of that time. I won't hate an entire family, for one person's misdeeds."

Milos stiffened, startled, as Rita perked up. "Wait, what?"

Lillianna shook her head. "That is a story for another time." She peered around the room. "Work is always being done to protect the citizens that reside here, so I must try to shorten this meeting." She moved back to her desk, taking a seat. "I wished to introduce myself for one and for two, to let your Alertian friend know that, even if nowhere else, he is still welcome here, in this place."

Alex felt relieved at that and Rita seemed to feel the same. Both Ari and Leon had small smiles on their faces as they watched a stunned, though trying desperately to hide it, Milos.

"Can I quickly ask what type of Demon you are?" Rita asked, curiosity clear in her voice.

"Certainly." She placed a hand on her chest once more. "Though I wouldn't advise asking those you do not know." She chuckled. "I have no set species name, the rest of my clan and people having either been killed…or disappeared many years ago." She took a deep breath and slowly moved her hand in a strange gesture. "From what I remember, though, I am called a Demon of the First."

"Demon of the First?" Rita tilted her head, confused. Milos narrowed his eyes.

For Alex, though, the name felt strange, familiar in a way that didn't make sense. He KNEW he never heard it before, especially since it was such a simple phrase, but…

"A general history question for you all. Do you know which beings were created first?" she asked, getting more than a few confused glances.

"According to ancient records salvaged from millennia ago, it is believed that humans, in their limited capacity, but powerful sense of intrigue and freedom, were created first. However, they could not wield what we, or this world, I suppose, calls magic. So, to counterbalance that, Demons were created. Those first Demons, wielding the power of magic bequeathed by ancient gods that may or may not exist now helped settle the balance of the world. In those records, the Demons were called the Demon of the First." Lillianna shook her head. "Beyond that, I do not know the truth beyond what I have told you, or what that may mean. Most historical records of times before two thousand years ago have been long lost."

Alex furrowed his brow, and realized she was right. Of the history books he remembered reading from the Grand Duke's library, very few talked about life before a thousand or so years ago, and the few that did were almost beyond repair.

"Oh," Rita muttered as the woman nodded.

"But, onto other topics." She peered around once more. "I have been told by Valencia here that you only just arrived. On top of that, you, Alex, know Riviera."

Alex blinked, surprised, as he turned to her. Seeing that she was waiting for a response, he nodded.

"I see." She pulled something out of her drawer, writing something on what seemed to be paper...maybe Vellum? It was hard to tell from where he sat. "Riviera, please, take it from here while I work."

"Of course." Riviera stood, bowing slightly to the rest. "My name is Riviera, a friend of Alex's and a once slave of the Grand Duke of Lilliay. My true designation, though I'm not sure HOW related it is, is Riviera von Reisan Asmodus the third."

Milos actually stumbled at that, shock crossing his face, followed by confusion. "The lost prince?" He narrowed his eyes, hand on his sword. "I heard rumors that the third prince of the Underlands was kidnapped many years ago...are you...?"

"I still have my signifiers." The man nodded as Alex stared in utter confusion. "You are correct, I was kidnapped by a servant of my father's. I managed to escape, but the family was told that I was killed. I fled toward the south, managing to escape to the duke's, who recognized me and took me in as a 'slave'." He nodded his head. "I hid my signifiers and changed my appearance so that, even if Martinets were to come, the duke would simply explain that I was a child of one of the other slaves and he had forgotten to record my new signifiers." He sighed. "Of course, that only lasted so long."

Alex stared, not sure what to say, but the words spilled out. "Wait, that's why you were separated from the other slaves when the house was attacked, why they were treating you differently."

Riviera nodded, pained. "I'm so sorry about that, Alex."

Alex looked away, lips pursed.

"Once I saw you escaped, I begged your mother to help me get to the sanctuary. She wanted desperately to look for you, but the few remaining Martinets continued to track us down. We had to leave." He winced.

Ah…Alex glanced down at his hands. That's why Martinets weren't after him for a while after fleeing home. They were chasing Mom and Riviera.

"I suppose in dragging their attention away, you did give Alex time to escape," Rita muttered. "But…"

"It was a long journey," Mom said, her voice shaking with pain. "Every time I thought of going back and finding my son, thinking we were safe, we were attacked. I decided to get to the sanctuary and, once Riviera was dropped off, I would go and return to find my son, but…"

"I did not allow her." Lillianna spoke evenly. "We were not aware that those of her lineage were still alive and we couldn't risk her leaving for a son that may or may not be still out there. I will apologize for that, since it can sometimes feel like one is a prisoner when they can not leave for their own protection." Her attention drifted to Mom who looked away. "Especially since they have been here for about three weeks now.

"She did almost manage to slip away a few times." Riviera chuckled before it died. "She was quickly caught and brought back."

Alex turned toward his mom, who was holding herself close, shaking. Oh… He noticed as she suddenly straightened, that facade back in place that he was now starting to recognize. That's why she was so cold.

"Mom?" He leaned forward, trying to catch her attention.

She quickly looked away and he frowned. He pushed even farther. "Why aren't you even LOOKING at me? I…you were searching for me…"

"I'm so sorry." Tears trailed down her cheeks, startling him, the facade crumbling slightly. "I thought…I wanted so badly to find you, but I had no choice but to keep going…keep running—"

"There is always a choice," Milos cut in, words cold.

Alex jerked, turning just as Milos walked over, footsteps clacking loudly in the suddenly silent room, expression frigid.

"Your son was desperately looking for you and you just ran. All to keep a royal safe, you abandoned—"

"Don't you dare…" Mom jerked up, wings snapping from her back, black as night. "Don't you DARE say I abandoned him!" The pain in her voice gave Alex pause as she clenched her fist so tightly against her blouse he could have sworn he heard faint tearing. "When we first escaped, I tried desperately to look for him, but we were attacked. I was so badly wounded, I barely managed to escape because of Riviera." She slashed her arm out. "Do you know what it's like? Feeling like both your body and heart are being ripped to shreds? I thought my little boy was DEAD!"

Alex stiffened, horror racing through him as she collapsed, head in her hands, sobbing.

"He was all alone, in the Underlands without signifiers. He's a smart boy, but the Underlands are cruel. Every time I had enough energy to try to search, Martinets or other Demon hunters were upon us." She took shuddering breaths. "To be honest, when I heard an Alertian descended, I almost gave up hope. If you found me, I probably would have just thrown myself on the blade, but…" She shook her head. "The next thing I know, I'm hearing rumors about a strange Demon, but by that point, we were almost to the sanctuary."

"It was everything I could do to keep your mother going." Riviera spoke up as Mom's voice finally died into quiet sobs. "She was able to fly over the straits, but…" He shook his head. "She didn't recover physically until she arrived." His gaze shifted to Milos, a heavy sadness filling his expression. "Though, from the way you spoke…I suppose that was from personal experience?"

Milos's expression became stony and hard to read. He turned

sharply, walking back toward the door. He leaned against it once more, facing away.

No one said anything and Alex wasn't sure what to say. His mom thought he was dead? How could he even respond to that? He found himself watching as his mother broke down again beside him, loud heaving sobs echoing out as she continued to whisper with gulping gasps. "I'm sorry, Alex. I'm so sorry."

It wasn't like he could say it was alright because it wasn't. Yet, it hurt seeing her like this. She had always been strong. For her to be so vulnerable? It sent a sharp pain through his chest.

No one was saying a word and he desperately wished they would, but he understood the silence and, as he sat, he found himself leaning against his mother, feeling her shuddering shoulders and the familiar warmth and a sense of strange relief flowed through him. She hadn't abandoned him. The facade she put up... it was hiding this, wasn't it?

He closed his eyes and softly started to sing. "(Come little one, listen to my voice. A gentle soul sings of a choice. Hear my call and follow me so, I will love you forever more. Let the waters sing of the time, when memories and love intertwine. Forego the past and reach for the life, that both hold so dear with the coming time.)" He wasn't sure where the words were from, maybe he overheard the song before, or maybe he was just making it up as he went, but as the last note rang out around the room, he opened his eyes.

A gentle silence fell over everyone and the sobs faded into quiet sniffles. "You still remember his song." Mom's voice was weak and hoarse. "Your father's lullaby."

Alex froze, thoughts flying at his mother's words. Father's? He hadn't heard father's voice in a long time, so why did he remember?

Alex paused, noting the others' attention on him. He couldn't help but feel a little off. He should have felt embarrassed, but the emotion didn't seem right. He didn't sing that often, but, considering Mom loved his voice, he figured it was the best thing he could think of to calm her down and let her know that he didn't hate her. To think he ended up remembering Dad's song... He swallowed thickly. He hadn't thought of his father much. He died when Alex was so young that Alex would have no reason to. Although something about his other half seemed to remember and he felt a little warm at the thought and memory.

Sure, he was a little upset with his mother, but it was understandable what she went through.

"Holy…" Rita breathed, seeming to break the silence. "That was your father's?"

Mom let out a quiet chuckle as she wiped at her eyes, sitting upward once more. She gently pulled Alex into a side hug, startling him as she leaned her head against his, her wings gone. "It was. I would remember my husband's words any day and his tune. Thank you, Little Angel. I know I have a lot to make up for, but I want you to know that I love you, with all of my heart. Just like your father did."

Alex wasn't sure whether he felt even more embarrassed or more relieved as he let out a breath, relaxing into her hug, mind running a mile a minute.

"That was the Demonic tongue," Milos whispered quietly, catching Alex's attention.

"Indeed." Lillianna spoke, a strange tone to her voice.

Alex glanced toward her, just catching the pure shock on her face.

"Young one, you have a beautiful voice. I can see why—" She cut herself off and shook her head. "A dangerous one too." She turned to Riviera and snapped her fingers. He seemed to jerk, as if in a daze.

"She's right." Milos spoke, clearing his throat and pointedly avoiding Alex's gaze. "This is the first time I've heard you sing more than a few notes, it is very different."

"It's very pretty." Suzuha spoke softly, expression lit in awe.

Rita was, for once, strangely silent, watching him. Other than his mother, she was the only other one who heard him sing more than a few notes and her silence was even more telling than the others' words.

Alex found himself curling in toward his mother in embarrassment, who chuckled softly, brushing some hair from his face.

"Well, now." Lillianna tapped her finger on the desk, as if to recenter herself. "This is a good thing to know and something that can be extremely useful if necessary." She peered over the group. "I wished to have this conversation in this chamber due to the delicate nature of the situation and all the parties involved."

"Well, yeah, an Underland prince, a bunch of powerful Demons, a Vulfulas, an Alertian and a witch…" Rita shook her head, clearing her throat. "That's a mess and a half, if I've ever heard one."

"You're not wrong." Lillianna actually chuckled at that, standing once more. "I would give you a letter with my seal, but, unfortunately, people tend to ignore what they don't want to see."

She nodded toward Milos. "So all I can say is stay low and take your time to get to know the people and they will grow used to you. In the meanwhile, you can stay with Valencia in my estate to the north of here."

Alex slowly pulled away from Mom, smiling. "Thank you." He nodded his head, getting one in return from the woman.

"Now, you all must get going. Make sure none of this information leaves this room. The people here are unaware of Riviera's true status, Alex's abilities or his mother's circumstances. They only know she is a winged Demon that arrived with a human, nothing more, nothing less."

She swept back toward the table. "Also, while I try to keep my history quiet, it is a secret that others have heard. I suggest you not spread that either, it isn't necessary to avoid, but it's something I would ask you not to talk about." She gestured, as if telling them to leave.

Ari and Leon stood up first, heading toward the doors. They opened them, looking back at the rest of the group. Alex stood up, helping to pull his mom up as well. Mom smiled at that, fixing up her posture, though she couldn't do much about her reddened cheeks. Alex noted that she continued to hold him close, head almost resting on his.

Riviera bowed and stepped out, glancing over his shoulder. "We will talk again another time." With that, he waved and headed out. Rita, Suzuhah and Milos glanced toward Alex before following, stepping out of the doors as they closed with a clang behind him.

# Chapter Four

Rita watched quietly, noticing how Alex's mother, who had been pushing him away before, was now holding him close. She supposed it made sense. If his mother thought he was dead then saw him alive and realized that she could have found him, she would have felt awful. Rita knew that's how she would feel.

She glanced back toward the room, thoughts flying a mile a minute. They went from knowing nothing, to learning way too much at once, just adding more questions. It seemed to be a pattern as of late that she wasn't too keen on. She found her thoughts slipping, back to the past, when she first heard Alex's voice. For a brief moment, she was brought back to that time, when her parents were there, smiling and happy, when all she wanted to do was scream after their death, his singing was a comfort. This time…hearing it again, the waves of remembrance and grief hit her like a Drega. It was all she could do to stay silent. She had no idea what he said, but the song felt both powerful and gentle. She shook her head, pulling herself from those thoughts to deal with another time.

"So, what now?" she asked, hands on her hips, half forcing her normal no nonsense attitude.

Valencia pulled away, glancing toward her. "None of you are prisoners here. It's up to you what you want to do." She paused as Rita raised an eyebrow.

From the sounds of it, that was EXACTLY what Valencia was and Lillianna even mentioned it. She held no doubt they were probably in a similar situation considering Milos was with them. "Though, Milos, I believe is your name?" It wasn't hard to tell she was hesitant on those words. Milos just nodded. "I would advise you to stay with someone else while here, both for yourself and the people here."

"That is understandable." Milos nodded.

Alex glanced toward his mother, seeming hesitant. "What about you? She said we could stay with you…"

She smiled, reaching hand forward, lightly resting it on his head. "I have some duties here to take care of. Why don't you take a walk around town? There is a lot to see here. I'll find you all later to show you where to rest." She pulled away, digging into her pocket and pulling out some gold. "Here, use this to purchase yourself some things. I doubt you've eaten anything since you've arrived besides what I gave you all yesterday, so get something to eat as well."

Alex's eyes widened and he took the proffered money, clearly grateful. "Thanks, Mom."

Valencia's smile was proud, yet sad. "Of course, my little angel." She leaned down, kissing him in the forehead. He jerked, startled, as she pulled away, chuckling. "I'll see you later." With that, she waved, quickly rubbing at her eyes and turned, wings sprouting outward as her whole form changed. She shot into the sky, disappearing rapidly.

Rita watched Alex stare after her, a strange expression on his face. "So…" She leaned forward, poking him in the arm. "Whatcha going to do with that?"

He jerked and turned to her. "Uh, not sure. I mean, besides eat, like she said."

"Well, I know what I'm going to do." Suzuhah, now clearly in his male form, stretched toward the ceiling. "I'm going to spend some time relaxing. It's been a long time since I've been here."

"You're not going to give a tour then?" Milos crossed his arms over his chest. Rita noticed how both Ari and Leon were already gone. He must have been talking with them during the exchange.

"Why would I do that?" Suzuhah huffed. "The last time I was here was over six years ago. A lot changed in that time."

Alex chuckled. "How about just where the center of town is? Then we can break off from there."

Suzuhah paused before shrugging. "I can do that."

Milos shook his head as Rita stopped herself from snorting. The boys were something, that's for sure.

Suzuhah gestured, glancing briefly toward Rita. She joined him as

Alex and Milos followed a few steps behind. Alex was watching everything in a sort of wonder while Milos was more than a little guarded, tugging at his hood a little to better hide his appearance which made sense.

"So, what are you going to do, now that you are here?" Suzuhah asked, glancing toward Rita with a surprisingly serious expression. "I mean, I'm not even fully sure why you and Milos followed Alex this way. I'm grateful and all, but you two don't seem the type to stay here, especially Milos."

"I'm not sure," Rita admitted, glancing back toward Alex once more as he pointed something out to Milos, who was clearly trying NOT to be amused by his attitude and cheer. Alex seemed more relieved now that he knew what was going on with his mom and the situation in general. Though Rita couldn't help but feel more tense, it made her wonder. "But, I think I'll figure it out. I said I would stay by Alex, so…"

"What about your trade? Do you still want to be a seer?"

"Right, I forgot I mentioned that to you." Rita glanced toward the ceiling, the day stones twinkling brightly so high above made her cover her eyes slightly. "Maybe someday, but I would have to get to the Overlands first and I highly doubt that's possible here. At least, not easily."

Suzuhah didn't respond right away, causing her to turn back to him. He was staring down the street, the pleasant waft of ocean water cresting over the road from what was probably a nearby air vents. "I joined you all since I don't know what else to do, but…"

"Then why not stick around?" Rita leaned forward, hands behind her back, relaxed. "I mean, we like having you around and I enjoy talking to you about potions and stuff. Plus, I mean, I don't think any of us have any idea what we are doing now. For Alex, his goal was to find his mom, which he's done. Milos? Eh, I never know with that lout, and for myself? Well…" She shrugged, smile weakening slightly. "So, nothing wrong with all of us trying to figure it out together."

Suzuhah watched her quietly before letting out a breath through his nose. "Geez… Alright, fine. Plus, Alex needs to learn how to use his wings, watching him actually somewhat irks me."

Rita let out a laugh, getting looks from Alex and Milos before she managed to stifle it. "Okay, that's valid." She glanced back toward Alex, who cocked his head slightly. "Maybe we can do some training later. Maybe you can even learn from some of the Demons here. Who knows?"

Suzuhah grinned before turning around, walking backward briefly to talk with all three of them, clearly taking her advice in joining them for a tour. "So, the sanctuary is pretty big, from what I remember. I mean, it is the remaining Demonic safe zone, so it has kind of become the capital for those who are free." He shrugged. "In other words, you can literally find almost anything or anyone here. So, yeah, like you said we could probably find all sorts of Demons who would want to help Alex, though only a few would actually have wings. I don't know how they get products if they specifically are a sanctuary, but it's not something I question. So, since I know this place the most, I'll be a designated tour guide for now, contrary to what I said earlier."

The rumbling of Rita's stomach jerked her from her amusement at the sudden but appreciated switch in attitude. Alex chuckled quietly behind his hand as Milos raised an amused eyebrow.

"Shut it." She huffed, pushing down the blush as Suzuhah grinned. "It's not like I'm the only one hungry, we kind of skipped breakfast."

"She is right." Alex glanced over, a smile falling. "I didn't really realize, but food sounds good right now."

"Right this way then." Suzuhah saluted, grinning before turning and taking a right at the next intersection.

Rita scurried after him, trying and failing to hide her embarrassment.

~ * ~

Milos walked quietly behind the group, his thoughts narrowed down to concentration. It seemed Alex became accustomed to the amount of Demonic energy in this place, but that was not surprising. For himself, he had gotten used to it, but the occasional spike due to his presence did not help.

It was taking all of his will-power not to pull out his sword and skewer the creatures on the road as they walked. Talking with Alex helped as the boy tended to come up with a lot of things for distraction. He also probably noticed Milos' discomfort even with the cloak to hide his features, knowing Alex. Still, now that they were heading for food and Alex joined Rita and Suzuhah, he was left to his thoughts. He was not so dumb as to fall behind, but his attention was constrained.

If he tried to do anything following his lineage, he would be dead in seconds and yet, he couldn't leave either. It was clear, even to him, that though Lillianna was accepting of him there, she was probably not so with his fleeing. An example being Alex's mother.

"Hey, dingbat, are you even listening?"

Milos paused, glancing toward Rita, who had her hands on her hips. "To you? No."

"You are such a lout."

"So, not a dingbat?"

"Gah!" Rita growled before letting out a heavy sigh. "Okay, so, now that I clearly have your attention."

Milos was half-tempted to tune her out at that, but continued to listen. "We were figuring out where we want to eat. While I'm a fan of having something other than fish, I figured it would be best if we all find out what the others wanted."

"Well, you know my answer," Suzuhah responded after a moment of silence. His gaze flitted to Milos and Rita. "I mean, if you guys are okay with it."

"I don't suppose that there is a difference?" Milos raised an eyebrow. "I believe you mentioned that the three of us had a stronger life energy so…"

"I mean, you're not wrong." Suzuhah debated before glancing toward Milos. "I mean…"

Milos twitched at that. Of course. "How about we decide food for the rest of us and go from there?"

"Good idea." Alex cut in, literally stepping forward between them. Milos hadn't even noticed he was reaching for his sword. He quickly moved his hand away as Suzuhah watched him warily. "You were mentioning some delicacies?"

"Yeah." Suzuhah frowned before shaking it off and turned. "Have you ever tried chicken? Or, more importantly, steak?"

"Steak?" Rita asked, eyes wide. "Wait, really?"

"Should I know what that is?"

"Uh, yes?" Rita stared at Alex as if he had three heads. "How have—" She cut herself off as Milos shook his head, joining them.

"Is it really that surprising, Witch? I rarely had such delicacies."

"That's…Wait, really?" Rita blinked. Milos just nodded, grimacing slightly as he swiftly pushed away the burgeoning memories. "Huh? Well, then, if they have that here," she turned to Suzuhah. "Show us the way. Stat."

"Yes, ma'am." He saluted, clearly trying not to laugh. Rita rolled her eyes as Alex hid a smile. Milos sighed and shook his head. How did he end up in this crowd again? Oh right.

He followed after the others as his thoughts drifted. Now that he was here, what was he going to do? He was here, this was the place all Alertians sought after. It was a legend only spoken of by his mother. He paused at that, brow furrowed as the feeling of warmth and blue eyes met his gaze before they were quickly replaced with practically black pits of ice. He quickly shoved the thought off. They had also talked about it, though more with a greed that…he shook his head. Even THEY couldn't find this place, so now he was here, now he could prove himself and yet…

His gaze flitted to the group before glancing around. It was clear that it was only because of Alex, Rita and Suzuhah's presence that he wasn't being attacked on sight. He didn't miss the occasional glance or glare sent his way.

If anything, it made him want to know why Lillianna of all people was accepting of him. He vaguely recalled hearing of Demons of the First. It was only in old storybooks, legends passed down through the years. A distant memory tugged at him and he shoved it away. To meet one who was accepting of him, even though she was there for the human-demon war? He found himself fascinated.

Maybe that would be his goal for now, learn as to why she was accepting, even though she was from that time. What did she mean by the war being caused by one of the Alertians? It was true that Alertians led the assault on the Underlands, which was why they won the war in the first place, but…

"Milos?" Alex's voice pulled him from his thoughts, causing him to glance toward the boy. He joined him once more, watching him quietly. "I suppose you would have a lot on your mind."

He wanted to shake his head, say no, but he found himself pausing at the worry on Alex's face. He sighed. "I am distracted." Sure, that was the word he could go with. "I do apologize."

Alex shook his head, seeming a bit relieved, though Milos wasn't sure why. "No need for an apology. I figured I would ask." He glanced ahead before turning back to him. "Thank you for…uh…" He seemed to pause, flinching. "I mean, okay, I'm not sure how to phrase this but, I guess, defending me?"

"You are right, you are not phrasing this correctly. What are you talking about?" Milos let a hint of confusion fall into his voice.

Alex winced and smiled sheepishly. "Yeah, I meant in there, when Mom and Riviera were telling me what happened. You…well, for one, I've never seen someone snap at my mom."

Milos pursed his lips.

"At the same time, I appreciated the fact you did it because, well…" He let out a sigh, smile dropping. "I was kind of thinking along the same lines."

He shifted from foot to foot and that's when Milos realized they stopped outside of a building. He could see Suzuhah and Rita talking to one side, peering up at something inside the building. "I thought she abandoned me and, well, hearing that she saved Riviera and didn't…" He trailed off and Milos relaxed.

"I suppose I shouldn't have snapped the way I did." He started, hesitant.

Alex shook his head, but Milos continued, "However, I suppose I can't just sit there when a mother is saying such things in front of her son." He peered to one side, looking toward where he knew the water was, past all the stone crafted homes and walkways. "I suppose, being somewhat attached to you like the rest, I couldn't just not say something. That would be asinine."

When there was no response, Milos turned back to see Alex had perked up, smiling broadly. "Really?"

Milos resisted the urge to roll his eyes. "Do I need to repeat myself?"

"Rita would ask you to." Alex chuckled, but seemed to relax. "I'm not Rita." He shifted, expression softening to a warm one.

"Thanks. I needed that. It's nice to hear, considering how beautifully unnerving this place is."

"That's an interesting, if accurate, choice of words." At Alex's chuckle, he waved it off. "However, I doubt it's the first or last time."

"Well, either way, I appreciate your help and friendship." Alex grinned at that as Milos twitched at the boy's wording. Alex's lips downturned as he peered over the surroundings, seeming annoyed. "Though, the people here could stop with the glaring...even Rita and Suzuhah have noticed." Alex sighed and shook his head, gesturing. "Come on, let's get inside at least."

So, they had noticed. Milos wasn't sure whether to find that comforting or worrying. He trailed behind Alex, thinking over what the boy said and his response.

It had been almost instinctual, but he knew the reason. One he didn't want to think of and would not think of. Right, if he could just get out of here and return home, he could tell them of the passage. He could take down this sanctuary. With such prestige, not only would he prove to THEM, his family, that he was a capable Alertian, he would also be able to protect the others, protect Alex, Rita and their little group of misfits.

He supposed that was what his goal changed to at this point. It was weird to think his goal, seeming so easy when descending into the Underlands, changed so drastically.

He followed Alex into the building, noticing as the boy behind the counter stiffened upon the two of them entering. He glanced back and forth, seeming utterly confused.

"Yes, yes, ignore the lout and dingbat, like I was saying. I'm going to have the chicken cacciatore."

"Um, but..." The boy spoke up, stammering. Milos tilted his head slightly, noting the faint waft of Demonic energy. Another half Demon? Fascinating. "We...uh...that's an Alertian. I can sense him from here."

"Yes, and?" Rita rolled her eyes. "If he wanted anyone here dead, heads would already be rolling. Speaking of, can I also get the egg rolls? The pork ones?"

"Nice segue." Alex chuckled, walking over.

"My specialty." She grinned as the boy watched them all warily before nodding.

"So, this is the menu?" Alex glanced up. "Are we eating here?"

"Nah, I figured we would get our food and sit outside." Rita shrugged. "Suzuhah mentioned there was a park nearby that's usually pretty quiet during the day."

Alex nodded before turning to the boy, who glanced toward him, wary. Alex smiled. "Ah, sorry. I don't even know what some of this stuff is. Any recommendations?"

Milos stepped forward, only slightly surprised to see the boy relaxing as Alex spoke. "Oh, uh, sure?" He glanced up. "I usually recommend fish meals, but I suppose you probably want something else?"

Alex nodded, peering over the menu. Milos followed his gaze, surprised when he found a certain dish there.

He hadn't had that in ages…

"Alex, you mind?" he asked quietly, causing Alex to glance over.

"Oh, you know what you want?"

Milos nodded, turning to the cashier, who, while relaxed, was still a little nervous. "I will have the garlic butter steak."

"Oh, uh…we're o—"

"Oh! I heard that steak is pretty good, I think I'll try it too." Alex perked up, glancing back toward the boy, a strange expression on his face. "Make that two please."

"Wait, there was steak?" Rita stared up and pouted. "Shoot, I didn't even see that."

"Really? That's why I led you here." Suzuhah shook his head, chuckling.

"But there were so many options!"

Milos ignored the banter to one side as he noticed the hesitation on the Cashier's face. It was clear he had been about to say no to Milos. If even Alex caught on…

"Yes. Of course." He nodded and quickly jotted everything down.

"Thanks." Alex smiled, causing the boy to nod, quickly hurrying away. Milos didn't miss the hint of red.

This wasn't the first time and, after hearing Alex's proper singing voice, he wasn't surprised that someone, especially anyone with Demonic blood, would be flustered.

It was something he would have to talk to Alex about later when they had a moment. They touched upon it when they first met, but he supposed, now that he had a better understanding, he might be able to better figure out what was going on.

"Well, that was a hassle." Rita rolled her eyes, arms crossed. "I mean, did you see the way he was watching Milos the whole time? I mean, come on, I love the idea of slapping the lout, but that? That's just ridiculous."

"You should try it sometime." Milos spoke up, peering sidelong toward Rita. "I suppose that would be good training to see if you can actually hit me, something we need to get back on."

"Oh right." Alex winced.

"Training?" Suzuhah perked up.

"Yeah, it was something we were doing before meeting you. Kind of hard to continue when we were hiding, well…" Alex gestured toward himself as Suzuhah nodded.

"I'm guessing Milos was doing the training?" He turned to Milos. "Now I'm curious. I don't get to go all out in my Vulfulas form often, what do you say to a one on one, for training?"

Milos felt a sudden surge at the thought, a smile slowly curled onto his lips. "I suppose it's been a while for myself as well and I need some time to deal."

"In other words, blow off some steam?" Rita grinned before her expression softened. "But, uh, isn't it a bit unfair? Suzuhah is literally a beast that can shoot lightning."

"Yes, and?" Milos turned to her, using her words back on her. She raised a finger to argue before letting it drop with a groan.

"For once? I legit don't have an argument simply because of the sheer stupidity of it."

"Oh, come on, Rita. You know you want to see it." Alex grinned, getting a glare from the girl. He turned to Milos. "Just, she's right," he paused and turned to Suzuhah. "To be honest, I'm not sure which of you

I'm more worried about."

Suzuhah actually appeared annoyed at that.

"As much as I do appreciate the idea and words. I suppose it would be best to hold off." Milos peered over his shoulder, catching a few eyes that were watching their group. "As Lillianna said, I suppose I should lay low and take some time."

Alex winced before glancing around. "Well, we can't do it here anyway. Why don't we eat for now and maybe look for a place you two can fight later. There should be someplace nearby. I mean, Demons are known for instinct and stuff…" He winced. "So I mean, it's definitely likely there would be a place to settle disputes, though this isn't one."

"It's something to consider." Milos finally amended, letting out a sigh. "It is also something I would rather the community not be there for."

The others seemed to agree, because they all fell silent, waiting for the food.

It took a while and, Milos had no doubt, it would have never happened if it was just himself.

"You know?" Rita glanced over. "The people here don't seem to mind Alex, probably because of his mom. It would probably be better for the lout to stay with you."

"That's what I was figuring." Alex shrugged. "No offense, Rita, but you and Milos do NOT work well together…"

"Not offended in the slightest." Milos and Rita spoke at the same time, only to pause.

Suzuhah snorted as Rita slapped her face with her hand. Alex just laughed.

Milos, on the other hand, wasn't sure how to respond, finding himself both annoyed and somewhat impressed at the timing.

"Ah-hem…" Rita cleared her throat. "Where is he anyway? Does it seriously take that long for food? According to Suzuhah, this is supposed to be a faster location."

"Those two did buy steak," Suzuhah pointed out.

Rita rolled her eyes, hands on her hips. "Yeah, and? We ordered a while ago. What, are they having a conversation in the back or something? Catching the darn things?" She shook her head and sighed.

"So, uh, yeah, where did Ari and Leon go?" Alex spoke up as the silence seemed to lengthen after that, words almost stumbling out of his mouth to break the tension.

Milos turned to him, pulling away from watching Rita's heavy disappointment in bemusement. "I told them to enjoy themselves. The people here don't know them, and are probably not aware of their connections. I figured they should have some time to walk around before things get messy."

Rita's smile through her palm caught him by surprise, unlike the sound of footsteps as the cashier returned, carrying a bunch of bowls and pots. He watched Alex specifically, not looking at the others. "Your food, sir." He bowed his head.

"How much?" Alex reached into his pocket as the boy hesitated.

"Uh...twenty-five gold?"

Milos frowned slightly, was it cheaper or more expensive? It was hard to tell. Alex nodded, handing it over, though Milos did notice the way he cringed, looking dejectedly at the gold as it left.

*I guess it was a lot,* he thought.

Alex took the food, contained in what seemed to be cheaply made pots. He seemed to wince in pain from the heat, but ignored it, turning to the group. "Suzuhah? Mind showing the way?"

"Fine, fine." He waved and hurried out the door. Rita followed with Milos a step behind.

He heard a sound and glanced back. The boy grabbed Alex's arm and was whispering something to him.

Alex, in a rare moment that Milos found unnerving, pulled away and turned toward the boy, glaring. "I appreciate the words." He spoke through gritted teeth. "However, that MAN is my friend and ALLY. So shut up and leave us alone." At that, he swung around and stormed out, moving past Milos.

Milos quickly stepped back, not wanting to get in his way.

Alex, angry? It was practically unheard of. Milos wasn't even sure he wanted to know what could have caused it. He hesitantly followed, only slightly curious.

"Oh, took you long—" Rita's mouth snapped shut as Suzuhah's eyes widened.

"Oh, what did that poor bloke do to piss you off?" Suzuhah spoke up.

Alex let out a breath, slumping his shoulders as he handed the pots over, Suzuhah and Rita quickly took them, clearly not wanting to worry him more as well.

"All the glares and interactions have been getting to me." Alex shook his head. "I shouldn't have snapped, but…"

"What did that boy say to you?" Milos spoke up, arms crossed over his chest. He knew Alex needed to get it out, the boy would let it fester otherwise.

He hesitated before sighing, turning to Milos. "He said that…urgh…I'll paraphrase slightly. A person like you shouldn't be here and someone like myself shouldn't reduce myself so low as to be working with you." He twitched at that and Milos felt his grip tighten on the sword hilt.

"Oh, you have GOT to be kidding me." Rita spat, glaring back. "Considering it's you, I'm guessing the words he used were not as friendly." Alex shook his head as she clicked her tongue. "People should mind their own damn business, shvite like this is what pisses me off."

"I can understand why he would say such a thing." Milos gestured. "Alex obviously would have standing here—"

"Shut it," Rita snapped, causing Milos to actually snap his mouth shut, surprised as she got right into his face. "I am SICK and TIRED of 'standing' this and 'position' that. It's the reason that my parents are dead." She pursed her lips, pulling in a deep centering breath. "A random freaking stranger should not be telling any of us who we should be hanging out with or who we talk too."

"Rita's right." Alex turned to Milos, seeming to no longer be as angered. "I don't get why people always act like that around me, but I suppose it doesn't matter. You've helped us a lot since we all joined up, they have no right to say anything about it." He sighed. "Sadly, I don't think this is going to be the last time."

"You're right." Suzuhah spoke up, arms crossed over his chest, expression even. "I don't remember this sort of animosity when I was last here."

Rita clicked her tongue and turned to Suzuhah. "I hope this place you know is away from these people, because I am THIS close to slapping someone."

Milos kept his mouth shut, not sure how to feel about everyone's words. Sure, they mentioned it before, but… It was strange, he supposed he wasn't used to hearing such things before now, or ever, for that matter.

"Yeah, this way." Suzuhah gestured, walking toward an alleyway between buildings. Milos shook his head, pulling himself from his downward thoughts. They moved quietly through the city, a mixture of annoyance, wariness and other emotions swirling around the group.

It was strange, they didn't need to defend him. The people here had every right to feel the way they do. He was an Alertian, nothing more, nothing less.

And yet, he knew well enough that the people he was with didn't see him like that. It made him curious. Did they actually see him as something or someone besides an Alertian?

Did he want that?

His thoughts kept ricocheting back and forth. He swore he found his determination as they arrived at the sanctuary, but as he continued to stay with the others, he found himself uncertain. He was supposed to be a weapon, but… He placed a hand to his head, grimacing. Gold hair spilled over his shoulder, the red chain clinking in his ear, barely hidden by the cloak which he felt was barely doing anything.

He was an Alertian, that was always his goal, to prove himself, and yet, at the same time, he wasn't sure he wanted that anymore.

He needed to speak with Lillianna again, he needed to know why she said what she did.

"Here we are." Suzuhah's voice caught his attention. He slowly pulled his hand away to peer over. To one side, slightly hidden between buildings, was a white gate that Suzuhah pushed open. Rita stepped in while Alex glanced back toward him, gesturing.

He hesitated before slowly moving forward, Alex a step behind, as Suzuhah closed the gate.

Milos was surprised he noticed the place at all, considering how well it disappeared into the background.

The little area was actually bigger than he expected. And, it was beautiful. A spring curved through the ground, the ground itself, instead of rock, actually had something he hadn't seen in the Underlands before.

Dirt and clay and green as emerald grass.

The air was sweet with the scent of flowers that lined the sides, and a single tree, slightly old and crippled, but still alive, sat in the middle near some stone benches.

"Whoa…" Rita glanced around, shocked. "I've never seen some of these plants before."

Alex just seemed stunned into silence.

Milos, however, found himself kneeling on one knee, hand gently feeling over the soft grass which tickled his skin. It was strange, the dirt clung to his fingers so much like above. It stained his hand, but he didn't much care.

If anything, it made him feel homesick.

"My mistress loved this place when we came here. There are other larger parks with more trees and flowers, but this one is just so quiet and peaceful." Suzuhah walked over, staring up at the tree. The boughs and limbs were bent toward the ground, almost sagging, but still holding strong. He reached up, hand tracing over the bark. "It's nice to be back here again."

Rita took a seat on the stone bench, pulling out her food while examining the little nook. Milos debated before deciding to sit on the soft grass, though he knew it was improper and he really shouldn't. He pressed his back against the stone wall to one side of the gate, not that far from the spring.

"Lout, what are you doing over there?" Rita called, catching his attention.

"Appreciating some peace and quiet, don't ruin it."

Rita huffed, but didn't bring it up again. Suzuhah joined her and Alex seemed uncertain where to go before just plopping down between them and pulling out his food. He paused, glancing between the bowls and feeling them, before handing one to Milos. Milos gratefully took it, noting the gentle heat from it, indicating it was still warm, and opened the pot, or bowl in his and Alex's cases, he supposed. It smelled wonderful and it very quickly made him miss home, something he quickly pushed away. He took a bite, noting just how delicate the flavors were, how the steak and butter just seemed to melt into his mouth.

Alex wrinkled his nose and frowned, poking at the inside of his bowl before shrugging and pulling off a piece of steak, taking a bite. Milos noticed as he chewed for a moment before quickly spitting it out, letting out a cry of pain. He reached a hand up as a bit of blood trickled past his lips. Milos stiffened as Rita jerked, glancing up. "Alex!" She quickly put her food down and hurried over.

Alex grimaced and shoved the food away.

"What happened?" Milos shifted over, narrowing his eyes.

Alex hissed. "My mouth…" was all he said. Rita hesitated before reaching up.

"Can I?"

Alex just nodded.

Rita lightly pulled at his jaw, glancing at his mouth before wincing. "Yeah, something cut in…" She paused and grimaced before reaching up. "Hold on." Two fingers reached in and Alex seemed more than a little uncomfortable.

Milos found his hand very quickly wrapped around his sword when Rita withdrew, holding a small metal shard coated in blood.

Alex paled, hand reaching for his throat in horror.

"What the—Are you kidding me?" Suzuhah peered over, anger flashing over his face. "That's obviously a big piece, there's no way someone cooking food would MISS that."

"They didn't." Milos spoke up, peering down at the bowl. It was cooked, just like his own, but as if just thrown on to give the appearance. To one side, he could see a white note sticking out.

"Here, drink this, it should help seal the wounds. Thank the HEAVENS I made some on the ship and that the shard didn't go in too deep or hit a blood vessel." Rita reached into her bag, handing a bottle over to Alex, who took it and quickly downed it, grimacing.

He must have been hurting, and Milos wasn't surprised. He pulled out the note and swiftly read through it. "Cursed Alertian, You should have never been born, scum of traitors. Don't you dare touch or stay by HIM.

You have been warned."

While most of the letter, he could have probably ignored, there was one line that hurt much more than he would like to admit and only solidified what he thought.

Alex watched him, hand over his lips as Rita dug into her bag. Suzuhah stood off to one side, arms crossed and foot tapping, anger flaring on his face as he glared toward the entrance, clearly wanting to move but holding still.

Milos felt sick, something he was not used to. His stomach twisted as he realized what happened. That meal was intended for him, but Alex, being Alex, gave him the warm one, probably not even realizing.

Alex carefully took the letter from his hand before reading it over. "Rita." His voice was deadly serious as he passed it over, the word only slightly muffled by pain as he wiped a bit of blood from his lips. The girl swiped it up as Milos steadied himself, keeping his expression impassive and form straight. He was not going to show he was shaken.

Rita stared at it before crinkling it up in her hand jerking to her feet. Without a word, she started heading toward the gate.

"Rita?" Alex got to his feet, his voice a strange mix of angry and calm.

"I have a few words…" Rita's fingers curled around the handle of the gate and Milos could almost swear he heard creaking with how tightly she was holding it. "A lot of words and a few potions to give to those bastards."

"Rita." Alex cut in, taking a step forward. Clearly, it hurt for him to speak, but he was. "Believe me, I want to do something too, but if we go back now and make a scene, it'll only make it worse for Milos. I don't want that. We'll tell Mom and Lillianna, they can do something, but if we go charging back, then…" Alex trailed off, coughing slightly as he quickly put a hand to his mouth, wincing.

Rita growled before slamming her forehead onto the gate, her shoulders slumping.

"Alex is right." Suzuhah walked over, putting a hand on Rita's shoulder. "And, hey, you are a witch and I'm a Vulfulas, we can get them back subtly another time, where it won't endanger Milos or Alex. For now…"

"I get it." Rita spoke through gritted teeth before slowly pushing herself up and hurrying back to Alex. "And you shouldn't have talked that much." She pulled out another bottle, clearly finding it quickly before shoving it into his hands. "Drink this and you…" she turned to Milos who stiffened, unsure how to respond.

He was angry for Alex, no doubt, but he also felt off because that had been for him, not the boy.

"Milos." Rita got into his face, startling him. "I saw Alex debating earlier and you both got the same thing. This was clearly meant for you. What would you have done if Alex hadn't taken it?"

Milos stiffened, surprised. That was usually something Alex would have noted or said, not Rita. Milos wasn't sure how to respond. He kept his mouth shut, unable to say anything because he wasn't sure what he would have done. No, he did, he would have remained silent, simply putting the food to the side and pulling out the shard later. But he knew answering with that would only end badly. Alex and Rita clearly already knew the answer anyway, especially considering the way Rita's face contorted at his silence. She clicked her tongue and turned away, glaring at the gate.

He subtly took a deep breath, trying to force the thoughts away, instead turning his attention back to the group.

Suzuhah was pacing back and forth, clearly not as angry as he was initially. "Okay, okay, so we'll deal with the implications of what they did later, but, for now, why would they even do that? It's completely impractical. Milos and Alex bought the same thing, they could have and did hurt Alex, so why?"

"Hatred." Rita spoke quietly as she squatted down next to Alex. "Hatred can completely twist a person… make them do stupid things. I should know." Her words were soft and it took Milos a minute before he pieced together why she said that. He winced, remembering the reason behind her parents' death, or more so, the one behind it.

Silence pervaded the once calm garden, Milos turned back to Alex, filling the silence. "How do you feel? I'm guessing the witch's potion is kicking in?"

Alex nodded, sending a grateful look toward Rita, who waved it off, before turning back to him. "Yeah, thanks." He paused. "I guess I'm glad I noticed before I tried to swallow it or something." He gulped. "That could have been VERY bad." He shook his head. "Still, this is ridiculous. They know nothing about you. Why can someone hate someone they've never met so much?"

That question lingered for a moment.

"I suppose it would be easy." Rita pushed herself to her feet, startling the group as she looked up toward the roof. "When all you've heard is horror stories, whether that be about Demons or Demon Hunters, then when you meet one, your perception is already twisted. Think about it, no one would imagine our group could function together, we're from completely different societies, cultures…we're completely different people." She turned to face them once more, determination on her face. "Could any of you have even imagined a group like us traveling together? I certainly couldn't, not before…" She trailed off before shaking her head. "We're the unusual and unusual can be terrifying."

"And where there is terror or fear…anger and hatred soon follow." Suzuhah spoke softly, looking down at his hands. "As I very much know."

"I guess." Alex winced. "I just wish that wasn't the case." He sighed and shook his head. "I've lost my appetite, but the rest of you still have food left."

"That food is going straight in someone's face to be frank." Rita crossed her arms over her chest. "I'll find something else to eat later."

Milos watched them quietly. He still wasn't sure what to feel, but warmth was not one of them. He closed his eyes, taking deep breaths before pushing himself to his feet. "For now, we should inform the sovereign and then I will be returning to whatever room we are directed towards. I believe your mother did state she would be returning to tell us more than just a few lines."

Alex nodded, standing as well. "I'll join you, I have a question for her." He glanced toward Rita and Suzuhah. "What about you two?"

Rita looked back at her still steaming plate. "Something a little… devilish." Alex seemed to shiver as Milos decided not to acknowledge the malicious grin on her face.

"I'll join you." Suzuhah spoke, a strange tone to his voice. "I want to check up on some things, I feel like there's more to this than meets the eye."

Rita nodded before looking toward Milos, who very much wanted to argue. "If you say this isn't necessary, I WILL force a potion down your throat to silence that voice of yours for the rest of the day," Rita said, glaring at Milos. "If you want to know, I'm doing this more for myself than you."

"Liar," Alex whispered under his breath, something Milos just faintly caught. Rita twitched, but didn't take the bait.

"Either way, I need to get ingredients and Suzuhah can show me around. I won't have to watch my back every five feet." She shrugged, arms crossed over her chest. "Plus, I can't help but find myself curious about this place and maybe I might find something to eat that isn't laced with something…after I take care of what I want to take care of."

"Do you want me to bring you over?" Suzuhah asked, not looking at them, inspecting his hand quietly. "I would need a little bit of food, but…"

Alex went to open his mouth before pursing his lips. "I would love to say we would walk, but…" He sighed.

He shook his head. "I do not believe we walked that far, returning back should not be an issue. Even if others were involved, I highly doubt they would attack in broad daylight?" He wasn't sure if that was the word, but sure. "Not after being subtle with what just happened and myself still under Alex's cloak. We should be fine."

"Glad you said we." Alex chuckled. He turned to Rita and Suzuhah. "We'll head back, are you sure…?"

"We'll be fine." Rita waved, leaning forward, her back bending in an arc. "Plus, you know I can take care of myself and Suzuhah here isn't exactly weak or defenseless either."

"I know." Alex winced, causing Suzuhah to sigh and shake his head.

Rita's smile fell as she stared at them. "Are you two certain? While people seem to be okay with Alex, Milos…"

"As long as we are careful and stay out in the open, we should be alright. I don't think they will do anything else, especially out in the open."

"I wish I had your optimism." Rita sighed before shrugging. "Alright, be careful and head back to Lillianna's house as soon as possible, or, at least, go to the main hall so they can lead you there."

"Can do." Alex saluted as Rita shook her head, amused.

Milos turned toward one of the other gates, wanting to be out of this place and away from that restaurant or whatever. As beautiful as the park was, he felt a little nauseous. He was growing weak.

Alex joined him, humming softly as he swiped at his mouth, the little bit of blood smearing slightly on his hand. Milos pursed his lips. Another shouldn't be injured because of him, especially not Alex, of all people.

He heard movement and turned to see Rita and Suzuhah heading out the gate they entered through, hurrying away. He supposed, like they said, they would be fine. A feeling of unease fell over him.

He did not like this.

# Chapter Five

Alex watched quietly, tongue occasionally poking at the thankfully closed wound in his mouth. It hurt more than he wanted to admit and he found himself grateful for his hesitation. Milos' silence at Rita's question spoke volumes. The man probably would have taken it in silence, simply so as not to worry the group. Alex found himself still more than a little angry, but that feeling calmed. Rita and Suzuhah would take care of it without making too much of a scene…now that Rita calmed down a little bit.

The air smelled sweet, but cloying, something he only noticed now as he paid attention. The area itself was beautiful, but he didn't feel that same warmth of safety he had upon first arriving.

He thought it was over. He was finally to the sanctuary, far away from people trying to capture or kill him and his mother was back. Yet, in exchange…he glanced toward Milos and then peered over his shoulder toward where Rita and Suzuhah left.

He was probably the only one besides Suzuhah who was accepted here. He wasn't sure about Rita.

The walk back was silent, their footsteps clanking over the stone and smooth roads, occasional stairs pulling them upward, back toward the white building they only just left.

What worried him was they were there for less than a day and this happened. Sure, they were all seen entering, but… He rubbed at his neck, wincing.

The only thing was, if the Sovereign was busy, he couldn't just say, oh, hey, there were metal pieces in his food. Most people would brush it off as an accident. He slowed to a stop, peering up toward the building in the distance. Milos slowed a few feet in front of him, turning.

Milos was as stiff as ever, and Alex didn't miss how he seemed to have returned to that appearance when Alex first met him. The coldness and distance; it was as if the man put a wall up, just like his mother did.

It irked him more than he would like to admit. He and Rita and the others finally managed to break through that shell, even just a little, and now it felt like they were a few steps back again.

He wanted to punch something, and he couldn't punch worth crap. He let out a long breath, glancing up the marble steps. "If she's busy, we won't be able to say anything. Bothering her for questions and saying something is up without proof besides the cut in my mouth would not help anyone."

Milos fully turned to him, watching quietly. It was obvious the man came to the same conclusion. His fists clenched tightly over the sword hilt before loosening.

Alex peered over his shoulder, their higher-up position allowing him to see a good way away. The ocean sparkled in the day stone light as white shone from stone and marble, descending downward in a mosaic of designs. Splashes of color caught his eye, just as it had on the way in.

He had been so angry, he hadn't even thought of what to say. He found himself taking a seat on a nearby stair, staring down the paths in thought, a gentle, if stale, breeze ruffled past, startling him. He was still not used to how much air was down here, how often the breezes blew through from a nearby vent.

Milos joined him a few paces away, staring out over the horizon as he stood there, an intimidating, if graceful figure.

The long blonde hair draped over his shoulder, the chain glinting, barely seen under the hood.

Alex turned away, peering at the people. A few glanced their way before moving along, others ignored them entirely.

It was then Alex noticed something and he paused, startled.

It was a part of life, so he was shocked he hadn't realized earlier, but no one here seemed to have signifiers. A few humans did, but…he peered to one side as a young girl skipped past, her legs formed to create goat-like appendages with a tail that wagged behind her as she bound through the streets, being chased by a giggling boy a few years older with the same features.

"Satyrs," Milos whispered quietly, probably following Alex's gaze.

Alex nodded. Neither had a signifier. They wore plain clothes and while the girl had her hair up, it was with a simple tie.

He turned his gaze, seeing a creature walk by below. It looked more like an animal than a human. It was a large four-legged creature who seemed to descend the steps with ease. It had a slender head and long feathery tail.

Milos stayed quiet this time and Alex had to wonder if he even knew what the creature was called.

He glanced up, watching the man follow the creature with his gaze, a strange hint of barely hidden shock on his face.

"You know what that is?"

"A Gazellet. An extremely rare Demon. We don't even know if it has a human-like form that some of the others do. It is a fast creature." He paused, and glanced toward Alex. "A lot of these Demons, I've only ever heard of from—" He suddenly cut himself off and quickly turned away. "They're distant memories."

Alex didn't press, just grateful to get information and to have Milos talking. He sighed and pushed himself to his feet. His stomach growled, his appetite, unfortunately, back. "Let's wait for a bit, see if we can speak with her later this afternoon. It will make it so it's not quite as awkward." He tried to find the word and ended up just throwing one down half-heartedly. It wasn't quite correct, but he couldn't think of an alternative.

Milos didn't argue, though Alex did note the way he shifted slightly, shoulders lowering just the tiniest bit.

Alex peered down the stairs before hesitating. He debated for a moment before turning to Milos. "We should eat. I know it's probably not the wisest after what just happened, but we can't starve ourselves either."

"Rita and Suzuhah have no doubt thought of that." Milos spoke, voice even. "It's safer for them to move about."

Alex pursed his lips, annoyed. "I don't want to just stay put either. That's not…" He trailed off.

He knew what Milos was talking about. He wasn't about to abandon his friend anywhere and he couldn't just go around with Milos, the way things were.

It was frustrating when the one thing he was just starting to accept about himself was not helping. He felt his shoulders slump, the distant smell of sizzling meat and fresh baked bread wafting up from the streets below, teasing at his stomach.

"Why don't you simply go? I will…"

"I don't think we should split any more than we already have. We don't know how to get to Lillianna's house, even if Mom did mention it, and you going alone, clearly, wouldn't end well." Alex gestured. When Milos didn't respond Alex slumped. "I would just like for ONCE to go to a place without all this hassle."

"There's no such thing. All places will have their…"

"What about the Overlands?" Alex peered up. "I know you don't like to talk about it too much, especially considering how often I ask you, but…"

Milos closed his eyes and shook his head. Alex pursed his lips and turned sharply away. He wished he could fly, he wished he knew how to use his wings at that moment.

He would have leapt off the stairs and took off. Unfortunately, that wasn't an option.

"I suppose food is the wisest option at the moment, especially if we cannot speak with the Sovereign."

Alex nodded, staring out once more before coming to a decision. He turned, walking past Milos, startling him. He passed through a courtyard he ignored earlier when staring up at the building before him in its grandeur. Now, he ignored it due to not caring as he walked up the steps. The marble felt solid and almost slightly slippery under his feet, his shoes were so worn at this point, he wasn't sure if they were even still viable, but he ignored it, stopping before a guard he recognized. "We're here to speak with the Sovereign."

"Sir, I do apologize, but you only just left and she is a busy woman." One of the guards spoke, bowing his head in what Alex saw occasionally, deference.

It made him twitch uncomfortably, stomach churning. "What if it is important?"

"I'm sorry, sir, even one of your status cannot enter at will. She may be available in the evening."

One of my status? Alex wanted to ask what he meant, but the guard straightened, peering past him. He probably spotted Milos.

Alex pursed his lips. He expected this, but it was still annoying. He spun on his heels and almost stomped down the steps, almost. Milos waited for him, watching with a raised eyebrow. "It was worth a shot," Alex muttered as he stepped past. "Come on, let's see if we can find a place that isn't going to skewer you on sight." He paused at that and felt the blood drain from his face. "Er…that's not a pleasant thought."

"That sounded more like something I would say." Milos actually twitched his lip up slightly in a hint of amusement.

Alex huffed, but didn't argue. They descended back down the stairs, taking a different route this time. Still, Alex's mind swam. What did he mean, of my status? Now that he thought about it, why was his mother not allowed to leave? "Milos?"

"Hm?"

"He mentioned my status." Alex turned to him, hesitant. "Mom wasn't allowed to leave to look for me. What could that mean?" He wasn't sure if he wanted to know, but he found himself asking anyway.

Milos stared at him quietly, deep in thought. "I do not know," he finally admitted after some time. "We know you are of a nyx or naiad blood, but we have yet to discover the other part of you."

Alex pursed his lips, peering down. Blood. It was always because of his blood. How was that fair?

"It seems we have a few questions to ask both your mother and the Sovereign." Milos' gentler tone met Alex's ears and he relaxed, nodding.

They walked in silence the rest of the way, finding themselves in a different part of the sanctuary, a veritable city at this point. Alex hadn't realized just how massive it was when he first arrived, but he supposed it made sense. It was the last stronghold of the Demons of the Underlands.

While much of it resembled the rest of the Underlands, stones of all sorts adorned the walls and along the streets, glowing gently. He could see heat stones glimmering under tables as warm food sat on top. A cart trundled down the road, a gentle waft of cold indicated it held an ice stone within. Another cart raced by and that's when he realized none of them were powered by the creatures used elsewhere in the Underlands, those squat slow, but powerful things that looked almost like goats from the books he read. He still remembered being so hungry, he saw them eating rock and thought it was edible. It wasn't.

But, no, these strange contraptions were controlled like the ship, with wind stones.

Alex pulled in a sharp breath in realization, staring in shock. Stones were used a lot throughout the Underlands, but here? It was a common commodity and a way of life, it seemed.

How had he not noticed before? Was he just not paying attention?

"Wait, that cart..." Milos spoke softly, seeming just as startled. Guess Alex wasn't the only one who hadn't noticed.

"How are there so many of these stones? I see a water stone over there, a bunch of heat stones under a fire stone," Alex murmured, peering back and forth as they walked.

Milos didn't say anything as Alex shook his head, finding a food stand. He walked over, a young girl sitting behind, talking to a customer. She turned to him and blinked before blushing brightly and bowing quickly. "Oh, sorry, I didn't see you."

"Oh, uh, it's fine." Alex quickly waved his hands. "Um, I was just wondering how much for two?" He paused. "Actually, make that four."

The girl glanced up. Out of the corner of Alex's periphery, he spotted Milos to one side, waiting nearby, almost out of sight. "Oh, um... Three silver each."

Alex dug into his bag, grateful for what Mom gave him. He handed her the appropriate amount, which she seemed to take gratefully, handing the skewers to him. They were heavy with what might have been chicken and a rare few vegetables, something Alex hadn't had in quite some time. He nodded, smiling, and walked away. Milos soon joined him and Alex didn't miss the gasp from the girl.

He felt grease drip on his hand and quickly passed two over. He took a bite of his, relishing in the tender meat, quickly wiping at his lips as some of the juice spilled down.

It was delicious. The vegetables tasted fresh and the meat must have been a new cut. He hadn't realized how hungry he was until the whole thing was devoured and he was eating the second one. It hurt a little to eat, but Rita's potion helped immensely, so it wasn't bad.

Milos finished his two with a similar, if more tame, speed. Alex could never figure out how you could eat something like that without making a mess and yet Milos tended to do it. Even Rita was always impressed, something she admitted to him once when the boat suddenly swelled while they were eating. Milos managed to pick up his soup and kept eating as both Alex and Rita almost face-planted into the soup that spilled over the edge. Suzuha managed to splash some on her shirt, annoyed. He needed to learn that balance thing or whatever from Milos sometime.

Still, he wasn't sure what to do. They couldn't keep wandering around the city, that was stupid, but Alex didn't want to stay in one place and he wasn't going to condemn Milos to that either.

He almost wished he was Rita or Suzuhah.

He shook the thought off, peering up toward the slowly dimming day stones. Had they been wandering around for that long? He supposed the day stones were already fairly bright by the time they left this morning.

What were they going to do? Was his mother back yet to lead them to where they were staying? They said to the north, but there were a few homes that way.

Alex let out a heavy sigh and turned, trying to remember his way back to the city center at least.

"Child, what are you doing out and about with this Cur?"

Alex jerked and glanced over to see a young man walk over. He appeared human in almost every way, except for the pristine crimson and gold feathers trailing over his arms and a long train of a beautiful tail swishing over his back, overlaying over and over. Red hair fell in a wave down his back, floating slightly and his eyes were a piercing gold as he smirked.

"An Airadon." Milos spoke quietly. "One of the few Demons with some control over the wind, though they themselves cannot fly."

"Astute of you, Cur." The man tilted his chin up, unamused, before turning to Alex and bowing slightly, hand to his chest. "I know of your mother and was surprised to see you out and about at this time. My name is Maritus, I believe you've met Sechrondes? She informed me about you, along with the rest of the council. Vile woman, but well informed."

Alex pursed his lips, not saying anything, annoyed. The man

straightened, shrugging off the cold response. "You certainly are a young one, fifteen perhaps?"

Alex twitched. "Seventeen, actually, almost eighteen." He bit back.

"Sorry, sorry, you grew up among humans, I forget that." He chuckled. "Yes, I suppose you are that age." His gaze drifted to Milos. He narrowed his eyes, the amusement fading slightly. "A young one as well, older perhaps by only a few years…" He shook his head, the hair flowing in a way that wasn't natural, as if a bit of wind brushed it to one side. "No matter." He turned back to Alex and bowed. "Still, you shouldn't dwell amongst the common people like this, it is unbecoming of one such as yourself."

Alex wanted so badly to ask what he meant, but he had no reason to trust the man in front of him. "You've only just met me." Alex finally spoke up.

The man blinked and raised an amused eyebrow, glancing between them. "Ah, you can't sense it?"

Huh?

He chuckled and pulled back, feathers fluttering on his arms, crimson and gold in the dying light. "I would figure an Alertian would have realized by now."

"His name is Milos." Alex spoke curtly.

One side of him, a side he was growing familiar with, seemed almost amused at this interaction, a very weird sensation.

"My apologies." The man did not seem very apologetic. "I am simply surprised. Most Demons know how to sense the levels of another Demon, how do you think we know how to interact with each other? Especially with such varied species? Though I suppose yours is quite chaotic." He tilted his head. "Not that it matters." He turned and gestured, tail curling around him. "Come, follow me."

Alex pursed his lips, he had no reason to follow the man, but he also didn't want to admit that he was lost and Milos wasn't saying anything. Plus, he was curious. Levels? Did that have anything to do with his status? He shifted closer to Milos, noticing as he relaxed slightly before nodding subtly. The two walked after the man, not sure what else to do.

He kept his hands behind his back as he walked, back straight. A few people quickly bowed their heads as he passed, similar to when they met Sechrondes.

"One of the matrons, or patrons, I suppose would be a better term." Milos kept his voice low. "It would make sense if he brought up the council. Who knew Demons had a council of all things."

"What did he mean about levels?" Alex kept his voice low too, ignoring the hint of contempt in Milos' voice. "I was thinking it might have to do with how everyone seems to make mention of my status or whatever."

"I've only briefly heard of it in notes. Most Demons are even in strength and ability, but a rare few hold more life similar to Lillianna." Milos paused, frowning slightly. "I'm not sure if the term is accurate, but they call it 'magic' in them. One such Demon was Satan." He stayed silent after that, but it gave Alex enough information for now. Maybe they were the same?

They moved up the steps, eventually making their way to the marbled courtyard of the chief. The man bowed, bringing one leg back as he extended a hand, the movement elegant. "I believe that is your mother?"

Alex blinked, startled, as Mom landed, shifting back from her blackened form, head raised in a strangely annoyed look.

"Maritus, I presume you have done nothing with my son or his charge?"

"Of course not." The man pulled back. "I am not Sechrondes. I merely spotted him in the lower district and felt it prudent to bring him back, the people are still not sure how to react to him, after all."

"I am well aware of that." Mother seemed to withhold a sigh, her long hair tied back, gently falling over her back, her posture still straight. "I am just surprised. You're not usually one to step into the lower districts yourself."

"I heard of his arrival and found myself curious, much like the others of the council."

Mom's eye twitched at that, but she didn't say anything.

"Either way, my job is done. As I suspected from one such as you, you have quite a beautiful son." At that, the man leapt.

Alex yelped, wind blasting past as Maritus leapt, landing lightly on a distant rooftop before taking another leap, tail, hair and feathers flowing backward as he disappeared quickly out of sight.

"Show-off," Mom muttered before shaking her head and turning to Alex. "He didn't do anything, correct?" Her gaze flitted to Milos before returning to her son.

Alex shook his head, a little unnerved. "He just said a few strange things."

"What things?" She narrowed her eyes.

"Something about sensing Demonic levels or something. Mom, what am I?"

The last few words were blurted out, though he hadn't realized until after he said it what he was asking.

Mom's entire expression softened. "Oh... my little angel." She reached forward and pulled him into a startled hug. "Let's talk about that somewhere more comfortable. Now that you've spoken with the sovereign, I'll bring you to where Riviera and I are staying, like I said I would do earlier."

"Together?" he asked, hesitantly.

Mother chuckled softly as she pulled away. "Not like that, dear. You must realize there is only so much land here, many people live together." She glanced toward Milos, hesitating for a long time before she spoke. "You should join us as well, it'll be safer for you."

Milos seemed somewhat surprised, though Alex just felt relieved. He smiled brightly. "Thanks, Mom, but what about Rita and Suzuhah?"

"I saw them earlier and told them where to go." She frowned. "They seemed to have been covered in something, but they seemed pleased with themselves." Alex blinked at that. "I was wondering where you went off to when Maritus arrived with you." She gestured, fully pulling away. "Come, this way." She led them to one side where a set of gates curved around the courtyard. A few guards stood to the side and bowed as they entered. Alex shifted in discomfort, but it didn't seem strange to Milos.

Was the man just used to this?

It seemed lavish to Alex, even though he had lived with the duke. He pulled his arms close as he peered around, noting they were walking down a road made of a different type of stone that felt softer under his feet. Flowers bloomed up on either side, surprising him. Large two story homes curled around either side where he could see movement within. Eventually, they came to one that looked much like the others. It was placed at the end of the street, standing slightly taller than the others. There were two guards in front of it, standing at attention.

Alex didn't miss the fact that both were furred around the legs, having legs shaped like the wolves he read about in books. Snouts poked out from underneath sturdy helmets. Both held pikes in their hands and nodded toward Mom, watching them quietly. Mom seemed to sigh at that

"Lupin." Milos' voice was soft.

Alex was now glad that he was with Milos, it was nice to have names to the different Demons they encountered.

They moved up the stairs, only to stop when the pikes lurched out, almost slashing into Milos if he hadn't leapt back, hand on his sword. Alex jerked, whipping around.

"Lower your weapons," Mom snapped, voice almost resonating. "He is my guest."

"But, my lady—" One of the lupin spoke up, only to be quieted by a searing look from Mom as Alex shoved one of the pikes out of the way, just avoiding cutting himself.

Both hesitated before pulling back, letting Milos pass. Alex stayed next to his friend, arms crossed in annoyance as they walked past. They stepped inside as Mom closed the door behind them before letting out a sigh. "I'm sorry about that."

"It's been happening all day anyway," Alex murmured, his annoyance slipping into his voice.

"I'm sorry, dear, but they aren't like you. Not many are going to forgive or work with an Alertian. The sovereign and yourself are one of the few exceptions."

"What about you?" Alex turned to Mom, who hesitated.

"You have to understand, I trust your judgement, but…"

Alex pursed his lips, frustration flaring through him. So even his own mother believed Milos was simply a dangerous evil Alertian.

"If you have a room in which I could stay, I will depart so you can talk in peace." Milos spoke up, voice even, startling Mom. Guess she already forgot he was there, go figure.

"Oh, yes." Mom hesitated. "There is a bath at the end of the hall upstairs. Just take a left up the stairs. You can use the second room after that, it's one of the guest rooms." Milos nodded and quickly left, hurrying away at a pace that made Alex worried.

As much as Milos portrayed himself as unwavering, Alex knew the man had his vulnerabilities. He wouldn't be alive otherwise. How much was all of this hurting him?

"Alex?"

Alex turned back to his mom, feeling that annoyance once more. "You never answered my question. You trust my judgement, but it's clear you still don't trust him. He saved my life!"

"I know that," she snapped, taking deep breaths. "I know what you told me, I get it. He obviously cares for you as much as an Alertian can, but it's not that easy."

"Why?" Alex asked quietly. "He hasn't done anything since he got here. He's done nothing the whole way here. He helped me figure out that I was part Naiad and could have abandoned Rita and me when we fled north, but he didn't. He helped me FIND you."

Mom pulled back, looking down at her shoes.

Alex felt a stab in his chest, pained. "And yet, you treat him like the people outside, with wary glances and hatred and…" Alex snapped his mouth shut, suddenly harshly reminded of his mouth, thankfully healed, but still smarting slightly.

"And?" She spoke softly.

Alex slumped.

When he didn't respond, she gently took his hand and pulled him to one side of the entranceway, away from the large stairwell. The door opened to reveal a cozy room with a lightly flickering fire stone in the middle. The room was warm, but not uncomfortable. Plush chairs of a fabric and design that Alex couldn't recognize sat to either side of a table. It was a quaint little room. Mom took a seat, gesturing for Alex to follow. He took the other chair, struggling to even look at his mother.

"Sweetie, please, talk to me."

"I…" Alex wasn't sure what to say. When he was traveling, he had so much he wanted to say, and when he arrived, he wanted so desperately to talk to her, to tell her about what was going on, but now that he had a chance, his words dried up, disappearing like a vented breeze.

He felt a gentle hand on his which was curled into his lap.

"My little angel. I'm trying to understand, so please tell me what happened to you." Mom's eyes were wet with unshed tears. "You've grown so much and I want to know."

Alex hesitated another moment before letting out a breath and just…talking. The words, once he started, kept going and going. He told her about his fear as he ran, not sure what was going on. His hunger as he had to rely on Ame and stealing. Meeting Rita and learning more about himself and the environment he was in. The attack by Divon in a bid to marry Rita, his first time turning into a Demon and eventually encountering Milos. It all came spilling out, word after word. He was trembling, emotions crashing into each other as he finally acknowledged everything that happened lately. The fear and hunger, the anger and sadness, every emotion felt like a weight that was slowly lifting as he spoke. His mother would occasionally gesture or ask a probing question whenever he faltered, her own expression soft and gentle.

"Mom, why did you never tell me?" He finally finished after mentioning what happened in the streets.

He could tell she was just as overwhelmed by what he said, but she reached forward, cupping his cheek as a thumb rubbed gently under his eye, coming away wet.

Was he crying?

"I couldn't." She spoke softly. "I decided, as soon as I had you, that I would find a way for you to try to live as normal of a life as possible. Your father agreed. Do you remember the word I used? All those weeks ago?"

Alex shook his head, as best as he could with her holding him. She used her free hand, finger lightly touching his forehead. His mind flashed back to the screams and heat of a fire, blood coating a black nail.

"Gret." Mom's voice snapped him out of the memory as she gently pulled away. "Such a simple term of the Demonic tongue. I never thought I would have to say it, so your father and I picked it for its ease." She sighed. "I suppose it was a good choice in the end. The word meant run." Alex blinked, startled as she smiled. "It was also the word we decided on that

what happened, and I don't believe for a second that their choices are because of this." She lightly tapped his throat with her pinky. "I'll work with you to control it, so you know when the hypnotizing properties emerge. Though, I suppose, your song is also where your strength comes from." She lightly wiped at his cheek. "Don't be afraid of your voice. It's beautiful, with or without that ability."

"Mom." He hesitated, choking through the word. "Why do you know all this? If you sealed me away?"

What he didn't say, however, was what settled in his mind. She didn't know him anymore. Could he believe her about him not affecting the others? She wasn't there when he was learning his abilities, she only learned through what he said. He wanted desperately to believe her, but a small part of him couldn't. How would she know so certainly anyway?

Mom sighed and gently pulled her head back, but didn't pull away. She was squatting in front of him, hair falling over her shoulders. "Because of who we are," she said. "I was hoping not to say anything, but I suppose I can't hide it anymore. Not if I want to explain to you. Plus, knowing you, you would probably find out anyway." She smiled at her weak joke.

Alex felt his lips twitch.

She hesitated and slowly pulled her hands away, staring down at them. "You know how the Sovereign mentioned she was alive since the Demon-human war, correct? How she was called the Demon of the First?"

Alex nodded, confused, though his Demonic half trilled in recognition. Horror slowly settled over him.

"I didn't know much about my father, nor my grand-father, but I certainly heard the stories." She winced, hand to her chest. "I guess it's the advantage of our long lives or the disadvantage." She shook her head. "I was born about fifty years ago, to two pureblooded Demons. I was born in secret, but our family was attacked and I was taken. I was able to hide who I was, passed around after my parents' death."

Alex heard bits and pieces of this, but Mom never said how long ago it was. Fifty? She barely looked to be in her thirties.

Seeing his confusion, she smiled half-heartedly. "Demons are much slower in aging. Some Demons age even slower, look at Lillianna as an example."

Alex nodded, realization dawning on him.

Mother hesitated, staring at the fire stone, lost in thought. After a long time, she finally spoke. "Do you remember? The name of the one who led the Demons during the war?"

Alex narrowed his eyes, confused on where this was going. "Yeah, Satan."

Mom's smile was weak. "He was a powerful Demon, a leader that could use his very words to cause chaos. He would fly through the skies and hurl fire into the earth…" she trailed off. "We don't really know the species, since he was the first leader to not be a Demon of the First, but he was also my great-grandfather."

Alex froze, his entire body locking up in shock. Wait, what? His mouth opened and closed as he realized just what that meant. The great warrior of the human-demon war, one of the last leaders of the Demons, was his great-great-grandfather?

Even worse, Milos' main goal was to kill a child of Satan. He remembered the man saying that at one point.

He shivered violently, tightly clasping his arms. Oh god, what was he? A child of Satan? A Nyx? Was he even still human?

He felt arms wrap around him and he choked.

"My little angel. I'm so sorry," Mom whispered softly, gently running her hands through his hair, knotted and tangled as it was. He tried to calm down, but he couldn't. He wanted to know, but now he almost wished he didn't know.

Was anything he did because of him as a person? Or his abilities? Should he apologize to them? Should he even tell them? He and his mother sat in silence as he felt a sob rip from his throat. Mother's embrace was both comforting and painful, filled with lies and warmth. What was he supposed to think? His Demonic half almost wanted to curl in, whining alongside him, a soft feeling pressed against his chest, slowly starting to calm him.

He relaxed into his mother's embrace, at least now he knew what was going on.

He just wished it didn't hurt so much.

# Chapter Six

It took a while for his thoughts to finally settle. He quickly wiped his cheeks, embarrassed. He shouldn't be crying.

"It's okay." Mom smiled. "What I said was a lot to take in, I'm glad, actually."

Alex peered down, pursing his lips before taking in a shuddering breath. "I'm…"

"I have other things to say, but I think that's enough for now."

Alex jerked and glanced up as Mom pushed herself to her feet, hands on her knees. "Wait."

Mom stopped, watching him quietly before nodding. Alex pulled his legs up onto the couch, wincing slightly as he realized he was staining the seat with what was left on his shoes. Mom didn't say anything as he crossed his arms over his legs, relaxing his chin against them. He stared at the fire stone, lost in thought. "You said that you didn't know what type of species we were. What do you mean?"

There was a long pause before Mom sighed. "Exactly what I said. We're not Demons of the First, but we aren't like other Demons. Your father wondered if it was a mutation, but there is no evidence. All records of our type of Demon were lost." She peered up at the ceiling, deep in thought before continuing, "About two thousand years ago, I would say."

Alex blanched at the thought. That long?

"So, you know as much as I do about what I am." She placed a hand to her chest, curling inward. "I know how to control it and what I can do, but that is all."

Alex pulled his gaze away, not sure what to think. So even Mom didn't fully know. Still, to be a child of Satan, the warrior of the human-demon war, was something, he supposed. "What do you know of Satan?"

Mother paused before chuckling quietly. "Just the stories. I only vaguely remember my mother and father, they were both from the same lineage as Satan." Alex blinked at that, not sure what to think. "So, yes, I'm pure-blooded. You can probably see why I am so grateful to have you. I didn't think I would be able to." She paused, shuddering. "Not that…" She trailed off and shook her head. "That is not something for you to worry about." She turned back to Alex. "He was very tactical, incredibly smart for even a Demon, surpassing many humans, in fact. He could fly like us, his wings able to carry him far, fast which was how he was able to cross the Underlands so quickly, only a few days, from what I heard, during the war."

Alex peered over his shoulder, thinking of his own wings. He couldn't imagine it. It took weeks to cross the Underlands on foot and his wings certainly didn't feel that strong, they only ever seemed to get in his way.

Mom watched quietly before she leaned forward, hands resting on his shoulder. "You mentioned that you only just started to learn how to fly, right?"

Alex turned back to her, nodding. She smiled. "Then, tomorrow morning, once you get some food and sleep, I'll show you, I have some time before I have to go."

"Where do you need to go?"

Mom paused, pulling back. "I have a lot of duties to the people here, considering I am one of the few fliers and one of the few who is strong enough to travel to some locales. Those duties pretty much tripled when you arrived, and I didn't have to stay here." She winced.

"A high level…" Alex spoke quietly, deep in thought.

Mom narrowed her eyes. "That's a terrible way to phrase it, where did you hear that?"

"Maritus. He said I should be able to sense Demonic levels."

Mom grumbled under her breath, startling Alex. "That man needs to know when to hold his tongue." She shook her head. "Indeed, there are ways to tell, but it's a little more complicated than that." She turned to him. "Never use the term Levels. That is a demeaning term that was outdated from the outset. If you need to use a term for it, I suppose status is alright, for it describes classes of Demons more than Levels which speaks of the individual, which has caused issues in the past. Anyway, from what I know,

Demons are made from what some might call magic. Magic is amorphous in form and substances, no one knows how it works, though some humans, such as the seers and psychics, have found ways to utilize it."

Alex's eyes widened as his gaze flicked toward where he supposed Rita was. That would match her being able to see the future.

"This magic is detectable if one pays attention. Alertians are well known for this ability, which is one of the reasons that they are typically so dangerous." She shook her head. "It's truly a miracle you met one with a gentler heart."

Alex couldn't argue that point. "But if Demons are made of this magic..." he poked at himself. "What..."

"Just like how humans can now wield magic, so can those like yourself." She smiled proudly. "When he says levels, I would call it something like an expression. Magic expresses itself in different ways which oftentimes lets you know a bit about the Demon in question as well as their strength." She reached forward. "It's somewhat rude to comment on someone's level, or specifically, their essence and abilities with magic. After all, some inherently have and wield more magic than others, Lillianna being a good example of a Demon with a lot of magic. But, for now, here, try touching my hand and concentrating."

Alex hesitated for a moment before reaching out and closing his eyes.

"It'll be a little hard since there is so much Demonic energy around but just focus on my hand."

Alex felt it settle under his fingers, shivering as a sudden warmth flared through the room. The hand felt hard, and he realized she must have shifted.

He barely stopped himself from opening his eyes. Milos could sense Demons even in human form and yet he couldn't even when he focused. He felt a little disgruntled, but—

He cut his thoughts off as he felt a gentle prodding, though he wasn't sure if it was physical. He reached for it, gingerly touching it. It was like feeling for his own Demonic energy, but this felt different. As he felt over whatever it was, he found himself entranced. It was like a warm fire, burning against his skin. Yet, it didn't hurt.

Sensations he didn't recognize filled his thoughts, a power and gentleness combined with fierce protectiveness. It was almost like something was wrapping around him.

"What do you feel?" Mother spoke softly, catching his attention.

"Warmth, protection…" He trailed off. "Strength."

"Correct." Mom's voice indicated a smile, her words holding a strange quality that almost reminded him of himself. "What you are feeling is my magic, my essence. Usually, it is best to do it without contact, because it can be overwhelming if one is not careful, but it's often easier with."

She pulled away and it felt like the connection was cut but he could just faintly feel something in the air.

He opened his eyes and jerked, startled. A reddish glow hovered around Mom's Demonic form as she shifted back to human. It slowly faded as he watched. He rubbed his eyes, wondering if he was just imagining it, but considering it was still there, just faded, denied that fact.

Mother's smile widened slightly. "There you go, you probably spotted the magic swirling around me. Each Demon is different in color, intensity and glow. It takes some getting used to, but you can eventually find it even when staring at those with Demonic blood."

"Is that different?" Alex muttered, watching as it flowed away. He noticed a bit of red humming in the air, drifting about, also fading. Was this what Milos saw?

"A little." She winced. "Due to the nature of human and Demonic blood mixing, it creates…interesting side-effects in regard to magic." She smiled and poked his forehead. "But I wouldn't worry about that. Contrary to what that man said, it's not necessary for you to work too much on it, it's something you'll slowly learn as you grow, especially now that your abilities are fully unlocked."

"What does mine look like?" He found himself curious. "I mean, yours is a wispy red almost like—" he cut himself off, debating.

He didn't want to say Maritus, but his thoughts flicked to the fiery red appearance.

"Yours is an ocean blue with gentle swirls of green." She spoke, a faint smile on her lips. "Every so often, I see dashes of a sunset, the daystone lights drifting into night and beaming off the water with their red and orange tints."

Alex felt warmth on his face as his mother waxed poetic. He quickly looked toward the fire stone, trying to shift his thoughts. It made sense and certainly explained how Milos found him all that time ago and, in the caves, back at the last island. "Is it there for humans with magic?"

"Yes, though very faint." Mother stood once more. "That friend of yours, Rita, I believe you said, she holds a good amount of magic in her, though it's clearly not controlled."

Alex wasn't surprised, she couldn't control when her future visions came.

He finally pushed himself to his feet, wincing slightly as he realized his legs fell asleep. He quickly shook them out, the pins and needles making it hard to stay on his feet.

After a moment, he let out a breath and turned to Mom who was grinning as she said, "I'm going to get dinner started, what…"

"Nope." Alex quickly shook his head. He still remembered how Mom set the temperature to one hundred and twenty-five degrees for four hours and fifty minutes. Or the time she set the entire room on fire trying to make bread. "Sorry, Ma, but I'm not going to have you cooking. I still remember the last time when you—"

"Oh, hush now." Mom lightly swatted at his head as he ducked out of the way, grinning. The playful banter helped to cheer him up a bit. "Fine, what would you suggest?"

"If we have food? Ari or Leon." He paused and glanced toward the main entrance. "If they are here. They know to come here, right?"

As if on cue, there was the faint sound of a door opening and footsteps. Alex walked over and peeked out to see Ari and Leon carrying a few containers. Ari spotted him and gave the faintest of smiles.

"Ah, those two. Yes, I saw them during my work. I notified them where you would be staying as well."

Alex stepped out, walking over to the duo.

"Master Alex, it is good to see you. Is Mistress Rita and Master Milos present?" Leon asked, hefting his containers.

"Milos is, I'm not sure about Rita or Suzuhah." He observed the containers, curious. "Are you making dinner?"

"Yes." Ari spoke quietly, watching him. "We acquired the appropriate ingredients."

"Good, don't let my mom help." He forcefully whispered, not trying to hide his words from her.

He felt a light thwack on the back of his head and yelped.

"Ignore my son. If you need anything, please, let me know." Mom nodded her head.

"Thank you, we may take you up on your offer." Leon was smirking somewhat as he spoke, watching Alex as he massaged the back of his head with a huff. "Firstly, where is the kitchen?"

"Oh, this way." Mom glanced toward Alex. "I'll see you for dinner, why don't you head to your room? It's next to your friends."

With that, she turned and gestured, leading them to a door near the stairs on the left. Alex watched her go, watching the ex-slaves leave with a heavy heart. The only saving grace was he was almost certain there was no way this voice of his could have influenced them, he barely knew them before Milos decided to have them join. He let out a breath before heading upstairs.

Mom said that they decided to come with him of their own choice, but could he truly believe that?

He came to a halt on the top step, finding himself rubbing his arm without much thought. He asked Milos to help him find his mother, and he did. Milos was stubborn, just like Rita, and yet, in a lot of ways, none of them were like each other. Could he believe his mom? Even though she really didn't know him anymore?

He hated this, he thought he was finally coming to accept his Demonic half, and it turned out he could have been controlling the ones he saw as friends. What would they think? Was he…?

"Alex?" Suzuhah's voice caught his attention, and he jerked, opening his mouth before jamming it shut. "Whoa, you were out of it." Suzuhah walked over, arms crossed over his chest, lazily leaning on one leg.

It was guy Suzuhah this time instead of the younger female version, Suzuha. The burns on his body were healing, which made sense, he hadn't used his lightning ability in a while.

Alex wasn't sure what to say. He was almost scared to say anything. "When did you get back?" he managed to squeak out.

Suzuhah raised his eyebrow and walked forward, leaning up toward him. "A little while ago. Rita and I noticed you were busy, so we just went our separate ways. Also, yeah, something is seriously on your mind. I'm not one to talk to, but…"

"It's nothing," Alex quickly cut in. "Just something Mom said. That's all."

Suzuhah pulled back. "Oh? Now I'm curious."

Alex clicked his tongue, of course it was Suzuhah who saw him so frazzled. Then again, he supposed Suzuhah would be easier to talk to than Rita or Milos and Alex was almost certain he hadn't influenced Suzuhah, right? "Suzuhah, why did you decide not to kill me back then?" He spoke hesitantly, holding his arm tightly.

Suzuhah seemed utterly startled by his words, narrowing his eyes. After a moment, he turned, without a word, and walked toward a doorway on the right. Alex almost felt a pained wrench, if he hadn't noticed Suzuhah's gesture to follow. He hesitantly stepped after him, moving into the room.

It was large with a huge bed near two windows. A desk was set to one side and a wardrobe was set on the other. The floor had a rug that seemed soft to the touch. It seemed Suzuhah had already made it his home, the bed a mess of bundled sheets. He took a seat, causing Alex to stand to one side, uncomfortable. After a moment, he took a seat in the plush chair next to the desk, the door closing behind him.

Suzuhah crossed one leg over the other, leaning his elbow on it, chin in hand. "Alright, whatever your mother said must have gotten to you badly to ask something like that." Alex started, surprised as Suzuhah rolled his eyes. "We saw Milos briefly who explained the situation. I will say though, it was amusing watching Rita barge into his room and almost get cut." He grinned before the smile fell. "I'll answer your question if you tell me why you asked to begin with."

Alex clamped his mouth shut, startled. Considering how playful Suzuhah usually was, it was always a bit of a shock to see him more serious. The steely golden gaze met his, making him shift in uncertainty. He trusted

Suzuhah, the boy certainly could have killed him, but did he trust him enough to say this?

"Have you ever heard of Sirens?" He finally spoke up, words hesitant.

Suzuhah blinked, probably startled at the non-sequitur. "That's a change, but, yes. My mistress mentioned them. They supposedly lived millenia ago, even before the great devastation two thousand years ago. No one knows when they disappeared. The Nyx and Naiad are thought…" His eyes widened. "To be descended— wait, are you saying…?"

"I'm not a siren." Alex quickly waved his hands. "I am part Nyx."

Suzuhah let out a breath before furrowing his brow. "So, why do you bring it up?"

"Sirens are said to drag sailors to their death through their voices." Alex tentatively spoke up, trying hard not to curl into the chair.

Yeah, he was kind of glad he wasn't talking to Rita or Milos right now. He wasn't sure he could face them.

Suzuhah seemed deep in thought, gazing around before landing on him. His attention drifted to Alex's throat, and he froze.

Silence filled the room to the point that Alex almost wanted to run, but he held fast. Though that might have been fear as well, keeping him in place.

"You're singing." Suzuhah turned his attention to his face. "I'm not human, nor am I Demon, so Demonic effects usually don't impact me unless it's physical, that's why seers create us, or so my mistress said." He stared hard at Alex. "Are you saying your voice has the same hypnotic qualities of the ancient Sirens?"

Alex couldn't say anything, tongue stuck to the roof of his mouth, so instead he looked away, unable to deny the words, even if he wasn't completely certain of them.

"Oh." Suzuhah spoke after a bit of silence. "Oh boy. Yeah, that's going to be problematic. How strong is it?"

"I don't know," Alex admitted. "Mom said it's still growing, but are you certain you can't be influenced by Demons?"

"I'm certain." Alex slowly turned to face Suzuhah, surprised to see the gentler expression on the boy's face. Suzuhah peered around before standing. With a single step, he shifted, the room filling up with his sleek fox-like form. The wings pulled into his side as he lay on the ground, gold eyes watching him quietly.

Alex hesitantly stood. He yelped when Suzuhah lashed out, catching him with a paw. He panicked, only to stop when he realized there were no claws digging into his side. His movement did, however, cause him to crash into the Vulfulas' side. The fur was soft, if a little oily.

"To answer your question, if you really aren't certain," Suzuhah spoke up, his two voices mingling together in a gentle rumble. "You're too gentle and trusting. I may not be able to see magic like Demons, but life force often tells a lot as well." Suzuhah settled his head on his paws, peering at him as he curled around Alex, who sat on the floor, unsure what to do. "You've killed, the tang of blood sits there, but it is subdued and who, in this world, hasn't killed at least once?"

"No one should have to kill," Alex whispered, staring down at his hands, remembering, with distaste, the first time he killed as a Demon, the crippled and twisted bodies of the Martinets outside of Rita's home.

"No, you are right." Suzuhah breathed out, ruffling Alex's hair briefly with the warm air. "As for your voice, I can hear the strength, but I don't find it entrancing like the others seem to. It certainly is stunning, but I think that's just because you're a good singer. Don't you dare think I'm doing this because you influenced me, it's kind of insulting."

Alex winced, not sure where to put his hands. "I didn't even…"

Suzuhah's long tail curled around, the appendage settling over Alex's legs, warm and comforting. "Of course you didn't think about that." Suzuhah sighed. "I mean, you just learned about this dangerous ability and now you're like this." He gestured with his head, wings flicking over him briefly. "You're too much of a good person to hypnotize anyone, even by accident. Maybe someday, but at this point?" Suzuhah snorted. "I'm more worried about you shooting me in the wing with water than you controlling my, or anyone else's, thoughts."

"But…"

"Oh, shut it and relax." Suzuhah rolled his eyes, seeming strange with the fox-like face. "Do you know what? I don't know you all THAT much, however, from what I do know. Rita and Milos would both probably be offended at the idea that you controlled them, not because you might have, but because they believe in the choices they have made. Those two are stubborn sons of…" Suzuhah trailed off and Alex couldn't help the weak chuckle.

"They are something." Alex furrowed his brow, finding himself relaxing against Suzuhah's side, the fur comforting and warm. "But, like you said, you don't really know us much, you're doing a lot to help me right now."

Suzuhah chuckled, expression twisting upward in the facsimile of a smile. "True, probably a remnant of my mistress." The smile faded. "But it's also fairly simple. You saved my life on that last island. You've trusted me enough to allow me to eat, though you had no reason to after I attempted to kill you. All of you have accepted me as one of your own. It's been a long time since I've felt that." He sighed, closing his eyes, head curling around, gently pressing against his, the fur surrounding him. "So, I guess, seeing any of you distressed makes me want to help how I can and considering all of the shit that's happened today? Well, I expected someone to snap."

Alex hesitated before reaching up, wrapping his arms around Suzuhah's neck, letting out a breath of utter relief. "So, you are doing this…"

"Because of my own decision-making, not some hypnotizing bullshit." Suzuhah actually nuzzled into his side before pulling away, out of his grasp, settling onto his paws again. "I'm comfortable right now and you need some rest, I can feel it."

"What? You want me to rest here?"

Suzuhah opened his jaw in a yawn, teeth gleaming in the waning day stone's light. "Do whatever you want, I'm going to get some rest before dinner, and it's been a long time since I've been able to sleep in my Vulfulas form. Plus, well, it's kind of comforting since my mistress loved when I did this for her when she was upset, so it's nostalgic."

Alex peered around, chuckling weakly as he realized Suzuhah had kind of trapped him, a wing resting gently to one side. Nostalgic, huh?

A yawn suddenly escaped and the relief of knowing that at least one of his allies wasn't doing this because of his voice caused him to relax.

To his surprise, sleep took over as he rested against the soft fur of Suzuhah's side, the tail curling gently over him as his eyes fluttered closed in the warm embrace.

# Chapter Seven

Rita frowned, hands on her hips. Milos was a few steps behind her, silent. They were summoned for dinner, but, when they stepped out, Milos mentioned that Alex wasn't downstairs. That tracking ability was always stupidly impressive. Still, it made her wonder if Alex somehow managed to fall asleep in his room. It would make sense; those beds were way too comfortable.

However, when she checked what should have been his room, according to the small plaque on the door, it was empty and practically untouched.

"Guess he wasn't there."

"This way." Milos gestured down the hall and Rita huffed, stomping over.

"That dingbat, he should have waited until after we ate. We're not his alarm." Her words were cut off as she opened the door, only to freeze.

"Well, that explains a lot." Milos' voice held a hint of surprise as he peered in. Rita couldn't argue, scrabbling for her notebook and quickly sketching in the scene. Suzuhah, in Vulfulas form, was fast asleep, curled around Alex, who was pressed into Suzuhah's side, lightly gripping at the fur. A wing hung halfway around the boy, the long tail twitching as if in a dream.

She quickly finished her quick sketch, reminding herself to polish it later, and knocked on the door frame. "Hey, dingbats! It's dinner time!"

There was a faint grumbling from Alex and a huff from Suzuhah before Suzuhah's long neck uncurled and he lifted it, blinking before spotting them.

In a flash, he switched to human form, causing Alex to collapse onto his side with a startled yelp and a loud thud.

Rita winced as Suzuhah, cheeks red, quickly turned, facing away from Rita and Milos. "Right, sorry about that." He hurried to Alex's side as he rubbed his head, sitting up.

"You didn't have to wake me like that." Alex's voice was almost a whine, almost. Rita chuckled as Alex shook his head and looked over.

For a moment, his blue eyes flashed with hesitation, and he stood, quickly turning back to Suzuhah. "Still, thanks for that."

"No problem. Just don't talk about it again," Suzuhah muttered, turning around and hurrying toward the door. "Right, you said dinner, let's go get dinner." He hurried past, Milos stepping out of his way in amusement.

Rita turned back to Alex, who watched Suzuhah flee before facing them. He seemed nervous, mouth pursed into a thin line. He smiled after a moment, but it was shaky at best. He gestured, not saying anything before heading out the door.

"Uh, you're not going to say anything about what we just saw?" Rita put her hands on her hips, causing the boy to pause. He shook his head and hurried after Suzuhah.

Rita blinked, confusion taking over.

"Did something happen when you two were out and about?" She turned to Milos. "I mean, besides the obvious."

"Not that I can recall." Milos shrugged, a slight tilt of his lips showing his worried frown. "We met another Demon, but other than that, I believe it might just be all the events of the day and speaking with his mother."

"That makes a lot of sense." Rita sauntered to the stairs. "Well, we should head down." She peered over her shoulder, red braid hitting her shoulder-blade lightly. "Last one down has to ask Suzuhah to cuddle with them." She grinned, taking off.

She heard a grumbling from behind and then footsteps as she took the steps two at a time.

She let out a yelp as Milos leapt, sliding down the railing, both legs brushing past her as he kept balance with his hands, blonde hair whipping behind him.

"Hey!" Rita leapt on the other railing, skort bunching slightly as she slid, the metal of the railing making her go faster.

Milos pushed off, rolling onto his feet as Rita dug into her bag, feeling over each before recognizing what she was looking for and tossing a bottle at him. It splattered against his back, causing him to stumble as she used the movement to catch herself, barely avoiding being flung from the railing. A scabbard lashed out, causing her to trip, almost tumbling over.

She managed to catch herself with her hands instead of slamming into the ground, Milos already hurrying to the door in a walk that made him look regal, if not for the way he was holding his nose with distaste, some of his hair stained with the potion Rita threw at him. She pushed herself up, the dirt of the flooring spattering on her clothes, and raced forward, getting to the doorway at the same time as him.

Alex, who probably just arrived, jumped, turning to them as they both shoved passed the doorway. Milos, to her distaste, was a step ahead of her.

"You…"

Milos smirked, pulling his hair over his shoulder to get the stickiness from the blonde locks. "Don't have to ask for a cuddle. I'll make sure to get a sketch for you."

Rita felt her cheeks redden as Alex glanced between them, sweat beading on his forehead. "Do I want to know?" he asked hesitantly before slapping a hand over his mouth.

Rita frowned, confused. It wasn't an odd question.

"Not particularly." Milos shrugged, watching with narrowed eyes. "No need to slap yourself, it wasn't a stupid question."

Alex didn't say anything, just brought his hands down, smiling sheepishly.

"What happened to you two?" Valencia hurried over, startled. "And what is that smell?"

"I'm wondering that myself." Milos tugged at the strand of his hair, fingers getting caught in the tangles.

"I may have thrown a glue bomb at you; it was the first thing I could grab that wasn't dangerous." Rita shrugged before turning to Valencia, who crossed her arms over her chest with a disapproving look. "If it's any consolation, he tripped me, which is why I'm like this." She gestured toward herself, though as the disappointed look remained, she felt herself wince, starting to feel a little embarrassed. Milos's expression also briefly flushed as he seemed to realize how they acted in a stranger's house. "Ah…sorry."

Thankfully, Suzuhah spoke up. "Well, at least you realized. Also, you threw stinky glue at him?" Suzuhah —oh, right, female Suzuha— chuckled, leaning back in one of the chairs as she waved.

The room itself, now that Rita was paying attention, was a large dining room with windows to one side letting in the meager day stones turning night stones light. Light stones hung over the ceiling, casting a gentle glow over the long table, wooden chairs placed at even intervals beside it. Ari and Leon were already seated, watching in startled silence, along with Riviera.

"It's…"

"And what was that about asking for a cuddle?" Suzuha raised an amused eyebrow as she giggled.

Rita did a double take as she could have sworn she saw the flash of sheepish embarrassment on Milos' face at their antics. Rita was tempted to lift a middle finger to him, but held off, even more so after that, though she did feel heat on her face. "Nothing," she muttered, taking a seat at one of the chairs.

"Here." Alex reached forward toward one of the glasses, filled with water. His fingers twitched as he pulled the water out and carefully spread it on the glued strands, getting a grateful look from Milos.

"My boy, that's some amazing control." Riviera's voice caught Rita's attention as he watched, awed.

"My little angel." Valencia clapped her hands, eyes sparkling. "You already know how to control water! You are much farther along than I thought."

Alex was blushing brightly, hair somewhat covering his face as he worked, only she and Milos happened to see it, the faint amusement on his face.

"It is appreciated," Milos said, pulling at the now wet locks, the glue dissolving. Alex nodded before flicking his fingers.

Rita yelped, hearing another from Milos as a trickle of water splashed into her face.

"That's for antagonizing each other in someone else's house.

Again." Alex huffed; arms crossed over his chest.

Rita glared, noticing Milos do the same, his face as wet as hers. She quickly grabbed up a towel as Suzuha snorted.

"And then he does that." Suzuha gestured, chuckling.

"I suppose it was one way to clean them up a bit." Valencia's voice barely hid the faint amusement.

Riviera was just outright laughing, not even hiding it.

"I had to do something with the water." Alex shrugged as Rita placed her towel down, Milos doing the same, the tips of his hair damp like hers.

Rita wanted to argue, she did, but she couldn't come up with anything. Considering Milos stayed silent, he had the same predicament.

"Well, this is one way to arrive." A gentle voice rang, catching everyone's attention. Rita turned and almost jumped as Lillianna Ren, Sovereign of the Sanctuary, stepped in. She looked as elegant as before, her movement graceful and refined. She was smiling in amusement. She briefly noticed Alex blink and rub his eyes, staring at Lillianna with a strange expression.

"Sovereign!" Valencia stood, startled, nodding her head. "We didn't expect you tonight. I thought you would still be working."

"I can come to my own home occasionally." She crossed her arms over her chest. "I'm not always going to sleep in my office. I loaned it to Riviera and yourself when you arrived, due to the limited space and your positions. I extended the offer to the rest of you." She peered around at the group. "How are you finding it so far?" Her gaze flitted briefly to Milos.

"Good?" Rita managed to speak up, surprised she wasn't tripping over herself.

"I am very glad I didn't throw the water on the floor," Alex muttered under his breath. Rita had to agree.

Lillianna observed the table and raised an eyebrow. "Oh, which of you cooked?"

There was a moment of hesitation before Ari and Leon raised their hands.

Lillianna walked over, taking the remaining seat at the head of the table. "Well, then, let's not waste this delicious-looking food. We'll talk after we are done, so eat up."

She pulled a plate over, scooping what looked like chicken onto the plate, along with some vegetables. They were seeing all sorts of specialty food down here.

Rita hesitantly followed suit, the others slowly gathering their own plates in stunned silence.

The food, to none of Rita's surprise, was incredible. The two managed to make great meals with the meagre supplies they had on board, so with fresh food? Rita may have eaten way more than she should have.

"Definitely my compliments to the chefs. I am somewhat glad mine was on vacation." Lillianna chuckled, wiping at her mouth daintily. Leon seemed proud. Ari bowed her head, somewhat embarrassed. Lillianna put her napkin down, hands in her lap. "Now then, since I have some time, how was your first day in our fair city?"

The mood very quickly soured startling Riviera, Valencia and Lillianna, though it was harder to tell with the last woman.

Rita crossed her arms over her chest. "Fair city?" She clicked her tongue. "I mean, sure, it's beautiful, but the people here are worse than dingbats."

Milos sighed. "My apologies for her words."

Rita glared as he seemed to carefully respond, clearly thinking over his own.

"You see, when we left after speaking to you, we decided to partake in the food here." He seemed to debate for a moment, only to jerk, glancing over as Alex nudged him, nodding.

Milos shook his head and turned back to the trio. "As you surmised, I am not liked here, and I can understand that…"

"Not like it makes any sense," Rita muttered. "They don't even know you." Her thoughts flashed back before a grin crossed her lips. "Though I doubt they will cause any problems in the future. Their main stove got…kind of melted. Too much heat I suppose?"

Suzuha barely withheld the snort as Rita thought back to the potion she carefully poured into that kitchen, and the resulting soot. After all, it didn't damage anyone, just some important equipment.

Lillianna raised an eyebrow but thankfully didn't press. Milos simply looked at her, seemed to decide not to bother and continued, his lips twitching. "However, my lineage speaks for itself." He turned back to the group and Rita almost missed a flash of a strange expression on Lillianna's face before it returned to careful curiosity. Geez, everyone had a poker face like Milos, it was kind of annoying. "Alex and I ordered similar food at one location. Probably the one Rita spoke of. He kept what was supposed to be mine." Milos hesitated.

"There were metal shards in it that I almost swallowed," Alex broke in, eyeing his mother warily.

Valencia was on her feet in seconds. "WHAT!" She pretty much vaulted over the table. Alex yelped as she quickly checked him. "You're not badly hurt, right? You didn't actually swallow anything? Those pieces of…"

"Calm yourself, Valencia. Let them continue." Lillianna raised her hand, watching them quietly, eyes narrowed, amusement gone. If Rita wasn't stunned, she would have thought she saw a flash of fury on the woman's face, though it was gone so fast, she wasn't sure. "I believe they have more to speak of."

Valencia slowly pulled away but kept her hands on Alex's shoulders. Alex glanced toward her before turning back toward Riviera, who seemed carefully neutral, and Lillianna, whose cheerful appearance was now gone. Rita shivered, she could see where the Sovereign part came into play.

"We found a note under the food, saying that Milos should stay away from me and that he should have never been born."

Milos twitched at that.

"That was the worst, but over the day, I think it was only because I was with him that we didn't get attacked."

"It was close." Milos' voice was hesitant, low.

Wait, seriously? Considering Alex's reaction, turning to him in shock, he hadn't noticed either.

Lillianna steepled her fingers, hiding her lips though it seemed she was straining to keep her expression neutral as Valencia squeezed Alex's shoulders, doting on him worriedly. The sight tugged at Rita's heart, distant memories of her parents doing the same made her want to tear up, but she quickly blinked it away.

"I knew there would be some animosity, but to attack so soon and to hurt Valencia's son in the process? That is not a good sign." Lillianna's gaze flicked around the room. "It is something to keep in mind, moving forward. Though I thank you, Rita, for… stopping that from happening again in the future. I can't have fights breaking out in this city, especially amongst such powerful fighters." She seemed to pause, fingers white from how tightly they were steepled. "Milos, stay close to your allies and continue to cover your signifiers. It's the best we can do for now until they learn to trust you."

Milos pursed his lips, fingers trailing through his hair as if as an afterthought, still a little damp from Alex splashing him in water. "I will certainly do what I can." He spoke after a moment.

Lillianna nodded, an odd expression on her face. "I do apologize. I really do. You are not to blame for the atrocities of your ancestors, but it seems many here have forgotten that." Lillianna sighed, rubbing her temples before pushing herself to her feet. "I have some considerations to make. I think tomorrow it would be best if Alex here meets the council. They will want to speak with him anyway." She gestured. "I would typically send Valencia, but I need her nearby to discuss some things, so a woman named Erin will guide you there. She might appear frightening, sarcastic and will probably startle you, but she's a good woman and will guide you safely."

"But, Sovereign, the council…"

"I am well aware, Valencia." Lillianna turned to Alex's mother. "Which is why I need you there and Erin will be here to pick them up. We have to quell any thoughts, and Erin is as neutral as can be. If they hear his story, we might be able to convince them to persuade their constituents not to get involved with any of the party he brought with him." Her gaze swept over the room. "We have a lot of powerful people here; it is not something I am considering lightly." She closed her eyes and let out a breath. "On top of that, with so many of us in one location. I fear for the safety of the lands themselves, but that is another matter to discuss at a later time."

Rita pursed her lips. A moment later, the familiar tingling crashed over her, and she barely suppressed a cry as she grabbed her head tightly.

Another future vision?

She wasn't sure where she was standing, but she suspected it was the Overlands. The sun beat down, searing her, before vanishing in the blink of an eye. The ground was covered in dirt and what she suspected was grass, a few trees springing up around. They began shaking, sputtering. Limbs flailed as people she didn't recognize, of cultures and colors she never saw, looked up and around, bewildered and worried.

Then she noticed it, a piercing song filling the area, almost like a cry of fear and desperation. The very air was shaking as the earth suddenly screamed, sending her stumbling as cracks slashed across the ground, ripping up dirt and trees like they were nothing. A loud CRASH echoed from nearby as a large building of metal splintered to the ground…breaking through it and disappearing out of sight.

Alex, wings flaring out, swept down, catching her just as the ground crumbled below her, and she watched in abject horror as the people around her all fell, reaching, grasping, desperate. Their screams of utter fear pierced her ears. A large hole opened like a crater, straight down into an abyss of black where they disappeared. Suzuhah flew beside them, carrying Milos on their back, who was peering down in a quiet pained silence, hair cut short, signifier seemingly gone.

Wind whipped through the air, stinging her eyes and slamming into them as rain screeched down, crashing over more earth which splintered and broke. She could hear the screams and cries. Pleas for help were promptly silenced.

The ground shattered.

The city she could see in the distance, larger than even Raynout, crumbled, falling away, disappearing in a blink.

It felt like the whole world was vanishing before her in roiling chaos. It was a living hell that did not seem to end. Suzuhah's and Alex's wings stuttered, barely keeping them aloft as the wind howled and cried.

"We were too late." Suzuhah's voice rang through them as he swept past, dodging around a sputter of rock that almost crashed over him, crumbling down into the void.

"Dammit…" Alex cursed, startling her, but not really. "Is there really nothing we could have done? Nothing?"

Milos stayed silent as she spoke. "I don't know," Her voice sounded exhausted, tired. "They did this to themselves. We warned them, we TRIED and yet…"

Her words were lost as an explosion of heat flared up. Alex tried to dodge, letting out a screech of pain as they were sent tumbling backward…backward…

CRASH!

Cold stone lay beneath her as the headache subsided and she slowly sat up, shaking her head.

She felt a presence beside her and glanced over to see Suzuha helping her up, expression showing recognition.

"Rita?" Alex's voice reached her ears, and she glanced over to see he was standing, hands on the table and only slightly younger than the future vision she saw. Was it a future vision?

Or a nightmare?

"Sorry." She forced a smile on her face, still trying to parse through what she saw, her mind spinning and aching. "I guess I'm more tired than I thought." Milos narrowed his eyes, unbelieving, as Suzuhah's fingers squeezed into her shoulders.

"Young lady…" Lillianna's gaze was firm, but gentle. "I may not know much of the seer's class, but I do recognize when one receives a vision." She watched quietly. "Considering your reaction, I ask that you tell me what you saw. Visions, even wild ones, are important."

Rita pursed her lips, remembering the pure hell she saw. She wanted to explain, but every time she opened her mouth, the horror of it slammed over her like a tsunami. "I…I can't…" She found herself stuttering, unable to say the words, startling both Milos and Alex. She wasn't one to hesitate and yet just remembering what happened sent her into a mental panic. She knew she should tell Lillianna, but the words just wouldn't come.

Lillianna's gaze softened, seeming to recognize something in her expression, a flash of pain and realization settling in her gaze before she sighed. Rita wondered, for a brief moment, if she even had to say anything or if Lillianna already knew somehow. "Well, I think that's enough for today. All of you, get some rest. I will speak with you in the morrow." With that, she swept out of the room with a grace that Rita didn't think she would ever be able to manage.

She heard footsteps as Milos squatted in front of her. Gaze serious and voice low. "We need to talk."

She didn't want to, but she took his hand and, with Suzuha's help, stood.

Riviera and Valencia watched as Alex came over as well, expressions worried. After all, he only saw her visions once, compared to Milos. Suzuha was a seer's creation, this was fairly normal, probably.

"You four, rest. We will see you tomorrow." Valencia gestured to Riviera who stood and left alongside her.

Alex watched them go with an odd expression before turning back to her.

"Let's go upstairs," she said after a moment. He nodded and gestured. Milos rolled his eyes, but stepped ahead, leading the group. Ari and Leon watched before starting to clean up, leaving them to discuss. Soon enough, they found themselves upstairs, having picked a random room to talk in. Considering Alex's amusement, it turned out to probably be his, though Rita wasn't sure if Alex actually saw his room yet, so…

She took a seat on the bed, organizing her thoughts, as Milos leaned against the doorframe. Suzuha plopped on the floor as Alex joined her on the bed, curious eyes watching her as she thought over her words. Her racing thoughts slowly calmed as those around her remained quiet, their presence comforting.

After a few minutes, she finally found herself able to speak. "I know I said I couldn't talk to Lillianna, and I couldn't, the words just didn't want to come out, but…" She shook her head. "I need to tell someone, and, for some reason, I got a strong feeling that she already knew. Sometimes I wonder if Demons can read minds." She glanced toward Milos who winced.

"Some can, from the records. I don't know which, however."

"Great." Rita peered toward the window, settling her breath before she continued, "I don't know where I was, but I think we were in the Overlands. There was a large city of metal and people of all sorts wandering around." Her voice came out hesitantly.

"That sounds right." Milos pursed his lips. Alex blinked, startled. His expression grew contemplative as Rita continued, "Suddenly, it was as if the world just… broke. The land was being destroyed." Rita glanced up, eyes narrowed. "It was as if the entire world was shattering around us. The Overlands were crumbling into the Underlands."

Horror flashed on Alex's and Suzuha's faces as Milos narrowed his eyes, but didn't budge.

Rita hung onto his expression, trying to keep calm. "We were avoiding it because Alex and Suzuhah could fly, but even that was barely doing anything because of the weather battering us from all sides." She took a breath and let it out. "Though, the worst part was the conversation…"

"We were talking during all that?" Alex asked cautiously as Suzuha watched her with an almost sad expression.

Rita nodded and told them what she could remember of the conversation, though it was fairly seared in her brain. "I said they did this to themselves. That we warned them…" She trailed off. "What is this? What caused it? It was as if the whole world had destroyed itself and we knew the reason and were unable to stop it."

"You're certain it wasn't a day nightmare or something?" Alex asked hesitantly, though it was clear even he didn't believe it.

Rita wanted to, she really did. She didn't want to believe that a future like that existed, and she wasn't even aware of what could cause such a thing. "No," she finally whispered. "That was a future vision. I recognized the feeling before it hit."

The other three exchanged looks. Milos let out a breath, eyes closed in thought before he spoke. "It's something to keep in mind, but from the sounds of it, there is still time until that." He opened his eyes, meeting hers. "Do you have a general time frame, besides the fact that Alex could fly?"

Alex looked away at that as Rita pursed her lips. "Everyone did look a bit older, though I'm not sure if it was really by a lot." Her gaze flitted to Milos, noting the difference. She only got to see the future Milos briefly, but he was different, and not just because of the short hair.

"Then, yes, there is time to figure out what caused that and hopefully stop it." Milos peered towards the nearby window, not looking at anyone. "As much as there are parts of the Overlands that I would be HAPPY to do without, it is still my home. I wouldn't want to see it destroyed in such a way."

Rita nodded as Alex gave her a tired smile.

"Hey, as Milos said, we still have time. For now, I think it's best if we worry about it later." He lightly touched his shoulder. "I mean, I can't even fly yet, so it's gonna be a while till I'm able to fly through a storm like you described, especially carrying someone." He chuckled before turning to the others. "I don't like it, but at this point, there isn't much we can do about that."

Rita huffed. "I should be saying that, not you."

"That's why I'm saying it, because you aren't," he teased. getting an amused snort from Milos who quickly covered it with a cough.

Suzuha just chuckled, swinging her legs back and forth.

Rita shook her head and stood, hands on her hips. "Well, I've changed futures in the past and, while some of them did still come to pass, not all of them did so." She pumped her fist. "If I ever figure out what causes that, you can bet your arse I'm going to stop it and you three are helping me." She pointed around. Suzuha giggled behind her hand as Milos just raised a bemused eyebrow. Alex smiled; expression soft as he nodded.

"That's kind of obvious," Suzuha piped up, grinning.

"Way to spoil my grand monologue," she muttered. Alex chuckled at that as Milos shook his head. "Well, whatever, it's not like we're going to be in the Overlands for some time, so, yeah…I think…" she cringed and stuck out her tongue. "Milos is right, and I hate to say that."

Milos just smirked, causing her to glare at him.

"Still, what now?" Suzuha pointed out, plopping down beside her. "Let's see, not even counting an apocalyptic future, we've got…" She put her hand up, fingers extended as she slowly curled them in with each point. "A Demon who doesn't know how to Demon." Alex snorted, but didn't argue. "An Alertian who is basically going to get shanked as soon as he takes two steps outside. And a witch who is allied with both. On top of that, there is a powerful group of people who govern this place who are interested in our situation, and we also have a princeling of the Underlands in our midst. Did I miss anything?"

"No. No, you didn't." Alex winced, his expression hesitant for a moment before he continued, "That's a lot, admittedly."

"You think?" Rita gave him a look, feeling a mix of emotions at the thought. Man, this was so messed up.

"My situation is fairly simple to rectify." Milos gestured. "At this point, I have no reason to leave except for that meeting tomorrow and, maybe, to train, which I should be able to do here."

"I mean, that's true." Alex frowned.

"We can worry about that later." Milos peered around the group. "It would be best if we focus on what we can work on." He turned to Alex, eyes narrowed. Alex stiffened, smiling sheepishly.

"Ah, you mean, me?" He gestured before slumping. "I guess it would be better to learn how to use these abilities." He glanced over his shoulder, lost in thought. "I'm kind of unnerved though. The sooner I learn how to use my wings, the sooner that future becomes possible."

"However, forgoing learning your wings won't change anything," Milos pointed out and Rita found herself unable to argue, frustratingly enough. "So, tomorrow, we're going to start practicing. I know she mentioned meeting the council, but we won't worry about that until it happens. Suzuha, you are going to help."

"Me?" Suzuha glanced over, startled. "I mean, sure, I kind of expected as much, but it seems a bit soon." She paused before shrugging. "Eh, fine. I would rather get it over with. I do want to spend some time going around town on my own anyway."

"You can." Rita glanced toward Suzuha. "After all, you are not exactly combined with us, per se, plus, you've been here before, so they know you."

Suzuha nodded, a grin on her face. "Exactly."

Alex peered at her quietly before relaxing. "Thanks, Suzuha, Milos."

Suzuha waved it off as Milos nodded.

Rita stood, reaching toward the ceiling in a long stretch and barely suppressing a yawn. "Well, I'm going to relax here for now and I would rather NOT have everyone in my room at the moment, so shoo."

"I think this is my room, actually," Alex pointed out, startling her.

She blushed and smiled sheepishly.

Milos actually seemed to snort at that but slipped out.

"Right." She quickly headed toward the door as Suzuha waved and hurried out. She peered back toward Alex, noticing his gaze flitting between them.

He spotted her and his expression relaxed. "Good night."

"Night, Alex." With that, she hurried to her room, letting out a breath. She peered out the window as she stepped into hers, the day stones fading into night. This was going to be a weird few weeks, wasn't it?

# Chapter Eight

Alex awoke to a knock on his door. He groaned, curling into the sheets. They were so comfortable after the last few weeks. Sure, he liked the soothing sound of the waves and water, but the beds weren't exactly anything noteworthy. He heard the knock again and huffed, sitting up. "I'm coming." He grumbled as he pulled himself out of bed, somewhat unsurprised to see Milos, already up and changed. Suzuhah stood behind him, yawning, but awake.

Guess it was time to start.

He pulled his clothes on, slapping the belts over his waist before heading downstairs. There was a faint sound of sizzling that caught Alex's attention. He frowned and, waving that he would be there in a minute, he hurried over to the kitchen. That burning smell…it couldn't be…

His thoughts were cut off as he peeked inside to see Mom running around, panic on her face as the oven glowed brightly with a fire stone.

"MOM!" Alex yelped, grabbing whatever was nearby to extinguish the flames. He heard footsteps and heard a yelp and a surprised grunt. Soon enough, with Suzuhah and Milos' help, they were able to turn the oven off and suppress the flames from damaging anything else.

Alex, sweat coating his face, glared at his mother who put her hands together with a pained, if sheepish expression. "Sorry, honey, I thought I would try to make you breakfast."

"Mom, we've discussed this." Alex huffed, managing to tug out the lump of charcoal. He wasn't even sure what it was supposed to have been.

Milos curled his nose up as Suzuhah actually laughed.

Mom pouted.

Alex found himself relaxing as he threw the coal lump into the trash and turned to her. Strangely, this felt familiar and almost relieving. In so many ways, it seemed his mother was completely unrecognizable, but this?

This was something that she always did and, in some ways, it kind of reminded him that she hadn't really changed. It was just his own perception.

Still, in some ways, even now, it was hard to compare his sheepish and slightly singed mother with the dangerous winged Demon from before. "You okay?"

"I'm fine." She waved it off, walking over to him and ruffling his hair. "Thanks for the help."

"No problem. I smelled it and guessed you tried something like this again."

"Am I that obvious?" His mother chuckled, but relaxed, gaze flicking to Suzuhah and Milos. Milos' expression was even, though there was a hint of amusement. Suzuhah was just grinning widely, hands behind his head as he watched. "Thank you both for your help as well." She paused at Milos before turning to Suzuhah. "May I ask why you all are up this early? The meeting with the council isn't for a while and I did say…"

"Training." Suzuhah shrugged.

Mom glanced at Alex, worried. "What type?"

"Flight." Milos let out a breath, staring at her quietly. "Suzuhah here is a Vulfulas, and I assumed you would be too busy to teach your son such a thing."

Mom bristled at that. "Actually, I set time aside to catch up with my son and help him." She hesitated at that. "However, as much as I say that…" She let out the heaviest sigh Alex heard in a while. "Lillianna wants me to help coordinate the meeting with the council, as you heard yesterday." Her gaze met Alex's worry on her face. "I know I promised I would teach you, but this is important as well. So, I hate to admit it, but Milos is right." She glanced side long toward Alex with a soft expression as Alex blinked, startled at the use of Milos' name. "I wish I could show you what to do, but I barely convinced Lillianna to give me enough time to try to make something for you. I can, at least, give some pointers."

"That would be appreciated."

Her gaze flicked to Milos, a hint of surprise clouding the features before her eyes narrowed. "Speaking of, Alertian, why are you so determined to help my son? I'm not oblivious."

Milos stared quietly, grip tightening slightly on the hilt of his blade before the fingers slowly unfurled. "I have my reasons," he said simply, startling Alex. "However, if it's any consolation, I hold no opposition to your son. He is..." Milos actually paused, brow furrowed. "A close acquaintance."

"You mean friend?" Suzuhah teased. Milos sharply looked away. Alex chuckled at that before glancing at his mom. He paused, noticing the strange expression on her face.

"I see." She spoke softly, with an odd intonation. "As long as you mean no harm to him, I will accept your presence... and your willingness to train him in my stead."

"Mom." Alex cut in, confused and annoyed, briefly noting a flare of red around her.

Milos turned back to her before giving a surprisingly deep bow, blonde hair falling over his shoulder, the metal of the chain clinking softly. "I appreciate the gesture of confidence." He straightened. "I, as such, have no wings, but I do know the flow of magic. If you could tell me how the two balance, that will suffice."

Mom hesitated for a moment before pulling away. "The magic is inherent." Her voice was even, almost clipped. "It is not something that needs thought about. The coordination of the wings is what is necessary. Demons, such as my son and I, create wind currents to sustain our flight. It is why I was able to get to your ship as quickly as I did. Teach him first how his wings work, then worry about the magic that courses through them."

Alex stared at his mother, utterly confused. What did she mean? His wings were separate from his other abilities? Or did she mean something else? Also, why was she being so rude? She seemed so relaxed with Milos even just a few moments ago.

"Mom, what the heck?" He leaned forward, almost breaking their conversation. "You are being really weird."

He felt her gaze before her eyes widened and the redness dimmed out of sight. She winced and turned back to Milos, who clearly was about to respond. "I do apologize. I guess instinct kicked in, especially since it was in regards for my son's safety. I did not mean to be rude or offensive."

Milos seemed a little taken aback, clearly not sure how to respond. After a moment he seemed to shift back to stoic as he spoke. "Understood."

Wait, what? Alex glanced toward Milos who nodded. "I… appreciate the apology. As for your words of advice, that's what I needed to know." He turned to Alex who wasn't sure what to think. "Are you ready? We'll grab some breakfast and get started."

I am so lost, Alex thought before turning back to his mom, who gestured. "There should still be some sausage in the cold room." She leaned forward, pulling him into a quick hug. "I'll see you later, my little angel. I wish you luck." With that, she glanced toward the kitchen once more before hurrying away.

Alex watched her go, grateful she at least apologized, only to jump slightly as footsteps reached his ears and he felt a pat on his shoulder. He turned to Suzuhah, who gave a gentle expression of warmth. "She's a kind soul. I know how hard it is to resist instinct; it was somewhat admirable she acknowledged her fault."

"She is…" Alex felt his lips twitch up before he turned to Milos. "So, food, then training?"

Milos shook his head as they grabbed some of the sausage and leftover toast. After quickly cooking and chowing down on the filling meal, they found themselves outside. The day stones glowed brilliantly over the beautifully trimmed garden in the back. There were some light stones and heat stones keeping the plants thriving and he heard and felt occasional sprays of water falling gently over the area.

Suzuhah shuddered before stepping to one side. In a flash, causing Alex to cover his eyes, golden fur expanded, catching the surrounding lights and glimmering faintly. Suzuhah sat down on his haunches, wings settling onto his back as the tail curled around him. He was large, quite large in this form. Alex remembered how he filled the room when he transformed before to comfort him, but it was another thing to see it under the glow of the day stones. He easily sat on his haunches, a good foot above Alex, wings almost as long as Alex himself. He wasn't as large as the drega Alex and Milos fought in the ravine, but he was close.

Milos just stared for a moment, shook his head, and stepped to one side. "Alex, switch to your Demon form."

After the last few weeks, it was fairly easy to pull on the feeling in Alex's chest. He twitched, tail lightly thwacking against his leg as the wings fluttered. He peered partially over his shoulder, head slightly heavier from what he guessed were the horns. The black and blue wings spread out to either side. Unlike Suzuhah, he didn't grow in size, the main differences were the wings, which were almost as long as he was tall, which made them so cumbersome. Yet he was still about the same height as Milos, maybe a little shorter.

Footsteps caught his attention as Milos stopped before him. "Alex." Alex turned to him only to pause. For a brief moment, Alex could have sworn he spotted a flare of white and silver before it promptly vanished. He blinked, barely hearing Milos' next words. "See if you can bring your wings in front of you."

"Huh? That's…"

"It's possible, just try it," Suzuhah called, causing Alex to purse his lips before nodding and focusing, pushing the image to the side. He knew where the edges were because of Rita's and Milos' help ages ago. He slowly shifted them forward, letting the joints move. He grimaced slightly at the awkwardness before finally getting them in front of himself, the tips of the wings crossing each other.

Milos nodded, a faint smile on his lips. "Relax."

"How?" Alex huffed. "You want me to relax like this?"

"You are thinking too much about how odd it is." Milos gestured. "Your wings, just like your magic, are just extensions of yourself. Let your Demonic half have a little more control."

Alex pursed his lips. He hated the idea. Sure, he came to accept his Demonic half, but…

He yelped as he felt a faint THWACK on his back and stumbled slightly. He felt his wings shift, curling even more around him as if in protection as he glared over his shoulder toward Suzuhah. The long tail curled back as a grin formed over the fox's face.

"That works." Milos chuckled, catching Alex's attention. He paused as he peered forward once more, noting as his wings slowly pulled back, almost like a curtain. "Did you notice?"

Alex paused at that, frowning slightly. Notice how his wings moved? It seemed strangely natural. He sighed. Right, Demons relied on instinct, he kept forgetting that thought, even though he was reminded just that morning.

"Well, time to actually learn about your wings." Suzuhah extended one wing out as Alex turned. "Our wings are different, mine is more resembling one long bone, yours is more similar to a bat's wing, with smaller bones throughout. However, functionally, they both work similarly, especially if you create your own wind currents."

Alex paused, extending his own wing out as he examined both.

Faint scratching sounds caught his attention, and he peered over his shoulder. Wait, when did Rita get here?

Rita peered up and waved. She sat on the steps to the house, book in her lap and pen in her hand as she sketched away.

"You slept in," Milos called, a hint of amusement in his voice.

"I wasn't the one who needed to be up," Rita responded with a grin. "Don't mind me, go ahead and get back to what you were doing."

Alex shook his head as Milos stepped forward, gesturing. It was fascinating, learning the differences and similarities. As the day stones grew brighter, Milos took a step back, gesturing to Suzuhah to show how he would take off.

Alex watched, curious, as Suzuhah got to his feet, muscles rippling. The wings extended out, tilting in a strange way that caught Alex's eye. A moment later, Suzuhah slowly beat down. "I'm taking this slowly, so pay attention."

Wind started to swirl as with one long thrust, Suzuhah leapt into the air, the wings catching down before curling back up. The force of wind blew at Alex's and Milos' hair and pulled at their clothes. Alex saw Suzuhah take flight before, but this was stunning. He felt his own wings twitch and flutter, almost as if his Demonic side wanted to follow through, feeling the wind against him. Suzuhah circled above, long tail curling around to complete the circle before he, wings extended, slowly settled back to the ground, wings beating to catch himself briefly before he landed again.

"Well, I have never seen a Vulfulas so close, but that was quite beautiful." A voice caught everyone's attention and Alex found himself whipping around to see a woman standing in the doorway. Rita yelped, almost dropping her supplies as she turned, staring upward.

The woman was tall, far taller than any woman Alex ever saw. Short cut red hair curled around a would-be pleasing face, if not for the long scar cutting through one eye that was milky white compared to the other hazel one. She clapped her hands, long nails clacking against each other. "So, this is the party with which the council is supposed to meet." She peered around as Alex shifted. He felt his tail curl, his wings bristling in discomfort. Something about this woman irked him, as pleasant as she was being.

"Oh?" She turned to him, her gaze flicking to his tail before she turned back to him. "I suppose your Demonic side is sensing mine." She grinned, fangs flashing briefly in the light. A flash of brown curled around her, before it faded. Alex frowned. At least now he was catching glimpses, but only getting glimpses of what Mom talked about the night before was annoying. He briefly wondered how she figured he could sense her, but she was a Demon, it was probably some ability of her. Alex noticed Milos was off to his side, fingers grazing his sword as he watched.

"I suppose you were selected to guide us to the meeting?"

She nodded, bowing to the waist. "My name is Erin, though that is simply the name that is easier for humans to pronounce." Her gaze flicked between Rita and Milos, staying on Milos. "Lillianna said she mentioned my name to you all, so that should clarify who I am. Though I suppose an Alertian would not struggle with one's Demonic name, would he?" The words were said in an almost sweet manner.

Alex felt a hiss rise in his throat and promptly squashed it down.

"Considering you took us by surprise, you should not be surprised at this reaction." Suzuhah shifted, settling back into his human form, staring dead at the woman. "Shouldn't we go? I don't think anyone is interested in standing around, talking."

The woman looked at him before turning on her heels, leaving. Alex noted, uncomfortably, that he couldn't hear her footsteps.

"What was—Who the hell was that?" Rita stood, annoyed.

"From what I could gather? Probably a species of Tacirapax, also known as the silent predator." Milos slowly uncurled his fingers from the grip on the hilt of his sword. "It's clear why they are called that."

Alex pursed his lips, his wings settling against his back. For some reason, he did not feel comfortable switching back to human form and no one was saying anything about it. He knew he should. He usually hated staying in Demonic form but something about the situation, the tension felt through the group and everything that happened lately made him tense. A large part of him was not letting him switch back and, for once, he decided to listen to instinct. It was easier and everyone in this city seemed to know who he was anyway, he had no reason to hide.

Rita pushed herself to her feet, shoving the stuff back into her bag as she patted herself down. "Well, that's unnerving." Her gaze flicked to Milos. "Even you…"

"I noticed about a moment before she started speaking," Milos admitted. His gaze on the door. "But…"

*Great,* Alex thought. Just what they needed.

He shook his head, walking ahead. A grunt sounded from behind and he glanced back to see his tail curled around Milos' arm. He quickly pulled back, surprise and embarrassment racing through him. Milos waved his arm out, stepping even. "You need to learn to control that." He waved out his arm as Alex winced.

"That's easier said than done. Unlike wings, tails have a mind of their own." Suzuhah spoke up, only a slight chuckle in his voice as they headed back up the steps, Rita only a few ahead, listened curiously. "They pretty much are in tune with the emotions of the one in which they are attached. Some can control it, but I would not trust those people." Suzuhah peered ahead. "I would be more trusting of someone like Alex where it was clear their tail was showing how they felt. That's probably how she could tell you and Milos were sensing her."

"Urgh…" Alex huffed. "That's embarrassing to think about."

"It explains a lot though." Rita peered back, expression even. "And it goes back to the whole instinct over thought thing. Speaking of, is your instinct telling you to stay a Demon? You would have normally changed back by now."

"Yeah." Alex peered back over himself, glaring briefly down at his tail before turning back to Rita. "I…something is telling me not to."

"Alright." Rita nodded, seeming to accept it as they walked through the house to the front door where the woman was waiting. She stared at them with a bemused smile before turning and continuing down the road.

They hurried after her, passing by the Sovereign's imposing marble building and down some steps. It almost looked like they were about to walk through town when the woman suddenly took a sharp right. Alex shifted to the other side of Milos, after noticing a few looks his way that turned to stares. Still his instinct told him not to change, that it was safer to be in Demonic form. He was starting to hate the feeling. Suzuhah walked a few steps behind with Rita in the lead.

Their steps were hesitant at best and everyone was quiet as they moved after the woman. Soon enough, they arrived at another large building, not as grand as the Sovereign's, but still beautifully designed. The woman walked up the steps, opening the door before gesturing. Rita stepped through, shoulders back and gripping her bag tightly. Alex found himself shifting closer to Milos as Suzuhah stayed behind them, expression strangely neutral.

The inside was a long, large hallway with doors on either end. All wood and stone with intricate designs and an arching ceiling. Alex could hear faint conversation from one of the doorways near the end of the hall. Erin walked forward, opening the door with a flourish before stepping inside.

Alex only got a quick peek before silence fell over the congregated group. Inside there were five people, all of whom he met at least once since arriving in the town. He winced, feeling almost palpably the energy, his mother talked about before. He was somewhat grateful, in that moment, that he remained in Demonic form. It felt a little easier to handle.

He felt his tail settle around him, lightly curling around his leg before he forced himself to step forward, feeling it twitch back behind him. His wings ruffled uncomfortably.

"The cur is joining as well?" Maritus, the airadon, spoke up, the long red hair floating as if pushed by a breeze as he leaned on one elbow. "This is not something I expected."

"It is fine, Maritus, Milos is Alex's guard, see it as nothing more."

"Lots of fine guards, and... men." Sechondres smiled, teeth glinting as she eyed Alex and Milos, her gaze flicking briefly to Suzuhah as she licked her lips. "I don't see any problem with them joining us. It is a meeting regarding their situation in our home, after all."

Alex briefly noted as Erin took a seat on the left-hand side of the room, close to Lillianna. The room itself was large with windows lining one side, letting in the day stones' light. Light stones dangled from above in curling tapestries of color that startled Alex. They were usually only blue or white, but these had many different hues. The table was wood that Alex didn't recognize and, around it, were different styles of chairs, some high-backed, some leaning toward comfort and some, like his mother's, that seemed like it was put together only recently. He wasn't even sure why his mother was there.

To one side were four chairs that Alex assumed were for them. Rita plopped down, taking a seat as if this didn't bother her in the slightest to be in a room full of powerful people.

Alex... Alex felt like he was going to puke. The magic he felt since arriving swirled around this room, almost heady, making his head spin. It called to his Demonic form, keeping him firmly in place. Faint flashes of colors drifted off each, vanishing only a moment later. He turned toward Mom, noting her familiar red, just a little clearer than everything else. He felt a hand land on his shoulder and took a deep breath, recognizing it. With a nod, he walked over to a seat which seemed to have an open back near the base for his tail. He settled down, the colors fading as everyone settled in. Suzuhah leaned over Rita's seat, arms crossed over the back, clearly watching the assembled crowd instead of taking the remaining one. Milos stepped up next to him, eyes narrowed and back straight.

His fingers trailed over the hilt, but didn't grip it. Alex wondered how hard it was for Milos not to react to what was in front of them. Alex placed his hands in his lap, fingers curling as he peered from person to person. There was Sechrondes, the naga smiling in a way he saw those in the red stone district portray. Maritus, who was curling a finger in his hair as he leaned against the palm, had a curious expression on his face. Ludwig, the short older man who was staring at Milos, that pressure from before there, filled with hatred. Erin, who was checking her nails, and then Mom and Lillianna. Mom gave him a soft smile filled with warmth and a hint of worry. Lillianna's expression was pleasant as she placed her hands in front of her on the table. "Well, now that everyone is in attendance." She nodded toward Erin. "Thank you for retrieving them."

"Of course, Sovereign, it is my pleasure." Erin nodded her head, respectful.

Lillianna gestured around the group. "I believe all of you here have met each other in one way or another, according to our newest advisor." She gestured toward Mom, who was watching quietly. There were nods and shrugs around the room before Lillianna continued, "So, I believe we will move to the point of this meeting." She turned back to Alex, eyeing him quietly. "With the arrival of Valencia's son, thought to be dead, an Alertian…" Energy swirled up at that word, but Lillianna pressed on, voice firm. "Here under my protection, and a Vulfulas that survived without his mistress, there are many who are concerned about the fate of our home."

"Of course," Ludwig cut in, glaring toward Milos. "An Alertian is as welcome here as a barnacle-encrusted steak is in someone's mouth." He turned toward the group. "They are not to be trusted, and it is inconceivable that—"

"Old man, we get it." Erin waved her hand, getting a look from Ludwig. "All of us are aware of the Alertians' betrayal of our kind. While none but Lillianna," she bowed her head toward the woman before continuing, "our Sovereign was there, we have all heard the tales. However, he comes with a child thought dead, with magic we cannot comprehend."

"Speaking of…" Sechrondes stared at Alex, her gaze drifting from the horns to his wings before meeting his gaze. "A blue winged Demon is practically unheard of and to be the son of our Valencia, of a lineage thought destroyed in the war, it is quite…fascinating. After all, Valencia attained her seat due to her personage and heritage which puts this young man into an interesting position."

Alex felt himself bristle, his wings fluttering. A hand landed on his shoulder and he slowly relaxed. "You're speaking like I'm not here," he finally said, annoyance slipping into his voice. "I know of my lineage." His gaze flicked to Mom before returning to the group. "I only came here because I knew my mom was here. I'm not really interested…"

"Boy, this is a bit more complex of a situation than I think you realize," Maritus cut in, gazing at him.

"He's not Boy, he's Alex. Geez." Rita crossed her arms over her chest, frowning. "Look, I get you are all powerful Demons, but—"

"Silence," Ludwig snapped, causing Rita to suddenly shut her mouth, startled. "You are only here because you follow the Boy. Keep that tongue in your mouth."

Alex's fists clenched and he felt the nails dig into his shoulder before relaxing. He wondered if Milos was doing that for comfort, or for himself. He didn't particularly care either way.

Still, he didn't respond as the man turned back to the group. "He and his companions are still young, they have no means of understanding our history, our laws. So many have already been broken with their arrival. This is inconceivable."

Silence filled the room for a moment before Mom spoke up, voice slightly shaken. "Laws that none knew until arriving? Of course, my son and his comrades would not know…".

"Valencia, dear, you've only been on the council for a week or so for a precarious reason. While we appreciate your words, now is not the time." Sechrondes spoke, gently, before she waved a hand. "However, I do agree with Valencia's words. Why condemn those who do not understand? Plus, we all know, from experience, the disadvantage of angering those who—"

"He's but a child," Maritus interrupted.

"You take children too lightly." Erin tilted her head toward Maritus, hazel eye gazing at him quietly. "Many a child fought in the war a hundred years ago, which is why so many of us are still alive today, still have a home of our own. Do not underestimate a child, especially one who traversed the very Underlands to get here."

Maritus stared at her quietly before shaking his head.

"Well, then, what of the Alertian?" Sechrondes gestured, curious. "That was one of our reasons for this meeting."

"The cur? I don't care one way or another, as long as he does not harm any within this place, then I don't mind his presence though I would prefer him under watch or lock and key." Maritus' gaze flickered to Milos before turning back to the group. "Though, I will say, I am itching to test his capabilities, you all can sense it as well, can you not?"

"Maritus, that is not something we will speak of." Lillianna's voice cut off Maritus' slow smirk as Alex blinked, confused.

"Alex." She turned to him. "Why don't you tell us a little of your journey here, so that those here may understand the situation a little clearer."

Alex hesitated, glancing toward Rita and Milos, then Suzuhah, who gave a nod, expression just as neutral as before. He took a deep breath, turning back to the group. As he stared from person to person, he felt almost small. These beings... something in him told him they were all powerful, was it because of that strength that they were a council? Or was it something else? He had a feeling it was a mix of some things he wasn't aware of but in that moment he didn't much care. He felt his wings ruffle, uncomfortably close to the back of the chair. "What, exactly, do you want to hear?"

"How did you meet the Alertian?" Erin spoke up, staring right at him. "And please, do be truthful." Her eye narrowed onto him. "A lie is not appreciated in this room."

Alex pursed his lips. "I was attacked by some Martinets who caused the destruction of Rita's home. I managed to flee to the outer parts of the town where Milos found me." Alex hesitated for only a second, thoughts flashing rapidly. "There was some... miscommunication." He stopped himself from bringing his hand up to his cheek. "But he let me go and headed back toward town to find out more. Later, he caught up with Rita and me when we were traveling through the Eagle's Crag and helped me fight off a Drega that attacked us. We traveled together after that." Alex glanced toward the group, keeping his expression as even as possible. None of his words were a lie, per se, but he knew if he mentioned that Milos attacked him at first, it would be a whole different story, or when he was resting, the second time. "He helped me figure out where my mom went and helped keep us alive during the journey across the ocean. I owe him my life at this point."

"Same." Rita put one leg over the other, gaze stern. "And, no, I'm not going to stay silent. As much of a lout and a dingbat he is, he is not some murder-crazed monster like you all think he is. Sure, he's an Alertian, but he's the main reason most of us are still alive.

Ludwig's expression turned sour, but he didn't comment on Rita's interruption.

"And you, Alertian, what is your reason for being here?" Erin turned to him. "Clearly, you have these two at your...beck and call."

"I am thoroughly offended at that statement," Rita snapped, but everyone ignored her, gazes on Milos.

Alex felt his wings flutter, barely stopping from clipping Milos' side, annoyance flashing over his face once more. If anything, Alex was the one who had that ability, not Milos.

"They told you why I'm here." Milos' words were careful, his fingers curling into Alex's shoulder, side almost pressed to Alex's arm. "With the boat gone, due to the Aqua Wraith's withdrawal, I have no means of leaving, nor any intention to…" He trailed off for a moment before shifting his stance, pulling his hand back. Alex immediately missed the contact. "I am here to make sure no harm falls upon Alex or Rita and, in extension, Suzuhah."

"Appreciated," Suzuhah chirped, getting a sigh from Alex. Milos twitched, but didn't respond.

"If I wished to attack anyone, I feel it would have been apt to have already done something. After all, my presence is well known in this sanctuary at this point, even with the concealment we have tried to utilize."

Erin pursed her lips as Ludwig tilted his head up. "You lie." He spoke, voice dripping with venom.

Actually, as Alex watched, he could have sworn something dripped from his fingers and down his lip, some splattering onto the ground, sizzling slightly.

"He is not, in fact, lying." Erin spoke evenly; annoyance clear in her voice. "None of his words were a lie."

Milos' gaze flicked to her as Alex stiffened. "Right, Taripax can read the body language of those around them to learn who to be wary of."

"Well informed, I see." She stared at him with a narrowed eye, the milky white one almost more unnerving than the hazel. "But, yes, as much as I hate to say it, you are correct."

"Erin, this must be a sham." Maritus gestured. "You see that blonde hair, that red signifier, a signifier of that blood red has not been seen in…"

Milos blinked, a moment of confusion passing over his expression, something Alex only noticed because he was watching him. Maritus' words were interrupted by Sechondres. "Maritus, dear, it has been many years since any of us have seen an Alertian, nonetheless had one in our midst. It could simply be that this red is now a common signifier among that line.

However, crude such a thing is."

"Crude?" Rita blinked, glancing around. "Wait, do signifiers not exist for Demons?"

"You are correct." Lillianna spoke up this time, causing a silence to fall over the group. "Signifiers are a human-made creation and something that is believed to have started after the cataclysm that occurred two thousand years ago. It is not something Demons need nor have a desire for. It is a befuddling item to many of us, even now, though many an escaped slave has tried to explain its importance."

"Jewelry should be worn however you want, not as some tag to show who you are." Maritus huffed, a bangle clanking over his wrist as he waved it. "Still, we do understand some of the basic concepts, and know, more importantly, about the signifiers of an Alertian, for obvious reasons." His gaze snapped to Milos. "Such a shame, too, for such golden hair to be marred by not only that putrid length, but that red chain."

"I think the length looks stunning, but I digress." Sechrondes waved. "Correct me if I am wrong, Alertian, but the length indicates your duty as an Alertian, does it not?"

Milos pursed his lips as Alex blinked, glancing toward him. He hadn't known that. "It is."

"Really?" Rita perked up. "I wondered why you had such long hair." A strange expression crossed her face, and she frowned slightly. "So…what did…"

"You didn't know?" Erin spoke up, glancing over the group. "My, that is something most Demons know. If you see an Alertian with hair cut short and a red chain curling over it, it means they have killed and defeated a Demon. If you see one without the chain, which is unheard of in this century, it means they forsake their Alertian heritage. Which means, this one has yet to kill one of our kind or forsake his heritage."

"Which is part of the reason, begrudgingly, that we are accepting him." Maritus stared at him quietly. "Because it is tradition to cut one's hair with the bloodied sword that felled the Demon, according to our studies."

Alex felt sick at those words as Rita gagged, horror flaring on her face as her gaze snapped to Milos.

Milos stayed silent, not saying a word.

"To be around a powerful Demon like Alex…it is astounding that your Alertian instincts haven't kicked in yet." Maritus gestured, grinning. "Unless, of course, they are faulty."

Milos bristled and, this time, Alex felt a snarl curl up his throat. He shoved it down, though he didn't as miss the group of people in front of him suddenly shifted.

The somewhat uneasy air condensed into something heavier as everyone's lax postures became defensive.

"Little angel, calm yourself." Mom spoke, meeting his gaze, Alex almost paused as he noticed a flicker of red around her, that comforting red she showed him before, her magic. "We are not insinuating anything."

"Young man, you need to control yourself," Ludwig snapped, a few more drips of something falling to the floor with a sizzling splat. A flash of brown seeped from him, like dirt, the color shifting and fading into specks of cold green. Wait… why was he seeing this?

"Alertian, how are you ignoring this?" Erin hissed, nails curling into the table, anger flashing over her face for a moment. Blue…

"His NAME is Milos," Alex said, fingers twitching. A moment later, wind caught his hands, and he yelped as he was pushed backward, the chair slipping out from under him. He felt someone catch him by the arm, barely, as Rita and Suzuhah cried out.

His wings snapped out, halting his slide backward along with Milos' shifted gait, stopping them both from being blasted into the wall. Maritus stood, feathers flaring as the long-layered tail curled upward. This time Alex was certain, the curling blues and greens that swirled around him like a spiral was clear for him to see. He could almost feel it, the pressure. One hand faced them, his expression annoyed. "Do NOT forget who you are speaking with, child. You may be powerful in your own right, but we have been protecting this sanctuary for longer than you have been alive. Do NOT think of challenging us."

"Maritus, enough." Lillianna spoke as the wind died. Alex wondered how it was that, while he spotted flickers of color from the others, he didn't see anything on Lillianna. Was hers controlled? "From our knowledge, he has only recently come upon his Demonic powers. He has no means of controlling those energies, calm yourselves."

"My Sovereign, this is a mistake, if…"

"That is why he will be training here, under the council's watch."

Alex stiffened as Milos helped him forward, letting go against Alex's wishes. He needed the stable hand at the moment. Rita scurried out of her chair, checking them over as Suzuhah shifted in front of the three, posture almost defensive.

"I do not agree to that," Ludwig cut in. "I am sorry, Sovereign, but this is one thing I will NOT agree to."

"Then you do not have to, Ludwig." Lillianna faced him, almost staring down at him. To Alex's surprise, he seemed to crumple back slightly. "The four of them can be of great assistance to our home. I know you all desire to protect this sanctuary, this refuge." She spread her arms out. "From Valencia's words, the martinet's guild has grown in strength and it is not hard to assume that, sooner rather than later, they will find their way across the ocean."

"I'm sorry, Sovereign, but the only reason these four crossed was because of the aid of the Aqua Wraith." Maritus spoke evenly. "We all felt her presence when she arrived. Not many would dare cross those waters without aid such as hers."

"No…but we all know how tenacious humans are." Lillianna peered around the group. "Humans have a perseverance to them that we cannot and will never understand."

"We're all pure Demons." Maritus put a hand to his chest. "A pure Demon will always…"

"A pure Demon fell to a human." Mom spoke up, stopping the conversation. She stood, hands on the table as she peered around. "Humans WON the Human-Demon war. They are the reason so many of us are enslaved, so many are here. But humans are also the same ones who protected my son and me for years. Humans are the reason my son is still alive. There are many humans here who help keep this sanctuary running and safe. Do NOT underestimate humans."

"You say that because your son has human elements to him." Erin spoke, narrowing her eyes. "Sure, half-Demons have gained acceptance in our sanctuary, but they are not Demons, they cannot and will never be up to our capabilities." She stood as well, peering down. "Humans hold no magic, without our aid, they would have died long ago, millennia ago. Do not think, for a moment, that they aren't beneath us."

Mom snarled, her form snapping into the black winged version. Alex quickly shifted back as he grabbed Milos' arm. "You are so closed-minded! You've dwelled here, not even knowing or dealing with the outside world, how DARE you put a blanket statement over all humans."

Erin's form changed as well as she growled. The long incisors grew longer as her stance shifted. Two long black tails curled up behind her as her back arched. The nails sharpened into points as two long, almost flared ears curled around the side of her face. Dark fur covered her form as the piercing eye started to glow. "You stupid woman. You've been charmed by those humans. Look at yourself, you cower under them like some rat. You said it yourself, they have enslaved our brethren, forced them to perform and act like wild animals. They have even enslaved their own kind. What good are such creatures?"

"What good? Have you MET humans? Their creative spirits, their hopes and dreams, they do terrible things, but so do Demons!"

"We do no such thing." This time, Maritus spoke, the feathers having curled up over his form, his legs bending as if to spring off, only to reveal they changed to appear almost like some animal Alex read about. Wind whistled around the room.

Alex felt a little dizzy as colors flared and seemed to clash in the air, reds and greens and blues… almost as if their very magic was clashing as much as their words. "We are instinct, magic, we keep the balance of the world. If not for Demons, all life would be extinct. You would do well to remember that, Valencia."

"Now, now." Sechrondes spoke up, the fangs lengthening as the magic grew to almost intoxicatingly heavy levels. Alex felt it buffet at his skin, his Demonic form screeching quietly in a mix of panic and fury. Scales curled over her arms and face, the hair flowing backward as her tail crashed down on the floor. "Your instincts are flaring because of the child's emotions. Calm yourselves…"

"Oh, don't act like you're better than us, Sechrondes, you are changing and feeling it too," Erin snapped.

Alex gripped tighter onto Milos, noting as he grabbed his sword with one hand, the one Alex was holding. The other was to his head, fingers almost digging into his skin. Suzuhah pulled Rita behind him, posture low as a growl rang from his throat.

"ENOUGH!" Lillianna's voice cut through the growing argument as she slashed her arm out. Silence fell over the room. She and Ludwig seemed to be the only ones still appearing human. "I hear all of your concerns but now is not the time." She stood, peering over each person, a weight falling over the room. "I expected better of all of you. Control yourselves."

A feeling of disappointment fell over Alex, but it seemed that feeling was even worse for those around the room. Very slowly, everyone started to shift back to their more human-like forms and, for the first time since arriving here, he slowly let his own form drop, the wings fading at his back as the tail vanished.

Lillianna must have noticed, giving a very faint nod in his direction.

"Right, my apologies, Sovereign." Erin spoke, voice soft, bowing her head. "I let my instinct get the best of me."

"I understand." Lillianna spoke evenly. "However, now is not the time to speak of such things." She turned to Alex and his group, her expression softening. "Alex, Milos, Rita, Suzuhah, I must apologize on behalf of this council, it was not our intention to create such a scene or cause such distress."

Alex slowly relaxed, noting as Milos slowly uncurled his fingers from the sword. Alex hadn't even realized his tail had curled around Milos' waist to stop him, he only noticed by how Milos lightly rubbed his side, glancing behind Alex briefly to what was no longer there. Rita seemed to relax as well, adjusting her hat in the process.

"Well now." Suzuhah turned, hands on his hips. "I've only been with these three for a short time, but they behaved better than most of the Demons in this room who are many years       older than them." He tilted his head. "What does that say to you all?"

A few people bristled, but no one commented.

"It is as you say, Suzuhah." Lillianna spoke, voice even. "Tensions have been high since their arrival. I did not expect it to culminate in such a way." She peered over the group. "I think it is best if we all adjourn this meeting. However, first." She turned back to Milos. "Considering Milos, here, did not react or attack upon such a scene, I do believe we can trust that no harm will come to our citizens with his presence." She peered from person to person. "Under my honor, I will advocate for his safety in our lands."

There was a moment of silence before Sechrondes shrugged. "I have no complaints about him being in our lands. To resist such magic even with who he is…I think it is fair to think that, as long as he stays with his comrades, he will only be an asset to our people."

"I cannot, in good conscience, allow such a being to remain here, but I will abide by whatever the council decides." Ludwig spoke, voice even.

Erin and Maritus stayed silent for a moment before Maritus stood, feathers flaring. "An Alertian in our midst is a sign of danger, it shows weakness on the council's part. You can simply hand him over to one of us in retribution for his sins." He narrowed his eyes. "If he bestows any harm onto the people of this fair refuge, then I will be the FIRST to come down on him and those by his side." Maritus' gaze drifted to Alex. "No matter who or what they are. I will not jeopardize the protection of this place for a few people who are…mostly human." He turned back toward Lillianna. "So, I vote for his incarceration."

Alex pursed his lips, feeling uncomfortable.

"Oh boy…" Rita's voice was soft, her hand in her bag. "How hard would it be to run away now?"

"Very." Milos' voice came out slightly choked, that hint of fear slipping in. Something Alex knew only because he knew him. He barely stopped himself from switching back into Demon form.

All eyes shifted to Erin, the final one to vote, it seemed. She peered toward Alex, Milos, Rita and Suzuhah, disgust flaring over her face for a moment. "They are humans." Her gaze shifted over the four of them again. "Other than the Vulfulas, they are abominations. However," She turned back toward Lillianna. "I will vote to abstain as I do not wish to partake in this conversation. I understand the good having them on our side can bring, but I cannot, in good mind, agree to having them in our midst. Thus, I will not take part in this farce."

"If that is so, Valencia will take your place." Lillianna's voice was even. "While she may not yet be fully indicted, she is still an honorary member of the council until such time. Do you acknowledge this?"

"We already know her stance, so I suppose my abstaining is null and void." Erin narrowed her eyes at Mom who stared quietly back. "But, I was aware of that upon making my decision."

"As long as my son is safe, I do not much care." Mom spoke evenly. "You heard my son. Milos kept him safe through the Underlands. He had so many instances to kill him, or any other Demon, but he didn't. Plus, I'm not sure if you are aware, but there was a report that the Martinet's guild building in Raynout was destroyed, releasing all the Demons held within. It was said that Milos was at the scene on the side of the Demons." Mom peered toward Alex. "Is this correct?"

Alex could only nod, unable to speak with the sudden pressure in the room, almost suppressing the light from the stones.

"We are decided." Lillianna clapped her hands, gesturing toward Alex and his companions. "I will speak with you four later, but, for now, you are all allowed to remain safe within our home which, though I have forgotten to speak of, you may call Azher."

The word rang, familiar, in Alex's head. It wasn't Demonic, so he wasn't sure how he recognized it but…

He stood to his feet as Maritus shook his head, tilting his head up, eyes directly on Valencia. "This meeting is, clearly, adjourned. But, know this, daughter of Satan. Your grandfather would be MOST disappointed in this outcome." With that, he stormed out the door, moving past the group as Milos stiffened. Alex barely noticed, considering the glare his mother sent after Maritus.

"Pulling up lineage like that is inexcusable. My son and I are our own people. This is a sanctuary, after all, you—" She cut herself off, seeming to notice something. "Alertian, what is…"

Alex jerked, peering over in time to see the tail of Milos' long hair disappearing around the corner, vanishing out of sight. He heard Maritus' squawk of surprise and jerked, peering out the door in time to see Milos vanish past the doors leading outside, Maritus watching with narrowed eyes. The man made a clicking sound with his tongue before moving away, opposite where Milos went.

"Okay, great, thanks, totally not nice to meet you all, but I have to go check on the lout." Rita's chair screeched over the floor as she hurried past Alex, gesturing to follow with Suzuhah closely behind.

Alex nodded, glanced back, briefly, his gaze meeting Mom's worried look before he sent a glare to everyone else.

"Rude." Erin spoke evenly.

Alex twitched, a faint hiss slipping from his throat. He almost felt a short snap in the air and he, once more, barely stopped himself from shifting. "You all have NO right to say that."

With that, he chased after Rita, thoughts flying a mile a minute. What made Milos flee now? It was when he heard that Alex's mom was related to Satan…did that mean anything? He wasn't sure what his friend was thinking right now, but he wanted to be there to make sure he didn't do anything stupid.

Or at least…try to stop him.

He hurried outside, noticing that Milos was already long gone, though he wasn't surprised with how fast his friend was moving. Rita and Suzuhah seemed to be in a heated discussion. He walked over, twitching.

Rita glanced back and huffed. "Fine."

"Thank you." Suzuhah pulled back, fur rippling as a long tail curled around them, the larger form barely fitting in the front courtyard which they stood as he flipped into his full Vulfulas form. "You know how fast he can move and how big this city is. Now, get on."

Alex blinked, startled as Suzuhah lowered his head, Rita huffing, but hopping onto the long slender neck. "You too, Alex."

"That's— "

"We don't have time to argue. That idiot is going to get himself killed, running out there by himself."

Alex couldn't argue with that, so, taking a deep breath, he leapt on as Suzuhah took off with a powerful leap and a surge of wings.

It was both terrifying and exhilarating, flying through the sky.

It would be nice if, one day, he could do it when there WASN'T a pressing worry.

"That lout better be okay," Rita muttered, bending low on Suzuhah's back as they swerved around above the city, large even from above.

Alex hoped that as well, his gaze flicking from place to place. If only he could sense like Milos, though, that would have been pointless, now that he thought about it. Milos wasn't a Demon, the magic around him or whatever would only have traces of Demonic stuff.

He clicked his tongue; all this stuff was stupidly confusing. He hoped to God that someday, it would make sense. In the meanwhile, they had a wayward Alertian to find before he got himself killed.

# Chapter Nine

Milos found himself dashing through the streets, focusing on the feel of the wind on his face. He needed to get away from the magic, the Demonic energies that wrapped around him, almost choking him with their weight and energy. He needed time to think, and being in this refuge was NOT doing it. He bounded up some steps, leaping over a drop and landing before pushing off once more, ignoring the startled cries of a young woman that he nimbly dodged around.

Soon enough, heart pounding, he found himself leaping on top of a stone cliff face, wind brushing past, almost pulling at his hair in a way that felt achingly familiar. The refuge swirled behind him, glowing in the day stones' light, but here, it was quiet. He caught his breath, staring forward. A long path curled forward through stone pillars. To one side, he could see a set of steps that seemed to descend into the village proper, weaving down in calm strokes. Strange plants like vines curled around the pillars lining the last bit of the path around a corner ahead, almost like finding a ruin in a forest. It was strange. He found his steps light as he walked forward, thoughts running faster than he could breathe.

He could see the edge of the Underlands, right before him. He stared at it quietly as the roof sloped downward, the day stones growing closer and less bright as they descended to meet the ground. The wall of rock was carved and, to one side, the path curved behind one of the pillars, he could feel that breeze once more.

Still, he found himself stopping, not wanting to move forward, but not wanting to go back either. He found himself sitting down, scabbard clattering on the rock as his thoughts finally ground to a halt.

Satan…that name rang through his head like a siren, the word echoing over and over again. That women– He shook his head. He had been tasked with capturing and killing a child of Satan. His siblings…all of those before him failed and yet here he was. Not only had he found one, but two and, on top of that, there was a vent to the Overlands, an escape right there, so much closer than the ocean from before.

So…why had no one found this vent in the Overlands? It felt large, the wind strong enough to remind him of training above when clouds rushed past.

He gritted his teeth, finding his head in his hands, though he wasn't sure when that happened. Part of him wanted to draw his hands away, sitting like this, head bowed, and face hidden. It made him vulnerable.

He couldn't be vulnerable, especially not here.

And yet, he didn't move.

Steady breaths came in and out as he finally thought through the last few minutes once more, compartmentalizing, organizing and finding himself at a complete loss.

Slowly, the shaking hands came down and reached for his hair, pulling it over his shoulder, links clinking as the red glowed in the bright lights around him. Another burst of wind wafted past, a smell he didn't recognize meeting his nose. His mouth felt dry, but he pushed it aside.

What was he supposed to do now? His entire reason for coming down had been right next to him the entire time. If he had just done it that day he found Alex for the first time, he could be home, lauded as an Alertian…as a hero. No longer seen as…he paused in his thoughts. Such an acclaimed thing would finally get him the recognition he deserved. He could make his father proud. He was his father's child, no matter what that woman said and yet… Yes, if he had just DONE it, he could be proud of his heritage for once in his life.

Yet, he didn't. He was now here, stuck in this god-forsaken Underland, in a sanctuary that was on the edge of giving him a death sentence or worse because of how he was born. The irony of the entire situation was not lost on him.

His fists clenched tightly, and he felt a growl curl up his throat. Emotions swirled up and he found himself promptly hating the feeling. His mind, once so calm and determined, was now a mess of muddled thoughts.

The fingers tugged and curled into the blonde locks, tangling and pulling. These stupid emotions.

A flash of a memory shot through him, a disgusted expression filled with loathing and the words echoing loudly in his mind said, "You should never have been born."

He shoved the memory away as fast as he could, but the woman's frigid gaze still stuck in his head. The black hair cut short, the piercing brown eyes that held no warmth, the upturned nose as she stared down at him. Shut up!

He found himself curling inward, trying to control his breathing and failing. He felt almost light-headed, energy swirling around him in waves. It actually hurt.

"Why you?" An older boy, one he would NOT call his brother, spoke, that same black hair long and flowing like Milos' own, yet more ratty and tangled. Cold blue eyes stared at him. "Father should have just abandoned you. You're not of Mother's ilk, you're a half-Alertian, nothing more. So why does he hold you in such high regard? You're not even part of the family, you're not a true Alertian, even if you are Father's child. You were born from NOTHING! From worse than a slave! So, stop acting so high and mighty."

Milos slammed a fist into the ground, his hand stinging as the memory whisked away.

A small part of his mind noticed a sudden spike of energy, of magic, but he barely paid it any mind, unable too. It took all his concentration not to delve back into the memories that plagued him, that he thought he pushed aside upon descending down here.

So, he was somewhat surprised when the sound of metal against metal caught his attention and something poked against the side of his neck, inches from the chain. The kiss of cold steel was almost recognizable. He slowly opened his eyes, one hand still gripping his long hair, the other firmly on the ground, a small trickle of blood catching his attention. "What do you want?" He spoke evenly, his voice holding no emotion. "I was simply sitting here, away from the village."

"You are still an Alertian." The voice was feminine and even. "And you are away from the young man you were traveling with. One of our gracious leader's children, a descendant of our cherished ruler. The leaders and their children are our top priority, and those like yourself threaten that.

As soon as we noticed you were away from them, we knew it was our time to deal with you."

Milos stared ahead, noting two figures on either side. So there were three of them. The swirl of emotions dwindled as he noticed the two to either side shift, long tails like a cat curled up and yet the features themselves were more reptilian in nature.

"So, three on one?"

"Don't think us a fool. We know of the Alertian's strength."

"So why did you not skewer me while I was distracted?"

"Because we are not like you filthy beings." The woman snorted, leaning forward, hair just brushing the back of his neck. It must have been long. "We have honor, which is why we are allowing you to talk before we execute you."

"Hm…" Milos let out a breath through his nose, his gaze still ahead as he slowly focused down, feeling the swirl of the three of them. Powerful… "I suppose you are some of the defenders of the village?"

"You don't need to know that." One of the two on the side hissed, breath curling up from their throat, visible. Internal heat production?

"Fine." Milos spoke evenly, his thoughts finally cut to a halt. He held no love for this town and, though he knew it wasn't Alex's fault, considering the boy had no idea who he was, he couldn't help but feel a hint of anger, of fury at how long he was wrenched along, how it happened again where he was pulled along by someone else.

He felt the person behind him stiffen, as if noticing something. "Wait, you!"

Milos sharply tugged out a dagger he rarely ever used, catching the blade at his neck as he pushed off with his other hand, swinging around the sword. He dropped the dagger as he grabbed his sword, slashing out, ignoring the clatter of the scabbard as it was flung across the rocks, slamming into a pillar. The pummel slammed into the woman's side as the other two lunged.

As soon as his foot touched down, he launched himself back, almost flipping out of the way of one of the Demons as the other spun, tail lashing out.

"Wait! Don't attack!" The woman screeched, almost scrambling back. She appeared lion-like with a long-arched back and feminine features, a minx. "He's…"

The next words were lost as one of the reptilian creatures, who Milos wasn't sure about, pulled back and launched forward, steam rushing toward him.

Milos twisted, ducking low and slashing out. The creature let out a shriek as he stumbled back, blood slipping from the wound.

"You filth!" the other one screeched.

Milos felt his mind shut down. Enough was enough.

His body moved without thought, spinning and dancing. The flash of steel swayed in the air, almost singing as it sliced. A faint scream here and pleading there was all Milos heard barely around the voice of death that curled over him. They would pay. ALL of them would pay.

It wasn't until the presence of the three of them faded that he found himself sliding to a halt. Something dripped, warm and wet, down his face. His arm ached fiercely, and his breath caught in his throat for a moment. The emotions that swirled through him promptly faded to a faint hum at the back of his mind. One that seemed content in that moment.

He slowly stood, noticing the three were gone, though there was a pool of blood to one side. He stared down at it in a mix of realization and resignation.

Who was going to believe him if he said he was attacked? No doubt, those three would spread word that he attacked them on the outskirts of town. Not even Lillianna's good graces would save him then.

He felt something bubble up in his chest, a strange, unknown feeling. A chuckle… that felt inappropriate, but he started laughing at the stupidity of all of this. That woman even seemed to notice something about him. What the hell was that about? She was SO enthusiastic to stab him then she suddenly didn't want to? What was that bullshit?

The sword stabbed down into the stone, chipping it, but not doing much else. He put a hand up, wiping some blood away, and winced through his laughter, noting the burn on his arm from one of those Demons. He heard the sound of wings as the bubbling giggles finally faded, no warmth in the sound even to his ears. He glanced up as something soared above, curling around. It took a moment for him to recognize the gold before the creature spun once more. Like a bullet, he dropped from the sky, a mix of screams and startled yelps of delight reaching Milos' ears. With a flash and a spread of wings, Suzuhah landed, paws catching his weight as he lowered his neck. Rita stumbled off as Alex jumped, barely catching himself as he stumbled. Rita stood, brushing herself off, a big smile on her face that instantly vanished.

"Holy shiesse, what happened?" Rita stared, shocked, as Suzuha switched to her younger form, the little girl staring around the place in a mix of confusion and dawning horror.

"Nothing…"

"If you say it's nothing for us to worry about, then I will cut you off right here." Rita stomped up as Alex peered around, his posture stiff. Milos turned back to Rita, who had her hands on her hips. "It was clear a fight happened, considering the blood on the ground and your cheek and the burn on your arm. Speaking of, give me that."

Milos pursed his lips before letting out a sigh and extending his arm out. Rita nodded and started bandaging, practically slapping the ointment on, to Milos' chagrin. "Now, mind telling us the truth?" As she asked, Alex stepped forward, peering at him worriedly.

He found himself tensing on the boy's approach and didn't miss as Alex suddenly stopped, uncertainty flashing over his face. "I'm…"

Milos stared at him quietly, only to yelp as he felt something poke his back. He whipped around to see Suzuha lean over, hands behind her back as she peered up at him. She relaxed, a faint smile on her face. "So, any particular reason why you are suddenly nervous around sweet little Alex?"

"Hey!" Alex yelped, horrified.

Suzuha stuck her tongue out as Rita chuckled, continuing to put a poultice on Milos' arm.

"It's…" He found himself hesitating.

Alex pulled his arm close before reaching toward his throat. "Does it have to do with what I am?" Alex hesitated. "I acted rashly in there and…" Alex winced, suddenly hesitant. "It's not because of…" He felt over his throat, as if it hurt, though Milos knew it wasn't damaged.

"I doubt the latter option is the case." Suzuha's gaze was stern as she stared directly at Alex. "I've told you; it has nothing to do with that."

Alex let out a breath and slumped. "Right."

"Okay, enough secrets." Rita pulled back, annoyed. "We'll get to you in a moment." Rita pointed to Alex, who blinked before turning back toward Milos. "I'm not dumb, there was a fight here. Tell us what happened so we can figure out what to DO about it."

Milos wasn't sure what to say, startled before he shook his head. "A couple Demons thought it was a good opportunity to attack me while my–" He cut himself off. "While I was away from Alex, and it didn't end well for them...or so it seems." He peered around to the area where blood stains splattered over the ground.

"Okay, great." Rita threw her hands up before letting out a sigh. "This is not going to end well for us."

"No." Alex winced. "We barely convinced the council to allow Milos to stay around with Lillianna risking her honor and this happens right after?"

Alex turned back to Milos, pursing his lips. "Especially after you just ran out. Why? Was it because of that woman's words?"

"Alex, don't worry about—"

"Of course I will!" Alex flung his hands into the air, frustration bleeding into his voice, startling the three of them. "You know how I feel about my Demonic heritage. So much has been revealed lately and, sure, there have been hints and signs in the past, but now it's all being confirmed at once! Plus, if it's bothering those I see as friends and..." he cut himself off before continuing, "Then I want to know WHY. What is so important about me being related to Satan?"

"I mean, besides the whole child of the leader of Demons that ruled and fought over a hundred years ago?" Suzuha pointed out.

Alex just sent her a look. She waved and pulled back behind Milos.

"I'm curious too." Rita stared quietly. "I mean, even I know about Satan, the Demon that led the armies during the human-demon war, whose death meant the defeat of the Demons. It was thought his line ended after that, though it clearly hasn't." Rita's gaze flicked to Alex and then back to Milos. "Still, why are you acting like a lout and making such a big deal of it? You've known Alex was a powerful Demon for a while. You've always mentioned how he has two types of Demon in him. We just never knew what the second one was and now we do. Why would this change anything?"

Milos didn't want to say anything, he wanted to keep his mouth shut, but the persistent looks from all three of them, a few filled with worry and concern, ate at him.

They shouldn't even be CONCERNED about him.

"It was my reason for descending in the first place." Milos finally spoke, his voice strangely soft and hesitant, startling all three of them. "My entire goal for descending down here was to capture and kill a child of Satan. Nothing else."

Alex's eyes widened as Rita snapped her mouth shut.

"Oh…" Alex squeaked out, clearly unsure how to respond to that.

"Are you…?" Rita stared, took a deep breath before growling. "Are you FREAKING serious? Your entire reason for coming down to the Underlands was to kill Alex and his mother?"

"I didn't know." Milos immediately found himself speaking, though he wasn't sure why he was defending himself.

"Well, duh." Rita started pacing. "Oh, this makes SO much more sense and makes this SO much worse."

Alex put a hand up to his cheek, staring at Milos evenly, his expression difficult to read, not that Milos could blame him. "Is that why you tried to kill me when we first met? Not because I was a Demon, but because you realized I might have been a son of Satan?"

Milos went to argue before stalling, thinking back on that time. The powerful waves of magic that he followed to Alex… Sure, it was his first Demon, but thinking upon all the Demons he met after, that magic had been different from later ones, almost at the same strength as whatever dwelled within the sprawling caverns of the mountain range south of Raynout. After some thought, he shook his head. "No…you were simply a Demon." The words were tired as they came out, but he couldn't help but feel both of them would understand what he meant.

"Well, I'll take that." Suzuha shrugged, startling him and the others. "Look, I've only known him as your defender and ally, not this psycho killer or anything. Of course, we now know the reason he's with us, but I doubt that's still the reason." Milos stiffened upon the look on Suzuha's face. "Right?"

Milos found himself shaking his head before he really thought about it.

Suzuha shrugged and turned to the others. "You can talk this all over later, for now, we should head back and make sure our friend doesn't get killed for something he didn't do."

Rita took a deep breath before slumping. After a moment, she shrugged and smiled. "Can't argue with that." She stared at Milos before gesturing. "Well? I for one am glad to finally know what's going on with you, and why you are here. I'll berate you later for not mentioning this, or for even thinking of it as an option, but that's for a later time. Suzuha is right, we should go."

Fabric landed onto them, startling Milos. Rita pulled back, grinning. "Might as well clean yourself up somewhat. We have to head back to town and Suzuha can only carry so many people." She peered around. "I will say, though, this place is beautiful, ignoring the bloodstains and all."

Alex followed her gaze, clearly trying to avoid looking at the damage, and a strangely nostalgic smile crossed his face. "Reminds me a bit of home." He shook his head before turning back to them. "Come on, let's figure out what to do."

He glanced at Milos before his expression turned soft. "I know now, even more so, that you only mean to help me. After all, you would have killed me by now if you truly meant to. Yet not only have you not, you have helped me learn more about myself. I'm not fond of the idea that you came to the Underlands just to kill Mom and me…but I also know that's not you anyway and things change. Thank you, Milos, for being my friend, not just some killer."

Milos nodded; his tongue stuck in his throat as they started walking toward town, Suzuha gathering up his scabbard and dagger, handing them to him with a quiet smile. "Here, you might need these."

Milos gathered them up, hoping he wouldn't but realizing his hope was probably very misplaced as he strapped them back in place, ready to meet his fate.

# Chapter Ten

"This is going to be so bad," Rita muttered under her breath, thoughts flying a mile a minute. Milos was walking behind her with Alex at his side, both of them quiet. Suzuha stayed behind them, hands behind her back and swaying side to side, a scene of picture-perfect innocence, if Rita didn't know better.

Milos' expression of utter surprise still lingered in her head, especially after Alex's words. For a brief moment, she could have sworn she saw a strange desperation from him, almost...hope. Why? She shook her head. She supposed it wasn't that strange. The three of them, and now Suzuha, grew close and she felt protective of both Alex and Milos. Yes, she acknowledged to herself, even after finding out Milos' reason for coming down was murder but a reason and something he actually did were two different things. She wasn't sure if it was because of...

Her thoughts were cut off as she suddenly stumbled, hand slamming to her head as that familiar wave took over.

Another one? So soon?

Screams caught her attention, but it was distant beyond the thick stone walls around her. A young woman stood before her, black hair chopped short and somewhat bloody at the tips. She had a wide grin on her face, eyes a familiar piercing blue. Milos stood before her, bedraggled, he was holding himself close, his arm broken, his leg shattered and blood seeping from the wound on his head that Rita barely managed to bandage.

"Oh, look at what they did to you, brother." The woman gestured, cocking her head. "Dad always said you would be the best of us, that you would make the Alertian line shine again, and look at you. Look at what those filthy Demons have done to you." She slowly walked forward, her steps measured and almost relaxed.

Milos didn't say anything, though Rita had a feeling it was more because he couldn't.

The woman took Milos' face in her hands before anger flared through her. "And they ruined your pretty hair too. Don't worry, big brother, I will murder them for you and bring you home." With that, she turned and stabbed forward.

Rita stared down, eyes wide as blood pooled. Milos limply turned around, and this time, Rita could see it…the bandages over his eyes.

The place they were in…

The chains curling down over the floor, clinging still to his wrists, having melted off.

Rita choked as the woman leaned forward, her cheek almost brushing Rita's, frowning. "I don't care that you are human. If you associate with such vile, disgusting creatures who would do this to my sweet big brother, then this is a death you rightfully deserve." And with that, she pulled out the sharp tainted sword and Rita let out a gasp, stumbling backward, slamming into Milos, who quickly caught her arm.

"Rita?" Alex yelped, leaning forward. "Are you alright? What happened?"

Rita choked, scrambling at her chest where a blade stuck painfully moments before. "Milos?" She stuttered out. "Do you have a younger sister?"

She wasn't sure why she asked. Of all the things in the vision, that was what she asked? But it wasn't like she was going to mention the jail cells around her, or Milos' state or that Alex and Suzuha weren't there.

Milos suddenly tensed behind her. "How?" He actually choked at that as Rita pulled away, turning toward him. His gaze met hers, that same blue as the girl in her vision, the same blue that had been lost because of…

"We can't let them incarcerate you." She spoke; her voice filled with conviction. The vision clung in her mind, the shattered remains of the proud man before her. "I WON'T let that happen."

"What does…" Milos' eyes widened. "Rita, you know what that infers, don't you?"

Rita paused before her eyes widened. Yeah, she did.

"It means your sister is coming here." Alex stared at Milos quietly. "Rita, are you sure…?"

"The structure was the same as what is architecturally found around here." She turned to Alex. "I could hear screams from beyond and I think there were Demons littering the ground. She even mentioned how the Demons did—"She cut herself off."

"What happened?" Milos narrowed his eyes, posture tense.

Rita shook her head, the red braid almost slapping against her face. "It's a vision I'm going to change." She pursed her lips. "So, is there anyone ELSE we have to worry about? Any other siblings that might arrive?" She took a step forward toward Milos, noting with no small surprise as he promptly took a step back. "Any OTHER secrets you want to throw out in the open while we're at it? I am ALL ears, Milos."

Milos outright winced at the use of his name and winced even harder as it seemed her words caught up with him.

He seemed to slowly recollect himself as Rita took a step back, giving him a bit of space. He opened and closed his mouth, clearly uncertain before he shook his head. "I have a younger brother as well, but he's too young for the initiation and all my older siblings besides one are dead." His gaze grew almost distant. "And he won't be coming down here again, he can't."

"Well, fine, as long as no others are showing up now. But that's not as important as making sure you DON'T end up in jail."

Milos and Alex exchanged looks before Alex gestured. "I mean, has there ever been a future vision you haven't wanted to change?"

Rita winced and nodded. "One…when we were looking for you, I had a vision of all of us escaping to the boat safely." She glanced at Alex. "And it did happen, but I don't know how, or if I changed anything by knowing, which worries me. What if I can't change it this time?"

Suzuha stepped forward, almost pushing between Alex and Milos, who stumbled to the side, startled. She looked right toward Rita. "Mistress was always worried about that as well." Suzuha spoke softly. "Sometimes, the future visions are just that, visions of a future you can not change. Other times, they are warnings, guides to help us forward. No seer knows which they are seeing and which they can affect. She always said, all one can do is try. Try for a future that is different from the one you see because giving up means that the future seen WILL come to pass, instead of MAY."

Rita peered at her quietly, catching her breath.

"Still, that future vision might be what we need to help keep Milos out of jail." Alex turned, expression shifting. "Lillianna has seen your future visions before and you still need to speak with her about what you saw regarding the world just kind of collapsing. She would believe us if we mentioned an Alertian coming to the village."

"But what if mentioning something is the reason Milos ends up in there." Rita gestured, not sure what to do.

"Then we get him out right away." Alex narrowed his eyes. "All we can do is try, like Suzuha said."

Alex turned to Milos, staring at him quietly. "Still, what can you tell us about your sister?"

"Or about the fact that you have one." Rita put her hands on her hips, annoyed. "Thanks for letting us know about that and about your other siblings." She shook her head. "Either way, we can't stay here dawdling, SO walk and talk."

"I didn't feel it was necessary." Milos almost seemed to pull back, only to yelp as Rita grabbed his wrist and tugged him along. "It is surprising that she would come this way."

"She probably heard this is where you went." Suzuha shrugged as Rita nodded.

"She definitely seemed protective of you." Rita paused, thinking back on the vision.

"Obsessive is more the word. Though not for the reason you think." Milos pulled his arm free but followed with Alex at his side. Rita saw so much more of him lately, it was stunning, but something she appreciated. He knew so much about them; it was nice to see other sides of the man that she came to see as a comrade. Even if it was rough TO see.

"Huh?" Alex blinked, confused as they stepped into town. Rita stiffened, noticing the looks right away as silence fell over the street as they walked.

Milos' posture suddenly shifted, straight and stoic, unlike the gentler, hesitant version from earlier.

Alex pursed his lips, staying even as Suzuha stayed a few feet back on his other side, hands behind her back, whistling, but watching. Rita turned ahead. "We'll talk about that later, let's go speak with Lillianna."

She walked forward, hearing the whispers and mutters. It kind of reminded her a bit of when Divon first started pursuing her. The hushed and snide comments of the other girls in town, but this was taken up a few notches. She, thankfully, with some quiet help from Suzuha, found her way back up the steps leading toward the Sovereign's meeting hall.

Though, it was clear she wouldn't even get that far as a blast of wind caught her attention before a figure landed before her, feathers flaring out. He stood, expression cold, as he peered over the group before locking eyes with Milos.

"Alertian, you are under arrest for the defilement of our town and an attack on our citizens. Come quietly."

Rita straightened, though it didn't actually do much, being shorter than Maritus and down a few of the steps. "We wish to speak with Lillianna. This is a misun—"

"Silence." Maritus turned his head down toward Rita. "We barely let it slide, however, some of Sechrondes' own people were critically injured and, when spoken to, we were told that cur did it. She has changed her vote to incarcerate."

Rita growled. No matter what, she would NOT let that vision come to pass. She knew what Suzuha said meant she might not be able to affect it, but...

No, she could. The vision before this one showed Milos with two eyes, flying on Suzuha and relatively healthy.

She took a step forward. "I DEMAND to see Lillianna. Milos was not the one who attacked, he was the one who was ATTACKED, and I will NOT let you destroy him."

The man seemed to narrow his eyes as Milos and Alex stared at her.

"I KNOW what you will do." She hissed, leaning up, staring straight into his gaze. Fear flared through her, but she didn't stop. "You will break him, piece by piece, destroy his eyes, tear out his vocal cords... All because no one would care, or so you think, and it will lead to your *destruction*."

She heard a voice choke behind her, though she wasn't sure whose it was.

Maritus stared down at her, eyes narrowed. "We are not savages..."

"Then let me speak to Lillianna with Milos free."

"I cannot and will not."

"Let us pass," Alex's voice cut in and Rita jerked, turning to him. He, somehow, switched back to Demon form, a strange expression on his face. Milos stared quietly, emotionless. Suzuhah switched to his male form, fur almost appearing to bristle even though he wasn't in Vulfulas form as he stayed beside Milos.

Maritus narrowed his eyes at Alex and took a step forward. "You have no say in this, child. I've already told you, know your place."

"Then, tell me *truthfully*, what do you do to prisoners you despise?" Alex's voice sent a shiver down Rita's spine, causing her to still.

She noted something odd about Alex's voice, there was a lilt to it she only heard once before, when he still lived with her and her family or when he sang.

Maritus paused, frowning. "Break them so they can no longer fight back, of course." Maritus' eyes widened, surprise on his face as if he hadn't meant to say that, before a strange understanding shot over him. "You are a Siren."

"Why do you say that?" Alex spoke quietly, that lilt gone, but a strange tone that Rita NEVER heard from her friend. "I simply asked a question, you answered."

Maritus glowered, the wind whipping up. "That just gives me more reason not to let you pass."

Alex snarled, his own wings flaring out, barely avoiding Milos who sidestepped them, startled. A single word pierced the sudden silence, a note hanging behind it almost as if both spoken and sung with a strange ferocity. "*He'let*."

The word rang across the courtyard, powerful. Rita grimaced as Milos seemed to stiffen, hands to his head. Alex's tail lashed up around Milos' arm, stopping him as he went to take a step back.

Maritus stumbled, feathers flaring out. Rita noticed a few other people in the courtyard, who had been watching the ensuing scene, suddenly turned and hurried away, their feet almost stumbling over themselves.

Alex hurried forward, rushing past Maritus, pulling Milos with him. Rita scrambled to join him as Suzuhah shot ahead, taking the marble steps two at a time.

They raced through the door, slamming it shut just as wind suddenly slammed into it, screeching and howling. "*Ackt veck he-venate!*" The Demonic words screeched out, echoing in Rita's ears.

Guards suddenly snapped to attention, a few pointing spears in their direction as they raced through the hallway toward the far door. Milos stumbled with them.

"Lillianna!" Rita shouted as she was forced to slide to a halt, right as one of the lupin guards sprang forward, skidding in front of her, spear almost at her throat. She could only hope to the high heavens that Lillianna was actually in her office and not exploring the city.

Almost instantly, they were surrounded, and Rita didn't miss how she, Suzuhah and Alex made a triangle around Milos, who was holding his head tightly, shuddering.

"What is the meaning of this?" a voice called out as the far door opened. At the end of the hall, standing proudly, expression showing nothing, stood Lillianna, Sechrondes slithered behind her, anger on her face, as Valencia shot out, horror on her expression. She went to rush forward, only to be stopped by two lupin guards who put their spears up in tandem, holding her back as her gaze met Alex's.

Rita gulped. Shit, she hadn't thought Sechrondes would be here too, though she had somewhat hoped Valencia would, it seemed it wouldn't matter.

"Let my son go!" Valencia called, voice absolutely echoing down the corridor. "This HAS to be a misunderstanding!"

"Valencia, silence!" Sechrondes' voice was dripping venom. "They must pay for hurting my people. Guards, what is happening?"

"These four suddenly barged in." One of the lupin spoke as he continued to hold his spear toward Rita. "Sir Maritus tried to catch them, but they broke through anyway."

"We needed to speak to you." Rita gestured. "This is all a misunderstanding. MILOS was the one who got attacked. He was defending himself! On top of that—"

"Enough." Lillianna stared down, expression even. Valencia and Sechrondes both grew quiet. Valencia stayed where she was while

Sechrondes tilted her head up, but didn't say a word. Rita stiffened, startled. "I will speak with them later, for now, lead them back to my abode, under house arrest."

Footsteps sounded behind as the door that opened almost silently, slammed shut behind. "I cannot agree to that, Sovereign." Maritus spoke up from behind, anger trilling into his voice. "It is dangerous to have a Siren remain around you. That boy must be silenced first. His Nyx blood was tainted with Satan's to bring back those damn ancient bloodlines. It is too dangerous for him to—"

Lillianna's expression shifted through several emotions in rapid succession before she tilted her head, interrupting him. "That is a matter we will speak of later. That boy is no Siren."

"He used his very voice to control me." Maritus pointed as Rita's gaze shifted backward toward him.

Alex was quiet, wings fluttering slightly, tail still curled protectively around Milos' arm. "And this one speaks as if she can see the future."

Lillianna actually showed a hint of frustration before she slashed her arm out. "I will SPEAK with you later. You are under no circumstances to send any of these people to jail, understood? Lead them back and guard the door yourself if you wish. This is a matter I must deal with directly."

Maritus pursed his lips before nodding. "Fine." He glared at their group. "Guards, bring them to the Sovereign's abode." The guards pushed and Rita stumbled back.

"Geez, alright, alright."

She turned, noticing as Maritus' sharpened attention remained fixed on Alex. Alex's gaze flicked to him briefly before he hurried past.

This was a right mess, but they weren't going to jail. She could only hope they did enough to stop at least that timeline.

She almost felt a need to pray for that.

# Chapter Eleven

The panic was so strong, he almost felt sick. Alex shuddered as they stepped into the house and were placed in one room. The lock clicked as footsteps sounded outside... not leaving.

Oh shit, oh shit. His hands snapped to his throat as Rita took a seat on the bed, head in her hands, as Milos actually sat on the floor, hands pulling his head down toward his knees. The only one who still seemed to be himself was Suzuhah, though that was clearly barely as he paced back and forth in the room.

"Oh, this is a mess. Such a mess," he muttered.

Alex couldn't deny that.

"Alex?" Rita's voice was hesitant when she spoke. "What did you say? What happened back there?"

Alex flinched, once more in human form, almost holding himself close. He unintentionally switched back to Demonic form and, upon hearing Rita's words, he found himself following along with his Demonic side. What Rita was insinuating from her vision was torture, almost worse than he saw committed on some of the slaves he passed. He was already not fond of Maritus, and when the man tried to deny Rita's words while out in that courtyard... Every part of Alex KNEW Maritus was lying. He could practically feel it.

So, he hadn't been able to stop himself when he started speaking, when that Demonic half that crooned quietly suddenly came up, almost entwining with his own voice. At the confirmation, it was all he could do not to attack the man, knowing it would do nothing for him.

"I told him to leave." Alex spoke softly, settling on the floor, hand to his throat once more. "That's all..."

"Bull-shiesse."

Alex slowly tilted his head toward Rita, who was glaring at him.

"He called you a Siren, I could hear the change in your voice. You know what happened."

"I don't," Alex cut in, finding his voice pitching up. "I mean, I know what my mom told me, but this was different. Mom said that my voice might have qualities that could persuade people, but I've never used it. I couldn't stop it, whatever that was."

Silence fell over the room once more as Alex felt that panic returning. Shit…they now knew his voice could do things like that.

"So you have a hypnotic quality to your voice?" Rita asked hesitantly. "How strong?"

"I think you saw." Suzuhah spoke up, stopping in his pacing. "And Alex is correct, that is the first time I've ever heard it that strong. Sure, when he sang before, it held hints, but this was full on Siren song. Though a weaker version since he doesn't know how to use it."

"Weaker?" Alex paled as Rita choked, staring.

"If I were to guess." Suzuhah's gaze met his. "Is it that surprising?"

Alex supposed not.

Silence fell over the group after that, none of them wanted to say a word. A thin sliver of light drifted through the small window to one side, slowly fading into the night stones. Still, there was no sign of Lillianna and tension was keeping all of them awake. Alex was somewhat surprised Mom hadn't checked in, but she was there when it happened, she was clearly worried. Maybe they were forcing her to stay out of it? Like how they forced her to stay here instead of looking for him?

At one point, there was a knock on the door before it was opened. Two guards quickly put their spears in as another placed a platter down filled with food and water. No words were exchanged as the door closed, locking once more.

Suzuhah, the only one who actually seemed to want to move around, handed the food out, quietly coaxing each person to eat. Alex nibbled on the bread, thoughts racing. Lillianna told him to keep that ability secret, so did Mom. And here he was, using it pretty much right away.

Rita was eating as well, though in a bit of a dazed resignation.

Suzuhah ended up settling beside Milos, slowly coaxing him to sit up. Milos tilted his head up, expression almost lost. He didn't look at Alex, just accepted the food and stared quietly at it before taking a bite. Suzuhah let out a breath, finally eating as well.

The silence that pervaded the room was heavy and thick with worry.

So, when there was quiet conversation outside and a knock on the door, Alex found himself almost jumping out of his skin, tense. He only half paid attention to the conversation but he could have sworn the voices were familiar. Something about being members of the household and having a right to speak with those they once traveled with or something. He wasn't sure. He glanced over as it opened to reveal the two spear-pointing guards… and two recognizable figures. Relief passed over his face, until he saw their expressions.

"Thank you." Ari spoke evenly, nodding to one of the guards. "We won't be long. Nor will we mention we were here."

The guard nodded, watching the scene quietly as Ari walked forward, Leon close at her side. The spears were still pointed inward, and it was clear they were keeping an eye on Ari, Leon and the party.

Ari and Leon's expressions were blank as they stopped in the middle of the room. Ari's gaze flicked from place to place before she spoke. "So, it's come to this." The words seemed almost a bit stilted from her lips, as if forced. She walked forward, squatted down on one knee and, hesitating for only a moment, while Leon stepped behind her, clearly standing in a way to somewhat shield the two from the watching guards. As soon as he did, she suddenly wrenched Milos up by his collar, her lips close to his ear, though just loud enough for Alex, sitting nearby, to hear. *"Are you okay?"* Her voice shot up in panic, though kept low. *"They have not dared hurt you, right, Master?"*

At the momentary shock on Milos' face, she shook him, though it was light, to an outsider, it was purposeful. Alex heard a snort from one of the guards who obviously heard the resulting clattering of Milos' scabbard and the faint grunt from Milos' lips.

He shook his head as Alex watched, hesitant. "Ari?"

Leon sent him a look, good hand on his sword, he subtly shook his head as Ari continued, this time clearly much louder. "How DARE you betray us like that!" Her words were once more stilted, clearly for the benefit of the guards before it dropped once more into a hurried whisper.

*"I'm sorry you ended up like this. We convinced the guards we were breaking our contract with you because we were unaware you would do such a thing, but they wouldn't let us see you privately, so we have to act."* She slowly pulled back. "Why would you attack citizens? Disgusting." Her voice was louder, but also harsher. Alex didn't miss the pain on her face as she spoke once more loud enough for the guards to hear.

"He was attacked." Rita argued, seeming to realize what Ari and Leon were playing at. "He was only defending himself!" Her gaze flicked to the guards who seemed to be watching Ari and Milos with amusement. Her voice dipped as she continued, *"He was on the outskirts of town when we found him. Alex protected us by using his voice, but the situation is tense."* Her gaze flicked to the guards once more. *"The people who attacked him, if we can figure out who they are and get them to tell the truth, we…"*

"She didn't speak to you." Leon spoke up, though he did nod in Rita's direction. Rita pulled back, annoyance flashing across her face before she seemed to catch her breath.

Ari let go of Milos, almost shoving him back. "Alright, we know what's going on now." Her voice was monotone once more, though her expression…it was hard to see from where Alex sat, but it was filled with worry. *"We'll get you out."* She mouthed before pushing herself to her feet, words loud once more. "So that's who we were really following. Who were these supposed people who attacked you? Maybe it would be better to join them, then we won't have to worry about being lied to or betrayed."

Milos seemed to catch himself, clearly still feeling a little off with the situation. In short words, almost faint, he described the group, specifically a woman who seemed to have been the one who started it all, at least, if Alex had to guess from the way Milos' face momentarily twisted in a hint of disgust.

Ari nodded, spun on her heels and stomped out, Leon right behind. The guards let her pass; spears pointed past the two long enough to keep anyone from thinking of escaping. One of them scoffed, amused. "Damn, she's scary."

"Hush." The other argued, causing the first to snap his mouth shut as Ari and Leon walked through. The two guards closed the door with a sharp snap.

Neither Ari nor Leon looked back as they left.

"Well now, that was different." Suzuhah stared quietly at the door.

"Yet, they might be our only option of getting out of this situation." Rita spoke softly, frowning.

Alex couldn't help but nod, leaning against the wall as he peered out the one window. "Hey, at least we aren't in jail."

He tried to smile, desperately trying to force the panic down from earlier, but it came out more forced than he wanted. "A slim chance is better than none."

The others hesitated before Rita sighed. "I wish I had your optimism." She fell on her back, arms spread as she let out an oof. "No one trusts us now, even though it's not even our fault. It's so stupid. Heck, Ari and Leon had to pretend to hate us to even get to talk to us. Talk about things being so messed up."

"I wouldn't be too loud about that." Suzuhah huffed, arms crossed over his chest as he tapped his knee, flipping to her younger form. "I think it would be best if we just keep calm and all that. Trust them a little."

Alex nodded and let out a breath, glancing toward the door. There wasn't much else they could do.

Time passed slowly without any words. Alex found himself curled up once more, half-asleep on the floor. Rita took the bed and Suzuha collapsed on the couch. Milos was still against the wall, staring down at nothing in particular.

Alex heard movement and glanced toward the door as the sound of shifting and a faint 'Sir!' reached his ears.

"Are they still within?" Maritus' voice echoed from the other side. Tension in the room suddenly snapped as Alex swallowed heavily, feeling faintly nervous.

"Of course, sir. They have no means of escape."

"I desire to see them."

"Unfortunately, we cannot allow that request. The Sovereign has not allowed anyone to enter besides the ones who traveled with them. You must understand."

"I've spoken with the Sovereign; she has allowed me entry to speak with the siren."

Alex felt tense and noticed as the other three shifted. Suzuha opened her eyes as Rita sat up, staring at the door. Milos' hand was on his sword, attention finally turning away from the floor.

"I need a written notice with her signature."

"I can and WILL send you to the jails if you do not let me through this instant. The siren is a threat to our people and our way of life. There has not been a siren seen since before the great calamity. For one to appear now is a sign of terrible things to come for our sanctuary."

Silence filled the other end as Alex slowly pushed himself to his feet. Was he really that big of a threat? Why did everyone want to call him that?

He heard movement, and almost jumped as Suzuha took his hand in hers, glancing up at him briefly. "You are no threat," she said faintly. "Ignore him."

Alex pursed his lips as a sigh echoed from the other side and the door swung open. Maritus, standing tall, walked inside, observing the group with a subtle distaste that bordered on disgust. He turned to Alex and walked forward, staying a few feet back.

The door remained open like before.

"Siren, what do you have to say for yourself?"

Alex pursed his lips, not sure. "I…"

Maritus narrowed his eyes at the word. "And don't even think of using your voice on me. A mere child, even a siren, cannot…"

"What do you want me to say?" Alex finally demanded, frustration brimming through. "I've done nothing wrong!"

"You manipulated and coerced an entire group of civilians and tried to do the same to me, all to defend an Alertian already deemed dangerous."

"He wasn't the one who attacked, we already told you that." Alex pressed, pulling his hand from Suzuha, gesturing. "We're just…"

The man suddenly smirked, causing Alex to snap his mouth shut. "So you agree that you did what I said? That you used your siren abilities to aid an enemy of the sanctuary. Am I hearing that correctly?"

Alex just opened and closed his mouth, trying to figure out how his words led to that.

"What the frick are you talking about?" Rita snapped to her feet, hat slightly askew as she stomped forward. "He never said anything like that!"

"But he didn't deny it either. That is proof enough and I do, of course, have eye-witness accounts."

"This is entrapment!" She put her foot down, glaring at Maritus. "I don't know what you are playing at, or why you think he's a threat, but he is my friend, and he would never do such a thing unless it was absolutely necessary. You are twisting our words."

"We shall see." Wind rushed through the room, causing Alex to quickly bring his hand up, only to still as something gripped his throat. He choked slightly, horrified to see the man standing right before him, hovering slightly, fingers curled tightly. "I WILL find out the truth, child. I won't let you destroy this home or my people." He grinned. "And you've given me exactly what I need to make sure you are never a threat to this land." With that, he let go and, with a flick of wind, disappeared out the door. There was a yelp from the other side as it slammed shut. A moment later, it locked.

Alex found himself shaking, staring at the door with slight horror. "What?" He choked.

He heard footsteps behind him, and he jerked as Rita whipped around, facing him, hands on her hips and expression serious. "He's trying to unnerve us." She leaned forward. "We just have to hope things work out. I haven't gotten any more visions, so…" She pulled back, hesitant. "I hope that means things are going alright. That there is a chance to make it out of this with all of us intact."

Her gaze flitted behind Alex, and he turned, peering at Milos, who had gotten to his feet, staring at the door with a tension in his body and a strange fear on his face.

"Milos?" Alex asked quietly.

The word startled Milos out of his thoughts, because he turned to Alex and seemed to relax, letting out a breath. "As much as I despise saying it, Rita is correct. Ari and Leon…" He slowly pulled his hand away. "They know what to do. We just…they need to find the information before that Demon can twist our words and the situation anymore."

Alex stared quietly, wondering if the term was being used literally or figuratively, considering the vicious tone. He put a hand to his chest, trying to calm his pounding heart. "Right…right."

"Plus, don't forget, your mom is here too. You saw how she was when we met with Lillianna back there. She was trying to help. She's not going to abandon you. You heard what they said, sure, we haven't seen her, but maybe that's because she can't come." Suzuha spoke up, hands clapping in front of her chest. "And Lillianna, in as difficult a situation as she is, is very much aware of what's going on. She seems like the sort that would want the full story and she doesn't seem like she believes all Alertians are evil. That might be to our advantage."

Alex nodded, letting Rita lead him back to bed.

"Milos, sit on the couch this time, will you?" Rita called, catching the man's attention. "I'm tired of watching you and Alex sitting on the floor, no matter how comfy the rug is."

Alex found himself chuckling weakly as Milos shook his head but seemed to follow along with her demand.

The night stones fully took over by this point and Alex felt his stomach twist with a familiar hunger. They barely got anything to eat. Sure, they got the platter of food, but he couldn't help but find himself hungry again, part of himself anyway, the other half wanted nothing to do with food at the moment.

He curled into the bed, Suzuha plopping down on the other side as Rita settled on the rug with a pillow from the bed. Milos, after some convincing, took the couch, laying across it, arm used as a pillow.

Exhaustion pulled at Alex, but the adrenaline of the day was still lingering in his veins.

He could hear the others shifting in discomfort and, after a long moment of hesitation, found himself humming softly.

He instantly cut himself off as he realized, horrified.

"Why'd you stop?" Suzuha grumbled, not even opening her eyes. "Pretty."

Alex hesitated, pulling it close. "I…"

"Alex, shut up and do whatever the frick you want." Rita's voice caught Alex's attention as she rolled over, poking her head up enough for him to look over the bed. "At least it's better than pure silence."

Alex blinked before lying back down. He did want to calm the others as best as he could, and he only knew one way. It seemed like they didn't mind.

He found himself humming once more, the notes echoing softly through the room, a gentle lullaby. Soft breathing caught his attention as he continued and he opened his eyes, the notes continuing to vibrate from his throat as he noticed the others asleep, shoulders relaxing.

He wasn't sure if he wanted to stop. It was calming for him as well. He closed his eyes once more, letting his throat vibrate with the last bits of the melody as sleep finally pulled at him, the last note fading softly as the gentle darkness took over.


Milos slowly opened his eyes, finding himself surprised. That was the easiest he fell asleep in a while. A dreamless, comforting sleep he hadn't felt in so long. He slowly pushed himself up, peering over the group as his long hair fell over his shoulder, chains clinking in his ears. Rita was still fast asleep, almost spread eagle on the floor, chest rising and falling in heavy sleep. Suzuha wasn't even visible in the sheets, having pretty much pulled them all around her. Alex was curled around a pillow, taking up the other side.

Light shifted through the window as footsteps echoed outside. That was probably what woke him, the feeling of an approaching Demon. He shook his head, for being prisoners, they sure were receiving one too many guests in his opinion.

"What are you two doing?"

A voice spoke, curious. It sounded like Sechrondes, he believed her name was. That Naga.

"Oh, sorry, mistress, we...um..."

"The singing was nice." The second voice sounded sheepish. "We found ourselves listening and..."

"So, you were asleep all night? I've heard of the siren's abilities, and you know how dangerous they can be."

"But it was so gentle," the first guard argued before clearing his throat. "I'm sorry, we know this is tough for you, Ms. Sechrondes, especially since it was your charges in this situation, but..."

"There are no buts." The woman's voice hissed. "That MAN in there hurt my darlings. I come to check on the situation and find you two staring at the wall, out of it with goofy grins on your faces."

"That is enough, Sechrondes."

Another voice echoed out, startling Milos. He didn't even sense her approach.

"Sovereign!" Scrambling echoed from the other side as Milos pushed himself up, debating on waking the others.

"Sechondres, do not look down on these men, it is very hard to resist the spell of a siren, especially if you are unprepared."

Milos pursed his lips, walking over to Rita and lightly shoving her with his foot. She sat up with a start as he put a finger to his lips and pointed. She turned as Sechrondes replied, "Even as a child? Preposterous. I heard Maritus' claim, but I am more worried about that Alertian."

"Which is why we are here. Guards, open the door."

Rita scrambled to her feet just as the door opened, showing two guards trying to fix themselves up. Lillianna and Sechrondes stood on the other side. Sechrondes' expression was difficult to read, but Milos could feel a sense of hatred rush over him. It took much of his concentration not to shudder. His gaze flitted between the two before Lillianna stepped forward, her movement as graceful as before.

For some reason, he found himself taking a step back from her, though he didn't FEEL any malice. It was disconcerting. Her gaze shifted toward the bed before turning back to Rita and Milos.

"I have been contacted regarding some information." She stared at them quietly. "I want to hear from you what happened."

"So, you can twist our words like Maritus did?" Rita growled quietly, staring at her, one hand in her bag, though she was clearly shaken herself. "Considering we weren't supposed to have guests; we've seen a heck of a lot of people come through those doors."

Lillianna narrowed her eyes. "Maritus was supposed to have no contact with you all much like Alex's mother. We've been keeping an eye on Valencia to make sure she does not try to sneak in contact, but it seems we should have also kept an eye on Maritus as well." She glanced back to the guards, who both shifted out of sight. "I will apologize for that, and it is something I will keep in mind. It would certainly explain some rumors I have been hearing." She turned back to them. "Now, explain. Sechrondes, here, would like to know what ‚happened."

Milos pursed his lips, unsure, but the feeling dissipated as she gestured, putting a hand out, expression softening just the slightest bit. "You have nothing to fear from me. I simply want to know all sides of the story."

Milos felt his shoulders relax as he responded, "I was at the edge of town." The words came out, almost without his say and he found himself stiffening again as realization dawned on him, the feeling of magic curling over the air, a sign of some sort of command as he continued speaking, "I needed some time to myself, away from the demonic energies of the sanctuary. Three Demons approached me and said, since I was away from one such as Alex, that they would deal with me. They cursed me for being an Alertian and one attacked me. I..." He found himself drawing to a halt, his mind feeling almost blank. A moment of panic surged through. "I suppose I defended myself."

"You suppose?" Sechrondes hissed, as she shifted forward, tail coiling beneath her. "Alertian, there is no suppose. It is either you attacked, or you did not. Which is it?"

Lillianna continued to stare at him as the pressure seemed to increase in the air itself, growing warm. Milos found himself flinching.

Rita's gaze met his worry clear on her face. Clearly, she couldn't feel what was going on. For a moment, he was almost envious of her inability to detect Demons. He mentally shook it off and stared straight at them. "I don't remember." The words sounded almost bitter on his tongue. "The Minx held a sword to the back of my neck and when I went to get out of the way, one of the others blasted steam at me." His gaze flicked to both women. "I just remember thinking enough was enough and then...my next memory is standing alone, with my allies arriving and the three that attacked gone."

Lillianna narrowed her eyes, but strangely, the pressure seemed to lift considerably.

"So, you are saying they attacked you first?" Sechrondes slithered forward, curling around the two so she was almost leaning against his back. "Do you honestly expect me to believe the lies of—"

"Sechrondes."

Lillianna's one word resonated through the room, stopping the three in their tracks. It wasn't necessarily a sharp tone, but it caught Milos off guard.

Sechrondes turned to Lillianna as she stepped forward, standing right in front of Milos, gaze meeting his. "Milos, do you know what Alertians are?"

"Lillianna, pardon my wording, but that is quite the stupid question," Sechrondes cut in, though her voice was slightly shaken.

Lillianna didn't even shift, her gaze staying firmly on Milos. "As you recall, I put down my honor that you would not harm anyone here, and not long after, this incident occurred. So, you must understand, my patience and my dealings are thin." She said evenly, "So, answer me, Alertian, do you know the truth of your ancestry?"

Truth? He stared at her, feeling slightly cowed at her presence, but he shoved the feeling off. "I'm a Demon hunter, plain and simple." He spoke, though the words came out softer than he intended. "Nothing more. I'm simply a weapon of the people."

"Bullshit." Rita spun on Milos, startling him. "Okay, well, maybe not on the Demon hunter bit, but I would say you are more than a weapon, as annoying as you are." She seemed to stiffen under the eyes as shifting sounded from where Alex and Suzuha were sleeping. Though Milos highly doubted they still were at this point. "Last I checked, you were as human as Alex or me, okay, well, you still get my point." She thrust a finger toward him. "I don't get why you have this mentality of being nothing more than a hunter, a weapon."

Silence descended over the room as she seemed to realize, and she quickly pulled back. "My apologies, Lillianna." She smiled sheepishly, though Milos could see some of the sweat drip down the corner of her cheek. "I'm just tired of this lout looking down on himself as being less than a person and all that."

"It is quite alright." Lillianna spoke up.

Sechrondes shifted back around, watching the group quietly, a strange gleam in her eyes.

"What's going on?" a tired voice called, catching almost no one by surprise. Milos' gaze flicked back to see Alex sit up, rubbing his eyes before stilling at the sight. "Oh…"

"I tried." Suzuha shifted, rolling out of bed and standing on her feet, padding over. "You all were being loud."

Alex sent Suzuha a glare, before his gaze shifted toward the others, nervousness taking over. "Um… what did I miss?"

Lillianna shook her head, before turning back to Milos. "I see." She seemed to debate for a moment before continuing, "It seems your line's philosophy has been poisoned over the years. Your friend here is right, you are no mere weapon."

"Then, that outburst?" Sechrondes asked quietly. "The one he spoke of that almost slaughtered my people?"

"Uncontrolled." Silence fell over the room at her word as Sechrondes stared at Milos. "My guess is that your line no longer knows how to control the gift you were given and, instead, it's been shifted as simply a weapon." She let out a long sigh. "I think I am now aware of what happened on the outskirts." She turned, clothes flaring out briefly in her quick movement. "Sechrondes, gather the others, there is something we must discuss."

Milos felt his throat close up as something in him tugged, desperate. He found himself taking a step forward, startling even himself. "What do you mean?" His voice came out harsher than intended. "Gift? Uncontrolled? I've never…"

"Knowing your state of mind at the current time and the tense situation, it is best that I do not say more." Lillianna tilted her head back to stare at him, but her expression was soft, almost painful. "I'm sorry." With that, she gestured, and the door closed with a click behind her as the guards closed it. Footsteps echoed down the hall as Milos stared, his normal calm broken as his thoughts churned and raced.

"I missed a lot." Alex pushed himself to his feet, walking over. "Are you two okay?"

"I'm fine, but…" Rita's voice reached Milos' ears as he clenched his fist tightly, almost shaking. "Clearly, the others know more about Milos than, well…"

"I do."

He spun on his heels walking to the other end of the room before catching himself on the couch, taking deep breaths as he sat. He put his head in his hands as he tried to calm his racing heart and mind. What did she mean? A gift that shifted to simply being a weapon? Uncontrolled? He spent years developing his skills and she says that?

Was it because of his blackouts? His moments of missing thoughts? He briefly thought through the last few weeks. When he first attacked Alex, he only remembered the sword suddenly piercing the stone. When he fought the drega, he remembered shredding through the wing. On the island with the mutated humanoid Demons, he found himself surrounded in blood, his mind eerily calm as Rita and the other two pulled away from him.

A few hours ago…

He found himself gripping his hair tighter as a faint horror fell over him. He always saw that as his focus dwindled down to the subject at hand, to what needed to be done, but what if…?

The Aqua wraith's words rang in his head as his mind wavered, "*A sword is a part of an Alertian. No matter how much you may try to dull it, it will always come back sharp as steel.*"

What had she meant, then? That he couldn't control it?

He felt the couch dip next to him and felt the familiar swirl of energy.

"Hey, Milos?" Alex's voice reached his ears, but he didn't move, his fingers twitching as he closed his eyes tight. His mind was such a mess. "If it's any consolation, I probably know how you are feeling right now."

Milos jerked at those words. "We are NOT the same." He shot to his feet, spinning on Alex, who stared up at him, startled, grip tightening slightly on the couch. "You are a Demon, a child of Satan." He growled, finding his emotions pouring out, unable to hold them back this time. "My entire reason for coming down here was right there, in front of me, and now it means nothing!" Alex's eyes widened as realization dawned on Milos at those words, and, yet, he couldn't stop speaking, talking, saying whatever came out.

"I've been told my entire life that I am to kill Demons, that if I didn't do that, then why was I even born?" He put a hand to his chest, the emotions surging as Alex's expression, strangely, softened. "Now I'm being told the ONE thing I was supposed to do, I can't control? The one REASON for being in this damn hell is someone who I couldn't kill if my life depended on it? That now I hear my sister may be coming to this land? How in the Underlands am I supposed to feel? What in the king's name am I?"

Silence filled the room as the breath left his lungs and he dragged it desperately back in. Alex pushed himself to his feet, staring at him quietly. "This is going to sound stupid, but you're Milos." He grinned. "And one of the few friends I have in this stupid place. I'm grateful we got a chance to work together."

Milos pursed his lips.

"And, seriously? Did you have to blow up on us like that?" Rita leaned forward, tilting her head up toward him as she grinned, relief flashing over her face as he glanced over. "I mean, I guess it's to be expected. You are always so stoic, but it was definitely surprising."

"Are you...?" He gritted his teeth, the anger searing through him.

"Of course you're angry." Alex gestured, letting out a breath. "I was too, remember?" Rita winced, pulling back as Milos' gaze flicked to Alex. "My mom lied to me my entire life and, even when I found her, it took you all to finally have her tell me a little of what was going on." He gestured with both hands. "I know exactly how you are feeling. It's frustrating, and makes you want to scream your lungs out." He pulled back, rubbing his arm, wincing. "Questioning everything you knew? It hurts."

Milos slowly pulled back, gripping his sword tightly, head bowed as the feeling of rage slowly drained out of him, along with what felt like everything else. What even was the point? "Right. You would know." He spoke faintly, not looking at anyone. He hated this, he wanted to just leave, but that wasn't an option.

"Well, an apology is always a good thing," Rita pointed out.

Suzuha let out a quiet snort.

"Rita." Alex huffed, annoyance leaking into his voice. "Seriously?"

"Just saying! He did snap at us and, okay, I get it, I really do, but it's Milos."

He wanted to just say he was right here, but where his words flowed out earlier, his tongue was now stuck to the roof of his mouth, unable to escape.

"Hey, get some rest." Suzuha peered up, catching his attention as she grabbed his hand gently. "I know you just woke up, but something like this? It's exhausting. Once we know a little more of what's going on and the situation, then we will talk."

He closed his eyes, slowly breathing in and out through his nose. Right, they were right. He found himself being led back to the couch, where he took a seat, curling against the arm.

Fear passed through him briefly, flinching in expectation, but nothing came. The couch dipped again, and he heard movement from the other side of the room as two people settled down on the bed.

Something slumped against him, and he almost jumped out of his seat before looking over to see Alex leaning against him, clearly still tired after being woken up so suddenly.

One part of him screamed how wrong this was, another side promptly said to shut up. He already made his choice.

He slowly started to relax, feeling exhaustion slam into him as he pulled a leg up, leaning his head against it as one arm dangled listlessly over the edge of the couch. His reason for being down here, when had it disappeared? Was he even still a Demon hunter if he felt almost no inclination to kill Demons?

Was he just that much of a failure?

"Milos?" Alex's voice was soft, startling him slightly. He didn't respond, but it seemed Alex didn't need it, having not moved, eyes still closed in half sleep. "Did…?" He seemed to hesitate for a second before he sighed. "You mentioned that people said your only reason for living was to kill Demons. I don't believe that for a second and I don't think you do either."

Milos felt his entire body freeze at the words as silence fell over the room. Alex shifted, head leaning against his shoulder as the words faded, clearly said as he was falling asleep. "No one is born for one purpose and one purpose only. Even slaves have a reason to live beyond their situations. I guess, finding out the reason is a part of living."

Milos peered toward Alex and let out a long and tired breath.

"He's right, you know." Rita spoke up as he briefly glanced over to see she was sitting on the bed, hands draped between her legs as she watched quietly. "Freedom. It's a strange concept, but I think it applies here too.

You've chosen this path, through your own free will, which means you are more than what you are born as." She sighed, peering up toward the ceiling. "Though, breaking away from that can be devastating."

Milos nodded, unable to respond. He saw the aftermath of her situation, of her breaking free. It seemed so simple back then, when he first descended, but now he felt more emotions than he felt most of his life and felt closer than he ever had, even…

He slowly tilted his head up, staring up at the ceiling without really seeing it. With the pull of everything going on, he felt his mind slip into a sort of half sleep, filled with unpleasant nightmares.

He just hoped they didn't show outward. He didn't want to hurt the others because of his own situation.

# Chapter Twelve

Rita leaned against the palm of her hand as she stared at the door, almost glaring at it. With all the intruders lately, at least she had answers on why CERTAIN ones hadn't appeared. Suzuha was playing with the fabric of the bed, clearly lost in thought. Alex and Milos seemed to have fallen asleep. She was somewhat relieved.

Milos' expression startled her, the pain in his voice and eyes. It's not something she saw from the man before and she could kind of understand why. A lot happened lately in short succession, and she honestly hated it.

It didn't help that they were stuck here, just sitting around, unable to do anything but wait and hope that things worked themselves out. She riffled through her bag for the fifth time since ending up in that little room, hoping to find something, though she knew there would be nothing different.

If only she had time to make some potions when she actually had ingredients. Either she had ingredients, but no time, or was able to find time with no ingredients. She sighed, shaking her head as another potion rattled against a bottle. She pulled her hand back out, grumbling under her breath as she continued to watch the door.

She wasn't sure how much time passed before she heard footsteps echo once more down the hallway. There was quiet conversation from the other side before the door opened, revealing four guards standing outside. "We have been tasked with escorting you all to the trial. Please, come forth."

One of them spoke as the two who had been at the door the whole time exchanged looks and the other three stayed back, spears at the ready. Rita pursed her lips but slowly got to her feet. Suzuha hopped up, hurrying over to Alex and Milos, tapping them both on the knee to wake them up.

Alex rubbed his eyes while Milos snapped awake, hand reaching for his sword before he pulled back, shaking his head.

The lead guard seemed to watch them, though it was hard to tell with the helmet over his face, before he turned with a clack of metal on stone, gesturing. Rita grumbled under her breath but followed Alex a step behind as Suzuha lightly shoved Milos, who was understandably tense.

They stepped out of the room and Rita winced as her stomach growled loudly. Right, they hadn't eaten much over the last day or so. Well, that sucked. The two guards at the door joined the other four to lead them out.

Soon enough, they were brought out of the front entrance, the day stones shining brightly above, beaming down at them and making her squint slightly. The light through the window had been dull in comparison. The path was lined with greenery. Two guards took the front while the other four followed at the back, keeping an eye on them, specifically Alex and Milos.

Alex seemed more than a little uncomfortable and Milos' expression was just hard to read.

It wasn't long before they found themselves in the plaza and she winced as she spotted a small crowd to one side, watching the procession. Hatred surged and even Milos seemed to stumble slightly.

Rita didn't even know hatred could actually feel like a force, but this one certainly did, and she wondered if it had to do with them being mostly Demons. She did spot a few humans in the crowd and noticed that they seemed to be watching in, not hatred. Instead, it was curiosity and almost concern, which threw her. She shook it off as they were led past and up the flight of stairs leading back into the great halls of the Sovereigns domain. Instead of going through the set of doors at the end of the hall, they made a sharp right into a smaller doorway, different from before. They stepped inside to find a circular room with a plinth in the middle. Six familiar Demons sat around the base with a few others sprinkled throughout, along with a few humans here and there.

Rita's gaze snapped to the plinth, and she almost went ballistic as she spotted manacles, two in particular.

She jerked, glancing over as Alex and Milos were suddenly shoved forward. Alex managed to catch himself as Milos went to spin, only to be grabbed by guards standing next to the manacles.

"What the…?" She turned back and forth as she felt Suzuha bristle beside her. "What is the meaning of this?"

The guards stepped back, gesturing with spears toward Suzuha and Rita. "Do not fight." The guard that led them spoke evenly, causing Rita and Suzuha to tense.

Alex shifted uncomfortably but let the guard slide the manacles over his wrist. Milos was a lot more hesitant, but, thankfully, the man seemed to realize it would be better not to argue right now.

Though Rita was beyond pissed, especially when she noticed both wince and recoil slightly as the manacles snapped firmly shut.

"To answer your question, Witch, precautions." A voice echoed around the chamber, a familiar one.

Rita turned to see the older Demon, Ludwig. He glared down at the group as Alex pulled back, nervous, and Milos stood straight, expression impassive. "Any Demon under trial must be put into shackles."

"Then, why…"

"Milos is an Alertian." This time, Maritus spoke, grinning from ear to ear as the feathers bristled in a non-existent breeze. "I feel like, for him, it is not enough precautions."

"We have already discussed this." Lillianna's voice echoed out, quieting the crowd as she swept to her feet, hands clasped in front of her. "But that is enough, we are all here for a unique situation. These halls are rarely used for their intended purpose, but they will be today."

She gestured, staring down with an almost impassive air that made Rita stiffen once more, a hint of nervousness flaring through. Now that she was looking around, Alex's mother was nowhere in sight. That was more than a little worrying and it was clear Alex noticed as well.

He swallowed heavily, tilting his head up, fingers twitching. Suzuha and Rita stood slightly behind the two, watching warily.

This was not what she expected, but she honestly hadn't known what to expect.

"Today, we discuss the fate of the Alertian, Milos, as well as his entourage, Alex, Rita and Suzuha." Lillianna gestured. "This design is one of human make, so a human shall be presiding over the trial itself."

She gestured to one side, nodding her head. A young woman stepped forward with short cut brown hair, a pen and paper in hand and watching quietly. "She has refrained from knowing the situation and, as the term goes, will be a judge. Those within these halls will be the jurors." She turned. "Will this be sufficient for everyone involved?"

"I still believe we should just do this the Demon way." Ludwig twitched. "Humans…"

"Those on trial are more human than Demon, the human laws remain intact for everyone involved, so we must abide by them. Plus, I am not a fan of the more atrocious and uncivilized version that Demons use." Erin spoke up from one side of the hall, inspecting her nails. "I find these human trials fascinating, much more than the bloodsport that is Demonic trials. I believe these to be the one GOOD thing humans have created."

Ludwig growled, but didn't respond.

Rita was just wondering what she meant and decided, if they got out of this intact, then she needed to do more research.

The brown-haired woman cleared her throat, staring down at the four of them. "My name is Veronica." She nodded her head toward the four, expression even. "Court is now in session." She pulled out some papers as Lillianna took a seat to one side and the others shifted, curious. "The crimes listed include assault and battery, traitorous acts, manipulation and coercion, as well as attacking a high ranking official." She peered up. "These are all serious claims that, if decided upon, deserve a harsh punishment." She put the papers down. "First off, can we have the prosecutor and defendants take the stand?"

Quiet chatter echoed through the room as Maritus swept to his feet, staring down at the party with a slight grin on his face. Rita glared up to him, her heart pounding in her chest.

She heard footsteps and jerked as more murmuring sounded out and looked over to see Valencia.

"Mom?" Alex choked as Valencia came to a halt before stepping aside. Her gaze flicked to Alex and Rita could have sworn she saw a flicker of a smile along with a wink before she turned. Behind her stood Ari, dressed in sharp clothing, her head held high. The chains still curled around her wrists but were slightly hidden by long sleeves. Rita glanced around, startled to not see Leon. He was always with Ari, where was he?

Maritus let out a sharp laugh. "A human? I'm surprised, Valencia, that is the best you could find?"

"It's all I need." Valencia spoke evenly, staring up at Maritus. "This girl has every right to defend those standing before you as you have to prosecute them. I will not interfere, clearly having my own bias, but I will stand witness if necessary." She nodded her head and stepped up the stairs into the surrounding benches.

Rita watched Alex stare, it seemed like he saw the wink, his shoulders relaxing just the slightest bit.

"Maritus of the Airadon, prosecutor of this trial and Ari of the Humans, do you agree to a fair and legal trial under the laws bestowed by humans that are upheld within the sanctuary and beyond?" Veronica peered back and forth, both nodded, though Maritus with a faint smirk, like the Demon who caught the rat.

Rita REALLY wanted to punch his face in.

"Prosecutor, please make your claim." Veronica gestured.

Maritus bowed before staring down at the trio. "The evidence is quite clear. We are all aware of Alertians and how dangerous they are. Being the reason we are even sequestered to these northern lands. This one, clearly, is no exception." He stepped down the stairs. "Not only are there viable reports that he has attacked our citizens, but I have learned that he has attempted to kill those with which he journeys."

Rita stiffened as Alex jerked, glancing up in faint horror.

"On top of that, I was present when the siren, Alex, used his voice to coerce me to step aside, putting the sovereign in danger. I think the evidence is quite clear that those involved deserve the harshest of punishments."

Murmuring filled the hall as Veronica nodded, though her expression remained strangely neutral.

"Defendant? What do you have to say?"

Rita glanced toward Ari, worried. The girl wasn't one to speak, but there was a certain stance she held right now as her gaze flicked to them, staying on Milos before turning away. "I cannot deny the dangers of Alertians, for I have seen it myself," she started and Rita felt her heart stop, breath catching in her throat. "However, I have evidence pointing to the contrary of what Maritus says." She gestured behind her. "Regarding the attack on your citizens, there have been two incidents which have shown that, actually, it was the citizens who attacked the people standing before you." Quiet chatter filled the halls as a sheepish-looking male stepped out, one Rita recognized. "Before you stands a shop keepers from within the sanctuary. Please, tell them what you told me."

Ari turned back to him, catching the man's attention. He cleared his throat, not looking at the four of them. "The other day, I spotted the Alertian standing beside the boy before you…a powerful and rare Demon. I didn't want the Alertian to hurt anyone, so slipped some shards of metal into his food. I only later found out that Alex swapped the food to protect Milos and…" He winced and didn't continue. "Even if Alex hadn't taken and swapped it, I did attack them unprovoked, simply due to my own hatred. Yet, they did nothing in retaliation, even though they had every right too."

Rita tried incredibly hard not to react. She had, admittedly, put a potion in their workspace that MAY have stunk the place up to high heavens for a while and MAY have melted one of the stoves by accident…but it was far less than what was done to them, so it was completely fair.

Ari turned back to the crowd as the boy was quickly led out. "The iron shards in question are here."

She pulled out a few, startling Rita. She had just thrown them to the side. Had Ari scoured the courtyard to find them? "You will see blood still on them…from Alex."

Gasps filled the hall as Maritus frowned. "And what does this have to do with my claim of Milos attacking…"

"Everything." Ari, to Rita's surprise, cut in, staring straight toward him with her normal impassive expression, not revealing a thing. "These people were already attacked once within a place deemed a sanctuary. Alex, a Demon of stature at the time of the incident, was injured in the process, trying to protect his ally. And yet, they were still cordial WHILE meeting more Demons. The second incident, in which this whole thing is based off of, was staged."

~ * ~

Milos jerked, glancing over as Sechrondes suddenly surged upward, tail thrashing.

"How dare you, human." She hissed. "Are you saying my own…?"

"Silence." The judge snapped her hand down. "Do you have proof of such outlandish claims?" She glanced toward Ari, who bowed and gestured once more.

This time, Rita did a double-take as Leon helped a limping woman through the doors. She was a lion-like woman with a thick mane and was clearly heavily hurt. "She is willing to testify to the court. Miranda, please, tell them what you told us." Ari turned to her as the woman pushed away from Leon to stand straight in front of the crowd, not looking at Sechrondes.

"We received a note saying that the Alertian fled to the northern passage that leads to the vents. We were told that, if we bothered him, we would receive a reward. We knew we weren't strong enough to kill him, and that was not our intention." She glanced up, staring at the group. "When we arrived, we found him sitting on the ground, distracted. He didn't attack us, he just talked, even when I had a sword to his throat. It was when my comrade attacked that he finally responded in kind." She shook her head. "He never attacked first."

Rita noticed Maritus was about to speak when Ari quickly but succinctly continued, "Did the note specify who it was from?"

The woman's gaze flicked briefly to Maritus before she shook her head. Rita snorted. "Sorry, but, did you even get the reward? Because that's just rude if you didn't."

There was a flinch from the woman as Veronica cleared her throat, a sharp look sent Rita's way quickly shutting her up. She didn't want to ruin this, but she couldn't help it.

"So, not only were you put in a difficult situation by one you cannot name, but you also did not receive the proper recompense for your ordeal." Ari spoke evenly before turning toward the stands. "The note in question has been recovered, if you will." She gestured.

Leon stepped forward, placing a piece of clearly folded paper into the hands of Veronica before stepping back.

Maritus looked like he was swallowing acid with the way his

expression was contorted.

Veronica peered over it and nodded. "No name is inscribed, but this is clear evidence to prove our witness was aware." She did not say more, simply placed the paper down.

In that intervening moment Maritus cleared his throat and spoke, a slightly fake smirk crossing his face. "Even with such a note, the evidence is clear that he attacked our people after being under watch for said actions and, as a result, lead to life threatening injuries for three of our citizens."

"He attacked, after he was provoked, twice," Ari responded evenly. "After someone told these innocent people to provoke an Alertian, which puts them in a difficult situation themselves, as I stated earlier. I believe anyone who is provoked enough times, will lash out in what is called self-defense."

Maritus narrowed his eyes as Miranda nodded. "We believe that is what happened. He was mostly just dodging us until he got hit with a steam breath." She winced. "I don't remember much after that, the air became heavy and difficult to breathe and..." She shook her head.

"Thank you." Ari spoke softly. "It's appreciated, you can rest now." The woman nodded as Leon carefully helped her out. He returned a few minutes later as Ari turned back to the crowd. "As you can see, I hold proof that Milos never instigated the fights, nor is he the reason behind them. It was all in self-defense."

"Then, how do you explain the acts of coercion later?" Maritus lifted his jaw, staring down placidly. "This group came running into the plaza after having fought with Sechrondes' people, Milos covered in blood and expected us to just let them through to talk with our leader. Of course I was going to say no. However, that one," he pointed toward Alex, who recoiled slightly, "used his very voice to force the residents to flee and to paralyze me for a moment to allow them to get past. This is dangerous on all accounts."

"For that one, I am going to have his mother speak." Ari gestured, startling the crowd as Valencia blinked, clearly just as surprised. "His mother is one of the few aware of his situation. Can I have you please stand?"

Valencia looked around before getting to her feet, clearly surprised by this turn of events. "Yes?" Her voice wavered slightly.

"Please, tell us what you know of Alex's situation regarding his voice."

"You cannot use her as an example, she is biased in being Alex's mother, she will lie…"

"Demons, especially certain Demons in this hall right now, are able to detect when another is lying. If they speak up, then you have every right to argue." Ari's gaze shifted to Erin, who tilted her head up, but didn't reply. Rita couldn't help but find herself more and more impressed with Ari at that moment. The girl was always emotionless unless under rare circumstances and it was coming to her benefit now as she stayed calm in what was very much a divisive situation. Plus, she never heard Ari talk this much in her life.

Maritus snapped his mouth shut, a heavy frown falling across his face. Ari turned back to Valencia. "Now, please, answer."

Valencia nodded. "My child is descended from both me, a child of Satan, and my husband, who was an experiment created to develop half human half Demon children." Horror settled over the surroundings as Rita's eyes widened. Oh, she hadn't known that. Her gaze flicked to Alex, who was watching quietly, clearly unsurprised. "His father's half Demon counterpart was of Nyx blood, which, from historical records, date back from before the collapse with a possibility of being descendants from the ancient sirens." She shook her head. "We were unaware until a few years after he was born that my satanic side and his father's Nyx side may have reawakened those capabilities, so we put a seal on his Demonic half. It's only been within the past few months that he's actually been able to utilize and interact with his Demonic side." She turned to the crowd as Rita listened intently, stunned. "As many know, Demons have no control over their abilities while they are still young. For all intents and purposes, my child is only a few years old when it comes to his Demonic control. He only learned about three days ago that his voice had the capability to affect those around him and it hurt him." Her gaze settled on Alex, with a pained expression. "It hurt him deeply. So, I have no doubt, he only would have used it if it was an emergency, and by accident."

"And how do you propose we should believe…"

"You can feel the Demonic energy around him." Valencia cut in, meeting Maritus' eyes. "You can still tell it's growing, which should not be possible for someone his physical age, at least, not in the speed with which it is."

"There is very much the remains of a seal on him," Sechrondes said quietly, catching everyone's attention as she stared down at Alex. "I was ignoring it until you spoke. Even now, some of his powers are suppressed with the lingering effects of a seal, though it is weakening."

Alex froze, as Rita swallowed heavily, tongue almost in her throat. Wait, what?

Maritus looked outright pissed as Veronica looked around. "As a human, I am not quite sure of what this implies. Can I have a Demon please explain that is not directly involved?"

One of the Demons in the crowd raised his hand, a young male. "Um, basically? It means that for all intents and purposes, Alex is a Demon child, which means that he couldn't have intentionally used his abilities. Seals are almost unheard of, but they are said to be used on those with human blood so that their chance of survival increases. So, most likely, the use of his abilities was an accident."

Veronica nodded and turned back to the crowd, an interested gleam in her eyes. "I see." She didn't say more, though Rita could see Maritus' expression twist to outrage. "Prosecutor, do you have anything to say in return?"

Maritus quickly schooled his expression, straightening. Rita was finding the man had a lot of intriguing expressions, all of them punchable. "I believe that the situation is still being manipulated." He stared down at Ari, who wasn't even looking at him, her gaze on the judge and those surrounding her. "Ludwig, please, stand and tell the crowd her affiliation with those involved in this case."

Ludwig huffed but stood. "We should just strike them down where they stand, my blood is screaming to just deal with them." He stared down, nose up. "That defendant should not be trusted, she is a slave of Milos, the one on trial, and was seen coming off the boat with the others alongside the one-armed man who guided one of the speakers in. What proof do we have that they aren't just manipulating the situation to save their master so as to not be sold off again?"

Murmuring shot through the crowd as Veronica turned down to Ari, narrowing her eyes. "Is this true?"

Ari stared back at her, expression even. "I did, indeed, arrive with MASTER," The word was said so emphatically but with no change in volume, Rita almost found herself startled, "but everything I have brought in and spoken of is through my own research alongside Leon and those I shall not name."

"See, proof." Maritus spoke smugly, staring down with a wide toothy grin. "A slave is…"

"Someone who has the same rights as Demons and other humans within these lands," Veronica interjected and this was when Rita actually got a better look at her and jerked, noting the thick bands around her wrists…not chains, but maybe at one point. "You used Master. Is this of your own will?"

"Yes."

Veronica's gaze settled on Erin, who didn't respond. Veronica's expression shifted slightly.

"What does that have to do with anything?" Maritus crossed his arms over his chest as Rita's eyes widened, realization dawning on her as she suppressed a grin. She could see the humans murmuring in the crowd, watching Ari with an appraising look.

"May I?" A woman in the crowd spoke up, catching everyone's attention.

Veronica nodded. The woman stood, staring at the surrounding Demons. "The importance of the term, Master, is not something to look down upon amongst slaves. Many of you were born or have always remained in this land. For those who have arrived through the waterways and escaped servitude, the term, Master, is only used through great respect. If you've escaped, no slave will use that term unless they hold the person in high regard." The woman bowed her head. "Your name is Ari, correct?" Ari nodded. "My guess is you were sold or given to the one standing before us."

"That is correct." Ari spoke evenly. "Leon and I were given as gifts upon Milos' descent into the Underlands. He saved us and, in turn, we both agreed to use the term, as appropriate for someone who has given us freedom, even though we did not ask or necessarily deserve it." Her gaze flitted to Leon before staring at the crowd once more. "You all know the implications of a lame slave. Look at my companion here. Do you honestly believe he would have survived this long, if not for these people's aid? Someone like him would have been abandoned long before this point."

Maritus scoffed, waving his hand before pausing as murmuring filled the hall once more, even a few Demons nodding along, staring straight at the missing arm in question. "Simple word play." He stared down quietly. "How did the arm get lost in the first place?"

Ari stilled, gaze flicking to Leon, who stepped forward. "A drega attacked us and went to drag me off. To save my life, Milos used his sword to severe the arm. That is the only reason I am not dead at this moment."

Maritus smirked as silence fell over the crowd. "In other words, he injured his own ally without a care or thought." He turned to the others, who were staring at Milos nervously. "Not only that, but even in self-defense, you saw the wounds on Miranda and the two with her. Those are not wounds of self-defense, but of someone who was seeking to kill. Who's to say how he will react now that we have put him on trial ourselves." He gestured, staring down. "He is dangerous, too dangerous to be let free to walk around Sanctuary. Even if we say he did respond to being provoked, a normal reaction is to fight enough to find a way to escape. Two of those who fought him came back with mortal wounds that took a lot of resources to recover from. It's a miracle they are still alive." He turned to Veronica. "Even if we can wave off the coercion, the Alertian's response was beyond what it should be, evidenced by his willingness to lop off his slave's own arm. Sure, you say it was to save his life, but there are many other ways that would have kept him alive. If the accused was able to slice off the arm, he should have been able to slice off whatever part of the body the creature had grabbed the witness with as evidenced by the precise and clean strikes on the victims." He leaned forward. "Since Miranda is still a witness, I wish for her to emerge once more."

Ari and Leon exchanged hesitant looks before Veronica gave them a sharp nod. After a moment, Leon left and carefully guided Miranda back in.

Murmuring settled through the crowd as Maritus spoke evenly. "As we have a few in the crowd who are doctors, as well as the medical reports, provided before this farc— Trial." He quickly corrected. "You will notice that the incisions across Miranda's body are precise and clean. Aiming at vital organs. Vital organs…which are different from normal humans. His abilities, as an Alertian first and foremost, are uncanny in their precision whether that be to kill or maim, something many of us have witnessed in the past, which means that it is impossible for him to have been unable to attack the creature in a way which would have released his compatriot. Instead of focusing down on the Drega, he instinctively maimed his own comrade. This is inexcusable and showcases the inherent dangers of letting one like him loose in our city. If he is willing to maim his own before finding a way to kill his prey, then what would that mean for our people?"

Veronica stared quietly down at the four of them. Rita swallowed thickly. Maritus had a good point with that. With Milos' skill, he should have been able to free Leon without cutting off the man's arm. Unfortunately, she wasn't there, only Leon, Ari and Milos were, and it was word against word.

Ari seemed a little taken aback, clearly uncertain how to respond.

"It was hectic." Leon spoke evenly. "The drega had taken off and was flying away, even with his precision and abilities, the closest thing he could reach in time was my arm."

"A valid excuse." Maritus spoke evenly, staring down. "Except, it is coming from one with direct bias from the accused. Even if it was the truth, that is a truth easily obscured by one's belief, not what actually took place." He turned to the crowd. "However, we have definitive evidence showcasing that, while in battle or under stress, he will succumb to the base instincts given to him by the accursed Alertian line. Sechrondes?"

Sechrondes stiffened and Rita felt a little uncomfortable as realization dawned on her. "Would you mind repeating what you heard from the accused in regard to the attack?"

Sechrondes hesitated for a moment before uncoiling, her long tail twitching behind her. For a split second, Rita could have sworn she felt the temperature of the entire room drop as her eyes flitted to Lillianna, but it quickly settled, making her believe she imagined it.

Sechrondes cleared her throat before speaking. "When the

Sovereign and I spoke to the accused, we asked what happened. He agreed that they drew blades first, however, after a certain point, he did not remember what happened, stating that he supposed he fought back. She shook her head as murmurings fell around the crowd.

"Thank you." Maritus straightened, a barely concealed grin crossed his face as he stared down. "So, not only is it proven the Alertian has no memory of said attack, while under that trance like state, he almost murdered three of our people. A similar state, most likely, having been what caused the maiming of his own allies arm. If he is able to fall into such a dangerous state, simply from being coerced, then how can we, as a people, allow him to walk amongst us? What reason would we have to believe he would not fall into it again due to some slight in the future?"

Rita swallowed thickly, horror settling heavy in her stomach. Things seemed to have been going well up until now, very well to be fair, but he pulled out something not even Ari could probably counter, and it was clear she couldn't because Ari, for the first time in this whole thing, suddenly appeared nervous, gaze flicking to Milos. The room was abuzz with conversation, a few eyes flicking to Erin, who hadn't responded at all, watching with an impassiveness that made Rita shudder.

That had always been a concern of hers as well and, clearly, of Alex's considering how the boy was eyeing Milos, whose head was bowed in seeming defeat, his whole-body drooping in despair. She clenched her fist tightly, gritting her teeth so hard she could almost swear they cracked. Was it not enough? Could she not change her or Milos' fate?

Six words rang out amongst the hall, a sudden silence falling over everything as Rita jerked, staring up in shock. Lillianna stood, voice echoing strongly, but not loudly, over the crowd. "I have an answer to that."

All breath left Rita's throat as a sudden dizziness fell over her. She wasn't sure if it was a future vision, or a current one, but she put a hand to her head, wincing as Lillianna's words sliced through the silence.

"I got a chance to speak with Milos before this trial, as dictated by Sechrondes, since, as you might recall, I put my honor on the line that he would not hurt anyone within this sanctuary."

Rita winced, slowly tilting her head up to face Lillianna as she continued.

"As one of the few survivors of the Demon-human war a hundred years ago, I know the truth of Alertians, their ancestors and the reason behind Milos' reckless actions and his inability to remember that will help prove his innocence." Her expression flashed to a pained and soft one for the briefest second, almost hard to tell.

Milos stiffened as Alex glanced back and forth, expression filled with worry.

She let out a long sigh, clasping her hands in front of her. It seemed the whole room was holding its breath, everyone watching her intently. "Many years ago, I was betrothed to an Alertian."

The words crashed over the group and Rita felt her eyes widen, hands snapping up to her mouth in utter shock, the only one who didn't seem to react was Ludwig who let out a sigh, shaking his head.

Her gaze solidified on Milos, who was stock still. "From ages long past, Alertians and Demons used to work side by side to protect the human and Demon realms. That was all destroyed when an Alertian corrupted the minds of humans. They brought death and destruction on our lands…even taking down and murdering his own brethren in his desires. We talk of the strength of the Alertian, but all Demons know that humans are weak of body, if strong of mind and creativity…"

Her gaze shifted to Alex. "And so, Alertians, or humans that knew of the Underlands when our worlds were still separate, married with Demons to create a line of humans with Demonic blood to protect the land."

"What?" Rita couldn't help but reply, slashing her arm out. "Alertians are part Demon? How is that possible?"

Milos…Rita never saw Milos so pale and shaken, stock still.

"Just like Alex. I do not know of what has happened with the Alertian line over the past one hundred years, but the one who stands before you is simply a child much like Alex, one who has the blood of a Demon, and was never taught how to control it except through force."

"That's…That's a lie." Milos' voice echoed through the chamber before he jerked, staring up at her, almost pulling at his manacles. "I am an ALERTIAN, a Demon HUNTER. I am NOT a Demon. Nor do I have Demon blood! I would rather you throw me in jail then say such things!"

Alex was silent, eyes wide, posture stiff. Rita swallowed thickly.

"You heard him," Maritus said quietly. "He would rather…"

"He has every right to know." Valencia cut in. "You can feel it too, now that Lillianna has spoken, the waves of energy seeping from him. I always figured it was because he was an Alertian, and staying near my boy. But to be honest, this makes much more sense. How else could humans have completely defeated Demons a hundred years ago? Unless the one leading was a half Demon." She gestured. "Which means, this poor child was forced to reject part of who he was and learn only to hunt down that side of him."

"He was made to believe he was only a weapon." Lillianna spoke quietly, staring down at Milos, who was shaking his head, metal clanking loudly from the blood red chain signifier. "Of course he would attack recklessly, or have moments of blackout, no one was willing to let him learn or to teach him. The fact that he didn't completely slaughter those around him, even after being provoked so much, by itself shows his restraint. Even full-grown adults will often struggle not to fall into trances when anger or fear overcomes them. To blame a child, especially a child who was forsaken and forced to loathe a part of him, is cruel. Note the energy within him, that force we, Demons, can all feel. You should all recognize it. Where Alex's powers were sealed, Milos' were simply suppressed due to sheer force of will, a feat not even most Demons can contend with. That is evidence enough that he is innocent in this case. After all, the one who sent the note willingly provoked a child who has already been broken by those who were supposed to guide and nurture him."

At this, Milos crashed the manacles down on the plinth, hair whipping up as he let out a shout, "SHUT UP!" It was the loudest Rita ever heard from him, and she almost found herself taking a step back as Alex stiffened, Suzuha suddenly shifted, defensive. "I don't want to hear it! I was born to HUNT Demons; that's the only reason why I was born! And now you tell me I'm a fucking Demon? Are you fucking insane?" The metal clanked on the ground as he crashed it down once more and Rita almost yelped, quickly covering her face as if she felt almost like a wave blast into her.

"MILOS!" Alex shouted, wings flaring out as he caught himself. A few shouts echoed through the crowd and scrambling met her ears. "CALM DOWN!"

Milos' gaze snapped to Alex, hair curling around him, almost snapping in a non-existent breeze. Breath hissed from the side of his lips, eyes narrowed, specks of white curled up the side of his neck. Alex jerked forward, pulling at the manacles as his wings flared out behind him, horns curling up as his tail lashed. "Please, Milos, stop," he pleaded. "Maybe that's not…"

"It is…" Milos' voice choked as he shifted. "You can feel it…no, you can see it."

Alex snapped his mouth shut, gaze flicking to the air around Milos, at least, it seemed to Rita, before he shook his head. "Then maybe you are." The words seemed to slice through Milos, the manacles almost shaking.

Rita peered to one side, noticing a few humans holding onto the chairs tightly while the Demons seemed to be holding their heads, reeling slightly, except for six. The leaders watched with varying hard to read expressions.

Though Maritus looked absolutely victorious, grin widening as the mayhem continued, practically proving his point. Rita shot a glare at him before speaking up. "Snap out of it, you lout!" She took a step forward, unable to get too close, though it was hard to tell why. "You don't think every one of us hasn't felt what you're feeling? So, what if you are a Demon? You are Milos, and we'll figure it out just like we've figured out every other stupid thing that's happened since we all met!"

Alex nodded, tail thrashing as he took another step forward, straining at the manacles.

Milos took a step back, the chains digging into his wrists with how harshly he was tugging, emotions flashing over his face.

"*Heavoleun mitte vend.*" Alex spoke, voice rang softly over the surroundings, causing Milos to still, the words reverberating through the suddenly quiet room. "*He-ven hue,* Milos. *Verist jit villen. Viet ackt fel fen.*"

Milos stared quietly as Rita blinked. What? What did Alex say?

Alex continued to meet Milos' eyes, almost desperate. "I know you know what I said. You KNOW the words came out of nowhere, but they are the truth. We ARE here for you." The words echoed softly around, almost delicate, the edges filled with the beginnings of a quiet song.

Milos shuddered and seemed to settle. To Rita's utter surprise, he seemed to collapse, knees crashing to the ground first before he stared down, the wind and feeling in the air dissipating. Silence slowly filled the room as Alex let out a tired breath, glaring at the metal before blinking as Suzuha stepped forward, producing a key from behind her back and unlocking it. Rita jerked and glanced over.

"I stole it."

She shrugged, tossing the key up before catching it in the palm of her hand, a strange emotion on her face. To Rita's surprise, and relief, none of the guards came over to put the shackles back on.

Alex shifted over, kneeling next to Milos whose hands were on the ground, head bowed, his whole body crumpled. Alex's wings curled forward, reaching around both him and Milos as if in a hug, partially hiding the man. He jerked, a heavy glare piercing into the surrounding crowd with a quiet fury Rita rarely saw.

"Are you all done?" He hissed, surprising Rita. "Nothing good has come from arriving at this supposed sanctuary. This is more of a hell-scape than the southern reaches."

"Well, I mean, I can't argue." Rita put her hands on her hips as she stomped forward before staring at everyone who caught themselves. She placed herself on the other side of Milos, defensive. "We have done NOTHING to you all and instead we've been hurt, attacked, manipulated, thrown on trial and, for what?" She slashed her arm out. "Ari, our FRIEND, had to dig to find research and prove our innocence and yet…"

Rita felt her tongue slam to the top of her mouth, and she shook her head, unable to continue. She heard movement and a click as Suzuha unlocked the manacles on Milos, who still hadn't moved.

"Why should we believe you?" Maritus finally spoke, staring down. "We all clearly saw how dangerous they both are. Even as children, an uncontrolled power is still…"

"Oh, shut up, air-head," Rita snapped, just done with this prick. "You and your molting feathers can go jump off a cliff for all I care."

"Airhead? How dare…"

A snort echoed through the room, catching him off guard. Sechrondes quickly looked away, hand to her lips, though Rita spotted the corners twitching upward.

"That was startling, to say the least, but things have calmed down." Veronica stood, straightening her clothing. "While, normally, such an outburst would be immediate dismissal and a retrial with much harsher judges, but…"

Her gaze landed on the four of them, Suzuha standing in front, hand on her hips with Alex and Rita on either side of a shell-shocked Milos, protectively huddling near him, though Rita would never admit it. Ari was glaring at Maritus, expression impassive, but angered. At some point, Leon must have brought Miranda back outside, because she wasn't there anymore.

Veronica just shook her head. "Considering the mental toll this trial has taken, as well as the series of events leading up to this moment, it is clear not much else needs to be discussed. All those in favor of condemning the four before you on the charges of assault and battery, coercion, manipulation and attacking a higher being, raise your hands."

Rita watched, dismay curling over her as one hand went up, then another and then a few more. Maritus crossed his arms over his chest, smugly as the count slowly increased, five… ten… twenty-three…

Was it not enough? Had she been unable to change Milos' fate? No matter what she did? The thought kept circling around and around in her head, no matter how many times she pushed it aside. She hoped and prayed that Lilliana's words would be enough to convince the people that they were not to blame for what happened, that Milos wasn't a menace to their people.

Veronica looked around before nodding and noting something down. "You may put down your hands." Once everyone did as she said, she gestured. "All in favor of relieving them of all charges just announced, please, raise your hands."

Rita stared quietly, feeling a heavy heartache falling over her as everyone exchanged looks, before one person raised their hand. The woman who talked about the importance of Master. Then the Demon and soon a few more raised their hands. Rita's eyes widened as Alex looked around, watching as he held Milos' shoulders. Alex's tail curled around his own waist like he did when he was nervous, and Rita didn't blame him. There were so many hands before and it was hard to tell how many there were this time. Was it enough? It looked way too close. Maritus' expression seemed to shift as, to Rita's surprise, Sechrondes raised her hand, then Erin. Maritus peered to either side.

"Why are you two…?"

"Because they are children." Sechrondes spoke evenly. "I remember as a child what it was like when my powers went crazy. I felt terrible, but there was nothing I could do and it was the same for you. We had the advantage of being around Demons to learn how to develop these abilities, they did not. And, well, that one is true, they have done nothing and all we've done is attack them through words or actions." Her gaze drifted down. "And I know my underling, Miranda, was telling the truth and it was clear she wasn't fond of what she did. And to be frank, your point became invalid regarding his blackouts now that we know it's due to his uncontrolled Demonic side."

Maritus' face twisted as Eren shrugged. "I didn't hate them or like them and that human had a good argument. She showed multiple pieces of evidence and, well, I do know a little bit about slave heritage." She tilted her head, eyes catching his. "They never lied. Can you imagine? Never even knowing you were someone you always thought you were supposed to destroy. I feel it is our duty, as elder Demons, to lead children like that. Though you very much clearly have a different opinion."

Maritus pursed his lips before glaring over the crowd, as if hoping to dissuade some of the hands. Ironically enough, the two leaders' words seem to cause a few more hands to raise that Rita could have sworn rose last time. Rita swallowed thickly. She lost count. How many raised their hands to jail them? Was it the same? Was it one less? It was too close to tell and it was making her extremely nervous. She tried not to show it, but she felt her hands slowly curl into fists to try to stop the shaking.

Veronica noted something down, staring before turning to Lillianna, whispering something quietly. All the Demons seemed to jerk, startled, and even Alex tilted his head up, eyes wide. Lillianna nodded, quietly whispering back, receiving a deep bow in return. Veronica wrote once more into the book and closed it. "The final verdict has been decided. Lillianna, our Sovereign shall speak of the decision for the four before us. If you will."

Lillianna nodded and turned to the group, her presence feeling overwhelming. It was hard to read her expression. Was it good? Was it bad?

Rita couldn't tell, but from the way Alex was twitching, staring up at her almost hopefully, she could only hang on to the belief that they did enough.

"The jury has decided... These children sought us out for help, sought me out for help." Lillianna stared quietly. "Even fighting their own heritage and truths. I find them not guilty of all actions spoken of in this trial."

"WHAT?" Maritus snapped, growling before catching himself and slowly fixing himself up, glaring down. "This is outrageous..."

"We have made the decision based on the laws of this land." Lillianna spoke, tilting her head up.

"We all heard, it was an even split." Maritus said, breath sharply inhaling through his nose. "Which means the vote..."

"Would have come down to me," she said simply. "This was as Veronica detailed and allowed, being the neutral judge and adjudicator. With it being close, I made the final decision. I said this once before, and I will continue to say this. My honor will continue to remain on the line for these children. They might be just what this country, these lands, need to make amends. It has been over a century since an Alertian and a Demon walked side by side. A witch and Vulfulas at their side as well? This must mean something, and you know this as well as I. For one with the gift as powerful as the ones before you, for them not to have caused more damage speaks of their character and strength of will far more than the damage that has been inflicted."

Maritus pursed his lips before storming out. Rita stared in shock before utter relief surged over her and, without even thinking, she pulled Alex and Milos into a tight hug, almost on the verge of giggling in delight, but managing to stop herself and just leave a smile instead. Alex yelped as Milos tilted his head even farther down, almost shaking. She heard footsteps, harried, before to her complete and utter surprise, Ari pretty much threw herself around them, relief clear on her face with the barest hint of a smile, even if it was strained.

Ari pulled away and squatted down in front of Milos, hesitant, before she reached forward, taking his cheeks. "They will figure it out." She spoke, catching his attention as Leon joined the small group, glancing over each of them worriedly. "Just remember, keep being you."

Milos slowly tilted his head up and this time, Rita could see the desperation in his eyes, on his face…it was heart-wrenching. It quickly vanished, covered in a placid mask. Ari and Alex helped pull Milos to his feet as Valencia hurried over as utter pain flared over her face. "I'm sorry, sweetie. I wanted to come sooner, but I wasn't allowed to see you… I tried, I really did…"

"I know." Alex spoke after a moment of tense silence before a faint tired smile crossed his lips, "Lilliana said they had guards keeping an eye on you all the time." Valencia slowly relaxed her grip on her chest. "You helped Ari and Leon, right? Thanks, Mom."

Valencia slowly pulled in a breath and, as she let it out, her body seemed to relax, a faint smile on her face. "Why don't I bring you all somewhere to get cleaned up and rest? I'm sure you all probably need some time to deal with what happened."

She peered toward Milos, a strange sadness settling over her. "Though, even with the acquittal, you should stay in Lilliana's manor, at least, until things calm down."

"Will they?" Alex asked quietly, gazing at her. "It certainly doesn't seem like it."

Valencia shook her head. "Maybe someday. For now, I'll see what I can do to make sure you all stay safe." She hesitated before carefully reaching forward, gently taking Alex's hand, checking his wrists. "When you are settled, come see me. Those manacles are meant to suppress Demonic energy, and I want to make sure you are okay."

Alex blinked before seeming to relax a tiny bit, nodding.

It took some doing, even with Valencia there, to act as a protector. Suzuha and Rita kept an eye on everyone as they moved. Leon stayed at the back, guard up and defensive. The other humans and Demons filed out of the hall through doorways on either side of the balconies, leaving them, strangely, in peace.

The walk back to the mansion was tense, a crowd still outside, many murmuring in shock when they saw the group walk out, not in chains. Quite a few shouted and hissed and, at that, Rita just stuck up her middle finger at all of the stuck-up a-holes. Promptly followed by a glare from Valencia which actually sent them scattering. She hovered near Alex, much like

Rita's mom used to do after she was upset by one of Divon's sudden arrivals. She shuddered. She hadn't thought of HIM in a while, the prick. As long as he didn't obsess over her anymore, she didn't want to think of him again. Still, it also reminded her of Mom and her thoughts soon drifted to her parents. She couldn't shake the memories as they returned to the mansion. The group of them walked into Lillianna's home before splitting off, either to go to their respective rooms or talk quietly to one side.

She stood in the entrance hall, staring up toward the high ceilings above, where light stones dangled and glittered.

She hoped this blasted place burned to the ground and brought all of these bastards with them.

Her memory flashed to the future vision, and she shuddered. Right…maybe not quite like that. But the sanctuary by itself? She kind of didn't care at the moment what happened to the people and Demons here.

# Chapter Thirteen

Alex's thoughts churned as they finally got back to their temporary home with Lillianna, Mom almost doting on him. Ari and Leon slowly pulled Milos away, saying they would keep an eye on him. Alex watched them go, thoughts flashing to the trial. A strange hatred seared through him, and he wasn't sure if it was from his Demonic side or his human. He took a steady breath. He spoke in that tongue again. Was it intentional? He wasn't sure. But, even though he didn't know much about Demons and what is required to sense them, he knew Milos, and it wasn't hard to feel the pain coming off him at the realization. Nor was Alex surprised when he noted the curls of pearl gossamer white curling over Milos' form like fog.

Still, he had called out to Milos, he couldn't remember the first words, but the others rang in his head. "Listen to me, Milos. Hear my voice. We are here for you."

He just hoped it was enough for now, until they could figure out what all of this meant. He nodded toward Rita and Suzuha. Rita was staring up at the light stones above and Suzuha had scurried away, muttering under her breath about needing a good nap. Mom gently brushed over his wrists, staring down at them quietly. "I hoped to avoid you ending up like that, but…" She turned fully to him. "I won't be able to stay here long. I will need to help calm the people and make sure Maritus doesn't do anything rash. Still, I wanted to make sure you got back safely."

Alex blinked, startled, as he felt a gentle warmth settle over his wrists. He glanced down, noticing a strange red curling over his wrists. The same red he remembered seeing when he was learning about his mother's Demonic energy. He felt almost invigorated for a moment, like a calm settled over him for the first time in a while. He tilted his head up, startled.

Mom's smile was gentle and filled with such warmth Alex wasn't sure how to feel. "I'm sorry I haven't been able to help you more, my little angel. I'm just grateful human ingenuity won out over Demonic instinct today. I could hardly bear to imagine if we had to utilize the Demonic means of trial. A blood sport more than anything." She shook her head. "Maybe someday, I'll be able to help you more, but, for now, I gave you a little of my energy, to help calm the burn of the manacles and help them heal." She glanced briefly to his waist before looking back up at him. "Your father's gift…you still wear them. I'm glad to see you've been taking care of them." To his surprise, she reached forward, lightly pressing a kiss to his forehead. "Stay safe and stay here. It'll be fine." With that, she nodded to him, turned and hurried away.

He stared, not sure how to react. His fingers settled on the belts around his waist. The belts his father left for him, that he had worn since he left home. Actually, he had worn them since before he left home. It was strange for his mom to bring it up, but the thought quickly passed as the feeling of wanting to move pressed on him.

Alex found himself in the gardens they were training in barely two days ago. He had been trying to learn how to use his wings, being taught by Suzuha and Milos…and now. He tilted his head up, staring up at the day stones, shining so brightly above.

He was grateful for his mom's aid. He hated them, the manacles. Some part of him loathed it with every fiber of his being. He never felt so repulsed before…no, he had, once, when he was strapped down in the Martinet's guild. He shook his head, letting out a breath. Whatever his mom did, the feeling quickly subsided where it was nothing more than a faint throb like a bruise.

His gaze flicked toward his wings, which folded into his back, not disappearing after they appeared. Right, he was still in Demon form.

He wanted to…he wasn't sure. Did he just want to flee? Run? Get out of here?

He found his wings expanding outward to either side, twitching. His tail was still curled tightly around his waist, almost making it difficult to breathe.

He found his gaze lingering on the distant roof. Milos helped him a lot with learning who he was and yet, he still didn't fully know or understand. Could he return the favor? Would Milos even want him to?

His heart thumped loudly in his chest, anxious and overwhelmed. All of this was just too much. He hoped, with getting to the sanctuary, that things would calm down and all of them would have time to rest, to recover. Instead, their situation only got worse.

*I want to touch the ceiling.* The thought seared through his mind, a humming voice echoing, familiar and no longer terrifying. His Demonic side.

*I want to leave, to be able to bring Milos, Rita...the others. I want to bring them with me, out of here.* The thought settled in his mind like a fierce cry, the goal solidifying in his head, so strong, it almost ached and hurt.

*I want to fly.*

It was that simple, he realized, it was part of the reason he longed for the Overlands. To feel the wind and heat on his face, to be free of all of this, to see the others no longer be strapped down by who they were. Freedom. He couldn't help but find the word strange, even now. But, he had a feeling he was starting to figure it out. He found his thoughts drifting to his mom, her Demonic form settling before them on the boat, the warmth of the energy curling over him only moments ago.

His gaze flitted to his wings as they ruffled, expanded out, waiting. He wasn't sure how long it would take, but he wasn't scared of the idea anymore. He relaxed, closing his eyes and, slowly, with a gentle flap of wings, he felt energy curl around him. For a brief moment, he felt light, and he snapped his eyes open.

His wings flared out on either side of him, feet a few inches off the ground. As soon as he noticed, delight passed over him, followed by surprise as his wings twisted and he found himself stumbling, barely catching himself as he suddenly dropped back onto the ground.

Still, he managed to float, if only for a moment. It was something he never thought he would get. He glanced back toward the house before frowning. After debating for a moment, he tried again, trying to capture the fleeting feeling he held. After some time of attempting, he found himself able to hover, but for only a moment. He sighed. He would practice more later, but he needed to eat. He hadn't realized until his stomach growled loudly in protest at expending energy when he hadn't eaten much the last day or so.

He hurriedly ran into the other room to grab something to eat. His mood was already lifted from both his mom's comfort and the proof of flight with the hover he learned. He grabbed up some meat and cheeses, wrapping them together before munching quietly on them, leaning against the counter as he did. His attention drifted out the window, fingers brushing over the leather belts around his wrists, fingers almost tingling with the touch. His mom mentioned they could have ended up in a bloodsport. He wondered what that meant. An actual battle? Or a trial of some sort? He shook his head; grateful he didn't have to find out and hopefully never would. For the first time since arriving in the Sanctuary, he felt relaxed. The worst had passed, and he could only hope Mom would stay true to her word this time.

~ * ~

Milos wasn't quite sure where he was, darkness pushed down at him from all sides, suffocating. Was it a lie? Did he end up in jail like in Rita's vision? He felt something in the back of his mind, something he always knew was there, but refused to acknowledge. Like a whisper of wind, it echoed nearby, and he shoved it away. He wanted nothing to do with it.

He HUNTED Demons. Wasn't that what an Alertian was? Had there been a time when Alertians were protectors instead? Like what Lillianna said?

"How dumb." A voice echoed back, a familiar male voice, one he hadn't heard for a while and thought he would never hear again. No… he shouldn't have been able to hear it again. They were in the Overlands, stuck. Even so, every fiber of his being tensed. "You have Demonic blood in you? Disgusting. Mom was right, why were you even born?"

"Brother? Are you a Demon? Oh, can I kill you now and take your head?" His sister stepped forward, steps light as she smiled, she looked just as she did before he descended into the Underlands, hair pulled loosely behind her in a braid as a smile curled over her lips, not cruel, but not gentle either. Why was she here? HOW was she here? "Maybe I'll put your head on my wall, or is that too gruesome? I don't want to be separated from you again." She took a step forward and Milos found himself trying and failing to step back. It didn't work, and soon, he found her reaching toward his throat, that smile ever present as she gently pressed a thumb under his chin, fingers on the pulse at his neck. "Why are you so nervous, brother? I wouldn't hurt you. Maybe I'll just keep you. Just like Father kept your mother until mother found you."

Milos managed to snap his hand up, shoving her away, finally stumbling back. She shook her head, tutting, as a familiar blonde form walked into view, leaning against her side and leering over her shoulder. The same voice as before, the one he hoped never to hear again, responded, "Why would you want that? He's vermin, nothing more than the dirt below Mother's shoe." Dark brown, almost black eyes seared into him with a disgust that bordered on murder. No smile crossed the chiseled features of his older brother. The cane in his hand tapped against the ground next to him, most of his support on his sister's shoulders.

Milos wanted to run, the dual looks of loathing and whatever it was in his sister's eyes made him want to flee across the span of the Underlands, as far as he could. He whipped around, attempting to dart away, only to still as a voice reached his ears, a simple song that kept him in place.

Alex's song drifted over him as the boy sang, legs kicking as he settled on a rock to one side, a river slowly shifting beneath him. Alex's gaze shifted to him and the song turned into a single held note that made Milos reel. He buckled, knees slamming into the ground as his hands covered his ears, whispered words of the Demonic tongue floated over him. He understood, but he didn't want to, he wasn't going to listen. Every fiber of his being screamed not to listen, even as the note turned into coaxing harmony that tugged at him.

"See? You can't even deal with one little Demon." Sister's voice reached his ears, her ponytail lightly falling against his neck.

"Why don't we take care of him for you?" Brother's voice brushed over his skin, feeling like poison on his flesh. "Stay the little vermin you are. I don't know what Father saw in you, but you are nothing, you will always be nothing and— "

"We'll prove it." Sister chimed in with a certain glee that bordered on insanity a second before a horrendous screech cut through the noise, the soft and coaxing tune suddenly shattering into a piercing note of agony.

It cracked through his mind like a whip, and he wanted to scream in pain. He couldn't look, he wouldn't, this had to be…"

Blood-coated fingers took his chin, wrenching it up to meet his sister's gaze. "I'm coming for you next, brother dearest."

Water crashed into his face, and he sputtered, eyes snapping open from the dream. He peered up to see Ari huffing heavily, bucket in hand as Leon lay over Milos' side, holding his hands down, pinning them under his weight. As soon as both saw he was awake, they quickly pulled back, letting out sighs of relief.

"Sorry." Ari spoke quietly as she pulled back, wincing.

Leon was already moving, helping Milos to sit up before bustling away, returning a moment later with a towel. The room was lit with the soft light of the day stones falling through the windows and settling over the familiar wood and upholstery of his new residence. Milos found himself startled as Leon started rubbing his hair, helping to get some of the water out.

It didn't feel bad.

"You were having a nightmare." Ari slowly put the bucket to one side. "We couldn't wake you and you were starting to hurt yourself." She squatted down, taking his arms in her slender fingers. He didn't miss the deep scratch marks he must have caused in the throes of… that.

Pain flared through him at the memory of the nightmare, the words and images still echoing and piercing into his mind. He felt something like a salve and glanced over to see Ari was digging into the bottle he gave her ages ago, carefully plastering it on his arms where the wounds were the deepest. He stared down quietly, thoughts finally, unfortunately, coming to a halt. There was nothing. No matter how much he wanted to say that Lillianna's words were a lie, he knew, for a strange fact, that they were true. He always thought his senses were because of being an Alertian, but…

He furrowed his brow. So why was it they all HUNTED Demons? If Alertians are Demons, if they have Demon blood, then why did they end up Demon hunters? Did it mean that….? What was he? If he had Demon blood, how strong and how much?

"Master, stop." Ari's voice reached his ears, and he slowly turned his head, realizing he was digging his fingers into his arms again, almost piercing the skin. He felt a hand on his skin and slowly let out a long breath, glancing toward Ari who was watching worriedly.

He slowly pulled his fingers away. "Thank you." He spoke softly as the two pulled back, nodding.

"I'm glad we could find the information." Leon spoke, moving around him and settled to one side. "We weren't sure we would be able to find proof, but Ari was determined."

Milos' gaze flicked to Ari, who was staring down at her lap. "Is that so?"

"I know you couldn't have been the one to attack, even before we talked to you," she said before tilting her head up, staring at Milos quietly. "When everyone spoke of what happened, I knew I needed to find and talk to the ones who attacked you." Her grip tightened on her clothes. "I wasn't going to leave you or Alex to your fates, not if there was an option out. Valencia helped me search for the ones who instigated it. I appreciate everything she did during that time, even though she was clearly being watched so as to not interfere with the proceedings."

Milos felt himself relax, a faint feeling of pride running through him as he focused on what she was saying, trying not to think of what he learned. "Then, I thank you once more. For helping me and the others, even if you didn't necessarily need to." He paused. "And I believe Alex needs to know how much his mother helped us as well. You might have been safer just not being involved...."

"I couldn't do that." Ari jerked up, staring hard at Milos. "Neither of us could. You are important to us, just as the rest of our little group is." She paused and pulled back, hands to her chest as she winced. "If that is okay."

Leon was tense, but was watching quietly, clearly curious himself. Milos felt his shoulders relax. "That is fine."

At the smiles on both of their faces, he felt that relief pass through him, calming the raging thoughts.

"Master, about what that woman said?" Leon spoke up, catching Milos' attention. "I know you might not be fond of the idea."

"I would rather not speak of it," Milos quickly cut in, sweeping himself to his feet, his fingers clasped tightly on the sword. "I have no interest in that."

"Don't you want to know more?" Ari asked, startling him. "She seemed to know something more than she was saying and, truth be told, it was only because of her speaking that you are now free. I had no defense against Maritus' words. But she did."

Milos' mind raced before he just nodded and spun on his heels. "I would ask you to stay here, but I don't know how long I'll be gone, so do what you will."

The two hesitated before bowing as Milos slipped out the door, heading downstairs. He could hear faint clattering from the kitchen and peered over, hesitating mid-step as he heard a familiar hum.

Alex.

He wasn't sure if he wanted to see the boy at the moment. It was overwhelming to think on, so he quickly shut the idea out and turned toward the doors. As unnerving as it was, he found his mind, as usual, focusing on the waves of energy leeching off the surrounding Demons. Was this because he was part Demon? Or was it actually because of his Alertian side? And what actually WAS his Alertian side? He wasn't sure anymore and it unnerved him. He shook it off, letting out a tired sigh as he headed forward, carefully opening the door, not surprised to see a familiar figure walking down the path toward the house. He hadn't planned to go far; if anything, he sensed the woman's approach and found himself meeting her where he could.

Lillianna's gaze met Milos' and she hesitated for a moment before gliding the rest of the way up on quick, yet quiet steps. The guards to either side of the door glanced back and forth, startled.

"I see you are willing to listen." Her words were brief but surprisingly kind.

"Not necessarily," he said, grip tightening on the sword hilt. "But I do need answers, and you are the only one who has been able to provide them, even if they are, in my opinion, utter lunacy."

"You…"

"It is fine. I can understand his hesitation." Lillianna waved toward the guard who hissed in disdain at Milos. "Come, let us speak in the sitting room. I will tell you what I know and remember. Maybe it'll give you some of those answers and relieve you a little of your confusion."

Milos didn't say anything to that, but found himself following, his steps only a smidge behind hers as they moved through the entrance into a side room. It held a comfortable fireplace with soft chairs and couches and a cozy atmosphere.

It did not help him relax.

She settled down in a chair, watching him, hands in her lap. "You may take a seat. I have no reason to attack you and if you attack me, I can defend myself from a child."

Her gaze met his and he shuddered as POWER emanated from her. He felt it before, but this time, he found himself almost immediately taking a seat, grimacing at the pressure slamming over his head.

"I do apologize." She spoke after a moment. "Considering your reaction during the trial, the fact that you are part Demon was not something you expected."

As he turned away, he realized he didn't feel anything, slamming away all emotions as he was always taught to do.

She actually seemed to flinch, hands grasping in front of her. "I'll start with how I know all this." Her eyes met his as she spoke, a genuine authenticity that somewhat unnerved him. "Many years ago, over a hundred years ago now, I was in love with one of your ancestors…and we were to be married, in human terms." She gestured. "You see, for the last couple millenia, from when Alertians first learned of the existence of Demons, we've had a truce, a deal. We would remain below, protecting the lands beneath and the Alertian would remain above, preserving their society and hiding our existence. To do this, when the eldest Alertian came of age, he or she was to be wed to a Demon of high standing."

She seemed to pause as Milos tensed. He never heard of something like this.

"It was one hundred and two years ago that I was supposed to marry the eldest, a boy that I met many years before and whom I fell deeply in love with." She met Milos' gaze. "His name was Xade Alertian."

She said the name as if Milos was supposed to know it, but it didn't ring any bells. Xade? How was he supposed to spell that? It was as if the name had a more Demonic flare to it.

When he didn't respond, she quickly looked down, a strange despair coloring her expression. "So, they don't speak of him anymore." She seemed to choke, putting a hand to her chest as she recovered her breath before turning back to him, expression once more neutral. "Xade was an Alertian of twenty and one years, much like yourself. He was compassionate, kind and believed deeply in keeping the peace between humans and Demons. His brother, however,…" She shook her head. "Farren Alertian was a cruel boy who was also too intelligent for his own good." Lillianna leaned back, tracing her hand through the air, as if drawing.

Milos did recognize that name, his great ancestor. "The Alertian who slayed the Demon King." Milos spoke softly.

Lillianna clenched her hand. "The Alertian who lost the name when he betrayed his siblings and, in secret, amassed the humans to attack the Demons." Lillianna's gaze was firm, and a flash of fury flared over her face. "He turned his siblings into traitors to humanity and had them slaughtered before they could respond and captured our land, through the use of ancient technology said to have been lost before the calamity some two thousand years ago. You know of the elevator, that is just one piece of what he brought down. The Demons were taken by surprise and, even with our strength, humans with their ingenuity and an Alertian with the power of a Demon King were difficult to fight back against. He struck fiercely and fast."

Lillianna's gaze shifted to meet Milos'. "He turned some of his siblings against my husband, saying that Demons should be for all humans, not just for the eldest child, and some seemed to agree. The division caused a war that devastated humans and Demons…almost leading to the collapse of both worlds. Eventually, we fled to these northern lands, but we were weakened, and humans created a stronghold in the capital city of Raynout."

Milos stiffened, noticing Lillianna's faint expression. "Yes, that city was once a Demonic capital, and it is now a place of fear and hatred for many Demons." She glanced down to her wrists where he could see faint markings. "Many a Demon was captured and enslaved. Those that escaped fled north and many remember the devastation your great grandfather wrought to our people." Her gaze flitted to him as her expression softened.

However, I hold no hatred for him, only a strange pity. Xade fought against him, managing to free me and defended my father to his dying breath, the whole time, telling his brother to stop, that it'll only bring more pain... and my husband was right." Lillianna shook her head. "The land above has been wracked with problems since the destruction of our civilization and the bond that humans and Demons once held has been destroyed. A simple flip will bring the whole country to its knees...all because of one jealous man."

Milos pulled back, loosening on his blade. "Which was how we became Demon hunters instead."

Lillianna stared at him quietly. "It is as you guess. With each passing generation, the blood of Demons has dwindled in your veins and the strength and fury of those below have grown. I have no doubt you are aware of what that entails."

He was... His mind flitted to Rita's future vision, when she talked of the world imploding on itself. It certainly explained why there was so much hatred for his kind, for who he was. He was a Demon hunter, a descendant who created this wretched society.

He heard movement and peered over as Lillianna shifted. "You, however? I feel an energy from you that doesn't indicate a degradation." Her gaze met mine. "Do you know who your mother was?"

Milos' thoughts froze in place. "I don't have a mother." He spoke almost instinctively.

There was a long, tired sigh. "My child, how old were you when she passed?"

"Why would you want to know?" Milos hissed.

Lillianna's gaze flitted to Milos, pain in her expression. "Because I feel my sister's presence."

Milos felt his heart stuttering for a moment, loud in his ears and throat. The words rang in his mind, and he quickly shoved them away. As he turned away, he could feel Lillianna's heavy gaze, freezing him to the core.

"Milos? Do you remember anything about your mother?"

He wasn't sure he could respond, not when he was thinking of way too much at once. So instead, he gripped the sword tightly, trying to calm his racing thoughts as a single flash of memory settled over him, of a beautiful woman with bright blue eyes, filled with warmth. "Blue-eyed." He finally spoke up, his shoulders tense, his back straight but not with pride, just anxiety and fear, as much as he loathed to admit it. "I have her eyes, Father always said that."

Without meaning too, he found himself pulled into Lilliana's warm expression. Milos felt like a child, and it unnerved him greatly. He wasn't supposed to feel that way. He wasn't a child anymore.

A part of his mind scoffed at that and whispered he was never a child, that was lost long ago.

"May I?" Lillianna's voice was soft, catching his attention once more.

She was leaning forward, hand hesitantly reaching toward him. Every instinct screamed at him to move, to chop, to DO something, but the expression on her face made him stop. It wasn't filled with malice or hatred or anything of the like.

Not disgust like his stepmother.

Not grief and pain like his father.

Not disappointment like everyone else.

He wasn't sure when he nodded, but she solemnly reached forward, lightly touching his forehead.

In that instant, everything seemed to click into place, and, at the same time, everything fell OUT of place. He was in the scene, and watching it at the same time, two presences, but one place. A soft song settled over him as he was held in soothing arms, familiar golden hair mingling with his own. The warm lap was familiar and comforting, even though the clothes felt scratchy.

Everything felt so distant and yet so familiar.

A voice, soft and delicate. "You look just like your father." The woman pressed her face to his, a proud little smile on her lips, noses almost touching. "You'll be safe here, away from them. My precious Milos, my sweet child."

A warm fire crackled, a real one, to one side as he curled against her body. A tattered, yet comfortable blanket rested around them as the woman hummed, hand lightly combing his hair. He was young, he knew that his smaller body fit into her side like a glove as she tightly hugged him back.

There was cold outside, the windows and doors rattling as wind howled, and yet, in that little space, it was cozy and safe.

He was a little older now, shivering tightly in thin clothes as two hands gently took his. The whispered words were comforting, if unrecognizable. Were they Demonic? He couldn't tell.

The hands pulled away as a wash of energy slammed over him and he found his arms wrapping around himself as familiar, yet not familiar words reached his ears. Who was speaking? Was this still a memory or the present?

"Focus, Milos, listen to what it says, it won't hurt you, it IS you."

The woman put her hands to either side of his face, or was it Lillianna? No, it was a memory, it was...it was his mother. "It's not something scary. It's something beautiful that your father and I both gave you. Listen to my voice, sweetie, I know you've heard horrible things about Demons, but it's not true. That magic inside you? It's precious. Hold onto it and it'll protect you just as much as it'll help to protect those dear to you. Alright?" Arms wrapped tightly around him, a heart beating faintly against his ears as she whispered, "I will protect you. You are the only one...the only one who survived. I won't let you die; I will do whatever I can to keep you safe."

He wanted to protect her too. That thought pervaded the memory, piercing through it, causing it to fade for just a moment as a sound reached his ears, a chocked sound of pain that wasn't his then the next memory solidified.

He was home, in that tiny little hovel that one could barely call a house, holding up the knives proudly, along with the rabbit he caught. His mother was startled, but took the rabbit, worry and pride settling over her face. "You don't need to hunt, Milos. We have enough..."

"But I want to help!" his childish voice rang in the room. "I've gotten really REALLY good with knives!"

His mother pursed her lips before relaxing. "You are helping, but I just want you to be careful."

Milos nodded, putting away the knives just in case.

The next vision, they were out on the street, his mother pulling him along, looking incredibly worried, bag flung over her shoulder. She was muttering something he couldn't hear as he tripped over his own two feet, trying to keep up with her longer strides. They rounded a corner, and she suddenly pulled to a stop. Milos tripped, peering around her leg as a line of Martinets stood before them. Hurried footsteps echoed behind and he quickly looked over his shoulder where more martinets came from behind, weapons held forward.

"Release the child, Demon. We have been authorized to kill in order to retrieve that child."

He suddenly felt his mother pull him close, the skies above a pitch black of a coming storm, hiding the sun. "You won't have him. I don't know how you found out about us, but…"

"The lady demands his return to his father's side. Do not interfere."

Mother tensed as Milos curled inward, confused. The lady?

Before he could respond, he heard footsteps then all Underland broke loose. He felt arms suddenly rip him from his mother's side as she spun, just as the other Martinets darted forward. The wind picked up as speckles of sleet and rain caught on skin and clothes alike. Quickly making the cobblestone slick. He struggled against the tight grip around his waist as he was suddenly pulled back, a few men stepping between him and his mother.

"Mom!" he screamed as the blue-eyed woman struggled against her captors, reaching for him, the Martinets wrapping rope and chains around her as she struggled against them with all her might. He kicked and punched, trying and failing to reach for his knives, only for one to clatter to the ground as the man twisted to avoid Mother's lunge.

She was tugged backward, almost howling into the air. "You are not taking my baby! GIVE HIM BACK!" She screeched, white curling over her back and face, as scales glistened in the torrential downpour. An echoing screech rang through the streets causing him to freeze. Silence met his ears, a stillness that was more eerie than anything. The grip was ironclad, but the man holding him wasn't moving. No one except his mother was as she broke free of the chains and rope.

Milos thought he saw the flick of a tail, of his mother's tall proud form before suddenly there was red where once there was a glittering white.

Movement returned once more in a flurry as the white Demon settled back into Mother, her gaze slowly drifting down to the sword pierced through her chest. The sword pulled sharply out, and she crumpled. Milos knew, he KNEW, but...

"MOTHER!" he screamed, his voice almost hoarse as the blood quickly washed over the pavement, causing little streams into the side ditches to form as a woman stood behind his mother's now crumpled form. Black hair clung to her face as she lifted her head up, a vicious smile curling over her lips. She leered downward before leaning down. Milos quickly closed his eyes as a sound he would never forget cut through the storm, *SHLICK*. He didn't look, he didn't want to look, pain...it hurt...

"Take the child to our house as instructed, I will be there in a moment."

"Understood." The Martinets spoke, pulling him away.

He didn't resist.

The next memory hit him like a ton of bricks as he watched the same woman as before, black hair damp from rain, walk into the house. He was brought to a lavish home where Father stood, frozen, his expression hard to read. The woman walked in, sheathing her sword. A smile cold as ice curled over her face and in her hands—

A head. The blue eyes now dulled and lifeless, the blonde hair stained red with blood. Horror. All he felt was pure horror and pain and rage and— He went to fling himself at the woman, only to be sharply pulled back by the Martinet still holding him. The scream of pain that ripped from his throat echoed in his ears long after it faded as the woman turned. "I have a new trophy for my wall. I DO hope you don't mind, honey." Her smile was a viper. Milos couldn't pull his gaze away from what was once his mother. His vision narrowed down to nothing but what was left of her. He only heard the choked gasp of his father as that woman walked away with a faint hum.

The next memories were all flashes, huddling in a corner, cold and tired, as people called his siblings laughed and ate nearby, his clothes stained with bits of blood.

Covering his head as blows landed, harsh though the fists were slightly smaller than his own. Everything hurt as they laughed and kicked and pummeled.

Cackling and hatred and disgust. That black-haired woman's face with her nose stuck up, peering down at him with such utter disdain and amusement, that vicious smile only coming out every so often when one of his siblings beat him in another unfair duel. Why? If she was going to torment him, why take him from his mother? Why do THAT to his mother?

A numbness settled over him. He barely flinched anymore. Staring blankly as tension grew amongst the others. Of another death reaching their ears of his supposed siblings. The ones who descended before him. Only one survived, but with a limp and his ability to fight gone.

His father…his father who argued with that woman, who tried to protect him from his siblings, eventually grew tired and frail. A sickness settled over him, bringing him to his bed where Milos heard him cry. His sobs echoing late into the night as he whispered Mother's name over and over in a pained apology.

Maybe if he became an Alertian, they wouldn't look down on him, he could fight back, he could end this. He could prove himself worthy. He could BE something. Maybe then it would stop the pain and hatred and grief—

Hands pulled away from his head and he found himself snapping up, fingers tightening on slender wrists in a strange desperation. They didn't move away farther, silence falling over the surroundings as he found himself back in the present, back in the room of a fake flame and an unfamiliar woman whom he only just met.

He felt something curl around him, a familiar feeling of magic, and instantly snapped his hands back, shooting to his feet as he whipped his sword out, pointing forward.

"What was that?" He spoke, voice barely staying even as the memories flitted through his mind, dragged out of a forgotten area he'd thrown them into.

Every part of his body was tense and coiled, that heavy numbness returning that being in the Underlands pushed aside.

Lillianna's expression caused him to still. There was heavy despair and pain, hands trembling slightly. He could almost feel something from her he couldn't understand, a rage, a pure unadulterated fury that WASN'T directed at him.

"Child…that was not a life you should have had."

He narrowed his eyes, shoving any emotions he felt to the back of his mind, where he hoped they would stay. "What did you expect, Demon? I have heard of some who can read their victims' minds, but it came as a surprise. Did you get whatever you wanted out of it?"

Milos was used to controlling his emotions, he had to. But the woman before him, the facade over her face was cracking with each breath. She put her hands to her face, outright shaking, startling him. "I felt it," she whispered. "Your pain and agony. Your desperation... all of it. Every blow and heartache... So, yes, I did get my answer. I now know my sister's fate."

Milos felt every part of him coiling, defensive, a growl settling low in his throat that surprised him. Lillianna pulled her hands down, her grief no longer masked. Her tears were barely being held back as she swallowed heavily, hands curling into her lap so tightly, they were white. Her next words were filled with utter rage. "They slaughtered her in the street as a trophy. They took you from her simply as another. They..." She took a sharp breath and, very quickly, the mask was back on, the emotions once more under control as she let it out. Her gaze met his once more, piercing, yet warm. "I am so sorry for your loss, for what no child, no person should have to deal with. Demon or human, you were just a child. You still are, in a Demonic sense, and I now know why."

She swept to her feet, unfazed about the sword at her throat. "You have lost so much. But I will say this. You are more of an Alertian, of a true Alertian like my husband, than those creatures you were forced to call family."

Milos was startled by the vehemence in her words, though her expression hadn't changed since she put the mask back on.

"At least the one she loved didn't betray her. It was that woman. She must have found you two and went behind his back to..." she shook her head. "At least he still loved her to the end, that he did everything he could to protect you. I suppose that is one saving grace. But, to know I'm the only one left." A strange exhaustion reached her as she looked back toward Milos. "I may be able to tell you a little of your skills, of what it means to be a Demon of the First. It sounds like you were the only child who managed to survive. Not surprising, considering Demonic blood is strong and our blood is even stronger. "

"Our?" He narrowed his eyes, though he already knew what she was saying. He had known since her first words, but a large part of him fought to deny it.

"Child, that woman in your vision? Her name was Verity. And you, dear Milos, are my nephew. My only other living relative."

Nephew. The word seemed to pierce through his mind. He was unable to deny it anymore, the truth before him.

Verity. The name rang through his head, the name Father repeated over and over again as despair and sickness struck him down.

He thought nothing of it at the time, just another consort, but now that he thought about it, Father never had consorts, even though, as a descendant of the Alertian line, unlike his stepmother, he could have. There was no love between him and his stepmother, a marriage of convenience and tradition, nothing more than what he gathered.

He let out a tired breath, the tip of the sword slowly dropping. "You…" His voice was filled with acid. "What could you teach me? Maybe I should have never been bo—"

Her blue eyes snapped to him and a strange understanding shot across her face.

"How dare you!" She surged forward, magic curling outward before immediately withdrawing. "My sister gave her LIFE for you, was desperate to protect you with everything she had, and you want to just throw it away?"

He met her anger with a stoic silence for a brief moment. The emotions shoved away as usual. "If what you say is true, then I am nothing. I was supposed to be an Alertian, a Demon hunter. If she was truly your sister, then it means she was a full Demon. Stepmother did what all Alertians do when they defeat a Demon. If my family's lineage involved having Demonic blood anyway, I'm more Demon than human. I would rather be dead."

Lillianna's energy surged around him, almost suffocating, but he didn't react as she seemed to seethe for a split second before settling back down, head in her hands as she let out a tired breath. "THOSE BASTARDS!"

The swear took him off guard as utter hatred roiled off her in such heavy waves, he almost wanted to take a step back. He slowly brought his sword down even more, unsure how to react to this.

He knew what happened, his trip to catch that rabbit caused them to be found. It was his fault that they weren't able to escape in time. That they were caught in the streets.

As if reading his mind, she slowly looked up to him and spoke. "Nothing was your fault. None of what happened to you was your fault. It doesn't matter what they said. You were a child, just trying to help your mother. You did nothing wrong."

He shoved the sword back into his belt, hair and chain clanking as it spattered over his shoulder in his movement. "We're done here." With that, he turned on a dime and stepped toward the door.

"Milos."

He paused, startled as the word echoed back to him, said so similar to that woman…no, Verity, his mother. Then he realized it was the Demonic tongue, a lilt to the words that caught him off guard. The name emphasized in a way he wasn't used to, harsh in areas that usually weren't and lyrical in others he hadn't thought possible.

Why did the Demonic tongue have to sound both harsh and gentle at the same damn time?

When he didn't respond, nor did he step forward, he heard the flutter of fabric and faint footsteps. They stopped a few feet back, but he didn't turn to face her as she spoke.

"Now I know why you are so attached to that boy." Her words were soft. "Just like with the witch and Vulfulas, with those two ex-slaves; you wish to protect those that are precious to you, to make it so they don't feel the pain you had to. You aren't heartless, no matter how much you try to be, no matter how much that tainted Alertian side of you says you are. Demons aren't pure evil. We are instinct, magic. You wanted to keep them safe because you felt a connection to them and that is important to remember. But it was not just your Demonic side that chose that. You, as a human, chose to protect them because you thought it was the right thing to do. It was a decision of your own, something you wanted to do, remember that my dear nephew."

Milos pursed his lips at her words, hesitating for only a moment before he shook his head. He had nothing to say to that. He threw the door open and stalked out, quickly passing a startled Rita before continuing out through the back doors and into a garden-like area behind the house. He kept moving, kept going until he found himself near the edge of the village once more, but in a different area, the closest one to Lillianna's place. He pushed against the wall, almost seeming to pulse with energy as he settled down, finding himself curling up, knees almost to his chest as the wave of emotions he shoved away, hoping to ignore, came roaring back. The memories he locked away long ago now swam in front of his eyes, taunting him. Why? What was the point of it all? What did his stepmother gain from doing that?

A memory, one so subtle and small, floated to his mind, a quiet conversation that he could only remember bits and pieces of, but...a few lines in her voice stood out. "I couldn't risk another overshadowing my children, so I had to take him in. After all, how dare my husband love another when I am all he needs. My beautiful children, you all will grow into strong Alertians and none will oppose you, especially no hidden consort's child."

"I hope he dies in those Underlands that took so many of my children. But, for now, I have to follow my husband's wishes, and he wants Milos to descend, so he must, no matter how tainted by Demonic blood he must be from that woman."

"Come back, Milos, it's boring without you."

A familiar voice reached his ears, his sister's, his youngest sister. Her smile had an edge to it that always felt off, her gaze locked with his as she always stood a little too close.

Then he was free to descend, to make his own way and prove himself and now...

He just wanted things to make sense, couldn't it happen just once in his life?

# Chapter Fourteen

Rita jerked to the side as Milos, a storm cloud of emotions, walked straight past her. She paused as Lillianna stepped out of the room he just left, staring after him with a heavy sadness. She seemed to notice Rita and she quickly schooled her expression. "Ah, Lady Rita." She spoke faintly. "I do apologize. You and Alex might want to speak with him later." Both of them turned toward the door as it slammed shut. "He…"

"You don't have to tell me." Rita put a hand up, other hand on her hip. "It was a bit much, mentioning a power like that out of nowhere. I'm not surprised he's acting like he is."

Lillianna nodded. "You are wise for your age."

"I'm a witch, kinda what we do." She hesitated. "So, I do have to ask. Though we are no longer on trial, I don't think it's safe for any of us to leave." She put her other hand on her lip. "However, I need to find someone to help train me in order to become a seer. And you know exactly why."

"I am well aware of your future visions, which you have yet to divulge to me." Her words were light, but something about them made Rita still. After a moment, she lightened and continued, "Unfortunately, due to reasons far beyond my control, all the seers have fled to the lands above in hopes to stop a future calamity." Rita felt her whole-body shudder at the memory of the vision and her words. "I believe you might have actually seen a portion of it in that vision the other day, if your complexion was any indication."

"Shvite…" She grumbled. "What is it with Demons and just KNOWING things?" She took a deep breath before letting out a sigh. "Yes, actually. The world was just falling, being torn apart at the seams." Rita glanced up at her. "And we knew why."

Lillianna paused at that. "You knew?"

"Our future selves did." Rita gestured, pulling up the details with surprising ease. "I was with Alex, Suzuhah and Milos. If the sun was any indication, we were in the Overlands. Suzuhah was mentioning how we were too late, and I was saying how they did this to themselves. That we warned them, that we tried…" Rita shook her head as Lillianna shifted her stance, expression hard to read.

"That is…" She peered to one side, clearly thinking something over before continuing, "That is more than I've heard from many seers who passed through here to go above. Most just spoke of the devastation, of the ensuing calamity, but you KNOW." She turned back to Rita. "I can surmise what happens, but I fear telling you will do us no good and might simply make the future come to pass. However, there must be a reason so many of our seers have received this vision. No vision is absolute, from what I have gleaned. For so many to have been warned, there must be a way…" She cut herself off and shook her head. "But now is neither the time nor place. You asked for aid to find the witches; I can give you that."

Rita stared up at her, a little shocked and also a little annoyed. If the woman knew WHY the calamity was happening, then why didn't she just say it? Yet, she could also tell from the look in Lillianna's eyes that she was not getting anything out of her. Rita didn't miss the heavy sadness that flashed across her face a moment before she spoke of aiding Rita and so, she let out a breath and shrugged. "If you don't mind. I would totally take you up on that offer."

"Of course." Her gaze flitted away. "I owe you all immensely. You and your chosen family are the reason that…" She shook her head

Chosen family? Right, Rita did see Alex as a brother and Milos like an obnoxious, but consistently reliable sibling. Like an ever-dependable older brother she never had.

She let out a groan. Great, hopefully, those two never heard her say anything about that. She wouldn't hear the end of it.

She heard a faint chuckle and glanced over to see Lillianna actually smiling. "I will get you the books and supplies you might need. Hopefully, we can help you all settle down. I might not be able to help you, but I do know ways to help your family. For our future, you all are important, I'll do what I can." With that, she nodded to Rita and turned on her heels, heading out the door.

She heard a sound and peered over as the door to the kitchen opened and she saw Alex peek his head out, curious. "Rita? Was that Lillianna?"

She nodded, spinning to face him. "Yeah, what are you…?"

"Making something to eat." He stepped out. "I felt something odd earlier. Was that Milos?"

"Yeah, he was acting like a lout…" She trailed off before sighing. "We'll have to talk to him later."

Alex seemed to spot something because he just nodded in seeming understanding.

That was Alex for you. Even if you didn't say anything, he seemed to understand. "So what now?"

Alex blinked, glancing toward her before shrugging. "No idea. I spoke with Mom earlier, but I'm not sure where she is now and while I would like to check on Milos, I'm not sure if that's a good idea right now."

"I think the lout needs some time." Rita peered towards the back garden. "Oh, hey, if you see your mom, can you ask her if she could guide me through town tomorrow?"

Alex tilted his head, confused, and Rita rolled her eyes. "Lillianna mentioned there were witches in the sanctuary and I wanted to meet them. I'm not dumb enough to go out on my own, especially on the same day as the trial, so, thus, tomorrow.

Alex shook his head, clearly abashed, a faint awkward smile on his lips. "Ah, that makes sense." He peered out the back door, debating. "I can do that." He turned back to her. "Do you…"

"I don't think I should be the one to talk to him." She cut in, voice sincere. "I think you should. He might respond better to you, considering, well, who you are."

Alex winced and it took Rita a moment to realize why as she quickly waved her hands. "I don't mean your Siren side or whatever, I just meant because you had a similar experience of finding out you were part Demon without anyone to help you, so you can be there for him where I can't."

Alex examined her for a moment before his expression softened in understanding. "Alright." He nodded. "I'll see you later, Rita."

"You know it."

With a wave, he hurried out the back into the garden and beyond, clearly knowing where to go. Rita watched him leave, lost in thought.

Lillianna, so far, was the only one who knew why the calamity happened and yet Lillianna wouldn't tell her. Was that to make sure she didn't know to change the results? Or was it something else? Some other reason. What about Alex and Milos and the others? She let out a breath. This was too much for her to deal with. She knew Alex would keep to his promise, but she wanted to leave today, so badly. With a shake of her head, she returned to her room. Maybe she could make some potions out of ingredients around the house. It would take her mind off the situation, at least a little.

~ * ~

It didn't take long for Alex to find Milos. The man was leaning against the wall of the cavern, a few weak day stones only a couple hundred feet above his head. Milos' gaze flicked to him, but he didn't respond otherwise, expression hard to read, harder than usual. Alex walked over, taking a seat beside him, sitting in silence. There was no reason to say anything at the moment. He knew Milos just needed some time and a reminder he wasn't the only one who had to go through this.

A small part of Alex was a little jealous. At least when Milos found out, he had people nearby who could help him learn. Alex didn't have that.

He promptly shoved the thought off, waving it away as stupid. He didn't envy Milos in the slightest. To have been told, probably all his life, that he needed to hunt Demons, only to find out he was one. Alex couldn't imagine it.

So, he sat there, one leg brought up in a quiet silence as he peered up toward the low ceiling of the Underlands.

He wasn't sure how long they sat there before Milos shifted, carefully pulling his sword out before setting it on his lap. For a moment, Alex felt a surge of panic about what he was going to do. Strangely, not for himself, but for Milos.

Thankfully, the moment passed as Milos' finger carefully felt over the middle of the blade. "This was my father's." Milos finally spoke, catching Alex off guard. "He held it specifically for me, until I was of age.

My brothers and sisters always called me out as being Father's favorite, even when he became sick." He winced as Alex watched him, noting as the man lightly tapped on his legs, as if whatever he was remembering was not good. He immediately stopped. "The only blood I have shed with this blade has been pretty much human blood. Up until our journey to this land. A small part of me can't help but wonder if that hesitation is because of…"

"Eh." Alex cut in, catching his attention as he flopped against Milos' side, startling the man. "I would say the hesitation is because you are a good person. Doesn't really matter that much, at least to me, that you have Demonic blood in you." He felt a smile cross his face. "Actually, it makes me feel relieved and like I'm not the odd one out. I always saw myself as strange, different from you two." Alex winced before peering back toward the path leading to their temporary home. "So, I guess I was kind of happy when I found out you were just like me. It meant I wasn't the only one going through this or trying to figure this all out. And, to be honest, it explains a lot of things about you. We always passed it off as just you being an Alertian, but looking back? I can kind of see the times when it might have been, well…"

"That side?" Milos' voice dipped, almost harsh.

"I…yeah." Alex lightly poked Milos' side, startling the man. "I'm not Rita or anything but maybe see this as a way to explain your life up until now. I found, once I accepted who I was, that it was easier to see where my powers differed from my human side. I mean, I'm still learning and stuff, but maybe you can do the same? Show how, yeah, you do have Demon blood in you, but you are also still human."

"You are not good at pep talks."

"So I've been told." Alex huffed as he felt Milos' posture finally untense, startling Alex into almost falling over, if it wasn't for Milos quickly putting a hand up to catch him, amused.

"Still, it is appreciated. I just have a lot on my mind." At Milos' words, Alex raised an eyebrow. Milos let out a sound almost like a huff, startling Alex. "Yes, I know a certain someone would be saying something about that, but it's not wrong." He turned away as Alex settled back. "It's going to take some time to come to terms with the situation, but I suppose a small part of me is grateful to finally know." He brought a hand up, peering at it quietly, as if seeing through the skin and bone. "Lillianna spoke of my mother."

Alex stared, stunned.

Milos didn't elaborate, and Alex didn't push, even though he was definitely curious on what Milos meant.

After a while longer, with the day stones starting to wane, Milos pushed himself to his feet, shaking his legs out.

Alex stumbled to his own, almost falling over as he realized how dead they were. Maybe he should have shifted a bit more.

"I suppose I should have been a bit more prepared for the answers I got, but I can't look down on them either. Answers are answers, whether I like them or not." Milos peered toward Alex. "Tomorrow, we'll get back to training."

Alex perked up, startled. "You sure?"

"For one, it's a good distraction, and for two, I might be able to figure a few things out if I'm helping teach you."

"Mom said she would help as well." Alex shifted, turning more to face him. "Would you be okay with that?"

Milos twitched for a second, frowning before letting out a long, tired breath. "Considering she doesn't seem to mean us any harm? Yes."

"I'll take what I can get." Alex chuckled, a faint smile on his lips. "Thanks, Milos."

"Don't thank me." Milos stepped ahead, startling Alex as the man picked up his pace, the words echoing back almost missed if not for Alex's sharper hearing. "I should be the one saying that, not you."

Alex felt a wide smile cross his face as relief settled through him. He didn't respond, not feeling the need to.

It wasn't much, but progress was progress. His stomach growled loudly, and he winced. They had been out all day, just relaxing near each other, and he was starving. Milos chuckled, diverting their walk so they were heading for the kitchen.

Grabbing dinner, they split ways once more, agreeing to meet up the next morning. That night, Alex finally slept properly. He wasn't sure why, but the relief of everything being over, of them having a time to relax and having someone else to work alongside he could trust made all the anxiety just…fade, at least for that day.

~ * ~

The next morning, Rita meandered into the dining room, rubbing her eyes tiredly as smatterings of ink clung to her clothes that just weren't going away. Suzuhah, in male form, watched her enter with a grin, arms crossed over his chest. Milos, to none of her surprise, was already awake, quietly cleaning his blade as he waited. She could hear sounds from the kitchen and peered over as Ari and Leon bustled into the room with Alex a step behind, humming a tune along with Ari.

Plates clattered on the table as Rita ripped into her omelet and bread with relish. She hadn't realized how hungry she was and, as usual, it was all delicious. The sound of clanking and chewing filled the air, but there was no conversation, which she was fine with.

She heard footsteps and peered back, quickly swallowing as the door opened to let in Valencia. She glanced around the room, clearly ready for the day, before spotting her. She smiled and walked over, giving Alex a quick hug on the way before stopping in front of her. "My son tells me you wanted to see the witches' district? I can do that for you today. Things have calmed down since yesterday, so there shouldn't be as much issue in going out and about. I could go with you. I don't think any problems will arise."

"Good." Rita chuckled. "So, have you had breakfast? It's delicious." She paused at the woman's nod before continuing, "okay, let me finish then we can go to the witches district, sound good?"

Valencia smiled at that, nodding. She glanced back at Alex. "Once I'm sure she's safely in the witches' area, I will come back to train with you. Rest for now."

Alex gestured in understanding as Rita quickly finished her breakfast, excited. She quickly grabbed up her bag and hurried toward the door, almost bouncing on her heels. Valencia smiled at the action before walking out the door, gesturing for Rita to follow.

Once they were a good distance away, the town quiet in the gentle morning light, Valencia turned to Rita, almost sizing her up. "Rita, do not mind me asking, but what, exactly, is your connection with my son?"

Rita almost tripped over herself, barely avoiding face-planting as she caught herself. Valencia just watched her, faint amusement slipping onto her face. "He's a friend." Rita let out a breath, resettling her thoughts. "He's the only one I have left, so I would say we're pretty close, but Alex is good at making friendships, even without that voice of his."

"He's always been a sweetheart." Valencia peered ahead, as Rita returned to keeping pace with her. "He didn't really have anyone his age where we lived and his experiences in the town were not the best. It was fortunate that a friend of mine was keeping watch for him." She shook her head and let out a breath. "I was so worried when he had to flee by himself. I thought I lost him for good. For him to show up with such strong companions and in a healthy state? I wasn't sure how to handle it." She turned back to Rita, her expression extraordinarily soft. "Thank you for keeping an eye on my son and for confirming my thoughts. I'm glad to know he's finally got people he can fall back on. It's a relief for me."

"You don't really need to thank me," Rita pointed out, frowning. "It was just what I thought was the best option." She let out a breath, pushing away the encroaching thought that slowly seemed to invade her mind.

At least he still had his mother.

She shoved it off and grinned, hands on her hips. "So, enough about this. You said there were places for witches like myself? I would like to see them. Probably a lot less judgmental than the Demons around here."

Valencia seemed amused by the topic, but didn't argue, turning and leading her out of the gates and through the plaza. It hadn't been long since they left and she could tell people were still about, listening as someone spoke on the final verdicts and the reasons behind the decisions.

It was clearly split. Those like herself seemed to be hesitant or unsure. A few seemed relieved. However, a large majority of those with Demonic-like qualities seemed frustrated or outright annoyed. One or two actually looked murderous.

Instinct…that's what Demons lived on. That's what they were. Humans were known to be more open-minded and it was clear to see as, while the humans seemed split and discussing the situation, pretty much all the Demons were against it. Though, it seemed to have faded slightly from when they left the building yesterday, as if a few had come to terms with it over the night.

Or, maybe it was just because of history.

She shook her head, letting out a breath as Valencia quickly swept her to one side of the group and down the stairs into the city proper.

Thankfully, she wasn't Alex or Milos, she wasn't as known, she supposed the term would be. Who knew she would be thankful for that.

Descending the steps, it wasn't long until she found herself being led into a more residential part of the city. She hadn't been here before, so it was a bit surprising. She followed Valencia, peering around quietly before they came across a few shops that caught her attention. Her eyes widened in surprise as she walked up to one, peering inside.

"I'll let you look around. This area is where a lot of witches and psychics gather. Maybe talk to some of them." Valencia's expression was soft as she gestured. "It is safe here. If you need any help getting back, let one of them know or ask someone to get me. I made a promise with my son to train him, so I can't stay." She paused. "Lillianna probably has some books kept away that those here don't have, so I'm not surprised she said she would find some for you, but she doesn't always understand that, sometimes, you just need to get away." Valencia winked. "You might be surprised to find who you might meet here. They really are lovely people." With that, she gave a little wave before shifting, wings slowly curling out as she grew just a bit into her full Demonic form. With a quick flap of the wings, she shot into the air and sped away, blowing Rita's hair back in the process. Rita watched her go, letting out a snort of amusement before looking over this part of town once more. She could already feel it, a difference in the air here. She just knew she would be fine.

It wasn't long before she was glancing through the different shop, heading into the first store that caught her eye. Inside was filled with all sorts of items she remembered being hard to get when she was at home. Her eyes widened at the clean lines of the shop. The shopkeeper was an elderly man with a calm smile and a gaze that did not seem to meet her own. "Welcome, it's good to meet a witch. I can tell you have already graduated." He gestured. "Come, anything you would like?"

Rita blinked and relaxed. To be noticed as a witch so quickly, but not shown any other regard was strangely nice. She went around, picking up some goods before slipping out of the store, finding herself wandering from place to place. There was even a little cafe where she could see different potions being brewed alongside teas. She stepped inside, taking in the sweet smell of honey and cinnamon. Stepping up to the counter, she found herself surprised to come face to face with a woman with long hair that seemed to curl around all the way down to her waist, as if it were another piece of clothing. Her legs were similar to the goats that pulled carriages in the southern regions. She blinked and smiled.

"I didn't know Demons could be witches." The words came out before she really even thought about them.

The woman chuckled, hand to her lips. "Dear, anyone can be, as long as they have some skill and work hard enough. My father is an acclaimed witch." She gestured. "He actually has a little shop farther down the street. Considering the smell on you, you probably stopped there earlier."

Rita blinked, thinking through her interactions before remembering the old man.

"Oh." She stared at the woman, eyes wide. "Uh, yeah." She dug into her satchel to distract herself. "Actually, I have a few potions I was wondering if I could sell. I need some more money to buy items for other potions."

"Of course, what do you have?"

Rita pulled out the last few bottles. "Let's see, a drought of sleep, a vial of acid melt and…I don't remember what this one is." Rita lifted it up, suddenly feeling incredibly sheepish.

She remembered throwing all her items in the satchel when she left home, but she forgot to label them after the fact and now the blue liquid floated languidly in a simple glass bottle without anything on it.

"Oh dear." The woman tentatively took it, inspecting it quietly. "Let me check something." She stepped to one side, where Rita could see a cauldron and the familiar pulley that allowed her to dump it if something went wrong. She let a few drops drip into the cauldron before grabbing a few things from the side that Rita couldn't recognize or clearly see from here. After a moment, the woman let out a quiet laugh and turned back to her, handing it back. "Here, you should keep this."

Rita took it, confused, as the woman smiled. "It's a potion to help with wounds. A powerful one, clearly given some energy by an accomplished seer. I don't know who you worked with, but I haven't seen a powerful potion like this in a long time. A few drops will seal wounds and pouring the whole thing will even help seal internal damage if there is any." She pulled away. "As for these two? I can certainly give you some money for them."

Rita carefully pocketed the potion, trying to think back to when she got it. She couldn't remember.

Did her teacher give it to her at some point? The last month had been a mess of thoughts, so maybe she did. Rita shook her head, taking the money gratefully.

"Please, come back." The woman clapped her hands. "My name is Trisha."

"Rita." Rita peered around the small cafe quietly, noting the cozy atmosphere. It was strange, a small part of her was reminded of home, the tension she was ignoring slowly dissipated as she saw a few people walk in, placing their things down before heading toward the table, talking animatedly. "And I think I will. Thank you."

The witch nodded. "And tell those boys with you that they are welcome as well." Rita stilled, startled. The woman's smile widened, still warm. "Many of us witches and prophets had an inkling you all were coming. There is a change in the air. The others and I have no qualms about the Alertian or the previous leader's child. You all are safe with us. After all, they are simply victims of circumstance and we all can sense great things from them, the shifter and you."

Rita stared at her quietly, only now noticing the same expression as the old man. She thought the woman was meeting her gaze, but she wasn't. "Are you...?"

The woman gestured, quickly filling out the orders for the group that came up to the counter, forcing Rita to step to the side. The hands and movements were practiced and even. Within no time, the group was taking a seat to one side as the woman turned back to her. "I got my father's gift, but it has left me without physical sight. So, no, I cannot see you, but I know you." She gestured. "There are many in this city much like me, but we live how we want. Maybe you'll meet my brother someday. He has the same gifts as I do."

Rita stared quietly, shocked.

In the south, such conditions would have been cause for death, or at least, solitude.

Here, it was different. She nodded, realized what she did and spoke. "I…yeah. I would like that."

She bowed her head and was about to berate herself when she noticed the woman seem to quirk her lips in amusement. With that, Rita turned and walked out the door, thoughts churning.

There was a lot to hate about this place, or so she thought, but, as she peered down the quiet street, the day stones glimmered above and people moving through the streets, chatter and a quiet relief settled on their faces. She wondered if she only really saw the bad side of it.

Ever since they arrived, they were thrust from one thing to another, none of them got a time to breathe or be able to see the better parts of this place, so they were led to believe there weren't any.

She found her feet leading her back home, taking in the sights once more. She knew she should ask for someone, but the comforting air of the witch's area put her at ease. Thankfully, there were no issues as she walked back, humming a faint tune as she meandered through town. She had never met someone visibly impaired before, but she was perfectly normal. As she paid more attention, she noticed the people in the streets, children played and laughed as a few parents, humans and Demons, watched. So far away from the courthouse and center of town, it was surprisingly peaceful. She spotted a few clothing stores and paused, pulling at her clothes.

She would have to come back again; hopefully, this wasn't just a one off. She would like things to be working out for once. She and the others desperately needed time to just relax and recuperate and maybe get a fresh change of clothes. Their traveling clothes had gotten worn and dirty over the last month or so and she hadn't had time to grab anything from home except the bare basics.

As she pulled herself from her thoughts, she found herself diverting away from their temporary home, heading instead toward the coast. Soon enough, she found a ledge which overlooked the slope that led down to the water's edge. There was a little path leading down it, but she didn't follow it. She settled down, feet lightly kicking back and forth, hat lightly being tugged off her head by a faint breeze that seemed to push at the water, causing it to lightly slap against the pier and stones so far below. She could see a few witches nearby, chatting quietly while a few young children picked a few of the herbs that seemed to cling to the nearby rocks with determination. In the distance, she could see the familiar towering walls of the path they traveled through to get here, a mountainous line as far as the eye could see. She briefly spotted something approaching from above, only to realize it was a winged Demon that slowly curled down above the village before landing out of sight.

That was probably how Valencia got here, over the barrier in front of her. Her fingers curled into the stone as her legs stopped kicking, her memories flashing back to the horrific future vision. Staring up at the gigantic wall before her, she wondered what caused the fall. How did it happen if it hasn't happened for over a hundred years or, actually, how long had Demons been down here before the war?

If so, how long had the Overlands and Underlands been a thing? She shook her head, letting out a huff as she pulled some hair away from her eyes. She was thinking too much, she needed to stop thinking about this, or even worrying, for that matter. Things would work out eventually anyway. Especially now that she had a place she can go if she wanted to get away from the others for a bit.

She would probably need it over the next...however long they decided to stay there.

# Chapter Fifteen

Alex stared up at the distant day stones slowly beginning to grow steadily brighter. Milos was off to one side, going through measured and slow sword movements, a strange concentration to the practice.

After Rita left, Ari and Leon left soon after to take in the sights, now that they were no longer trying to look for a way to save them. Milos had no problem with that and soon they were on their way.

Suzuhah decided to stay behind, mentioning how he was interested in seeing how the two of them would train.

It actually made Alex wonder; he had another form that he switched to when pulling at his Demonic side.

He never saw that with Milos.

He heard the sound of wing beats and looked up just in time to see Mom land, switching back to human form in the process. Milos jumped, before shaking his head and sheathing his sword.

"Hey, Mom." Alex smiled, waving. "Rita's all set?"

"She is. She'll be safe with them." She glanced between the two of them. "So, any questions before we begin?"

Alex paused and winced. "Ah, one question actually. Why is it that, well, I'm still somewhat human when I transform? Why is it that all the half Demons I met so far lean more toward human?"

Mom's expression softened. "That's mostly because human blood has an interesting property. Most humans aren't able to handle magic, which is what a Demon is mainly composed of. So, for those who survive, they tend to lean toward whatever side they feel more comfortable with. Due to society being the way it is, it isn't surprising that most decide to be human and acclimate accordingly. Because your abilities were suppressed, the power comes out in spurts, as if to make up for lost time." She turned to him quietly as he paused at that. "While those who are half are human, all of them will have some form of proof of their Demonic heritage, even in human form. Just like they will have some form of human attributes in the demonic form. Though for you two to be so strongly human, is… I have no way to explain it. As for Demons, over time, we acclimated to these human-like forms, but our natural state is that of Demons, it's rare for a full Demon to be able to maintain a half form like you might."

Alex pursed his lips before glancing toward Milos, curious.

Milos' expression was strange, as if a sudden understanding settled over him. "I have heard of that from certain people. Though I thought it was just a false idea."

Alex paused, noticing how he was once more gripping his sword tightly, hand flaring and curling as if unsure what to do.

Mom watched; her expression sad. "It's going to be hard for you to learn but sometimes learning and understanding are the most important things in trying to figure out how to move forward." She turned fully to face Milos, who stiffened. Alex watched a mix between confused and worried. "I think it's best for everyone involved, if we figure out how to pull out your Demonic side. I have no doubt you are opposed to this, but if you've been with my son this whole time, then you know sometimes you can't control it, even if you want to."

"Wait-what? You KNEW I wouldn't be able to control it and unsealed me or whatever anyways?" Alex spun on his mom, feeling a flurry of emotions flare through him. "That was…"

"At the time, I felt I had no choice." Mom spoke quietly, her gaze never drifting from Milos, who slipped one foot backward in a defensive stance. "It was either that, or risk you not being able to defend yourself. It was all a gamble. A gamble I thought I lost when I thought I lost you." At this, she finally turned toward Alex, pained. "But you are such a gentle child, I knew you would be alright."

Alex pursed his lips, taking a step back, unsure how to respond. His mom closed her eyes, clearly having expected the rejection for what it was. She turned back to Milos. "So, to avoid that again, it's best if we awaken your Demonic side in a controlled environment. That way, you can understand how it works and, if you want to suppress it, what to watch out for."

Alex peered away, not wanting to see either of their expressions. He couldn't argue. Knowing was what allowed him some sense of relief.

"Fine," Milos finally said after a long moment of silence. Alex didn't miss the slightly choked sound as he continued, clearing his throat. "What am I supposed to do? It took a lot of effort to figure out what provoked Alex."

"I think I know." Mom let out a long breath before Alex felt his tongue suddenly catch in his throat. Energy poured off as her skin rippled and with a sharp snap, her form shifted to the Demonic one, black wings uncurling as long sharp claws extended outward. "You have an obligation to finish."

With that, she shot forward, startling Alex into quickly covering his face. He heard footsteps and felt a hand on his shoulder just as he went to whip around. Suzuhah held fast, expression somewhat grim. Alex turned in time to see Milos slide backward, sword up, just catching Mother's claws.

"Wha…Mom!" Alex went to take a step forward, only to feel the grip tighten. He glared over his shoulder to Suzuhah. "Let go of—" he cut himself off as he noticed Suzuhah peer past him, watching with a taut expression.

"Just watch for now. If your mother was actually trying to kill him, this scene would be very different, can't you tell?"

Alex turned back, feeling the waves press on his mind, much like when he first entered town. It was concentrated and made it hard to breathe.

Milos' eyes narrowed almost to slits as he shifted before twisting the sword, the claw sliding down the blade as he spun out of her grip. She flipped, fast as lightning. Alex found himself observing her wings, how they twisted and convulsed, curled and snapped. Only to have his attention ripped toward Milos as he spun, almost dancing. At first, it was focused, but slowly, as he watched, they became more vicious.

Soon, the dance became even more deadly, and Alex  paled. Watching Milos now made him realize just how lucky he was that the man thought that killing him was not worthwhile, or at least, that the man just decided against it.

He saw a bit of blood splatter and the grip tightened.

He almost felt sick as Mom suddenly leapt into the sky, wings snapping out, pulling her barely out of reach as Milos spun, kicking off the nearby stone wall before leaping into the sky with a bound that was DEFINITELY not human.

Focusing even more now than ever before, Alex found himself stilling, noting as Milos' eyes glowed blue, a bright blue that seemed to shine over the edges, like licks of magic. When he landed, head snapping up, seeming to notice them, Alex's breath caught. The pupils were slits, almost like the snakes he read about in his grandfather's books. His posture was low, a hint of white curling right near the base of his neck, usually hidden incredibly well by the man's choice of clothing. Little licks of white and blue curled off him, magic.

Mom shot down, just as Milos kicked off. Alex stumbled back, stunned as wings almost brushed his nose, claws clanking hard against metal.

In the span of a second, Milos crossed the entire space in a single bound and it was terrifying.

"ENOUGH." Mom's voice cut through. "Focus! THIS is your Demonic side, don't shove it down, don't suppress it, understand what it is, how it feels then focus on your instinct. You wish to protect my son, not hurt him. Focus on that if you need to."

Alex almost heard Mom grunt, sliding an inch backward as he quickly stumbled out of the way.

Suzuhah frowned before suddenly darting around. With a flare, he switched to his Vulfulas form with a crash of lightning, wings snapping out as his tail lashed, curling around Milos' ankle. Barely giving it a second thought, the man leapt, using his sword to spin over Mom.

Alex froze as energy slammed into him. He felt sick. Before him was something just…wrong. Milos spun, hair flaring out as his sword whipped to one side, and a growl ripped from his throat.

"I think you pulled out more than you bargained for." Suzuhah spoke, voice echoing as Mom stiffened, her posture defensive.

"Alex, speak to him." Mom spoke quietly.

Alex could have almost sworn he saw Milos shift, his ears almost twitching, seeming just that little bit longer than they should have been. If anything, they seemed flared, more reminiscent of animals.

Up close, the differences were a bit more noticeable. The slightly more extended ears and neck that seemed to arch slightly, the white curling up his back that looked between a mix of fur and scales, the magic, that was the term, almost oozing off him, making Alex dizzy. For a moment, he could have sworn he saw the flick of a tail, much thicker than his own slender one, but it seemed to vanish in the same moment, as if suddenly pulled back in.

He tried hard not to breathe more than he had to, trying to pull away, only for Milos to shift as well, gaze snapping briefly to him with a demanding 'don't move'.

"He went from trying to attack you, to trying to defend you." Mom spoke quietly. "You have a little control, don't you?" Her gaze flicked to his back, probably having seen the flash of the tail as well. "But you are still fighting it. You only can control what's left enough to know who your ally is and who the enemy is." The pain in her voice spoke volumes. "I'm sorry."

The words seemed to cause Milos to spasm for a moment. "Wai…" Before Alex could say anything, the man kicked off. Mom let out a surprised cry as he flung himself almost over her, leg snapping out, causing them to crash, hard, to the ground. Suzuhah jolted forward, lightning flaring. Faster than Alex thought possible, Milos flipped, skidding back over the ground, sword almost dropping from his grip as he tilted his head back and let out a sound that Alex never heard before.

The strangely terrifying screech seemed to echo as Alex felt his entire body lock up. Suzuhah slammed into the ground, wings twitching as he tried and failed to move. Mom was just as frozen, wing tips barely seeming to move as even her tail lay limply.

He heard clattering as the surroundings suddenly became dead silent barely a second after. In the distance, a distance much further than he expected, he heard startled screams that suddenly cut through the silence, even as faint as they were.

Milos slowly turned, eyes still glowing as he slowly picked up his sword once more, standing tall, that flash of tail appearing and vanishing once more as he brought his sword up right over Mom's head.

Alex wanted to scream, to shout, to do anything. Yet, everything down to his hair felt paralyzed. Magic. This was some sort of powerful magic.

STOP! The mental scream echoed through his head as a sound of choked vocal cords echoed from his throat.

It was enough to catch Milos' attention in the silence left in his wake.

Milos stared at him; the pupils so thin as to barely be visible slits. After a moment or two, he slowly brought his sword down, but not toward Mom. He took one step, then another, seeming to waver. Alex didn't miss the very clear exhaustion.

Pounding footsteps echoed loudly over marble and stone as Lillianna suddenly leapt out the back door, almost bounding all the way across the space in the same single bound as Milos did before. She slid, barely catching Milos as he suddenly collapsed forward, the spell seemingly broken.

Screams pierced the sky as the racket of scrambling and clambering met Alex's ears, much louder than before. He found himself slamming onto his butt, horrified.

"I made it." Lillianna spoke tiredly, letting out a breath as she slowly lowered herself to the ground, bringing Milos with her. "Valencia, get Suzuhah inside. The two of you are going to be dealing with the paralysis for a bit longer, since it was focused on you two."

Her gaze flitted to Mom who slowly struggled to her feet, wincing every so often. Suzuhah still hadn't moved, barely managing to switch to his male form with a wince. To Alex's relief, it was clear his mom would be fine, she just needed time. With a few hobbling steps, the two managed to get back into the house. Alex found himself still struggling to move, but managed to snap forward, almost crawling over the ground, only slightly better off than how his mother looked. "What was that?"

Lillianna's gaze drifted up to him from where she sat, Milos' head in her lap as she gently passed a hand through his hair, untangling the chains. Alex watched as the blonde hair curled over him. He knew it was long, but he hadn't realized how long.

"That was the commanding scream." Lillianna spoke quietly, patting the place next to her.

Alex found himself settling beside her, exhausted. "It wasn't focused, so all it did was freeze everyone in place, but that wave was much farther than I think anyone would have guessed, even if they knew he could do it. That was the only reason I noticed and, being another of his kin, was probably the only one able to fight against it to get here. Don't worry, no one else is aware of where it's from and I have the counsel helping those who got paralyzed, so they won't be coming by to ask questions." Her gaze drifted around the scarred backyard. "I figured your mother would want to pull his Demonic side out, but I don't think any of us expected it to be strong enough to do something that even my sister struggled with at his age." Lillianna peered softly down at Milos. "The poor boy has been suppressing such power through sheer willpower alone. So much pain…" She trailed off, and, for a moment, Alex briefly saw past the mask to an expression of anguish before it quickly vanished. "No wonder his emotions are so stunted, I suppose the word is." She shook her head, fury flashing on her face. "Those bastards. This poor child never got a chance to understand what was happening to him."

What? Alex stared, confused. Lillianna shook her head, glancing toward Alex.

"He was staring at you at the end. What happened?"

Alex opened and closed his mouth before finding himself speaking, words almost falling from his lips, detailing what happened, how he felt and his last-ditch effort to try to stop him, only managing to get a sound from his throat, if that. It was a relief to get to speak after whatever that was. So, everyone became paralyzed? So, how was it he was able to say anything at all?

Lillianna watched him quietly. "I suppose even the smallest noise in complete silence sounds like an echoing church bell." She closed her eyes. "To break through such a thing is no small feat. You two are more impressive than I think most of us Demons have given you credit for. Is it because of your human halves? Do those actually make you more powerful than a typical Demon or human?" She shook her head, turning her attention back down to Milos. "Still, now we know he truly does care for you. You probably know, from experience as well, how powerful the instinctual drive of Demons are, especially when they are thrown into a frenzy. Your mother was right in what she did, but she underestimated the situation."

"How…?" Alex swallowed thickly. "Mom is supposed to be Satan's child or whatever, right? Isn't that, or wasn't that, the leader who fought during the Human-Demon war?"

"You are correct." Lillianna peered toward Alex, who was still. "Your grandfather, your blood one, was powerful and intelligent, but was a kind spirit as well. When he knew that the fight was no longer winnable, he defended the land, allowing the Demons under him to escape, including myself. A few stayed behind, to fight alongside him, including your mother and my sister. However, news soon arrived of his demise at the hand of the Alertian who started the war."

"Wait, my mother? I thought…"

Lillianna smiled. "How old do you think Demons live for? You have been called a child for a reason." She peered down at Milos. "Though he may appear to be in his twenties, to us, he is no more than a ten-year old child. You are seen as even younger."

Alex stilled at that, not sure how to think.

"However, you are also still human, so your life span will still be much shorter than a normal Demon's." Her gaze drifted back to Alex. "Your mother was incredibly young when she fought all those years ago, to the point she probably blacked it out, not wanting to remember, and I do not blame her."

"Then…" Alex snapped his mouth shut as Lillianna just smiled.

"We are called Demon of the first for a reason," she said simply, peering down at Milos with a strange expression that took Alex a moment to recognize. Pure familial love.

"You said your sister…"

Her expression grew sad as she nodded. "I only learned she survived long enough to have a child when I saw this one and finally had time to reconcile what I was seeing. I felt the sudden surge even so far away, though even then I wasn't certain." She shook her head. "And, of course, it confirmed all my suspicions and worries. It's a terrible feeling, knowing you are the only one left…to know the fate of your last remaining family…"

Alex slowly tilted his head down, seeing Milos sleeping quietly, his body seeming to relax under Lillianna's careful ministrations. The only one left, like his mother and Rita.

"I think I understand the feeling, just a little." Alex spoke softly.

"Rita lost her whole family, and Mom is the only one I have left, even Suzuhah was alone for so long because he lost the most important person to him."

"You have all lost a lot for such young children." Lillianna paused, her head slowly tilting up. "No, I suppose some of you really aren't children, even if your energy feels like one. You are still growing, but hardships tend to have a way of pushing someone to grow faster than they should. This one shows that more than anyone."

Alex frowned, wondering about that. Something about the way Lillianna spoke caused Alex to wonder. He knew what happened to Rita and Suzuhah, but Milos was always tight-lipped about his past, about the world above.

Alex had a bad feeling, an insect settling into his throat, as the thoughts pressed on his mind. Milos was a gentle soul with a viciousness and cruelty that could only be learned. So who taught him to be this way?

What happened to him?

Alex wondered if he even wanted to know.

"I wouldn't worry about it for now." Alex jerked, glancing up to Lillianna, who was watching him quietly. "What happened in the past won't change, but what we do with ourselves now will affect how we all move forward in the future. The fact that this boy cares about you all so much says a lot. The fact that the only one he hurt was your mother, not Suzuhah or you, even though Suzuhah was fighting him, speaks volumes. I hope you will continue to be there to support him. He will need it immensely, going forward, especially now that we know just how strong his Demonic side is that he's been suppressing and the fact that it's still developing, much like your own."

Alex let out a breath, conceding.

"Though, I might have to join you the next few times to make sure he doesn't go into a frenzy again, or, at least stop him if he does." She smiled, almost mischievous. "It helps being impervious to those paralyzing effects."

"So, you can do that too?"

"Yes."

Alex swallowed thickly as the woman chuckled tiredly. "However,

I don't much like to. I am old now and have seen much. It is a double-edged sword if not used correctly…and can lead one into letting their guard down." She leaned back, staring up at the ceiling. "You will know if I need to use it, though I hope that time is not soon." Her expression grew pained. "I want everyone to have a peaceful life as long as possible, and I will do what I can to give them that chance."

She turned toward him, hair spilling over her shoulder in delicate waves as she said, "You take after your grandfather in a lot of ways." Her expression softened. "But it's very clear you are your own person and I look forward to seeing your growth. I hope this time, this space, gives you the chance to get that."

Alex wasn't sure what to say to that, so didn't say a word. Lillianna didn't speak again, just swayed slowly side to side, humming a faint tune under her breath. One Alex found himself humming as well.

The sound echoed over the backyard, soft, gentle and soothing.

~ * ~

Milos' mind felt fuzzy and drained, his entire body screaming how wrong it felt. His skin itched in a way that he knew he couldn't scratch off. His tongue felt thick and heavy.

"You are awake."

A voice echoed from above, catching his attention. What was he laying on?

He felt something lightly poke his shoulder before a familiar voice said, "Hey, Milos, it's good to see you are feeling better."

Feel…right. He slowly opened his eyes, which hurt even though the day stones drifted to afternoon, the brightest part of the day had already passed. It felt like hours passed in a flash, though clearly, they hadn't. Lillianna peered down at him, hair falling around her in a wave, her expression strangely soft and familiar. His mind flashed to a familiar visage holding him tightly when he was younger, those same blue eyes staring at him with an emotion he couldn't quite recognize. There was a shift as Alex leaned over, worry and relief clear on his features.

"It's good to see you awake. You were out for a while. How are you feeling?"

He wasn't sure if he could describe it. He sat there, trying to figure out the words, only to find them disappearing like the breeze.

"Take your time." Lillianna brushed a hand through his hair, startling him. The familiar weight of the chain clanking against his back was gone and utter panic trilled through him. He found himself wanting to pull away, to search for it. "Relax." She spoke, her words somehow relaxing. "It's right here." She patted something to one side of her and he heard the faint clanking sound, as she frowned. "I, personally, don't think you need it, but I can never understand those born into a society that holds them in such regard, even after all these years." She shook her head as Milos slowly pushed himself up, not to grab it, just to recenter himself.

It was only then that a flood of memories came back, hitting him like one of Rita's potions. He grimaced, slowly peering over toward Alex, finally taking in where they were resting. It seemed he had been HE WAS moved to one part of the garden, a little away from the fight. Alex was resting against a nearby fountain where water trickled over, splashing into a small circular basin below. Lillianna sat, legs out and back to another stone wall that separated the garden from another area.

"Yeah, I know the feeling," was all Alex said, and Milos knew it was true.

A small part of him knew what was happening, but it was as if another side of him took control, one he always held down tightly with a leash. He seemed to snap in the presence of Satan's child attacking him or, no…if she was actually attacking him, he would probably be much worse than he was. He took a deep breath, taking stock of his situation.

Surprisingly, he wasn't hurt, but he felt exhausted, like he was fighting a drega the whole morning without rest, or when… He immediately cut off that line of thought, listening to the two beside him.

"You should rest." Lilliana spoke, pushing herself to her feet now that he was no longer using her lap as a pillow. "I will be here tomorrow when you are training again."

Milos stiffened, his entire body screaming. "I won't be doing that again," he said simply, words short and almost vicious.

"You will," Lillianna responded with barely a moment between words, her gaze firmly on his. "Because you need to. It is a miracle you have been able to restrain it as long as you have without training, but you are reaching your limit, and we need to get it under control now while we still can."

Milos felt his muscles lock as his heart pounded loudly in his throat at those words. Alex glanced away, clearly unable to argue with her assessment.

Milos wanted to, he really did, but he found a part of him acknowledging she was right.

He was exhausted and now he realized that it wasn't just physically. His mind was sluggish and his thoughts were staggered at best, downright dead at worst.

He finally conceded, his head slumping downward in a strange defeat. Long tendrils of hair fell over his shoulders, landing on his hand. He stared at it, not sure how to feel about the long locks.

Nothing. He felt nothing.

"Alex, why don't you get your friend to bed, he needs his rest. We will talk more tomorrow." There was a pause before she continued, a little softer. "And I believe all of you have a conversation that needs to be done. While no one was hurt, beleaguered feelings can cause problems in the coming days. When you are rested a little, talk to Suzuhah and Valencia. Understood?" He heard movement, but didn't look up. He felt a hand wrap around his shoulder, feeling the slender finger settle under his arm.

"Come on."

He heard a grunt from beside him but found himself stumbling to his feet. He wasn't sure if Alex was supporting him, or if he was walking and Alex was just leading, but eventually, he got to his room and settled back into bed. He heard a yelp and grumble followed by a faint shoving. He let go, the pillow soft under his head.

The sound of the bed resettling as someone stood up was the last thing he heard as sleep claimed him.

# Chapter Sixteen

Alex felt heat rise to his face as he quickly hurried out the door. He never saw Milos so…not himself. It was almost as if he was drunk, but Milos didn't get drunk. He had not expected Milos to pull him down onto the bed when he collapsed, though maybe he should have expected it, considering how tired Milos seemed. The fact he only let go after Alex shoved him away, however, was less expected.

It didn't help that Milos, in a lot of ways, felt safe. He let out a sigh and headed downstairs, the hunger clawing at him. It wasn't long before he found himself in the kitchen after checking on his mother and Suzuhah. Both seemed fine, though clearly a little out of it still. They agreed to meet up later to talk about what happened. Which was fine with Alex, he wasn't sure he wanted to talk about it right now.

He heard stumbling and peered over as Rita shoved the door open, adjusting her hat as her attention veered wildly around the room.

"Hey, Rita, what's wrong?"

"What's wrong? Didn't you feel that?" She stared at him. "I mean, I think I was on the outskirts of whatever that was, but feeling your body lock up is not comforting. It took forever to get back here since everyone was trying to figure out what happened." She shook her head. "The only ones who seemed to know were the council, and they were going around, trying to calm everyone." She waved her hand and grumbled. "And now I'm starving. Where's the lout?"

"Milos?"

"Who else?"

"Sleeping." Alex shook his head, finding himself a little amused.

"Wow, did he get his ass kicked today or something? Wish I stayed behind to see it then."

She swiped up a piece of bread and turned to Alex as he got to making a simple meal of soup.

"The opposite. He expended too much energy." His gaze flicked to her. "I don't know how far out you were, but it might give us an idea of how far Milos' cry was."

Rita froze mid-bite, crumbs falling as her entire body seemed to tense. She started coughing, choking on the bread as she practically threw it to one side. Alex barely caught it, expression sheepish as she thumped her chest. "I'm sorry, WHAT?"

"Yeah, the thing that paralyzed everyone. That was Milos."

"Alex, you are speaking shiesse." She stared at him. "I was a good half a mile away from the house."

Alex blinked and felt himself pale before chuckling weakly. "Well, now we know how strong the effect is…"

"Don't give me that without explaining what the frick you are talking about!"

Alex winced and nodded, handing the bread back before going into detail about what happened. Rita listened quietly, frowning occasionally. After he finished, he gestured, "So, yeah, that's the whole of it."

"Oh," was all Rita said as she slumped into her chair. "So, you are telling me that the two people who became intertwined in my life, are some of the most powerful beings on this freaking land? Are you KIDDING me?"

Alex winced. "Um…I wouldn't say…"

"Alex, you can literally control people with your voice and Milos just stunned half the freaking city! Because of a freak accident!" She cut herself off as Alex found himself recoiling, wincing at her words. "Right, sorry."

"It's fine."

Rita pursed her lips before turning back to her bread, munching on it quietly. "That's a lot to take in. It makes me feel…" She suddenly cut herself off, catching Alex's attention.

Made her feel, what? The way she was saying it felt almost painful. He never knew Rita to be self-conscious, but he could have sworn he heard a hint of that in her voice. She shook her head and grinned. "Well, at least I know we'll be fine if someone is hunting us down."

"We're not powerful though, both Milos and I are still trying to figure out how this works."

"And that's fine, but you have a baseline to work from. You just need to develop it." She shrugged; arms crossed. "I would take that over…" Once more, she cut herself off and pointed. "Ugh, now you've put me in a bad mood. I think I'll stay behind tomorrow to watch. That way, I'm not wondering, from half a freaking mile away, what's happening."

Alex smiled sheepishly as Rita swiped up a bit of food, grabbing a bowl just as he finished cooking and gestured. He rolled his eyes but poured some of the soup into it. She turned and with a little wave, headed up the stairs.

*Rita and Milos are so weird sometimes.* He shook his head, turning back to his meal.

She didn't wait for him to put on the chives, or let it cool a little, for that matter.

Though it was Rita, should he really be surprised?

~ * ~

Milos slowly opened his eyes, exhaustion still pulling him, but his mind ran a mile a minute, not allowing him to sleep a moment more. The day stones were starting to drift to night, and he found himself uncomfortable at having, once again, lost a good amount of time at something he hadn't intended.

He slowly pushed himself up, the bed creaking with the slow movement. His stomach growled and he winced. He peered down at his clothes and peeled them off, noting how sweaty they felt, clammy against his skin. He wasn't sure who did it, probably Ari or Leon, but he spotted a bowl of water to one side which he used to wake himself up, water splashing over his neck and face, clearing away some of the grogginess physically still clinging on.

He heard a knock on the door and glanced over as the door opened to reveal Suzuhah. The young man blinked and slowly appraised Milos up and down. "I suppose I should have waited to hear a response."

Milos felt his expression shift to one of cold annoyance and the boy quickly raised his hands, turning away. "I just came to let you know dinner's ready and that we should, you know, probably talk about that whole mess earlier. Plus, sleeping all day and night does not work, I can say that from experience." He paused. "And, with that, I'm closing the door." Suzuhah waved, awkward smirk on his face as he hastily closed the door.

Milos took a deep breath to center himself and quickly got dressed in whatever was nearby, a pair of trousers with a lower cut tunic. Nothing special, but comfortable when necessary.

He went to pull his hair into its typical ponytail and found himself hesitating as he went to curl the chain around tightly as usual. His hands shook as his thoughts flitted to the last day. The memories he pushed aside, now front and center. Lillianna's words about what it meant to be an Alertian, so different from what he grew up with. Rita's future vision about the destruction of the lands...of everything that happened since his descent...no, since his mother's death. It all hit him like a wave, and it was all he could do not to just crumble. He felt that familiar numbness and let it take over. He was afraid of what would happen if he didn't.

Realizing he was getting lost in his thoughts, he tugged sharply, pulling himself out of them. He quickly finished his task before heading downstairs. He could already smell the scent of roasted meat, though he wasn't sure of what the Underlands' version of it was called, and freshly baked bread. Stepping inside the dining room, it was easy to notice as Ari finished putting down the last plate while Rita and Alex chatted to one side. Valencia was just settling down with Suzuhah purposefully avoiding him.

Upon his entering, the conversation quieted as Rita waved. "Took you long enough, lout. Suzuhah came downstairs, all embarrassed."

"I said not to say anything!" Suzuhah yelped, peering toward her in horror as she grinned.

Alex just shook his head and waved. Ari nodded to him as Leon bowed, pulling out a chair for him. He hesitantly settled into it as the others got situated as well.

The clinking of silverware and the sound of eating quickly filled the room, along with Suzuhah's quiet grumbling.

As they were finishing up, Valencia spoke up, cutting through the quiet conversations and eating her gaze on Milos. "Alex, Suzuhah, Milos, once we are finished eating, we need to talk about what happened today. Rita, Ari, Leon, you are all good to go your own ways."

"And we can't stay, why?" Rita crossed her arms over her chest.

"I'm not saying you can't. I do apologize; it was not intended to sound rude. I just didn't feel like it was necessary to pull you into the conversation when you can all do your own things if you needed to. But, if you wish to join, that is fine, just be aware it is primarily between the four of us."

Rita rolled her eyes and sighed. "I did need to go clothes shopping and now's a good time as any, there should still be a few stores open at this time. Ari, Leon, mind helping me with that?" She glanced over to the two who nodded.

"Here." Valencia pulled a pouch from her side, handing it to Rita, who blinked, surprised. "Go ahead and have fun, maybe pick out something a little extra on me. And thank you for understanding."

Rita shrugged, but the smile she returned spoke volumes. "Hey, I get it. I already know what the conversation is about, and I can always ask Milos and Alex and Suzuhah how it went later. Might as well get some things done in the meantime, right?"

At that, she waved and hurried out the door as Valencia shook her head in amusement.

"Did you have to send her away?" Alex cut in, voice a little taut.

"Like I said, I left it up to them whether they wished to stay or not. It is still a conversation that we must have, no matter what." Valencia spoke, her words a little tired.

Milos didn't say anything, though a part of him wished Rita chose to stay instead. Yet, he understood. He wouldn't want to be caught up in the coming conversation either. He turned back to face Valencia, who had a long expression on her face. Alex glanced back and forth, almost a little nervous as Suzuhah remained silent, embarrassment clearly gone.

"I will get straight to the point." Valencia spoke quietly. "You lost control during your training earlier and attempted to kill me. It was only thanks to my son's intervention that you didn't stab your sword through my neck while I was paralyzed. Now, I understand how powerful the Demonic instinct is, but that is something that could have been prevented by you as well." She narrowed her eyes as Alex opened his mouth, as if to argue, only to purse it into a thin line as he turned away. "I need to know, for future, what is your grudge against me? Your murderous instinct was directed toward me, and me alone. I need to know this, in case something like this happens in the future."

"Maybe it's because you're Satan's daughter?" Alex spoke up, hesitant as he watched Milos quietly, who found himself unable to respond. "He was tasked with killing a child of Satan and, well, he doesn't really know you."

"I understand that, Alex. But that sort of hatred and murder is a result of more than just a task that needs to be completed. Even with Demonic instinct." She turned back toward Milos, a strange expression on her face. "As I was frozen, staring up at you, I saw it. You weren't seeing me. I've seen it before on Demons, especially slaves. You were seeing something else…maybe someone else. I'm not going to ask who, that is your business, but I will ask if this continues to affect you in the future, if I were to continue to aid you in training."

Milos stilled at that, frozen to the core. He ignored it, thought it a mere passing thought. However, thinking back on it, for a split second, in his mind of whirling madness and fury, was HER. That woman who took his mother away, who took him in merely to be able to control him, to control Father. Her black hair clinging to her face as the cold stare pierced into him, through him. Then the image vanished, once more replaced with the black scaled creature below him, a woman's face like carved obsidian with curling horns and long, pure black wings.

He hadn't thought it possible, but in his interactions with Alex, with how things went since they arrived, he saw HER in Valencia. Saw that woman, his stepmother, in her place.

He found himself clutching the chair tightly, only the creak of wood cluing him into the situation. He found himself letting out a breath, slowly relaxing as he peered up. Before him was a very different woman from HER. There was a gentle concern on her face, hair long and curled over her shoulder and back. He wanted to say it wouldn't happen again, but his tongue stayed glued to the roof of his mouth.

"You okay there, Milos?" Suzuha leaned forward, having switched to her little girl form, as she almost got up in his face. "I mean, you are usually quiet and broody, but this seems different."

Milos felt his eye twitch at that, but the tense muscles relaxed as he shook his head. "I'll be fine." He turned back to Valencia. "I have no answer to that right now. I still do not know much about this other side. I cannot be certain I won't react the same way next time."

"But Lillianna will be there, right? And you're learning to figure out how to control it. It should be fine." Alex gestured; words almost hopeful.

"Yet it would be best not to risk such a thing." Valencia watched him quietly. "I'll not engage in combat again, but I will stay nearby to guide you both on learning what being a Demon is like."

She glanced toward Milos, slowly peering up and down, her expression almost sad. "I don't know who or what I remind you of, but whatever it is, I am sorry. I had no intention of the sort, nor do I have any intention of hurting you or any of you." She shook her head before she swept to her feet. "However, it seems like there is no animosity between us when you are out of your Demonic instinct, so that, I will take with relief. I will see you all tomorrow." With that, she quickly left, leaving just the three of them in the now eerily quiet dining room.

Suzuha glanced between them before turning toward Milos. "I'm not Rita, I'm not going to ask any probing questions, but if you need to talk. I think Alex and I would be more than happy to listen." Alex nodded along to the words as Suzuha got to her feet. "Anyway, after that food, I am sleepy again. I think I'll get some rest for tomorrow." She waved and quickly left.

Alex peered over, just watching, curious. "Do you want to just chat? Not about anything in particular, but you have been sleeping all day, and I doubt you'll be able to rest much, so…"

Milos relaxed with a nod. Alex smiled, leading the way as they headed into the sitting room, the fire stone dancing to one side as Alex slumped on the couch and Milos took a chair. It was awkward for a moment before Alex spoke up. "Did you see that Demon in the crowd? The one with the curling horns? They kind of look like the sheep that exist in the Underlands."

Milos blinked and shook his head, relaxing. "Ah, you mean the Satyr?"

"That's what they are called, huh…"

The conversation soon evolved into the sights they saw from their limited time being there and soon followed with conversations on what to do next. Alex wanted to explore the town a bit, now that they didn't have to watch their backs anymore. Milos wasn't sure, but at that point, he was mostly just listening, letting himself relax to Alex's melodic voice.

## Chapter Seventeen

The next day dawned rather early with most of the members of the place up and awake. Ari and Leon were preparing breakfast already while Lillianna and Valencia left briefly to go about town to make sure the incident from the day before was settled. Alex and Milos pulled themselves to the large back yard. Suzuhah sat next to Rita, who was quietly parsing through her bottles. She pulled out her potion kit, fingers dancing over her late master's gift as the bag turned once more into a pot. She spotted Alex and Milos glancing over briefly and waved. Alex smiled back as Milos nodded. That was basically a smile from the lout, so she would take it.

She wanted to work on some medicine anyway. She hummed, poking at her new clothes. The clothing store had, thankfully, still been open and so she was exploring her options. She would have to drag the boys there later. The new hard leather boots crisscrossed up her leg to right below the knee. Cotton stockings, thick enough to help with the chill, continued up to mid-thigh and were connected by straps to her short skort. The white blouse had long flowing sleeves and a green overdress sat comfortably around her waist, cutting in half at her hips and flowing down on either side to give her mobility. It was fancier than her normal fare, but comfortable and warm.

Suzuhah picked out some things themselves. A simple dress with a belt and shoes for the female form and a nice pair of trousers and a vest for the male form. Rita watched in fascination as he threw the vest on, nodding to himself before switching to the little female form, the dress swirling around her. She would ask how the clothing stayed on, but she decided that was one magic she would have to ask a seer about, and even then, she wasn't sure she would ever really know.

She peered back out as she settled her supplies next to her, watching. She hoped that scream or whatever from yesterday didn't happen again. Being frozen stiff for a good minute or so was NOT fun and could be very problematic when making her potions.

She paused, her thoughts flitting to that morning when she woke up and headed downstairs. She had been heading to the sitting room to get some time alone with the fire stone, only to come across Alex and Milos seated on the couch…fast asleep. She couldn't help but mentally coo at how adorable the scene was, with the two of them more relaxed than she'd seen in a while. While she would normally grab out her sketch pad, this time, she simply closed the door with a quiet click to let them rest. She teased, but there were some things she would leave well enough alone.

She heard a faint hum and whoosh. Alex switched to Demonic form, wings fluttering as he tried to angle them to lift off the ground.

Milos was watching, his expression harder to read than usual. Though she did notice a bit of exhaustion on his face that hadn't been there before, contradicting the faint smile on his face. The chain was tied tighter than usual around the long ponytail, almost tangling with itself to keep it all in place. She reached up, fiddling with her ribbon, deep in thought for a moment before shaking it off. They were far enough away where neither would interfere with the other and it seemed they didn't mind her watching.

She started to brew, glancing over every so often when Suzuhah would help by putting an ingredient in just before she asked him to, clearly knowing what to do.

She heard a yelp and peered over once more as Alex caught himself, hopping on one foot for a few paces before he managed to get his wings closed with a huff.

Milos let out a snort and gestured, saying something that was hard for Rita to hear. Alex just gave him a look before slowly extending the wings once more. With only a moment's hesitation, he twisted the wings and leapt upward.

Rita stared, blinking in surprise as, instead of falling back down, he hovered there, wings slowly beating up and down, hovering him in the air. Though his back was turned to her, she could feel the excitement radiating off him. He tried to spin, only to yelp and crumble, crashing into Milos as his wings caught.

Milos quickly shifted, catching Alex as the wings contorted oddly, almost seeming to tangle, which Rita knew wasn't possible.

Suzuhah winced beside her as she did another stir without really thinking about it. "Yikes," he said. "That's going to hurt later."

"What happened?"

"He tried to twist too quickly and whatever wind caught on the wings and tugged them the wrong way. It's more of a sprain than anything, but not fun to deal with."

Alex pulled himself free from Milos, wings twitching out as he grimaced, feeling one hand over his shoulder and peering back toward his right wing, which seemed to be struggling a little. He grimaced again before slowly unfolding it.

Thankfully, it seemed to be fine and, soon enough, they went back to what they were doing, though Alex was clearly a bit more careful.

Rita finished her potion, placing it in a bottle before moving onto the next. After a couple hours of Alex finally getting comfortable with hovering, Lilliana returned. Alex, seeming relieved to finally get time to rest, settled next to Rita, leaning back on his hands with a groan as his features shifted back to human form.

Milos seemed tense as Lillianna walked over, her posture elegant as usual. She nodded briefly toward Rita and Suzuhah before settling in front of Milos. Valencia sat beside Rita, not getting involved, but clearly there to help if needed. Though her gaze did occasionally flit to Rita, amusement crossed her face as Rita worked. Her smile toward Alex was soft and Rita didn't miss how Alex returned it. She couldn't help but feel a little jealous as she focused once more back on her potion. With everyone around her, a small part of her felt underwhelming…and it was frustrating. Milos, Alex, they were both descendants of powerful Demons. Suzuhah was the creation of one of the most powerful seers beside the grand-seer that Rita remembered hearing of.

The grand seer…it had been a long time since she thought about meeting them. It used to be her goal, but she barely thought about it after her parents' death. It was strange, it had been a driving force and now it was nothing more than an afterthought.

She paused, feeling a strange familiar tug and, this time, focused on it. She NEEDED to figure out how to control whatever this was. Usually, she felt the tug and found herself diving in somewhat unwillingly. This time, almost as soon as she felt it, she mentally dove after it.

Strangely, she felt calmer this time as she found herself talking to Alex. They were in the streets of the sanctuary and both seemed comfortable, relaxed. Peering ahead, Rita spotted Milos and Suzuhah. Alex waved to the two, a bright smile on his face, and hurried forward.

She tilted her head, peering off into the distance where she could see the distant crack in the mountains, they journeyed through to get to sanctuary. The day stones glimmered brightly, sparkling off the water and distant rocks. A faint smile felt like it crossed her lips in the vision, a gentle breeze blowing at her hair as an odd smell wafted to her nose, one she couldn't quite recognize.

She found herself pulled away, frowning slightly. What was that about? There was nothing happening, just a gentle scene. She felt a strange uneasiness settle over her at the end of the vision, which didn't make sense to her. All she was doing was staring out over the water. Sure, it was nice to see Milos and Alex and all of them being able to relax in the sanctuary, but...

She shook her head and sighed. At least this time, she didn't collapse, already seated as she was. She couldn't control it this time either, but she was able to at least sense it coming and settle down enough to prepare for it. She would just have to remember that for next time. She pulled herself from what she was doing, focusing on what was happening. Thankfully, it seemed like no one noticed, which relieved her. No reason to tell anyone, after all, there was nothing TO tell. Plus, she held no control over these visions, so there was no point in mentioning that she avoided fainting for once. It wasn't exactly an achievement.

Plus, it wasn't violent like most of hers were. Would she be able to control one like that? She wasn't sure and she didn't want to worry the others, so she held her tongue.

Alex leaned forward, elbows on his knees as he watched Milos and Lillianna, curiosity clear on his face. Rita followed his attention, seeing that Lillianna was talking quietly with Milos, before shifting her stance, gesturing. Milos seemed uncomfortable, something Rita never thought she would see on the man's face. Eventually, however, he slowly nodded and untangled his sword, laying it on the ground. Rita blinked in surprise, that was new.

She exchanged glances with the two beside her as she whipped up another potion.

Milos took a deep breath before slowly seeming to focus. She felt Alex stiffen beside her, narrowing his eyes almost in worry.

Lillianna suddenly shifted, instantly behind Milos, grasping his arms just as Milos went to kick away. His eyes glowed and Rita could have sworn she heard a faint growl.

"Control it!" Lillianna cut in. "We are instinctual, but we are rational. You know what it feels like, slowly let it go. You've been keeping it on a tight leash this whole time, slowly let it go. I've got you."

"Shut it," Milos snapped, voice almost hissed.

Rita almost dropped her spoon, the wood clanging harshly against the metal of the pot as she did a double-take at the words. Suzuhah let out a sharp whistle as Alex stiffened in shock beside her. Did she seriously just hear MILOS of all people being rude to Lillianna? She heard faintly bubbling and quickly whisked, focusing back on the potion while keeping half her attention on Milos, not wanting to get thrown off again.

Lililanna didn't respond, just held tighter as Milos struggled, unfazed by the rude comment.

Rita found herself wanting to get up and didn't miss how Alex was tightly holding his knees, almost ripping through the cloth. However, neither moved as Milos slowly stopped struggling.

Lillianna sighed and let him go. "I understand your hesitation to let it go, especially after years of suppressing it, but you'll need to learn how to do it." A faint smile crossed her face. "But, little steps. I will be content, for now, with you showing a bit more emotion, however vitriolic and rude it might be."

Milos pursed his lips, shoulders tensing at that, clearly upset.

Lillianna continued, "While you won't be working with the rest of the council like I originally planned, I will continue to work with you until you are able to feel comfortable with letting go of that inhibition. You will feel much more comfortable once you allow yourself to be yourself. We will go over this, every day, for a few hours, until you feel comfortable enough to do it without my presence." Her expression softened as her gaze slid to the rest of the group. "Hopefully, the next few weeks will be enough to give you all time to settle and to get used to our sanctuary. However, stay as long as you like."

She nodded, lightly patting Milos on the shoulder and walked over to the three of them. "That extends to all of you. I know it was a rough start, but I want you all to feel comfortable enough to call this a home. You may leave whenever you like. Just let one of us know and we will find someone to lead you back to the mainlands of the Underlands." She turned back to Milos. "Now, let's practice a few more times. I'm not letting this end this quickly."

Rita chuckled quietly along with Alex as Milos' expression twitched with annoyance, followed by a hefty sigh.

Rita relaxed back into her potion, watching in amusement and relief as things finally settled into place. She glanced over to see Ari and Leon step out with trays of food, calling together a lunch before heading on their way to pick up groceries. Valencia continued to watch, relaxing with a faint smile as the day progressed without issue.

The day continued from night into day again and they soon fell into a rhythm.

Alex would practice with his wings in the morning with the help of Suzuhah and sometimes his mother and, in the evening, Milos would be coached by Lillianna, who seemed to have found a way to get around her responsibilities for part of the day. Some days, they would have time off and just relax around the house.

It was about two weeks later when Rita clapped her hands and peered from person to person, startling them into silence as they finished breakfast. "Let's go out today." She grinned. "I've been exploring town, and I think it's been long enough for them to no longer be up in arms about you two."

She paused, thinking over her last few days out and about. The conversations died down since and it seemed the council was leaving them alone. At least, her, and she was intrinsically tied with the others. Also, she hadn't seen Maritus much lately and she was more than a little relieved about that. She was a bit worried about Milos, but she had a feeling he needed a reprieve. His issue was more he had too much control and helping him to loosen up a bit might help for the next time he had training.

Alex shrugged, glancing toward Milos who still was eating. He finished his food, clearly spending time debating.

Rita didn't blame him; she couldn't find it in herself to call him a lout lately. Where Alex was slowly improving, hovering in the air when he could and slowly getting a feel for how his wings worked, there seemed to be almost no improvement for Milos. She wasn't sure if it was because he was resisting the idea still or if it was something else. Thankfully, Lillianna seemed to have the patience of a saint and was giving him time to actually work through it. She hoped, like she thought before, that relaxing for a bit would help.

Rita pulled herself from her thoughts as Milos heaved a sigh and pushed himself to his feet, having finished breakfast. "I suppose some time away from this place might do us all some good."

"I cannot argue with that." Suzuhah waved, as he munched on a grape with a faint grin. "I'm just glad most people don't know my female form, makes it much easier to slip out of the house."

Alex blinked before letting out a quiet laugh. "Of course."

Milos let out an amused sigh as he followed. She spotted the two guards to either side of the door, who did a double-take upon seeing the group leaving.

They were ready to put their weapons forward, but stopped after a moment and pulled back, watching the four of them warily.

Rita just let herself wave cheerily, barely resisting rolling her eyes as she turned and walked ahead, hearing the others' footsteps behind her, clanking on the cobblestone. She could almost feel them tense behind her as they opened the gate that led out of the home.

She slipped out with Suzuha chuckling beside her, humming as she skipped along. She peered back in time to see Alex gesture and Milos purse his lips before following.

She shook her head as they came across the large thoroughfare where she could see one or two people moving about and the rest glancing over before making double-takes.

Milos pulled up the hood of Alex's cloak, clearly having kept it. Rita wasn't surprised. Alex didn't have much need of it. Where most of the

Underlands tended to be cold and wet, it wasn't like that here, it was almost warm in comparison.

She had one place to start with followed by the main locations. She wound through the streets with ease before arriving at a rather large building, the stone cut to create simple, but beautifully designed windows. She could already see all sorts of clothes and linens hanging in the windows as she guided them inside. Suzuha chuckled, following behind, guiding Milos and Alex in. Rita didn't miss the expressions on the boys' faces. Milos' expression was deadpan as Alex blinked before glancing toward her in amusement.

"A clothing store?"

"We have been wearing the same drab clothes since I MET you. You both need a change of clothes desperately, and spares." Her gaze flitted to Milos. "The rips in yours are getting impossible to mend, even with Ari, Leon and I working together." Milos glanced down and grunted, clearly unable to argue. "Now, shoo. I know you two know how to shop, so pick your clothes then I'll show you to our next destination. Don't worry, you'll like it." She winked.

The two exchanged worried expressions before hesitantly moving into the store proper.

There were whole walls of clothes, racks upon racks of simple to beautiful designs. It seemed to be a communal clothing store and was rather busy with customers who, thankfully, didn't pay any attention to Milos and Alex, too busy with their own objectives.

Rita settled back with Suzuha, waiting with amusement as Alex and Milos wheeled through the aisles, clearly lost and a little confused. Rita knew she could help, but this was more amusing.

Thankfully, they eventually found some things that would work. Suzuha paid and then pinched her nose. "Why don't you get changed then we'll move on. Your old clothes stink."

"Rude." Alex huffed, but didn't argue, ducking back where he came from as Milos just turned, clearly more than a little annoyed. Rita shrugged. Suzuha was right. Suzuha giggled, amused.

Milos returned first. Rita wasn't surprised. He was efficient, if nothing else.

He wore knee high hard leather boots with a slight heel, which surprised her. Loose fitting pants with a thigh belt on the left. She could see a few knives and small vials strapped on that she recognized. Over a tan loose tunic was a long woolen vest pulled taut to his frame. It loosened at his waist trailing down to his ankles like two tails. She never thought of Milos as fashionable, but he certainly gave the same vibes as an overland noble with that fit, one more than willing to stab an enemy if they got in his way, but that was beside the point.

Alex returned soon after, wearing a pair of cotton pants tucked into thigh-high leather boots. A short loose tunic was held in place by the familiar three belts he always wore. A loose cloak of darker blue wound around his shoulders like a shawl, going down his back almost to the floor, clearly warm and comfortable.

She whistled, impressed, before snapping to her feet, noting the cloth bags in their hands that probably held the rest of their attire. She clapped her hands and grinned.

"Well, now that everyone's dressed, let's move along to the main event." She spun on her heels and hurried back outside.

She still had to show them the witch's district, after all.

It wasn't long before they were in the witches' district. A few people spotted Rita and waved before glancing at who she was with. Curiosity was clear on their faces, but no hostility.

Alex seemed to watch everything with a mix of curiosity and worry. Milos was as difficult as ever to read and Suzuhah was humming along beside her, watching with a faint smile and clear recognition.

Rita spun around and gestured with one hand on her hip. "Well? What do you think?"

"It's a street." Milos tapped his finger on the hilt of his sword, clearly annoyed.

Rita rolled her eyes and gestured. "Ugh, I don't know why I bother."

Her gaze flicked to the shop briefly before she headed to the cafe, she frequented a few times now. She knew her comrades and, while she found this area interesting, she wasn't sure if they would, so she decided to focus on the next best thing.

The bell rang as she pushed the door open, letting them inside the quaint little cafe. A fire stone flickered to one side in a simple fireplace as the tall woman from before tilted her head up from where she was handing a young couple their drinks. The couple glanced toward their group and quickly left, quietly putting their heads together to talk. The girl glanced over, appraising Milos and Rita could have sworn, blushed a little before the boy lightly swatted her playfully, getting a chuckle back as she poked right back at him.

Rita ignored them and walked up to the counter with a wave and smile. "Hello! It's been a while, but as promised, I brought my friends." She clapped her hands and relaxed. "And, if you don't mind, could I get my normal? The chai tea?"

The woman behind the counter chuckled quietly. "Of course." She turned toward the rest of the group and she paused for a long moment. "You three must be Milos, Alex and Suzuhah. It's a pleasure to meet you all." She bowed her head. Milos frowned, seeming to notice her lack of sight, but the others didn't seem to notice.

"Uh...hi? Sorry, who are you?" Alex glanced side long toward Rita, who blinked before smiling sheepishly.

Whoops?

The woman tapped her fingers on the counter, shifting her stance as if amused. "The apology is on myself. My name is Trisha. I am the owner of this place and have heard much about you, both from clients and from your friend here. She has much to say." Her lips twitched up in a smile as Rita put a finger up to try to stop her, only to remember too late and groan.

Suzuha laughed as Alex blinked, glancing sidelong toward her. Milos seemed amused.

Rita huffed. "My chai tea?"

The woman responded with a quiet giggle before stepping away, quickly brewing the tea together with a practiced ease, returning only a few moments later with the requested drink. Rita immediately took it, grabbed out a potion and handed it over. "Hopefully, this is enough to pay for all of us. Still haven't gotten around to getting more money. Admittedly, I spent most of it on clothing."

"Hm..." Trisha shook the potion for a moment before nodding. "A potion of restoration. This can be useful. This is more than adequate." Her head turned to face the boys as she put the potion to one side. "So, what can I get you all?"

After a moment of hesitation, Alex stepped forward, peering up at the board to the side of the woman's head. The words were written almost perfectly, and, to one side, Rita could see a ruler and stylus covered in chalk, as if Trisha only recently finished putting up a new drink on the menu.

Alex ordered a simple green tea with honey while Suzuhah asked for a latte. Milos went last, staring at the board almost nostalgically. "Many of these drinks aren't traditional to the Underlands."

"You are correct, Alertian," Trisha responded, the term, Alertian, for once having no hidden vitriol or connotation, from what Rita could tell. "I learned of some of these recipes from those who descended from the Overlands. Though a few of them are of our own brew. I think you would probably enjoy a Cinnamon Cappuccino. It's light, but delicious."

Milos seemed to think for a moment before nodding, mid nod he seemed to realize she wouldn't notice and said, "That will be fine."

The woman's expression softened as she turned away and started to work on the drinks. Not long after, she returned, the drinks almost full to the top. Nothing fancy but still smelling fantastic.

As she handed Milos his drink, she quietly, just loud enough for their group to hear, said, "Milos, you do not need to fear me or anyone in this place. We mean you and your allies no harm and apologize for those who wronged you all. I might not know the whole truth, but I know enough to trust my instinct. You are more than welcome here."

With that, she stepped back just as another customer came in and walked up. The child briefly peered over toward Milos before turning back to Trisha. "Mom and I want hot cocoa!"

"Of course." Trisha nodded to the group before helping the child, just as another woman walked in behind him, hand on his shoulder as she chuckled at his enthusiasm, only giving them a brief glance.

Milos watched for a moment, a strange expression on his face. Alex gently pulled him along to join them in relaxing on a couple couches set to one side. Rita settled back with her drink, observing the people coming and going as Suzuhah began talking about how he would come by the witches' district a lot with his mistress, though the cafe was newer.

It was nice, relaxing in a place that wasn't Lilliana's house. Rita watched with a faint smile hidden behind the lip of her cup as Milos and Alex began to relax as well.

The cafe was busy, people coming in and out quite a lot. A few Demons hurried in, glancing their way briefly. However, they seemed to turn away when Trisha spoke quietly and they nodded, shoulders releasing some tension. No one attacked them or targeted them. A few nodded toward Rita in recognition. She recognized a few and waved back.

It felt safe.

Soon enough, they left. Rita hummed along as she put her hands behind her back. "So? What do you think?"

"You asked that earlier." Milos spoke before hesitating. "But it was…"

"Nice?" Alex peered over, clearly just as relaxed as Rita. "It's been a while since we've gone out and, well, it's good to be able to walk around without people throwing hate our way, most of the time." He paused, spotting a mother hurrying away, dragging her child with concern.

At least it wasn't hatred, Rita acknowledged.

"So, do you think you two will be okay going out again?" Rita glanced toward them. "I have no doubt it might be helpful for both of you, and I know no one is going to target you guys now. Too many people know you. I really think it's time for us to, you know, find out why this place is called a sanctuary? I think it would be good for you guys."

Alex observed the surroundings before shrugging, though the way his eyes lit up, he seemed to agree with Rita. "I mean, I don't mind the idea. I'm kind of tired of being cooped up all the time. Reminds me a little too much of…" He cut himself off and shook his head, peering back toward Rita. "Anyway, thanks for showing us around, and you too, Suzuhah."

"Didn't do much, but sure." Suzuhah shrugged before lightly elbowing Milos in the side. "We still need to do a mock fight. That previous time doesn't count since it was kind of two against one."

Milos raised an eyebrow before shrugging.

"I will take that as a yes."

"If I said no, you would insist anyway."

"Good enough for me." Suzuhah chuckled before putting his hands behind his head for a long stretch. "Well, I agree with Rita, I think it's time for us to actually explore this place a bit, AFTER we drop the extra bags of clothes off back at Lillianna's place." He grinned as the others exchanged amused expressions and Rita chuckled. She honestly kind of forgot.

"You three should be safe now. Sure, there are always going to be a few annoyances, but I think a majority of people have come to terms with you all being here. They would be idiots to think you all would do anything at this point, so, relax a bit. I, for one, could use an actual vacation."

Rita snorted at that as Alex blinked and Milos shook his head with a sigh.

"Considering, I guess I have no say in this." Milos shrugged. "Knowing you all, tomorrow, you will be heading out and about anyway, so I suppose it would be best if I do the same." He peered around, watching everything quietly. "Maybe it—" he cut himself off, not elaborating.

Rita didn't ask. There were some things she didn't need to know.

"Well then. See you tomorrow." Rita chirped before darting forward. "Last one home is taking over dish duty from Ari and Leon!"

"Hey!" Alex yelped, throwing his bag of clothes over one shoulder as Rita chuckled, sprinting headlong up the stairs leading to the central plaza, giving herself that small edge.

It didn't help much, but it was amusing. Sadly, Milos didn't even try; however, he also didn't seem to mind either.

She shook her head at that. The lout was so hard to figure out sometimes, but that was fine.

# Chapter Eighteen

The next day, Alex and Rita went their own ways, leaving Ari and Leon to stay close to Milos with Suzuhah trailing behind, watching him. Alex found himself relieved to finally be able to get away for a while and do his own thing. He tried his wings on the stairs and ended up more hopping down them than anything. He frowned as he went to catch the last few and let himself leap forward, spreading his wings out. This time, they caught air and his eyes widened as he found himself drifting forward. He yelped, pulling his legs up just in time to avoid beaning a young man in the head, who ducked just in time.

"Sorry!" he shouted back, grimacing as the wind died and he stumbled to the ground, barely catching himself.

He huffed, wings snapping in and out as he peered in annoyance back to them before sighing. He would figure these things out eventually. He folded them in and continued on the way, winding through the streets of the sanctuary. Now that he could walk through, the place was huge. He spotted the inn they stayed in, a new group of people walking in, exceptionally nervous. A young woman and two male demons made more to resemble a thing he only read about...bulls or something? They were big men, but they seemed just as skittish as the woman.

He supposed there were always more people coming. He wondered how there was so much room, but he got a chance to observe the area and spotted the occasional house that clearly wasn't being used.

Maybe people didn't always stay. There was a way to leave the sanctuary, after all.

He heard movement and peered over to see Riviera walking through the streets, a bag in his arms and clearly humming along as he walked. Alex blinked, startled.

Riviera shifted his package and waved, hurrying over. "Alex, it's good to see you."

To the boy's surprise, the man pulled him into a one-armed hug. He pulled back with a grin. "Glad to see you finally out and about. I got worried after that whole trial fiasco." He paused and peered over toward the wings, appraising them. "Huh, I think this is the first time I've seen you in your Demon form."

"I mean, we haven't seen each other since the Grand duke's place." Alex gestured, relaxing slightly. "So, what are your intentions, anyway? I figured you would have left by now."

Riviera shrugged. "I mean, I don't have a throne to go back to." His expression shifted. "Don't get me wrong, I would love to go back and make some changes in this land, but not only was I one of the younger sons, I am also pretty much presumed dead." He shrugged. "That's a mess and a half to go back to and I don't think the Demons here are too keen to let me head that way either." He lowered his voice at those words. "I don't blame them, but it is a bit crass." He pulled back. "Well, I don't mean to keep you."

"I didn't have any plans." Alex shrugged.

"Then, a suggestion?" He grinned. "There is a little-known spot to the eastern side of the sanctuary, a little alcove that pokes out over the water. You might like it, there's a little waterfall near it." He winked and slipped away, humming along once more.

Alex shook his head, snorting. Some things didn't change. Riviera was the one who let him know about the little cave he finally found not that long before the events leading to this mess.

His gaze drifted in that direction, and he found his feet following the path forward. He wasn't sure exactly where he was going, but he generally knew where east was, and he had nothing better to do. He needed to get away from practicing for a bit anyway.

He wound through the streets until reaching the outskirts of the settlement. The last few houses out here were clearly on the newer side and not nearly as well developed or made. It wasn't a poor district, to be fair, since the main trade was mostly goods and services, not coin in the city, but this was probably on the…less skilled side, if he had to guess. He spotted a few children running past and noticed a woman to one side who appeared to be a seamstress, working away, her fingers wrapped in bandages.

He continued past and into a wilder area. It was quiet and he could see the land in the distance meeting the ground a good way away. He could hear the faint splash of water, different from the constant sounds of the ocean he was getting used to.

It didn't take him long before he found a thin path that led down the cliffside to a slight overhang. He slipped inside to see it was a small, dimly lit cave with light stone crystals embedded into the wall, reflecting a soft blue light around and off the faint stream to one side that poured over the edge into the ocean below.

A smile grew on his lips, reminded of the quiet times at home. He settled to one side, leaning against the wall and listening to the water trickle past, the faint hum echoing in his ears like a soft melody.

To be honest? It pretty much was like one. He hummed quietly to the song, peering out over the ocean where he could actually hear a song drifting to his ears, a strange chord of harmonies that eventually forced him to pull his attention away, beautiful and chaotic as it was.

His wings spread out to either side, flapping lightly as he peered at them.

He felt a sense of fear. If he learned how to use his wings, that meant they were closer to that future vision that Rita saw, and he was starting to wonder if that was affecting his practice.

He WANTED to learn how to fly. It seemed so freeing to be able to do it. In that brief moment where he was hovering, or not that long ago, when he was gliding, there was a strange joy that settled over him.

Alex found his attention pulled toward the entrance of the cave once more and felt his wings twitch. He hesitated before pushing himself to his feet once more. He carefully walked forward, one foot poking a little over the edge as he leaned forward. Below was a stark drop into water, a few stalagmites piercing up from the waves that crashed against rock and stone with a discordant echo. His wings fluttered again, pulling at him.

A small part of him, the side of him he was always hesitant to listen to, tugged at him, whispering in his mind.

He felt his tail lash, realizing he was drifting more and more into his Demonic side as the horns settled over his head. He went to pull his foot back when his wings flared. He felt a surge of energy, like the wind that always seemed to catch when he opened them.

With a shout and cry, he found himself tumbling out of the little alcove, wings tangling as he plummeted down toward the water below.

Panic surged through him, and he desperately tried to snap his wings outward. His memory flashed to Suzuhah flaring out his wings, beating down, tilting his wings back to glide and his mother, who slowly let them beat behind her to hover.

The rocks were getting dangerously close in the few seconds his mind had to try to come up with something.

Then he felt something tug and that song in his head screamed at him to let go.

He quickly shut his eyes just as he felt the wings surge outward on either side. Something caught and he felt something brush his leg, the sound and roar of the water close and echoing in his ears, calling to him. He opened his eyes just in time to feel the wings beat down behind him. He jerked and glanced over his shoulder, noting he wasn't moving. His legs brushed inches from the rocks, almost tearing into his trousers. The wings gently beat behind him, without much thought. They expanded out and he yelped, finding himself swooping forward. There was something both terrifying and exhilarating about what was going on.

Part of him wondered how he was supposed to get back up to the little cave, while another part wanted to continue gliding over the water that sang below him.

He found himself drifting a bit lower, fingers brushing over the waves as he was pulled along. He knew he was the one controlling his flight, he could tell, but there was something unreal about it that he couldn't put to words.

Instinct was the only way he could phrase it.

Then…he focused on his wings, trying to figure them out. He wanted to know what they were doing.

In that moment, he felt a strange disconnect and yelped as he plunged into the icy waters, thankfully a good distance away from the cliff so as not to slam into the rocky wall.

He quickly pulled himself up, letting out an annoyed breath as he got to the surface, hair plastered to his face and new clothes soaked.

"Well, THAT didn't work," he said as he peered around, wading over the water for a moment. He had to admit, it did feel somewhat refreshing, if it was cold.

He shook his head, frustrated. So he could fly...if he wasn't focusing on flying. Made TOTAL sense.

He grumbled in frustration and let out a sigh. He debated, thinking through his options on what that meant. His gaze drifted up the cliff. "Now, how do I get...?" He paused and shrugged. "I want to get back up there." He wasn't sure if it would work, but he said it with a strange determination, his voice echoing slightly over the waves that pulled at him.

As he stared up, paddling to keep himself afloat, he felt his wings expand out once more before he suddenly found himself shooting out of the water.

He knew that shouldn't be possible, but he quickly shoved the thought down as he focused on the cave, feeling the air whip past, frigid to the touch then...

"How the— how am I supposed to land?"

The words came out of his mouth just as he breached the entrance of the cave, and his wings pulled inward. He let out a screech and quickly scrabbled, catching onto the side of the rock as he once more found himself dangling over the edge. He scrambled to pull himself in, collapsing to the ground with an annoyed huff, finding himself shifting back to human form in the process.

Well, at least PART of him knew how to fly. He wasn't sure how he felt about that, other than seriously frustrated. It was learning how to be a Demon all over again.

He let out a long groan. Couldn't things be easy for once? Or at least, make some form of sense? It would be appreciated.

Soon, after a little while of catching his breath and letting his clothes dry in the safe enclosure of the little cave, he trekked back out. Hopefully, he wasn't too much like a sodden mess. He didn't want people to pay attention to him at the moment.

Thankfully, he didn't get that much attention on his way home and he quickly got changed. However, the feeling of the flight he did manage stuck with him, and he found himself pulled to the back courtyard once more.

He closed his eyes, remembering the feeling of falling and catching himself. The sensation of shooting up the cliff face to get to the cave...

The wings expanded once more, the transformation so much easier now, after all the weeks of training, both after and before they arrived. Alex let out a breath.

Okay, so, like when he was first feeling his Demon form, it was all thoughts and instinct.

Great, so...

He slowly opened his eyes. He jumped like he had been doing lately, which let him hover before. The wings snapped out, leaving him hanging in the air and he frowned.

With a nod and a deep breath, he imagined himself flying like Suzuhah. This time, he didn't let himself focus on his wings, he just allowed himself to concentrate on what Suzuhah looked like while flying, how his mom would hover in the air and shoot forward.

He kicked off, as if it was the ground, and felt his wings twitch and twist in a way that shouldn't have felt natural but did. He curved around and shot upward, coming even with the windows to the second story building. He blinked, a strange awe and delight settling over him.

He peered around. There...he wanted to go there. He spotted some night stones starting to glimmer off to one side, close to the end of the Underlands, only about a little less than a quarter of a mile from where he hovered. Then, he was heading there, wings twisting and turning and beating as if he was always able to do it.

He would have to thank Riviera later as he let out a whoop of delight.

Only to once more remember he didn't know how to stop.

The wrenching sensation in his shoulder blades and back was not one he wanted to experience again as he brought his hands up, catching on the stone, inches from his face.

Okay. He definitely still needed some practice.

He shook his head and pulled back, wincing as he shook out his hands, numb slightly from the slight impact against the stone. He had some words for the others. All that practice...and they didn't tell him to just visualize flying? They were showing him the mechanics but never once mentioned picturing oneself in flight. He grumbled to himself but decided not to mention his annoyance. Either way, he figured it out and they did help him in the end.

Still, it was going to take some time to get used to.

~ * ~

Milos peered around the streets, surprised to find no one was paying him any particular mind, just like the day before. Some still shot him glares, but most just continued about their day. He felt like just another face in the crowd, and, in a way, he was finding himself appreciating it.

He settled into a leisurely walk, quietly watching as Ari and Leon peered around. He could hear footsteps behind him, but he recognized them as Suzuhah's.

The ebb and flow of the Demonic magic around him settled a lot since his initial arrival. It was almost as if the magic was used to him, which he found a little unsettling at the same time.

Still, he wasn't going to argue about the effect. He watched quietly as people moved about, coming to and fro. Demons, humans; the mix was fascinating to watch.

He twisted his hand, staring at his palm for a moment before shaking his head and turning to Ari and Leon. "Did you find any nice places around here?"

They both exchanged a look before shrugging.

"Do you want to go back to that little park?" Suzuhah stepped forward, swinging his hands like he was his younger female form. "It's probably still quiet and clean."

Milos tilted his head back, debating before nodding. Suzuhah gestured and started leading the small group through the streets. Soon enough, they came across the same small courtyard they were in when they first arrived. It seemed someone was keeping it pristine. The grass was soft, the little stream trickled quietly through, and the tree was still growing proudly, giving slight shade from the day stones. Milos settled onto the grass as the others took seats around. No one talked, but no one needed to. He found himself leaning against the wall, closing his eyes as he listened.

Unlike at the home they were using, here, he could faintly hear quiet conversation from people walking around outside.

There was talk about dinner plans, a new game, all sorts of things.

The peace and calm felt serene after so much had already happened. He peered at his hand one more time, staring at it quietly. He still had yet to come to terms with the idea Lillianna was his aunt, that he was a Demon. He couldn't argue it at all, but his mind still kept rejecting anything about it. He hated the feeling. On one hand, he wanted to just let go, but on the other hand, he was so used to curtailing the part he always thought was just a part of being an Alertian, he no longer knew how to let go. It was as if his very being would fight back.

Even when instinct was pulled out, when Lillianna would 'attack' him, he still couldn't bring it fully out. He wasn't sure what else he was supposed to do or what he could do at this point. He heard movement and peered over, startled, as the clink of the gate sounded and opened, revealing a young woman. She froze upon seeing the little place was full of people.

"Ah, I didn't know anyone was here. Sorry."

"No need to apologize. It's not a private park," Suzuhah called from where he lay on the grass.

The woman frowned for a moment before shaking her head and stepping in, closing the door behind her. She nodded to the group, staring at Milos for only a moment longer before walking up to the tree, a faint smile on her face. In her arms was a basket that she put to one side. It was filled with gardening equipment.

She pulled out a few things and started carefully walking around the tree, humming along as she worked. Milos watched, curious.

Gardeners weren't a thing down here. The only other garden he saw was the one by the boatman that was used for food.

He watched as she hummed along. While not nearly as powerful as Alex, he could feel hints of magic from her voice. A few of the withering plants slowly started to unwither as a few more leaves sprouted from the tree.

"A druid." He spoke before he thought much about it.

The woman paused before peering back at him. "I've always used the term Nymph, though I suppose druid is perfectly fine too." She stared at him quietly. "For an Alertian, you don't seem as scary as the stories tell." She paused. "Both the old and new ones."

"He's not." Suzuhah spoke up as Ari and Leon shifted, Ari frowning slightly at the woman's words.

"It's hard to tell sometimes." The woman spoke up, fingers dancing over the bark of the tree. The long dress that hid her arms fell back to reveal patches of green curling up to the wrist hidden by a pair of gloves. Her hair, now that he was more observant, was more like a mix of vines and leaves, soft to the touch. A single bloom was settled into her hair to help pin one side back, out of the way.

"Fair." Suzuhah sat up. "Do you maintain all the gardens around here? I don't remember seeing you before."

Her smile grew as her attention drifted to Milos once more. "I only arrived recently, from what I gathered, only a week or so after the Alertian and his party."

There was no fear on her face, only relief. She turned back to Suzuhah. "I and many others that arrived after them owe their group our lives. So I have no qualm with him or you all." She nodded toward Ari and Leon, her fingers reaching up to her neck briefly. Ari's eyes widened.

"You are…"

She just smiled, but didn't respond.

Milos furrowed his brow, pushing himself to his feet. He was about the same height as the woman, who turned to him.

Milos observed her quietly before realization dawned on him. "You are one of the Demons within the Martinet's Guild. I recognize that magic."

Her smile widened even more as she nodded. "We all fled toward our homes, where we were sold from or taken from. We realized quickly that it wasn't an option and heard the Martinets were focusing on the group of people who helped free us. So, many of us took our chances and fled North. I and a few others arrived with the Aqua Wraith, lovely woman, while a few others tried different paths." Her expression grew pained. "All I can say is, thank you for freeing us and giving us that chance, even if not everyone made it."

"Then, if you were a slave—"

"I do not wear signifiers, many Demons do not." She pursed her lips, hands brushing her neck again. "They remind me too much of a past I would rather forget, and I wasn't born with them."

Ari and Leon stiffened at that, exchanging looks as Milos froze. Wasn't born with them?

"Well, enough of that, I didn't think I would get a chance to meet one of the people who helped rescue us, so thank you for that."

She glanced back at Milos, a faint smile on her face. "I think there are a few others that would love to meet you and thank you as well. After all, it was you and the other boy…Alex, I believe his name is." She stared at him for a moment longer.

Milos wasn't sure, but a part of him felt almost a little intimidated by this woman and he couldn't for the life of him figure out why. She leaned up on her tiptoes, staring curiously, her green eyes glimmering with amusement. "You are very cute, you know that?" With that, she quickly grabbed up her things and hurried away. "Ah, anyway, I'll let the others know to meet you here, bye!" she called back, quickly running out.

Milos heard an amused snort from Ari and a chuckle from Leon. Suzuhah was outright cackling.

Milos didn't realize his expression until Suzuhah called, "Your face! I WISH Rita was here. I have never seen you flabbergasted before; it's gold!"

Milos quickly adjusted his expression, pursing his lips.

Demons were…why were they all so WEIRD?


To Milos' surprise, whenever he found himself back in that little garden, just wanting to experience a little of home, he ended up meeting the young woman. The second time, she hurried away without saying a word, only to return, to Milos' startled gaze, with a young man with a long curling blue tail that was thick at the base and flared out at the end, fin-like ears and burns on his wrists where Milos could see more fins folded down, flicking occasionally as if in water. Thin lines for gills settled against his neck on either side, also somewhat damaged from what must have been a chain.

The young man's eyes lit up upon seeing him and peered at the young woman. She just smiled and nodded.

The man hurried forward and quickly swiped up Milos' hands, a bright smile on his face and a whisper of a voice saying, "Thank you."

Milos wasn't sure if the young merman spoke or not, but he heard it anyway. The fins for ears flared in delight.

"Artorios, I think that's enough." The young woman chuckled as the young man stared at Milos with what seemed like awe. "You are overwhelming him."

"You can tell?" Suzuhah called, clearly amused as he sat back, watching the whole exchange, clearly also trying to hide his own surprise. Milos hadn't been able to convince him to go elsewhere so the young man followed him today as well. At least Ari and Leon decided to do their own thing.

The woman chuckled. "It's pretty obvious."

"Never is for me. Though, I guess Demons are different. Alex always can tell as well."

Milos sent Suzuhah a strong glare, only to pause as the hands quickly pulled away. The young man stared at him and quickly bowed. "Sorry."

The young woman sighed as the man stared at Milos for another moment before suddenly darting away.

The next time, it was just the woman. She smiled before walking up to the tree, fingers dancing over it. A leaf uncurled from a dying branch, the bark becoming just that slightest bit less brittle. Milos just found himself watching, confused at how the magic he could clearly feel from her was so gentle.

Just like with Alex, the Demonic power he was so used to being a danger and something to destroy was instead used to create, it was fascinating and a small part of him found it almost beautiful. Suzuhah, as usual, was staying nearby, watching. At this point, Milos was used to the boy following him to keep half an eye on him. Ari and Leon separated to do their own things after the second day when Suzuhah mentioned he would keep an eye on Milos.

As annoyed as Milos was, he understood why they did it. Alex and Rita just gave him space as well. He was not in the mood to argue with them. Especially since Rita would often end up in the witches' district and

Alex tended to spend time with his mother when he wasn't training with his wings.

On the fourth day, she didn't come, and Milos found himself feeling a little off about it. He had no idea why. He wanted to relax in a place reminiscent of the Overlands, not be distracted, but...

Suzuha observed Milos, kicking her legs back and forth with a strangely serious expression on her face.

The next time the woman returned, clearly tired. She smiled upon seeing him and relaxed, to his surprise, next to him, fingers dancing over the grass which bloomed just that little greener than before. "So, I asked and the old keeper of the garden that used to maintain these places died not long before you all arrived. So they were all dying when I and the others arrived. I will say, this one is my favorite, even though it's the smallest. It's just peaceful." She peered up at the tree as the day stones' light danced through the leaves, faux warmth settling over them.

It was then, as they sat there, that Milos came to a quiet realization.

He didn't know the woman's name.

"Kara."

Milos blinked and peered over.

The woman didn't turn, just smiled quietly as she stared at the tree. "I never told you my name. It's Kara." She peered down at the grass once more, fingers curling between the strands as her palms settled on the ground. "Short for Karashieda, but I prefer Kara." She smiled faintly before she shook her head and pushed herself to her feet. "Artorios won't stop talking about meeting you. It's created some contention with the few that remain opposed to you and your family, but I think it's been helpful."

Suzuha hummed as if in agreement. Milos narrowed his eyes. She nodded her head toward him. "Honestly, just speaking well of the one who saved us is barely touching the surface of what many feel we owe you all for, though you might feel differently." She peered up once more. "It's so much more peaceful here, but it's also odd, not having to always be at the mercy of another. For pain to not follow your every step. Many still haven't come to terms, but each person takes their own time to recover from their paths." She tilted her head, hair brushing over her shoulder. "At least now we have a future we can hopefully influence for ourselves." With that, she quickly spun on her heels and walked away.

Suzuha watched her, a strange curious expression on her face. She almost looked like she wanted to chase after Kara but didn't. "You meet the strangest people."

"I'm starting to realize that." Milos watched her go and pushed himself to his feet. "So, about that spar."

Suzuha blinked before her grin widened and she giggled. "Yes! I've been waiting for this."

"Oh, really?"

The grin turned fox-like. "The last time with Valencia didn't count, I still want that one on one. So, edge of town?"

Milos decided not to argue, and she suddenly leapt off the seat and, in the same movement, wings expanded outward, brushing the leaves as the Vulfulas lowered their head and gestured. "Get on already."

The mix of voices echoed in Milos' ears as he shook his head and went to walk away, only to find himself wrapped in two claws, surprisingly gently, and lifted off the ground in a swoop.

Instead of fighting, he found himself just sighing in recognition as Suzuhah let out a booming laugh. Milos grabbed the talon and just simply said, "Let go."

"Sure." With that, the talons unclenched, giving Milos just enough time to swing as Suzuhah dipped downward, long neck lowering just enough for Milos to swing onto the Vulfulas' back. As he did, he briefly saw the flash of green below, standing near the door of their little garden. The woman jerked and glanced up, eyes wide in a mix of awe and wonder. Their eyes met and it was then Milos who caught that her cheeks were a bright red just as Suzuhah twisted in the air and shot away.

He shook his head and leaned low to reduce the wind that beat over him. It was so odd to feel such strong wind in the usually windless lands, but it also gave him a sense of nostalgia.

It wasn't long before they arrived to one side, the long tail curling lazily around the great creature as they bent their head down, letting him leap off with ease.

He took a few steps to resettle himself as he pulled out his sword and turned.

The Vulfulas grinned, the skin almost flaring for a brief moment as sparks settled over the oiled fur. "So, ground rules, everything goes. It ends when one of us either taps out or shouts Enough. Sounds fair?"

"Don't call out too early then." Milos felt himself relax a little, fighting was something he was definitely more used to. Unlike Alex, he didn't much mind the burn and bloodshed was sometimes necessary.

"Well then…" Suzuhah leapt, tail snapping forward. Milos jumped to one side, sword catching the teeth just as the Vulfulas snapped down, tail missing by a mere inch.

Milos spun, sword flaring out, sliding and sparking along the teeth as Suzuhah snapped their head back, just avoiding the roundhouse kick. Milos caught on a bit of fur and pushed off the shoulder, leaping up into the air as Suzuhah whipped around, wings almost catching him as he pulled his legs up.

With a sharp snap, the wings closed, shooting the Vulfulas up into the sky as lightning seared over the body, flaring forward. Milos' eyes widened and he mentally cursed, caught in the air like he was. He twisted the bolt of lightning crackling inches from his skin, causing his hair to stand on end as the metal of the chain clanked, reminding him of just how much metal was on him. As soon as he landed, he kicked off, just avoiding another crackle of lightning searing down from the sky, wings spread wide as Suzuhah curled around, tail almost connecting with their maw to form almost a moon.

Milos felt tingles run down his spine and, while usually it was concentrated, he couldn't help but find himself almost having fun as Suzuhah called out. "You dance too much!"

"Well, I have to do something when you are constantly flying," Milos called up, finding himself grinning, his steps even lighter as he shot across the path, and jumped, using a nearby rock to launch up, managing to catch Suzuhah by surprise with the leap.

Himself as well, but he quickly brushed it off as he managed to slice some fur from the side of Suzuhah's face.

"Hey! Careful there," they called, as two talons snapped out.

The sword twisted, the flat of the blade used to give Milos the opportunity to leap over.

He felt a faint surge that was immediately familiar, and a moment of panic flared through him, only for him to get distracted as the tail caught him around the ankle. He yelped as he found himself hanging upside down as Suzuhah grunted.

He kicked upward, feeling the blood rush to his head. He was not used to being upside down like this. Suzuhah let out a yelp, the tail loosening just enough for Milos to twist and wrench his leg free, falling through the sky once more.

He twisted, feeling something flare out behind him. He slammed the sword out, catching a nearby rock and holding on tight with both hands as he jammed the sword in, slowing his fall enough where he could let go and land. He wasn't sure what hit first, but he winced slightly.

"You okay?" Suzuhah called, only to yelp as Milos wrenched the sword free and twisted, spinning and throwing it up toward him.

Milos blinked, staring in pseudo surprise as the sword soared through the air. Something he KNEW shouldn't have been possible. Suzuhah twisted at the last minute, only to let out a cry of pain as it sliced the edge of the wing, piercing through the thinner membrane. Suzuhah managed to catch themselves, but they stumbled onto all fours, shaking their heads. "Enough."

Milos, who was already preparing to leap forward, paused, and finally caught his breath.

Everything ached like a nice warm-up workout, and he found himself crumbling, one knee and hand on the ground as he caught his breath.

He smelled the sharp scent of what he could only call the smell of a thunderstorm as it faded but still clung around. He glanced up as Suzuhah limped forward, holding his arm tightly. "What the hell was that at the end?" He raised his eyebrow, his gaze settling behind Milos as he frowned. "I could have sworn..." he shook his head and turned back toward Milos. "Last I checked, it's not NORMAL to be able to throw a freaking sword like an arrow shot from a bow."

"It's not." Milos stumbled to his feet and grumbled. "And now it's gone."

"It didn't go that far." Suzuhah gestured with his head. "It's right over there, I know because I can still smell my blood on it. Speaking of...

OW! You know wings hurt when they are injured, even if it is just the membrane and not the muscle."

"You said anything goes and it seems like a superficial wound from what I can tell on your human form."

Suzuhah just grumbled, but didn't argue as Milos walked over, picking up the sword. It felt so heavy in his hands, which threw him. It felt so light only moments before. Sure, he was used to his sword feeling like an extension of his arm, but it felt different during the fight. He shook his head and quickly cleaned it of the blood before storing it away. "Let's get that checked. I don't want Rita nagging me."

Suzuhah snorted, but didn't argue as he settled down. Milos pulled out what was left of his ointment, tossing it to the boy. He carefully pulled his hand away from the cut on his arm and quickly plastered it on, grimacing.

"Still going to have to get it inspected you know."

Milos just sighed, settling onto a nearby rock, the tingling of his limbs indicating he had already started a good workout.

"Also, that landing was impressive. I didn't realize how high I brought you until you forced me to let you go." Suzuhah glanced over. "How do your wrists and legs not hurt?"

Milos didn't want to admit that everything ached. "Fighting flying creatures is incredibly annoying. Thanks to the Overlands there are very few Demons and creatures that can actually fly."

Suzuhah's expression fell. "According to some books my mistress managed to get, that wasn't always the case. There used to be more, but they all died out. Not sure why." He shook his head. "But then, it feels like everything is just so—"He cut himself off.

Milos didn't respond, just sat in silence, letting himself recover for a few minutes. Whatever that was, it was over.

"So, round two?"

Milos huffed in amusement as Suzuhah's expression stretched into a cheeky grin, throwing the ointment back toward Milos. "Last time was a draw, in my opinion."

"I believe YOU were the one who called Enough?"

"For both our sakes." Suzuhah waved as he shifted one leg back.

"Because my wing is damaged at the moment, doesn't mean I still won't be a worthy challenge. Second time's the charm, after all."

Milos felt a faint grin cross his face as he pushed himself to his feet. The fights in the past were never just for 'fun'. It was either life or death or a test of some sort. It was nice to let loose and not be forced into becoming a Demon or whatever and he wasn't necessarily worried about killing Suzuhah. The creatures could take care of themselves well enough.

With that, they shot forward for round two, his short break enough to get him moving again and he wanted to move, to feel the familiar ache and burn without any worry of danger.

# Chapter Nineteen

Rita crossed her arms over her chest as she watched Suzuhah limping in with Milos a step behind, holding a badly twisted arm, hair barely held in his always way too tight chain while more burn marks criss-crossed Suzuhah's collarbone.

She didn't even need to ask, she just let out a huff, blowing some hair from her face. "Sit down, you two, over here. Now."

Suzuhah immediately sat on the couch in the sitting room, switching to her female form to shrink down a little, smiling sheepishly and attempting to appear more innocent.

It didn't work.

"What did you two do?"

"A mock fight or two."

"Or three or four or…"

Milos sharp gaze wasn't enough to stop Suzuhah from responding as Rita just glared at him before sending said expression toward Suzuhah.

"Why am I not surprised? You are SUCH a lout." She pointed straight at Milos. "Do you at least feel better now?"

Milos' confusion was very much evident. Rita rolled her eyes. "You've been annoyed the last few times you've done training, so I figured, considering you don't appear to want to throw a fit, something changed this time."

"I think it's because it was just for fun." Suzuhah shrugged, before wincing. "Admittedly, we did get a bit too rowdy in the last fight, which was why we, uh, had to stop."

"Ah-huh…" Rita's deadpan spoke volumes. "Now, sit." She gestured toward Milos, only having to tilt her head up slightly as she dug into her duffle. She pulled out two bottles as he finally listened and handed them over before quickly inspecting Suzuhah. She ignored the faint gagging as she worked, quickly fixing up a few deep cuts and resetting Suzuhah's ankle. She wasn't too fond of that, but she knew she couldn't let the little girl naturally heal like that. She wrapped it before switching to Milos who finally settled onto the couch next to Suzuhah just as she heard footsteps.

"Oh geez." She heard Alex's voice as his footsteps rang behind her. "What happened?"

"The two were louts. I mean, I know boys will be boys, but they decided it was fun to fight each other and not hold back."

Milos stiffened, as if to argue, only to slump. Suzuhah didn't bother trying.

Alex seemed to pause in his steps before letting out a faint chuckle. "I can't imagine."

"Right?" Rita inspected Milos, who was begrudgingly letting her work. "What did you do to your wrists? I swear, if you weren't Milos, I would think your entire body was shattered by something."

"I mean, he did fall from about fifty feet in the air…"

"WHAT!" Alex yelped as Rita stilled. She slowly tilted her head, glaring at Suzuhah who suddenly gulped.

"His fault, not mine."

"You were holding me upside down." Milos said simply.

Rita slowly breathed in through her nose and out once more.

"You two…" Alex's voice said it all in that moment. His next word both startled Rita and made her feel a little woozy. "Sleep."

Milos stiffened, expression almost betrayed as Suzuhah shot a glare toward Alex, shaking her head violently. "Doesn't wor—" She cut herself off, putting a hand to her head. "Holy…it's a lot stronger when it's focused on you…"

Rita watched, noting that both of them seemed to be fighting Alex's siren's call as she was going to name it and, to be frank, she did need them both to sleep. She could only imagine how strong it was on them if she was feeling a little woozy and sleepy and fighting in this state would not be good for either of them.

She dug into her pouch as Alex's expression shifted to a hesitant one, almost nervous. Thankfully, the powder she made earlier was still in the pouch. She pinched it and tossed it at Suzuhah and Milos.

The powder, combined with the siren's call finally forced both of them into a peaceful slumber as the two slumped against the couch, bodies relaxing in sleep. She let out a breath, putting the bottle back into her bag before shaking her head to wake herself up.

"Well, that was probably not the best way to do it, but they needed to sleep anyway to recover from their injuries so I suppose it will have to do." She glanced toward Alex whose pursed lips told his discomfort. "Don't worry, your voice is not controlled, they'll understand. If they get angry, I'll take the blame." Rita shrugged. "And let them be angry, it's their own fault for getting that injured before having someone check their injuries."

Her words seemed to be enough as she noticed Alex's tense shoulders relaxing. "Yeah, I guess." He turned to her. "I really do wish I knew how to control this but…" He put a hand to his throat, clearly conflicted. "It seems like I'm not, well, at the point where I can do anything about it, at least, according to Mom."

Rita shrugged. "Then don't worry about it. Honestly? You've only used it to help and, come on, you only just learned you can do it. Stop worrying already. I mean, look, when focused on Suzuhah and Milos they were still able to fight it. It's not absolute or anything, it's a suggestion and last I checked, our crew tend to ignore suggestions at the best of times."

Alex blinked before letting out a snort. Rita grinned before turning back to the duo. She heard a faint groan as she told Alex to hold Milos' arm steady as she worked. "Well, hope he's okay with a splint for a while." She grumbled. "Thankfully, I've been talking to the Demons around here. Supposedly, you all heal much faster than normal, but this is still probably going to take two or three weeks. The darn lout."

Alex just smiled tiredly. "Well, it's quicker if we knew what would make it easier for him to heal, like water for me."

"I guess we could ask Lillianna." Rita pushed herself to her feet. "Still, that should do it for now. I will say, I'm a little envious, a break like that to his wrists and arm would take me months to heal. Alas, I am only human."

"Now you are laying it on thick."

Rita chuckled but couldn't help feeling a hint of pain at the thought. She was able to play it off as a joke, but it wasn't, really. She wasn't like the boys. She couldn't heal quickly or anything. She wasn't a Demon and, for the first time in her entire life, a small part of her wished she was.

However, she quickly threw the thought off, remembering the pain both Alex and Milos had to go through for their Demonic sides. Quickly, it helped her settle back, reminding her it was alright to just be normal sometimes. Less to deal with in that case. "Isn't that my job?" she joked back as she realized Alex was starting to give her a worried look, considering how long it took her to reply. She pushed herself to her feet, brushing down her skirt. "All joking aside. They should be fine now. I just wonder how long the sleep will last." She put a finger to her lips. "Considering they got hit with both your siren voice and my sleep powder." Rita didn't miss Alex's wince and she made a mental note but continued, "I wonder if you could possibly stop Milos from hurting himself more until he heals."

"I'm some sort of Siren, not a miracle worker."

"Ah, true." Rita chuckled before clicking her tongue. "Not gonna lie, I wish I could just pick and choose when I see the future. I would love to see if he actually listens to us and lets himself heal."

Alex sent her a sympathetic look as he settled to one side of the living room they had taken up. From what she could gather, it healed a lot of conversations so far, between Alex and his mother and between Milos and Lillianna. She was okay with it being a simple fix-up in her case.

"Ugh…that sucked," Suzuhah grumbled, startling the two of them.

"That was fast," Alex muttered as Rita nodded.

Suzuha rubbed her eyes as she pushed herself up. "I told you; it usually doesn't work on us. Seriously, though, if that is an inkling of what sirens were like in the past, I'm glad I was born now, though that sleeping powder certainly didn't help matters. I only woke up so quickly because of what I am." She paused. "I was also already tired, which didn't help."

Alex snorted at that as Rita chuckled, peering over to her. "Hey, Suzuha? Did your mistress ever tell you how to see future visions?"

The light-hearted tone and smile faded as Suzuha stared at her before shrugging. "She only said that she usually couldn't control it, but, supposedly, powerful seers can. Something about utilizing the magic that usually dwells within the Underlands, probably thanks to Demons, and meditating. I mean, obviously, there's more to it or my mistress would have been able to do it, but…" Suzuha paused and shook her head.

Rita leaned back, thoughtful. She wasn't a meditator, but she vaguely remembered her teacher mentioning something like that. A vague memory flashed in her mind as she was brewing a potion, sweat pouring down her brow as her teacher stood to one side, watching, her old, wizened smile filled with amusement as she spoke.

"Anyone can brew a potion, but to be able to brew a potion and stay calm when there are distractions is a much harder technique. Imagine me jabbering away while you are trying to sleep or relax. A good seer can tune out what's around them and focus on what they are doing, the magic of the potion. Maybe the magic around them, though most joke about that. Ah, speaking of, I met this wonderful young man today, mentioned he was interested in becoming a prophet, I wonder if he had the talent for it. Though it usually is from a line of people, that's not always the case. Oh, am I significantly distracting you? Well, I guess we have work to do, you forgot the eldritch root."

Rita cursed in the memory, having sufficiently been distracted by the ongoing talking. The woman sighed, her smile falling. "Rita. This is important. If you ever want to be a seer, to meet the Overseer, then you need to know how to calm your mind, ignore what's going on around you and concentrate. I know, for a fact, that it will be important for you in the future. You need to know how to control yourself, in order to control your future."

Rita pulled herself from the memory, blinking as realization dawned on her. "She knew… She REALLY knew," she whispered quietly, feeling a sudden sense of overwhelming pain, and a hint of rage for a brief moment. "She could see the future too."

"She?"

"My teacher." Rita snapped, before realizing and quickly pulling back. "Ah, don't worry about it." She pursed her lips, staring at the fire stone flickering to one side. "I just remembered something from a long time ago, a couple months now. It was such a small memory that I'm surprised I remembered, but I think Suzuha's correct. At least in attempting to control the future visions." She pursed her lips. "But if they can see the future, then why don't they try to change it?"

"Not everyone has the strength or ability to change what they can see," Suzuha said softly, catching Rita's attention. "Just because you know of a future doesn't mean you know how it happens, or how you can change it, or if you will want to." She shook her head, fingers curling around an inch above the bandage on her arm. "My mistress knew her fate, but no matter how she struggled, she couldn't find a way out. That's why I don't know how to..." she cut herself off, peering toward Rita. "From what I've gathered, you've changed many future visions you've seen already, and I can only wonder...how? Why is it that you can change your own fate?"

Rita stiffened as Alex stayed silent, eyes wide in surprise. Rita suddenly wished she was Milos, sleeping peacefully at the words. "I just do what I can." She shrugged, barely stopping her voice from shaking. "I don't know what to say."

Suzuha pursed her lips before letting out a sigh. "I know. I just can't help but wonder." She shook her head before slumping back down. "I think I need to go back to sleep, it's been a long, long day."

Rita watched her settle against Milos once more. Rita felt Alex's gaze on her and spun, forcing a smile on her lips. "Let's let them rest, we'll figure out what to do later." With that, she slipped around Alex, who didn't try to stop her, worry on his face. She hurried away, thoughts churning.

She shoved them all away. They weren't necessary or wanted, so she was just going to ignore them. She soon found herself in her room once more, the door closed with a snap and settling on her bed. She stared at the floor, tracing over the soft rug under her feet.

She was never necessarily GOOD at taking a deep breath and not concentrating on some tasks. Meditation wasn't really her thing, but she couldn't help but remember the future vision she saw when they first arrived. Of the lands above crumbling into the lands below, destruction everywhere. The vision where there was nothing happening.

She wanted to have more control over what she saw, even just a little. She remembered the feeling, having paid attention to it the last time it happened. She knew it would take some time, but she had her own training to do.

She wasn't going to be left behind by the others, she had her own job to do to keep them safe because they were family. She settled on that thought, a faint smile crossing her lips. She could finally acknowledge it. They were definitely more than friends; they were the family she lost and she was going to make sure she didn't lose her family again.

If that meant doing something she was never able to do before? Then she would at least try.

She wasn't sure where she got the incentive to dive in headfirst like she was, but she wasn't going to argue with the results.

She closed her eyes and settled down. She remembered her teacher's words on how to meditate, focusing on everything around her and slowly tuning it out until it was just the bed under her, and immediately her attention was broken by nearby conversation as Ari and Leon passed quietly by.

This was going to be a long evening.

# Chapter Twenty

Alex watched. His mind flickered briefly to his mom, and he let out a sigh. She was always so busy lately. Sure, she was able to stay with him for a little while but just recently she told him she had got a mission from Lilliana to check some odd goings-on to the south. He missed her already, which in some ways felt weird and in others felt normal. He heard movement and peered up as Milos awoke, twitching only slightly before he pushed himself upward, shifting Suzuha, who slumped onto the arm of the chair, but didn't wake. Milos pushed a palm into his face, wincing as he tried to bring up the other one.

"Yeah, Rita said it would take time to heal. How are you feeling?"

Milos blinked before his gaze snapped to Alex, annoyance crossing his face. "Was that necessary?"

Alex winced, smiling sheepishly as he pushed his fingers together awkwardly. "It wasn't intentional, it just kind of slipped out?" His words went upward in a slight squeak at the end and he quickly cleared his throat. "Look, we both know you needed it. I think you've been too stressed lately, so…"

Milos didn't argue, letting his arm relax back onto his leg. "I suppose you aren't wrong." He peered toward the fire stone for a moment.

"You have been calmer the last few times I've seen you, and you enjoyed yourself today, even if it was a little…" Alex brought a hand up, doing a so-so motion, unsure what word to use. "You get the idea."

Milos shrugged, not arguing.

After a moment of silence, Alex pushed himself to his feet, catching the man's attention. "Well, I'm glad to see you are feeling a little better. However, you better be careful with that, and maybe talk to Lillianna to figure out how to help the healing process." He paused. "There are, after all, some benefits to being part Demon."

Milos clicked his tongue, but his attention did shift to the arm now securely tucked into a sling. "If you say so."

"I think I have a right to say this, considering." He pointed toward Milos. "And you know that."

Milos winced, quickly trying to hide it by pushing himself to his feet.

Alex shook his head and gestured toward Milos. The man conceded after a moment, following along with a heavy sigh. Alex led them back out the door they came through not that long prior. The sunstones were beginning to set, so he knew dinner would be coming soon, but he figured he could catch Lillianna still at the main hall. He walked down the path, followed begrudgingly by Milos. The guards gave them a nod, but didn't seem to respond otherwise, clearly used to the group coming and going at this point.

Alex was relieved at that, relaxing as they headed past the gates and, not long after, into the main plaza. It was much quieter at this time of day, but there were still figures walking about. They glanced in Alex's and Milos' way but paid no attention beyond that. Hurrying up the steps, Alex stopped at the guards.

"Business?"

"I wanted to speak with Lillianna."

"She is busy at the moment. Unless it is urgent, we can convey the message."

"I had a question regarding her Demonic heritage." Alex gestured.

The guard shook his head and sighed. "Unfortunately, that is not seen as 'urgent'. Not knowing how being a Demon works is not qualified as an urgent matter, though it can be situational and problematic." His gaze flitted between the two of them before settling on Milos, spotting the splint, but not making a comment. "She will be out in about a half hour. If you want to wait, you can wait here."

Alex debated for a moment before shrugging and settling against the wall to one side.

"Is this necessary?"

"We wouldn't be doing this if I didn't think it was. It's for your own good anyway. Suzuha once told me we have to be careful regarding our healing when we are injured. We need to know what can boost your healing before we actually do it, so you don't accidentally heal. It shouldn't be an issue, but more just to make sure there are no complications. I guess that's the word."

Milos grunted, but didn't argue, settling down against the wall, not sitting, but leaning against his good side instead.

Alex chuckled, watching quietly as people came and went. He didn't see any of the council, which seemed strange to him, but he didn't mind. To be honest, most of them kind of made him feel weird. Not that they were bad, but he wasn't used to the amount of magic or whatever they let off, so it was a relief when they weren't nearby.

Thankfully, it didn't take long before the doors opened to reveal Lillianna. She took two steps before suddenly coming to a stop. Barely a second later, she was next to Milos and Alex had to blink to confirm she didn't teleport herself.

"What happened?" She knelt down, inspecting his arm like a worried mother. "How did you get hurt?"

"He was having a mock fight." Alex glanced side long toward Milos. "Suzuha and Milos didn't hold back. They got a little two rowdy and weren't paying attention."

"I'm fine."

"The arm is broken in two places."

Wait, two? Alex did a double-take as Milos stiffened, wincing in the process. "Huh? How did…?"

"The way the magic is wrapped around the arm," Lillianna said simply. "It's something I learned a long time ago, not something that can be taught." She leaned back, glancing side long between them. "I'm guessing that friend of yours, Rita, helped bandage you up? She is good." She reached a hand forward, splaying her fingers over the arm. "Hm, I think a little bit of light will do the trick." She smiled faintly. "When the day stones rise tomorrow, head toward the edge of town and rest against the wall closest to the day stones, it might feel a bit overwhelming, but you'll be surprised how helpful it can be."

She pushed herself to her feet, reaching a hand down and, to both Milos and Alex's surprise, hauled Milos up from under the arm. He stumbled to his feet, leaning against her for a moment before shifting to straighten himself.

"I will at least ask, how badly did Suzuha come out?"

Alex went to speak, only to stop as Milos shrugged, seeming a little flustered, which caught Alex's attention more than the question. Milos never got flustered and a small part of him was grateful Rita wasn't here. She would never stop nagging Milos about it.

After a moment, Milos recollected himself and spoke. "I did damage his wing." He paused, as if debating before continuing, almost hesitant.

Alex stared, trying not to at the same time. Milos being hesitant was not something he was used to.

"I am aware of the strength of Demons, is there something different about Demons of the first in that regard? They aren't talked about much."

"Very." Lillianna gestured and began walking back toward their home. Alex quickly scurried after as Milos hurried down the stairs. "Demons of the first are some of the oldest known Demons in recorded history and many believe them to BE the oldest. They contain powerful magic that many believe to be the ancestor of most Demons. Though I am not so certain on that saying. The strength of our kind has dwindled since ancient days, much like the sirens of old." At that, she gestured toward Alex before continuing, "However, we still maintain many of the skills of those times. We are incredibly attuned to the natural surroundings and can use them to our advantage for great speed and strength and, as you can recall, there is also our commanding scream, very different from the Siren's call. Some have the ability to read the minds of willing creatures, a rarer few can read those unwilling." She gestured toward the guards as they approached the house once more. The two quickly opened the doors and she stepped inside. Alex didn't have to turn to tell that Milos' expression was tense at best and, more than likely, completely closed off.

Lillianna stopped as the doors closed behind them. She seemed to observe the place for a moment before letting out a breath. "There is a reason our line was the one that married into the human Alertian line for so many generations. As you recall, many Demon Human children do not survive birth. That is usually due to the conflicting nature of humans and Demons, but a powerful Demonic blood will often overcome the limitations of human blood. Though, not even that is completely fool-proof." She paused, shaking her head. "However, I believe that is not what we were talking about." She turned to them. "That is why I wanted to help you pull out your Demonic side while we can. The fact that you've managed to suppress it for so long shows an incredibly strong will, but it WILL break through eventually and if you can't control it, you might hurt those important to you without realizing."

Alex stiffened at that, startled. Sure, it happened in the past and she wasn't wrong, but being told, to your face, that it was the case felt different.

"I control it just fine," Milos cut in, voice cold.

"If you could, then you would not be asking the question." Lillianna spoke simply, staring at him impassively.

Milos shifted slightly as Alex watched, not sure how to react to the situation. He almost felt like he was cutting into something that should be private. He quietly slipped backward a few steps, glad neither had really noticed him do so.

"It was a simple question, not one that held any implication."

"If you truly believed that you would not be getting defensive." Lillianna gestured. "I am not blaming or berating you, I am REMINDING you of the implications. You have been suppressing it so long, you don't know how to let go, but we need to find a— "

"That is…"

"Not necessary." Alex jumped as a young girl's voice spoke up.

He jerked, glancing toward the living room where Suzuha peeked her head out. "You guys were loud, and I was just waking up." She walked out, staring at them as if she wasn't a young child at the moment. "If I am right, forcing him like this isn't going to help. He will let go when he feels ready." Her gaze flicked to Milos. "When he can relax and not feel the pressure of training."

Lillianna stiffened, a realization dawning on her. For a brief moment, so brief, Alex was sure he would have missed it if he wasn't staring right at her, she seemed horrified. It just as quickly vanished, replaced by a rather impassive expression. "I see." The words were curt, but a little strangled. "I suppose you are correct." She nodded toward Milos. "I suppose I was a bit harsh on you of late. I believe that was mostly out of a sense of worry and understanding on my end. Demons are not known to be patient, our instincts often lead us more than our thoughts, but that often has its downsides too. While our instincts are always spot on, they aren't always the correct course of action." She took a deep breath and let it out, glancing between the group. "And yet, humans are often too patient, the irony of their shorter lives and our much longer ones is not lost to me." She turned on her heels. "Either way, Milos, as soon as the day stones light tomorrow, head toward the edge of town like I said, let your instinct guide you, it'll tell you what to do. Heal up your arm as best as you can so that you do not need to worry." With that, she headed upstairs, quickly leaving their sight.

Suzuha smiled quietly, walking over. "Did that help?"

Milos just gave her a look while Alex chuckled weakly, though he couldn't help but find himself a bit confused. "Did Lillianna not know? Or realize?"

"She did." Suzuha said, leaning back a little to stare upward. "It's just that, her worry was clouding her judgement. She needed a reminder more than anything that she was being too hard on us, on Milos in particular. That's all. Sometimes a reminder is all one needs when their own bias and concerns overshadow their more rational thoughts."

Alex pursed his lips but didn't argue, understanding where Suzuha was coming from.

It certainly answered some questions, but it also felt like it added so many more.

"Well, I think I'm good for tonight." Alex peered towards Milos. "Maybe you should get some rest." He paused as his stomach growled and he smiled sheepishly. "After we have dinner."

Suzuha giggled at that as Milos just shook his head, seeming to relax the slightest bit. It was enough for Alex.

# Chapter Twenty-One

Milos stepped out the back door, the night stones just starting to vanish as he walked past the little makeshift garden. It wasn't long until he found himself at the edge of town, glancing toward the nearest day stone a couple of feet above. The ones down here were usually much more faded than the ones above. It made sense though, they were connected to the light of day. It certainly helped to be able to at least have a better idea of timing, but he could only wonder how they existed considering just how thin the layer between the Overlands and the Underlands were and the nature of the Overlands.

He shook his head, feeling a hint of warmth as the first rays of light slithered from the stones, starting to beam down. He settled against the wall, underneath the nearest one and found himself resting on the ground, leaning his head back, metal clanking against rock. He relaxed, watching as the day stones slowly started to glow warmer and warmer and felt himself close his eyes. He wasn't sure why he listened, why he was doing this, but a small part of him wanted to know, because healing always helped, but partially because he found himself wondering if this was part of the strength of his Demonic side. Alex used water for strength and recovery, was it truly warmth and sunlight that did the same for Demons of the first? Why? Especially when Demons have always lived in the Underlands.

The way Suzuhah spoke yesterday, was so certain that he would release his Demonic form if he was relaxed. She knew something he didn't, both Lillianna and Suzuhah did. It bothered him.

He thought through the fight from the day before, the sword, the landing…he shook his head before letting it practically slam backward. The chain dug into the back of his head as he tilted it back, peering upward. Did he WANT the Demonic side to be let loose?

The question, which was once very solid and easy, NO, was now much more uncertain. She was correct. Holding it in wasn't going to help anyone, but letting it go was— he couldn't do it. Everything in him rebelled.

He focused inward, feeling the warmth settle over him. The day stones didn't often give warmth, just light, but here, it felt like a soft cushion or blanket.

A tiny part of him immediately recoiled, but the rest settled in, finding himself relaxing against the stone.

It was a half sleep. He was aware and awake, but at the same time, it was a rest that felt so much like a sought-after nap after a long day. He found it weird, since he just woke up, but at the same time, he didn't.

It was as if he was a cat, and the thought seemed just that little bit funny to him. He hadn't seen one of the furry creatures since before he descended. Strange, considering all the dark spaces they tended to get into.

He didn't realize he was shifting until he felt a faint tug on his splint, pulling lightly at his neck. Reaching a hand up, he untied it, feeling the wrap drop onto his lap as he stared down, startled.

The day stones' light settled over the arm, almost too warm through the bandages and he quickly found himself untying them. Rita could yell at him later, but he was used to tuning her out.

As he unraveled the last piece, he stared at the once bruised and damaged arm.

It was lightly bruised, and still ached, but he felt the pain lessen as he sat there, just like Lillianna said. The warmth was there as well, just subdued. He wasn't sure how much time passed, but eventually, he heard the faint sounds of footsteps.

Looking ahead, he spotted Alex settle down in front of him, faintly smiling. "I figured I would find you out here. Rita's going to be so annoyed with you." His gaze flicked to the arm. "Feeling better?"

Milos didn't want to admit it. Knew admitting it would confirm to him the side he would rather not, but he still found himself nodding. Alex's smile was faint as he settled beside Milos, peering out over the city. "So, light huh? You heal with the light of the day stones?"

Milos pursed his lips, lightly feeling over his arm. Milos, with his limited medical knowledge, could feel it was healed greatly from yesterday. The damage that would usually take months to heal was gone in a few hours of relaxation. Something he rarely found time to do before he descended.

He paused at that. He always healed incredibly fast, compared to the others. Where he lived, it was usually filled with sunlight and when he could, he would often step out and try to get as much as he could while avoiding the others. He just put it off to being an Alertian and didn't look any deeper, but he probably should have. If Alertians had Demon blood, that meant the ones who took him in did too.

No wonder people would always look at their line in wonder and awe. To have the aspects of Demons without BEING Demons was thought to be unique and unheard of.

Clearly, it wasn't unique.

If he knew more about this, if it was a thing he was raised with, what would it have been like? What if he hadn't left that day? What if they hadn't been found?

He shook the thought off. He should have gotten up, but he felt no inclination at the moment.

A faint hum reached his ears, and he glanced over. Alex hummed along to some tune, relaxed. He could tell the hum had some siren properties, just like always, but he didn't feel annoyed at it, it was almost comforting, a lullaby.

He relaxed against the wall, peering out once more. The silence and quiet humming enveloped the two and he felt his tense muscles relax. The hum, the light, the warmth, the sheer calm... it was something he hadn't felt in some time. He could feel a thrumming under his skin, could feel a coolness settling over parts, like a comforting embrace and felt a pressure on his back as something settled against his leg. It felt safe. Then it all stopped as a grumbling sound reached his ears. Milos was NOT going to admit that it might have been him.

Alex blinked out of surprise before chuckling. With a single movement, he pushed himself to his feet and turned to Milos, only to pause. His gaze flicked to Milos' side as the pressure against Milos' back faded. Milos pushed himself to his feet, the coolness that wrapped around him receding, as if tugged away. Strange, he felt comfortable for the first time in a while, like he wasn't trying to hold anything back or be someone else. He didn't necessarily remember letting anything go, but now he suddenly felt a heaviness in his chest.

"I could have sworn…" He frowned, before shaking his head. "Well, I guess it's probably lunch time. I could do with a good snack, you?"

They headed back, grabbing some lunch to a grinning Rita's amusement, followed by annoyance, followed by utter confusion.

She grumbled as she pulled away from inspecting his arm, shaking her head. She didn't elaborate and eventually pulled Alex aside to join her in going to the witch's district, leaving Milos to himself.

It wasn't long before he found himself heading toward the familiar garden. He lightly opened the gates, hearing a quiet conversation from the other side. He peered through, spotting a familiar visage standing in front of the tree. It was as if she was talking to the branches, palm lightly pressed against the bark.

She seemed to pause before peering over her shoulder, long hair brushing her collarbone. Their eyes met as a smile crossed her lips. She turned and gestured. "You can come in, no one's going to bite." She chuckled. "It's good to see you again, Milos. How did yesterday go?"

Milos hesitated before finding himself stepping inside, letting the gate swing closed behind him.

He didn't say anything, and she seemed fine with it, turning back around. "Considering you are walking around and perfectly fine, I'm going to assume you are alright. I will say, I was startled when I saw that creature take off out of nowhere. It's not something I'm used to witnessing. I believe it was called a Vulfulas?" She shook her head, hand pressed to the tree once more. "It was…there is always something to watch with you and I find myself awed, I suppose, every time." She dropped the hand to her side and turned fully to face him, once more smiling softly. "Do you want to join me for a bit? I only just arrived not long before you."

Milos shrugged, but didn't feel like he wanted to argue, settling down against the wall, quietly watching as she worked. They settled back in silence, but it was a comforting one, similar and yet different to when it was him and Alex. This time, he didn't feel that change, the day stones much farther away and the hum no longer a coaxing comfort.

He found himself staring at her quietly. It seemed like this was natural to her, taking care of what little nature managed to blossom down here, and he found himself somewhat captivated.

He shook it off. He was observing a Demon, just like when he observed Alex or Lillianna, nothing more.

So why did he keep coming back here? He understood why she came back, but at the same time, a small part of him didn't.

He quickly squashed the questions down, feeling over his arm like Rita did before, quietly marveling at the healing. He supposed that was one of the few benefits from this curse of his.

"Will you be here tomorrow?"

Milos jerked, glancing up as Kara squatted in front of him, pulling a piece of hair behind her ear. She wasn't super close, but close enough to thoroughly startle him that he didn't notice her approach.

She stared at him quietly and he found himself shrugging. She chuckled and pushed herself to her feet. "Artorius said he wanted you to meet a few of the others, so I figured I could bring a few more people, but I also figured I should ask you first. Would that be alright?"

"I'm not interested." Milos shook his head.

"I figured." Her expression softened. "Gratitude isn't the easiest thing to accept, it's sometimes difficult even to give it." She shifted back, dress swaying gently against the leather boots as she brushed it down. "But I think you should still meet them. Maybe not here, but I think you should come to our section of town." She paused and then shook her head. "You know? Never mind. As much as they might wish to thank you, advocating for you is more than enough. Sorry I asked." She peered toward the gate for a moment, debating. "I do hope, however, that you will continue to meet me here. I promise, I won't tell the others. I'll tell Artorius to stay quiet about it. I know he will."

Milos felt himself relax at that as she nodded to him and said, "I'll see you tomorrow then?"

The words were almost hopeful, and he found himself actually opening his mouth to respond, startled by the certainty in his voice. "Of course."

The smile he received was as bright as the day stone he was up against only an hour before, filled with warmth. She quickly waved and left, almost darting out the gate. Milos shook his head.

So weird. Why was he acting like this? This place was getting to him.

~ * ~

The next day, he found himself back in that little garden, staring up at the day stones high above as he settled into the grass, the little stream gurgled and hummed nearby, passing through the area before disappearing underground. The creak of the gate caught his attention, and he turned as Kara stepped in, quietly closing the gate behind her before turning.

She blinked before smiling brightly upon spotting him. The basket hung over her arm, covered in a white blanket. She walked over, brushing her dress to the side before settling next to him, placing the basket between them. "I'm glad you came." She spoke, brushing a flower twined through her hair— his thoughts cut off as he realized it was part of her hair, the stem curling back to mingle in with other longer strands.

Observing her more closely, he noticed the flowers all curled up in her hair, white and pale blues like the flowers of the Underlands, the ones Rita would sometimes talk about.

"Hm?"

Milos' gaze flicked to meet hers, realizing he hadn't responded. There was a glimmer there, as if she knew well enough what caught his attention. "I did say I would come." He finally spoke up, getting an amused chuckle in return.

"You certainly did." She reached down, tugging off the white blanket to reveal what seemed to be food. "I figured you would, so I made us some lunch. A little picnic, or at least, that's the word I've heard from Overlanders while in Raynout." Her expression grew distant for a moment before she shook her head. "The idea always sounded nice. Relaxing in a park full of life, enjoying a meal with someone impor…" She cut herself off before continuing, her cheeks a little pink. "A friend."

Milos raised an eyebrow. He certainly heard of picnics before, but he never went on one. Too busy with training and…he pushed the subsequent memories away, nodding his head.

She seemed to perk up, laying the blanket down before doling out the food. "I wasn't really sure what you liked, so I made a bunch of different things. Hope you don't mind."

Laid over the blanket were a variety of items, from sandwiches to pastries to salads. He raised an eyebrow. "Is that meat?"

She blinked and nodded; amusement hinted in her voice. "While we don't typically eat meat, we are aware it's important for others, so we don't mind making it." She picked up a sandwich that seemed to be more jam than bread. "This is my favorite, while not many fruits thrive down here, there are a few, one of which is this mableberry. It's a hardy fruit that doesn't need much light, but it has a tangy sweetness that I have just come to love. Here, try some." She picked up another sandwich, this time more carefully filled with the jam before handing it to Milos.

Milos hesitantly took it. He hadn't heard of that fruit before and while he felt uneasy, he took a bite anyways.

To his surprise, and quiet amusement, the burst of flavor was exactly as she described, and he soon found himself taking another bite. When he glanced over, the beaming expression caught him as he noticed a long line of white flowers settling over her shoulder, one he knew originally was more like vines. He stared for only a moment, remembering having read about that. How dryads were able to reflect not only their own well-being, but of the earth around them through their appearance. She dug into her own sandwich with relish, a little of the jam smearing onto her face. She quickly wiped it away with her thumb, a bit of pink on her cheeks as she tried and failed to eat a bit more carefully after that.

They sat in silence while they ate. Milos hesitantly let himself try a few of the items in the basket. He kept expecting something, poison, metal shards…he wasn't sure. But it never happened, and, with each bite, he grew more relaxed.

Soon enough, they finished. Kara placed the blanket back into her basket before staring up at the tree in the middle that Milos could acknowledge grew quite a bit since they all arrived.

"Did you have a favorite?" Her words were soft, hesitant and Milos found himself turning back to her, noticing she wasn't watching him, only the tree. Yet he knew the question was directed toward him.

He debated for a long time, longer than he knew was appropriate, before finally saying, "The mableberry."

She blinked, clearly startled, before turning to him. "You sure?"

He nodded. "It was unexpected, but I do want more."

Her hair was now more flowers than anything, the delight obvious as she clapped her hands with a bright smile. "I'll make sure to make more then!" She popped to her feet with a bit more zest than was usual for her, humming a faint tune as she did. "Thanks. I had fun." She paused, peering up toward the day stones. "I have to go, but let's keep meeting here, alright?" She turned to him. "Maybe, in time, you can come over to my place." Her cheeks bloomed a dark pink, almost red as she stuttered out. "I mean, if you want. But you know what? Never mind." She cleared her throat, the redness fading as she relaxed. "I'm more comfortable here anyway so, let's just keep meeting here, if that's fine with you."

He only hesitated for a moment, parsing through her words and actions, before nodding. She quickly nodded back and hurried away, the gate creaking as she left.

Milos watched her go before shaking his head.

What a strange woman...

# Chapter Twenty-Two

Milos found himself pulled back to that little garden almost every day after that. Every time he found himself getting frustrated or scared by Lillianna's tutelage, he was there and so was she. Sometimes, they would just sit on the grass in silence, enjoying the other's company. Other times, she would bring food, and they would have what Milos tentatively called a picnic together. It was the quiet moments that helped Milos to relax. It was simple, natural, and, in that way, it made him wonder why he felt so comfortable.

Milos tilted his head back, peering up at the day stones as Kara brushed her dress forward to sit beside him. "You are thinking of something." It wasn't spoken like a question.

Milos debated for a moment before glancing toward her. "Why do you meet with me?" She seemed startled and confused; hand paused as she reached for the picnic basket. He continued, "I know you said I, and the others, helped you all escape, but you have all returned the favor and you have your own life, your own home. What is your reason for coming back to meet with me?"

She stared forward for a moment, her face carefully blank before she shrugged, pulling away from the basket to lightly feel over the grass between them. "Because I feel comfortable here." She spoke quietly. "I feel grounded, like I can be me. I don't need to talk if I don't wish, I don't need to do anything if I don't want. I can just be me." She tilted her head up, staring up at the tree. "At first, I wasn't sure, but soon, I realized I was right, all that time ago when you freed us. You are a gentle soul. Someone I find myself feeling safe with. Even though you are an Alertian, you don't look at me any different, which is a strange feeling." She turned to him. "It's curious, I was always told to be afraid of Alertians, but while I can feel strength from you, I don't feel anything that makes me want to run. You feel sturdy, like a tree that has grown even through the darkness of the Underlands…like this little one." She turned back to the tree. "So, I come back here, because I want to know more, to relax and learn more about you. I want to be in your presence in a place both of us appreciate. Nothing more."

Milos watched as a hint of pink flushed over her cheeks and she quickly turned away.

"Uh, anyway, I brought more jam. I figured you could give some to your friends and all." She quickly rummaged in her basket and by the time she turned to him, the pink was gone, replaced with a smile.

He nodded, gently taking it from her, thinking over her words. He wasn't sure how to feel or what to even think, so instead, he said, "Thank you."

She seemed to understand the extra meaning behind the words, both for the answer and for the gift as she nodded, the smile turning warm and gentle. After, the two just relaxed, listening to the occasional quiet chatter from outside and the faint bubbling of the stream.

He thought over her words. He didn't look at her any differently. He supposed that was true, Demon, human; He was so used to both that their features were not a bother to him. They were beings. Kara reminded him a lot of Alex, but, in a way, she also felt so different from him in her mannerisms and tone. Milos could even acknowledge that he often found himself watching her. Her graceful movements and the occasional white flower petal that would drift down from her blooming hair.

He relaxed, taking a deep breath. He also felt comfortable here, just like she did, and in a way, knowing she was comfortable with him made him feel warm. He wouldn't mind meeting her more often, he decided, even though he knew he had subconsciously already made the decision. He didn't push or pry about her home or where she lived. It wasn't his business.

"I will be here every afternoon." He spoke before even really thinking about it.

He saw her turn towards him, surprised before she seemed to relax. "Then I will make sure I am here as well."

He nodded and they once more lapsed into silence, this time unbroken and calm. He heard shuffling before something fell onto his shoulder. He stiffened before glancing side long. Kara's head rested against his shoulder-blade, her eyes were closed as she hummed a quiet little tune. The soft flower petals pressed against his skin, the aroma a pleasant mix that he couldn't quite describe. He noted, with surprise, that the part he always kept strained seemed to uncoil, the tension fading. He slowly relaxed, letting her rest there as he turned his attention back to the tree and the magic curling around them and the city.

# Chapter Twenty-Three

Days passed into weeks as the group settled into life at the Sanctuary. Rita continued to visit the witches' district while Alex interacted with his mother and Riviera, slowly growing more and more used to following his instincts, his flight expanding minute by minute, much to his delight. Suzuhah occasionally would have mock battles with Milos and, other times, be found just walking through town, observing the folk and occasionally playing the innocent prank or two. Milos soon almost daily found himself with Kara, the two chatting or relaxing in silence. He would bring some drinks with him from Ari, who simply winked at him with amusement and seeming knowing and Kara would bring a variety of different foods. Lillianna no longer pushed Milos, but she did quietly watch and observe, often giving out pointers or outright directing certain training, but never as intensely. However, soon, they all started to notice how busy she was and the strange worry settling over her as the weeks turned into a month.

Ari and Leon settled into life in the town, and, to Milos' surprise and hidden happiness, Ari was dressing in something other than the plain rags she always wore, a much more lady-like appearance more common with the noblewoman of the Underlands. It would certainly explain why tea was starting to become her drink of choice and what she would often give to him to bring with him. Leon picked out a nice cloak that hid his arm and a scabbard at the side he could pull a sword from. Ari pulled her hair up out of her face, a smile now starting to cross it more often. The two of them were growing more and more like the individuals Milos saw in them and he felt proud whenever he saw them.

Then, a little over a month later, it all changed.

~ * ~

Rita settled back as she walked through town with Alex next to her, humming a little tune as he flitted along, literally springing forward with his wings fluttering behind him. She chuckled as she peered ahead, spotting Milos and Suzuhah talking to one side. They seemed to be conversing rapidly about something, or maybe it was just Suzuhah talking and Milos was listening.

She waved as Alex chuckled, the wings collapsing back and disappearing as he hurried ahead, meeting up with the two.

She paused, finding herself freezing in place as her gaze slowly slid to the rocky walls to one side.

What the...her vision? She wasn't sure how she knew, but something in her head rang like a siren. It was so simple, a common event, but everything lined up, the view of the crack in the wall, the interaction between their group, even the sounds of chatter filling her ears.

That uneasy vision she saw over a month ago. It caught up with her and she couldn't understand why.

She peered toward the coast, frowning. She shook her head. That sense of unease from her vision ratcheted up a few notches and she couldn't help but feel sick to her stomach. Alex and Milos both paused, a frown crossing Alex's face as Milos' gaze snapped around, as if trying to spot something.

Something was wrong, and Rita couldn't figure out what it was. The air felt heavy, and her head suddenly ached something fierce.

She recognized it instantly, a vision...she stopped, eyes widening as she purposefully paused it to piece through the options. No, it was multiple. She grabbed one at random, tugging it forward.

*She found herself slipping and sliding as blood coated the ground, almost stumbling over a body. She could hear shouts behind her and looked forward just as a woman, a very familiar woman, swung around and smiled, her hair cut short and bloody. The day stones glared down, hitting high noon. "Can't let anyone go, sorry." With that, she slashed outward.*

The vision flipped without her control, twisting immediately into the next vision, even as she tried to pull away from the sudden onslaught. A feeling settled over her she couldn't describe as the next one stabilized.

*She was back-to-back with Suzuhah, surrounded by what looked like soldiers, if the metal was any indication, their metal glinted in the noonlight. They reminded her of the guards that walked the streets of Raynout. She could hear shouts, and she was desperately throwing bottles like nobody's business, but she quickly found herself out, only a shaky stone bottle in her hand she was holding like a club. She could hear Suzuhah's pained gasps behind her. Screams and cries of pain and fear rang in her ears. "Dammit, we should hav— "*

*"Rita!" The voice startled her enough, she turned to spot an arrow shoot through the air, slamming into a body, a familiar one.*

*She stumbled back, holding onto Suzuhah as the young man shuddered from the piercing arrow, having pushed her out of the way. She looked up to see Milos and Alex to one side, bloody. Alex's wings were twisted, strange shackles clamped over the wings and neck, as he writhed on the ground. Milos was holding his own, but barely, a manacle hung off one arm that dangled at his side, his arm clearly unusable. He twisted, only to have something slam down on the side of his head. He recoiled and, in that moment, a chain snapped out, wrapping around his torso and neck. She never saw such agony on his face, only for the image to be blocked by one of the soldiers.*

*They tried. Alex and Milos wanted to—* the sword swung down. She never got to hear the rest of that vision's thoughts as another vision surged forward, *of scrambling up a stone path slick with water and ice. She couldn't see, no one could. There was probably another path, but they couldn't risk the more obvious one. She could hear stifled crying and shushes as she moved. She felt a hand pull her up and she let out a breath, spotting an exhausted Alex. Milos stood before him, tense and sword out. Suzuhah was nowhere in sight.*

*Neither were Ari and Leon.*

*She heard a cry and looked back at the path she was just on, where she could faintly see a few flickers of torchlight suddenly break away. The torch light extinguished as the constant running water wore the path so much, it broke through.*

*She lunged forward to try to catch the young woman behind her, a woman she swore she saw a few times with Milos and heard a sudden crack as the ground splintered under her. The reverberating scream from Milos caught her off guard.*

*"KARA!"*

*The utter fear in the woman's eyes as she plummeted down haunted Rita for only a moment before the earth crumbled beneath her. She heard a familiar chuckle and a scream from Alex that was suddenly muffled as the ground far far below rushed up to meet her, water reaching up like fingers, ripping out the ground above—*

"Rita!" She felt hands on her shoulder and jerked. Alex stood in front of her; Not a dead Alex, or a captured Alex, but the Alex from the present. "Are you back?"

Her breaths were short and raspy, her heart pounding out of rhythm in her chest as she jerked, glancing up toward the ceiling. She took deep shuddering breaths as panic rose. The day stones light was slowly growing stronger...heading toward noon. If she could hear, she wasn't certain, because her ears felt as if they were filled with leather.

"That was— You had multiple visions, didn't you?" Suzuhah asked from her side as Alex slowly pulled back, seeming relieved she was finally back with them. All she could do was nod, slowly pulling her head down, mind racing and spinning with not just the visions. Was it that soon? Was all that going to happen in a few days?

She spotted Milos settled behind Alex, watching her quietly, a hint of worry clear on his face.

All the visions blended together, and, for a brief moment, she felt her eyes water.

She died, three different times...and in the second one...

No, she wouldn't allow Milos and Alex to be captured. She wasn't sure what happened, what caused it, but she could tell they were in the Sanctuary.

"Something's going to happen." She turned, startling the group, and broke into a run, heading toward the main hall. "I don't know if they know, but we need to warn the council that something is coming."

"Rita! What are you talking about? Wait!" Alex's voice was breathy as he darted after her. Milos was immediately at her side, movement strangely graceful.

"The visions." She spoke simply, not having much breath. "The sanctuary is attacked. Martinets and I think Milos' sister." She paused, thinking through the last one. "And…I think there was also some kind of Demon involved. He sounded familiar and considering the water at the end." She shuddered as Alex and Milos exchanged looks.

The growl from behind her, however, confirmed her suspicions. "HIM?" Suzuha's voice was deep and pained. "That bastard decided to come after us? The same one who killed my master and tried to take Alex?"

Rita wasn't sure. The visions were all so similar and yet all so different. Either way, though, she had to warn someone of what she saw. There was so much death and destruction, each vision worse and worse. A part of her wasn't even sure why she was bothering. She was swamped with so many visions, pressing at her mind like a whirlpool, tugging at her and yet… she found herself shying away, barely getting glimpses of possibilities that didn't seem to improve. Why? Why was she getting this if there were no options but death?

She was grateful she woke up before she was hit by the others, she could feel more trying to get her attention, but she shoved them back. The future suddenly seemed very volatile. How could there suddenly be so many different paths? Suzuha's words from so long ago hit her. It was rare to be able to change the future, maybe because she WAS changing it, the future visions she saw were rapidly changing. All the visions clinging to her, were they still options?

There had to be one that would get them out. She just hoped all the others she saw weren't options, that they weren't real.

She skidded to a halt at the doors that had already seen so much, of their arrival, of the trial, of the truth of Lillianna, Valencia and Milos. She had to catch her breath, but, to her annoyance and relief, Milos was fine and quickly demanded to see Lillianna.

Clearly seeing their state, the guards nodded, opening the door, mentioning something about the council already housing an urgent guest. Rita caught her breath and hurried in with Milos at her side and Alex and Suzuha only a step behind, ignoring his words. Both of them stiffened briefly as shouts caught their attention, loud enough for even her to hear, though she couldn't understand.

It was in the Demonic tongue.

She didn't care, finding herself running right up to where the shouting was loudest and, instead of knocking, snapped open the thankfully unlocked door that led to Lillianna's main office.

Lillianna stood to one side, seeming ready to interject as Maritus and Eren argued. Sechrondes sat in a chair, massaging her temples and Valencia had her head in her hands.

To Rita's utter surprise, she spotted a very familiar, and clearly very tired, figure. The watery form of the Aqua Wraith was shaky at best, the hair almost like a straight waterfall instead of the normal waves. She was settled on the ground, water being poured over her head by the old man whose name she couldn't remember, but she knew was also part of the council. The Aqua Wraith looked haggard, as if she had also just finished a sprint.

The sight of the Aqua Wraith sent Rita's panic skyrocketing as her worst fears came to pass.

Those visions were from today, from only a little over an hour from now, when the day stones hit noon.

"What is the meaning of this?" Maritus snapped, turning to the group. "To just barge in out of…the impudence!"

"Oh, can it," she snapped, her voice pitched, and wavering, turning to Lillianna. "Something's coming. Soon."

Lillianna quickly put a hand up, eyes darting to the door. There was a faint click of distaste before the wind swung the doors shut with a click. "I am aware. The Aqua Wraith just arrived to inform us of the encroaching threat." She put her hand down, glancing at their group. "We just started the meeting to deal with the situation." Her gaze, as usual, was hard to read, but Rita could notice the slight narrowing of her eyes. "However, what is it that you saw?"

Rita caught her breath and straightened, adjusting her witch's hat. "Death, a lot of it." She spoke quietly. "There were Martinets, slaughtering as they went." That caused the group to still, silence filling the room as she continued, "I saw what I believe to be another Alertian, a young woman with short cut hair. She said she couldn't let anyone go. The citizens were being killed or captured in the streets. They didn't seem to care about

Suzuhah or me, but—" her gaze flicked to Milos, who stiffened, and Alex, who suddenly grew pale. "They did capture them." Her voice was quiet when she said it. "Then there was another vision of us and many of the citizens fleeing. The path crumbled and we all perished." She paused. "Though I believe that was caused by a Demon we encountered from the south, someone I would rather not meet again. He is a half Demon with control over water that can beat out the Aqua Wraith." She nodded toward the woman who nodded back. "And who, well…" she decided not to continue.

"Speak, child. What is it?" Sechrondes spoke, interrupting the silence, but it wasn't accusatory.

"He has an obsession with water Demons, especially Alex."

Alex shuddered next to her, and she saw Suzuha shift, pressing into his side in comfort.

"So, are you saying you had more than one vision? Because it sounds like you implied dying, more than once. That is unheard of," Maritus scoffed.

"It is not," Lillianna said quietly, staring at Rita with newfound recognition. "It has been seen a few times, when the world is at a turning point, the most powerful seers will receive visions, as has happened many times in the last 2000 years. Child, tell me, do you feel more? At the edge of your mind?"

Rita blinked, startled, and she couldn't help but nod.

"The high seer is but one of many who I have heard tales of having many visions. When the Demon-Human war came, we were warned by one such person, of the different futures she saw. None believed her…and you have seen the results." Her gaze flicked around the room. "It seems like something is coming, if the visions and the warning are correct, this sanctuary is lost."

"You are giving up already?" Maritus snapped. "Because of som…"

"I did NOT say we were giving up. I was saying this place was lost, not our people." Lillianna stood, just that little bit taller and Maritus cowed slightly, his mouth clacking shut. "We will evacuate those we can. All of you, be prepared to flee. We all knew this day would come someday; it just came sooner than we all would have liked. However, we still have a duty, if not for the humans, at least for our own people."

"So you are letting the sanctuary fall." Maritus pursed his lips. "You don't believe we can fight?"

Lillianna turned to Rita, startling her. "This might be challenging but see if you can focus on a particular vision. Do you see anything about us fighting back?"

"Why are you...?"

"Shut it." Rita stomped a foot forward. "Contrary to what you think, I've come to care for the people here." Her thoughts flickered to the two shop-keeps, the gentle aroma of the cafe she frequented, the men and women whom she had gotten used to talking to, exchanging potions and ideas.

She pulled back, feeling the pressure of the vision. She began to meditate like she had been practicing. She couldn't call on demand, but it was already there, so she just had to guide.

What if we fight?

*The image snapped into place, the Demons preparing as citizens lined the streets with pitchforks and other things. There were no kids or elderly, it seemed that they fled. It was as if the vision was in fast forward. She couldn't keep track, but it very quickly devolved as the first ship sailed through the gap, promptly followed by four more. Arrows seared through the air, covered in fire.*

*Water surged up, blocking the arrows. Streams cut through the middle, the ships suddenly shooting forward as arrows flew back, smashing into the first line as another wave of water pierced forward, only for a heavy blast of wind to shred across the front of their lines, the water dissipating in the winds, the two presences battling for attention.*

*She could hear shouts and turned in horror to see that Martinets, soaked in water, came out from behind, clearly having used the approaching ships to come in below and launch an attack from their blind spot.*

*Amongst them stood a familiar young woman, and beside her, was a young man with an orb in hand and a smirk on his face. "Ah, little lady, did you think you were the only one who could see? This place will fall, as I have foreseen."*

With that, all havoc broke loose as the group was bombarded by both sides. The blood that soaked the earth from before was bad, but this somehow was worse. She heard a scream as something was shot out of the air, the clank of chains followed by a heavy thump.

Chains, there were so many sounds of ringing chains and screams.

It was brutal and deadly, and she wasn't even sure how she was still alive.

At least, until she heard a cry of utter agony and despair.

She jerked, turning in time to watch Lillianna take a step back, an arrow in her chest. There was only a moment, where her form flickered, before a volley of arrows snapped forward, wind blowing only a moment too late.

A scream of rage vibrated through as a cheer echoed from the Martinets.

Bolstered by the powerful woman falling, they struck hard and fast.

It wasn't to capture; they were bent on killing and taking who survived.

One after another. Sechrondes, strangled by a chain as her tail thrashed.

Eren, caught in a trap, spikes spearing her prone body to the ground.

Maritus, so busy focusing on the wave, lost his concentration at Lillianna's fall.

The water speared up, piercing his chest.

Then, it was lost. The water roared forward, surging around the Martinets and slamming into the Demons and Humans still fighting.

Milos and the Alertian battled, just out of range of the wave, the young woman grinning widely, but Milos... not actually attacking her, seeming unable to.

She stabbed through his leg, causing him to crumple, giving her time to snap something on his neck. Rita wasn't sure what she whispered, but she could see Milos, whose body convulsed as he tried desperately to pull away.

Alex let out a song, his voice almost gone as he took over fighting the wave, tears tracing down his face as Suzuhah surged above, lightning *flaring down.*

*Then...she heard a crack.*

*She slowly tilted her head up, not watching the fight, not caring in that moment as she peered toward the roof so high above. She felt dust lightly brush against her face then...the world shook.*

*Another scream reached her ear*

*"This is the last place! If we take it, this land is ours. Keep fighting, men!" the psychic called, grin widening.*

*Rita continued to stare.*

*He didn't even realize, did he?*

*Then, the world shattered.*

She jerked, stumbling back, feeling a strong form behind her as Milos caught her.

That one was the worst one yet. "No." She spoke, voice almost hoarse. "Don't. I don't know why, but don't." Her gaze shifted to Lillianna. "The world...all I could see was that..." She cut herself off with a hefty gulp. "There was so much death then everything just shattered."

She couldn't describe it any other way. The earth shook like it wanted to break all their bones with a swift strike and then she knew no more. "An earthquake...so many deaths." She shuddered.

The thought of what she just saw, the flickers of memory of the previous visions, the many more pressing in her mind, haunted her.

She wasn't sure what to do. It seemed like it didn't matter whether they fought back or fled. Fighting back was clearly not an answer if the other psychic could see like her, though, clearly, they couldn't see everything.

She didn't realize she was wrapping her arms around herself until she felt a hand on her shoulder, squeezing lightly with another arm pulling her in close for warmth. Milos glanced toward her, letting go as Alex held onto her side, a faint, if tired smile on his face. Suzuha watched her quietly, a smile on her face as well.

Rita took a deep breath and let it out.

"So you are saying that not even fighting back will work? Even though it's just some humans?" Maritus spoke, absolute anger slipping through. He went to take a step forward when Valencia got in his way.

"Yes, that is what she said," Alex's mother said simply. " If she says that, I believe her. I have yet to hear her give a lie, and Eren can attest."

"I am a bit tired of all of you using me as a lie-detector," Eren said with absolutely no heat, just a strange resignation as she stared at Rita. "I also sometimes wish the ability wasn't so powerful."

Rita locked eyes with her and could feel that same resignation. Eren seemed to recognize her thoughts, of the hopelessness she felt weighing heavily on her.

"Well, all we can do, if that is so, is evacuate as many as we can." Lillianna spoke quietly. "Though, if— "her gaze flitted around the group. "I think we all now know why this might be a turning point for this world and recognize the repercussions."

The other Demons pulled back, even Maritus, who turned away in utter fury and, strangely to Rita, sadness.

That sadness seemed to cling to everyone, as if they knew something she did not, which wasn't surprising.

"Rita, are there no other options?" Alex spoke quietly; arm wrapped around her shoulder. "Nothing?"

She shook her head, feeling the weight of the visions.

"There has to be something." Suzuha spoke up, startling them. "Why would one get SO many visions if there wasn't a path that they could take to escape that horrid fate? You SUCCEEDED in changing your future, something my mistress couldn't do. So, by god, we're going to find a way to do it again. You know as well as I that there has to be one vision in there that tells of a chance to escape; otherwise, it is just cruelty incarnate for you or any other seer to get so many visions with no good outcome. Mistress gave up, I won't let you give up until we FIND that path. Understood?"

Rita stared at Suzuha, the little girl's expression was serious, a sentiment usual with her male form and, somehow, it seemed to hit harder here. She thought over what she said, startled as Alex lightly pulled her close.

"That's...yeah. Suzuha's right. We have to find something."

Milos simply nodded, but that was more than she expected from the lout.

"Well, damn, give me a minute then," Rita snapped, pulling the arm off her shoulder, startling the group. "I think starting the evacuation is a good idea, especially if we have time." She paused, furrowing her brow. "Wait, the psychic is just like me. He knows the different options we have, but he can only act on them—" Her gaze flitted to the day stones outside and she stiffened. "After an hour, because they will arrive at Noon." She turned back. "We need to take that time to get away from here. That was something I hadn't seen in my visions. We were taking secondary paths at the last minute or fighting back. Give me a sec."

She closed her eyes, praying she could dig through the visions like before. She felt a flutter and saw flashes of visions. A wave of water is crashing over the city. A blood bath as they tried to flee, obviously too late, arguments to stay, arguments to leave, indecisiveness—

She almost fell into the vision, startled as she saw herself gesturing. *"Go!" she shouted as people ran up a clear-cut path, lights from dim light stones bounced off the walls as the pounding of footsteps met her ears. She could hear the sound of singing, echoing through, and hear the swish of wings as she looked toward the exit. Suzuhah landed with a few more, flashing into form as the song finally faded. "This should be the last, but we have to go, the boats are here."*

*Rita nodded, glancing toward where the crack in the wall caught her gaze, imposing as it was, before turning and gesturing. "I can only hope this one works."*

*Alex simply nodded before they bolted through the crack. She looked back in time to see Lillianna nod before bringing a hand up and slashing down. She could feel the ground shake before rocks slammed onto the ground behind, sealing them off... for now.*

*She could only hope this worked. This HAD to be it, so many visions, she had to cling to one of them being right.*

She pulled from her vision, eyes wide.

She got enough hints from the visions that she had an idea. "I think I know."

"Well, spill," Maritus snapped. "Don't just give us— "

"Shush, Maritus," Sechrondes hissed. "Let the girl speak."

"We need to be quick." Rita looked around. "There is a main path, a well-lit one. We need to evacuate the citizens and everyone we can before the ships come." She glanced toward Lillianna. "I don't know why, but you stayed behind, destroyed the path behind us."

Lillianna stared before she nodded. "I see what you say." Her gaze flitted to the rest of the group. "You know why I would stay behind, and I believe you all will be doing the same, in varying ways."

The others pursed their lips as Maritus clicked his tongue but pulled back.

"You all, get the citizens' attention and direct them to the vent."

"They will argue." Rita spoke up. "In some of my other visions, the people argued, demanded to fight, pleaded that you all lead." She shook her head. "I never saw the rest of those visions."

"Arguments are likely to arise." Sechrondes rose into her imposing height. "Especially if the leaders themselves will no longer be leading." Her gaze settled on Lillianna. "Am I correct in assuming that?"

Lillianna nodded.

"So, you too?" Alex's voice was soft, catching everyone's attention, his gaze firmly on a tired Valencia. "You aren't going to come with us?"

Valencia turned to Alex, sadness settling over her face as she shook her head.

"I think it best we go." Eren spoke. "We have a job to do. Our citizens need warning, and we have little time." With that, she swept to her feet and hurried out the door, Sechrondes not far behind.

Martius huffed, but followed soon after, feathers flaring. The Aqua Wraith watched them quietly as Lillianna nodded and swiftly departed as well, leaving only the small party, the Aqua Wraith and Valencia.

Valencia paused for a moment before stepping forward and, startling everyone, pulled Alex into a deep and tight hug. Alex hesitated a moment before reaching up, holding her close.

"I'm sorry, my little angel." Valencia spoke, a little hoarse. "I need to stay. I need to stay in hopes that I can give you a chance to survive."

"But, why? Why are you all staying?" Alex asked, pained. "What reason is there to stay? You fled to try to avoid all this."

"We fled north. We did not flee the Underlands themselves. We never intended to."

Rita froze at that, realization dawning on her. Most couldn't get through the path above, due to lack of flight, and those who crawled usually died before they could make it across the ceiling of the Underlands to get to the central opening that led above.

Valencia could fly. She could have fled to the surface when trying to avoid the Martinets and she didn't.

"You never intended to." Milos gestured. "For some reason, Demons seem to believe they need to stay below."

"Tell me, Milos, can you feel it?"

Valencia slowly pulled away, but kept an arm around her son, holding him close as she looked toward Milos. "Can you feel the flow of magic around this place? Can you imagine all of it fading?"

Milos stiffened, eyes wide.

"We have our reasons, something all Demons of power can just feel, in their bones. With so few of us left, we need to do whatever we can to make sure it stays that way." She pulled Alex even closer, pressing her head to the side of his, closing her eyes for a moment. "My little angel, flee as fast as you can. I'm so proud of you, of the new family you've found. Please survive, no matter what, understood?"

Rita turned away as she spotted the tears settling into Alex's eyes before he spun, holding her tight once more. "Please…"

It seemed he didn't know what to say, but his voice became choked as he pleaded quietly.

Valencia hummed softly, a tune Alex sung a few times, as she lightly brushed his hair back. "I will do the best I can. Now…Gret…"

Alex choked, as the strangely solemn Demonic word rang over the room, but nodded, slowly pulling away. With that, Valencia pulled back, turning to the rest of them. "You know what I'm going to ask, but…"

"We'll keep an eye on him." Suzuha put her hands on her hips. "I don't think anyone here is going to let anyone else down."

Clearly, Valencia saw something in each of their expressions, because a relieved smile crossed her lips before she nodded to each of them and, with a single transformation, shifted to Demonic form.

Faster than they could blink, she shot out the door, leaving the group in a quiet and heavy silence.

Alex choked slightly, staring at where she was, his expression was more than a little broken and Rita didn't blame him in the slightest. She went to reach forward when Suzuha stepped up, grabbing his hands, startling him. "We should go." She spoke softly. "We can't waste time, we don't know how long we have before we lose the chance for that vision. Your mother will be fine. She's a flyer, she has means of escape."

Alex let out a breath, slumping heavily. "But I finally found her." His voice was pained. "Two months. That's not nearly enough time."

"What I would give to see my mistress again for a few minutes." Suzuha leaned up, startling him. "You had the chance many don't. You got a chance to talk, to reconcile. You got a chance to say goodbye. Not many have that chance. So, move. Your mother can only protect herself if she knows you are safe, especially this time."

Alex pursed his lips, clearly unable to argue. He nodded, glancing toward Rita and Milos, he quickly blinked away the edge of tears, resolute. "Rita, we don't have much time, but was there anything else important about your vision?"

"Firstly, what was that word she used?" Rita frowned. "Gret or whatever?"

Alex pursed his lips, looking away. "It means Run. It's the same thing she told me right after I fled my home to the south, when I first saw her as a Demon."

Rita winced and quickly shifted gears, deciding not to press. She thought over the vision again, her thought catching on one thing in particular. "Your song." She turned to him. "The siren's song. I think that helped garner people's attention and helped pull them along. People don't want to leave, this is their home, and, for many, this is probably their last refuge." Her thoughts flitted to the Demon shopkeepers she became friends with. The cafe owner and shopkeeper who would always check in on her. "I think we need your song, just to help convince them."

"But…"

"It's for their own good and it's not like you are forcing them," Suzuha pointed out, pulling her hands back. "Your song isn't strong enough yet to force anyone, it's like a suggestion, more than anything. They can choose to say no, and that's on them, but I think Rita has a good idea. Use your voice to catch their attention, to guide them. I doubt everyone knows how to get to the exit. I mean, now that I think about it, we don't."

Rita blinked and then felt a sheepish expression cross her face. "I may have forgotten to ask."

"You all did, but tis fair." The Aqua Wraith spoke up, startling all of them as she swept to her feet. Her form was weak and barely held together. She bowed and gestured. "I will guide thee, but I must returneth to the ocean soon after. I cannot join."

"I forgot she was here," Suzuha muttered under her breath and Rita couldn't argue, she completely forgot as well.

Speaking of..." Ari! Leon!" She looked around.

"They will be fine," Milos said. "They are most likely aware of the situation and I have no doubt will meet us where we need to go."

"I suppose." Alex glanced at the door. "It feels weird not getting them though."

"They are their own people." Milos walked toward the door, pushing it open. "They can make their own decisions, and I think they finally realize that."

Rita blinked and relaxed, realizing what Milos was saying as she slipped out behind him. "Aw...you are sweet."

"Don't push it."

"But you know I enjoy it."

She did, however, pull back, noting that, even though he was saying that he seemed tense, gaze flitting around and seeming unsettled. As if he wanted...no, needed to go. She supposed it made sense, especially since one of the people coming WAS his sister, something she knew unnerved him. It wasn't the time to joke back and forth, but the short moment was a relief to her frazzled and worried mind. The Aqua Wraith soon took the lead, her form shaking and shuddering as she quickly led them through the now empty courtyard. It was almost as if an eerie silence had fallen over the city, leaving everything with an odd feeling of unease. There were whispers and quiet panic, but nothing she could see as they stepped past the house, quickly picking up what little they had before moving along. Alex kept peering over his shoulder, clearly uncomfortable. Milos stoically stared ahead, but the grip on his sword indicated his thoughts well enough. If anything, Rita was kind of surprised he was going along with it. She figured he would want to fight as well, but she supposed, in her visions, she did see him hesitate against his sister. She wondered if that was what was causing him to hesitate now and flee instead of fighting.

Considering what she saw in the visions regarding his sister, she found herself unable to blame him and was a little terrified of the prospect of ever encountering her.

Rita wasn't sure how to feel. Her gaze drifted back over the city as they climbed a set of steps to one side; the stone was rugged and clearly not used often. Soon, to her surprise, she began to feel a light breeze and stopped as they arrived at the top of, now that she was paying attention, some very familiar steps, very close to where they found Milos after he fled upon learning of Alex's heritage.

She could see the stone pillars and the faint speckles of blood that stayed caked into the stone, never fully able to be cleaned up.

The way Milos stiffened also spoke a lot about the location.

She peered down the pillar lined path as they rounded the corner to see a cave, a very familiar one. Immediately, she recognized it, she could see the cave walls, smooth and bright with light stones placed along the edges. Her eyes widened and she nodded to the others. "This is it."

The Aqua Wraith smiled, her form almost fading into the ground and, without a word, she shot down the stairs, water droplets trailing behind her as she went. Following her path, Rita could already see a few people hurrying up the steps, those who had seemingly been prepared for such a time as this. They passed by the group, nodding briefly before diving into the cave with small bags. The first of the evacuees.

Alex turned, startled, before slowly facing the path once more. "Well, we know where to go." He glanced toward the rest of them and frowned. "How much time do we have left?"

Rita stared at the walls, and she couldn't help but have a feeling settle in her stomach, the answer almost falling from her lips as she said, "Forty minutes."

"Shit." Suzuha shifted to male form. "Then, I think it's time we got people's attention." His gaze flicked to Alex. "I'll fly above. I think someone should stay here and…"

"Don't worry." Rita glanced around. "I'm not a runner; I have a feeling I should stay here. It's where I was in the vision."

Alex, Milos and Suzuhah exchanged looks, but before any could respond, Rita put her hands on her hips and grinned. "I can convince people to go through, once they get here, and I already know where they need to go from here, you guys probably don't, so trust me on this."

Alex let out a chuckle before nodding. Milos just shook his head as Suzuhah let out a laugh, lightning flaring as he switched to Vulfulas form, the long writhing tail curling briefly around the party before he shot away, heading above the city, cries of warning echoing from his throat. No words were spoken, but the tone was like sirens echoing through the streets.

Milos darted away, clearly having an idea in mind, and a moment later, with a nod, Alex turned and hurried down the stairs after Milos.

Rita's smile faded as she stayed at the top, her thoughts and attention shifting over to the ocean, gaze firmly locked onto the distant crevasse.

The other reason she wanted nothing to do with gathering them was because she had a feeling the psychic was watching her.

The less she knew, the better. That might be their only chance to escape with their lives…and those important to them.

# Chapter Twenty-Four

Alex's attention drifted up toward Suzuhah, swooping high above. He glanced over his shoulder, debating before flipping to Demon form. He wasn't sure if it would work, but Suzuhah was already doing his part and Alex knew he needed to help. He had wings as well. He should be able to use them.

He closed his eyes, envisioning soaring beside Suzuhah for a moment before veering off toward the farther reaches. He felt the wings shift behind him and then let out a yelp as he shot upward. The wings beat behind him as he found himself hovering high above the city and, in that instant, he felt the weight of just how high up he was and a moment of panic set in, distracting him. The wings, beating calmly, suddenly stuttered, as if distracted and, with a cry, he felt himself plummet back toward the ground. Barely a second later, he let out a pained grunt as he slammed into the very familiar furred back of Suzuhah. The Vulfulas curved back upward. Suzuhah turned to giving Alex a bemused look. "You are lucky I spotted you when I did. Now is not the best time to practice."

Alex winced, repositioning himself to be on Suzuhah's back. Note to self, he needed more practice. If he got that easily distracted, he wouldn't be able to sing and fly. He let out a sigh. He could feel the wind brush against his wings but held them firmly to his back. As much as he wanted to switch back to human form so as not to be a bother to Suzuhah, he needed to stay Demon just to make sure the siren part of the song would work. He wasn't fond of using his siren abilities, but it had to be done to make sure people fled. He leaned forward, carefully holding onto Suzuhah's neck. "I thought we could make up more ground that way." He muttered.

With a whoosh of wind, they took off, the day stones gleaming brilliantly down above them, casting long shadows over parts of the water and the large city below. "Well, it's fine, my throat was starting to hurt, so maybe it would be good if you took over."

"You haven't been calling for that long."

"Look, shouting at the top of your lungs for any length of time is exhausting, now are you helping or what?"

Alex chuckled before nodding. He found his gaze flitting to the break in the large mountain-like barrier, so thin from here that it looked like nothing more than a sliver. Soon, boats would come through. Would they have enough time to even get everything done? Who was on it that made Rita so nervous? He shook his head, peering down over the city. From up here, he was reminded of just how big it was. How many people and Demons lived here. So many lives, uprooted in an instant.

He could faintly see people in the streets arming for combat, even as others tried to pull at them to leave. He could see the flicker of a long feathery tail land amongst the group, and, after a moment, those who were trying to run fled while those with weapons argued. This was a common sight throughout the city. He could see Sechrondes move through the streets, hurrying people along, as others headed toward the coast, much against her gestures.

It was so constant…

He wanted to save these people from their fate, save his little family. He knew Milos and Rita; they wouldn't leave the people here behind. It was obvious Milos wanted to fight, from the way his fingers lingered by the sword, to the tension in his shoulders to the agitated movement of his walk. It was so clear, and he wasn't alone.

Alex didn't want him to fight, he wanted them to be able to escape with their lives.

He didn't even really notice, not at first, but then the sound reverberated back to him off the distant stones as a keening music caught his ears. Words of the Demonic tongue drifted over the waves and city, both sharp and filled with longing. He recognized his voice, the lyrical waves of energy as it settled over him that he began singing before he realized. He barely stopped himself from cutting it off, letting his Demonic side take control as the song grew more powerful.

He wondered, briefly, how powerful the ancient Siren's song was if even he could feel the tug with his own voice.

*"Gret, fel kiem a leth. Allec fen vepons, jet neth. He-ven jit villen ah húe jite. Gret, Gret. Vieten ackt fel fen sach!"*

The Demonic words settled over him like a wave, the translation running through his head in tandem. "Run, for time is short. Drop your weapons, flee north. Hear my voice and follow me. Run, Run. They are here for your soul."

He let himself sing, eyes closing in concentration as the weight of the wings settled on his back. At that moment, he appreciated Suzuhah's help. He was not quite ready to fly, especially when he had to sing at the same time. His tail swished behind him and the horns sat heavy on his head. He could feel Suzuhah's wings beat and muscles shift under him as they curved over the city, warning the citizens as best as they could. It was all he could do to save as many as he could.

~ * ~

A beautiful, almost ethereal voice echoed from above, settling over the city like a curtain. Milos didn't even need to look up as the words resonated down to him. He knew it was coming, he knew Alex would be able to do it, but the words were still hard to resist enough to do his job. He wanted to fight. He hated constantly running. His hand settled against his sword as he raced through the streets, one of the only ones able to in that moment.

Many an eye drifted up to the sky, and he could almost swear he heard an echoing chorus from the surrounding waves beating against the shore to the south. The song faded in and out as Suzuhah and Alex flew above, circling the city, but that was fair. Alex's voice, as powerful as it was, could only reach so far on his own.

Milos spotted a crowd, armed and heading toward the coast, stopping in their tracks, hesitation on their faces before they seemed to relax. One glanced toward the sky, nodded and spun on his heels, heading up the path, slinging the weapon over his shoulder.

Others soon began to follow, glancing occasionally back to the sky before continuing back where Milos came from.

He didn't miss the somewhat glazing expressions he vaguely

remembered seeing the last time Alex used his voice to stop Maritus.

He shook his head. It was the right choice, according to Rita's visions, but he hoped the boy was ready for the repercussions, once everyone came to their senses. Then again, he probably was very aware of that fact.

Milos would just have to make sure the boy wouldn't get the full brunt of the people's ire.

Though, he supposed, the magic was more subtle than outright demanding, more of a suggestion than anything.

People could still resist if they wanted, though it took much more effort, as he was very clearly aware of. It was much easier to follow the suggestion than resist.

His feet led him to his destination, the little garden he frequented often. He didn't want to admit it, but his first thoughts had been to check on her. To check on Kara.

To his dismay, she was nowhere in sight. He peered around wildly but knew he wouldn't have the time to do a more thorough search.

With that, he hurried away, down the long slopes and steps to get toward the base of the city, where he could feel magic gathering.

He skidded to a stop at the top of some steps, peering down into the lower parts of the city. Many Demons were gathered below, along with a rare few humans. He could see the council members out and about, clearly trying to corral them as best as they could, clearly also struggling a little against Alex's powerful song. Lillianna stood by the coast, a tall silhouette, hard to see against the stone, but presence felt even from here. Valencia and a familiar woman of water stood beside her. Now that he paid attention, he could hear the Aqua Wraith's song, almost in harmony with Alex's, but just a little different.

From where he stood, it was hard to tell, but it seemed the very seas around the sanctuary were beginning to shift and move in a way that seemed odd.

It wasn't surprising though. There were two powerful wielders of water and, if Rita was correct, there was another coming, opposing them. One practiced in their abilities. He stared at the gap for a moment, his thoughts flickering back to Rita's words.

His sister. It would be around the time for her to descend down here. He wondered if she was on the boat, heading toward the city, like Rita said. He felt his hands shake at the thought.

He hoped, desperately, that it wasn't. As strong as he was, he didn't think he could beat her. Especially if he wanted to avoid revealing that side of him. He shook it off just as a voice reached his ears. "Milos!"

He jerked, peering over to see a familiar young woman, hair of leaves and soft branches. He could recognize that voice anywhere, he heard it so often lately. The sense of relief that flooded him surprised him, but he didn't think of it much as he turned to face her. Kara hurried up to him, Artorius and a few others at her heels. He could see some of them were armed. Kara's hair was tied back with a soft fabric. She was dressed, not in a normal dress, but in a tunic and trousers, hefty boots fitted over her feet were clearly new.

"Kara?" he asked, startled to see her and the others. "What ar—"

"We heard Alex's voice, much like before, and knew it was time to go." Kara spoke up, her voice soft and somewhat pained, but strong. "I was waiting for you at the garden, but I realized there might not be time, and I wanted to help." She tilted her head back. "Plus, that same voice led us to freedom last time, but we can tell not everyone is going to follow it." She stared into his eyes. "I know you, from the short time we've known each other. You want to fight."

Milos paused, somewhat surprised she did notice, since he hadn't said otherwise, nor pulled his sword out.

Kara shook her head, a soft expression on her face. "So, we will join you in whatever you decide to do." Her gaze flicked to the small group behind her. It was an eclectic group, all Demons of different varieties, one or two he didn't even realize had been captured so long ago. "We owe you our lives and freedom, everyone here will do what they need to try to keep you and your friends safe." She smiled. "Though, I suppose, you can take care of yourself."

Milos blinked, startled as she stared right into his eyes, no heat to her words, only sincerity. "And, well, Ari and Leon told us to meet with you. We met them a while ago, if you remember. When we first met? Ari and Leon were there, in the garden." She shook her head. "But, enough of that, I was going to find you anyway, because I want to be there for you, no matter what." She seemed to realize what she said, because she quickly cleared her throat and continued, "So, what is the plan?"

Milos found himself unsure what to do, surprised at the Demons before him. "I…"

"Milos, sir, we know you are an Alertian, but that doesn't matter to us because you have proven otherwise." Artorius spoke up, voice just that little bit stronger than its usually quiet tone. "Many might argue, say otherwise, but we know the truth, just as your friends do." His gaze flicked up as Alex and Suzuhah flew above, the song strengthening for a moment before fading into the distance once more. There was a sense of wonder, and he seemed almost galvanized by the song words a little stronger as he flicked back to him.

Though that could also be from the magic that curled around him. A water Demon strengthened by a powerful water Demon's song…fitting.

"Lead us."

Milos peered over the small crowd of Demons, unsure what to do. He understood what they were saying, but he worked alone. It took a long time for him to get used to Rita and Alex, but it was becoming easier lately. His gaze flicked to Kara, whose soft smile was filled with encouragement and a strange emotion he couldn't name.

He felt something in him crumble. With a sharp breath, he gestured a handout. "Fine. No, we are not fighting. However, even with Alex's song, many will still try to fight, we will corral the last of them and fight anything that approaches. We only have…" he peered toward the sky, doing his best to calculate, but could only guess. "I can only guess about twenty minutes. As soon as the boats breach through that passage, we need to run, to head north, no matter what." His gaze flicked around. "That means leaving behind those who are too stubborn to leave, we need to evacuate as many as we can, those who won't, have made their own choice…and their own demise."

He expected hesitation at his words, he was blunt, and he knew it sounded almost uncaring. But they simply nodded, straightening slightly, as if preparing. "We will be the last to leave, we will defend the back line for any that manage to get to land quickly. We don't know the extent of what the ships will bring. Understood?"

"Yes." The crowd nodded, a mix of solemn and proud.

Milos hesitated. "I'm no leader." He spoke simply. "However…"

His gaze flicked up to Alex once more, trying so hard to save everyone, to Rita, desperately controlling her abilities to find a way out of the situation, to Suzuhah flying above, endlessly, saving the last thing he had left of his mistress.

The least he could do was try to lead a rag-tag group of people to help in their endeavors. "For their sake…" he found himself muttering under his breath before turning to the crowd. "Split into groups of two or three and quickly head through the streets. Do not carry weapons, you need speed at your disposal. The fastest will head to the outskirts to bring as many as they can. There are a few who are disabled, they might be aware, they might not, I know some of you have encountered these people, find them and help them north."

His thoughts flicked to the shop-keeps Rita met and he nodded to himself. "Two of you, head to the witches' district, they were probably already aware, but you might be able to get more people to aid you. We have fifteen minutes then we must go north ourselves. Now, go."

The group nodded, glancing between themselves before breaking off. Artorius saluted, nodded to Kara and quickly departed as well.

Kara stayed put, turning back to Milos. "You aren't getting rid of me that easily." She spoke simply. "I'll use the parks to try to keep an eye on the situation. There are some trees near the coast that we can use to watch out for those approaching."

Milos stared, startled, as the woman smiled. "I might not be a fighter, but I have my own strengths. I may be a dryad, but I also know a little of scouting. It was my way of staying sane whenever I was caught."

She closed her eyes, one knee to the ground as her fingers lightly grazed the earth. He saw sweat begin to bead on her forehead and her body shake slightly before she suddenly pulled away, out of breath and swaying.

He quickly knelt, catching her as she fell against his side. She blinked, gazing to him before relief settled over her. "It's been a long time since I've had to do that. I forgot how exhausting it is." She paused, leaning into him for a moment, seeming to relax, startling Milos. "You smell really nice." Her voice was soft, quiet. She seemed to realize what she said because, barely a second later, warmth flared up her cheeks and she desperately stumbled to her feet, clearing her throat. "Uh, ah…right, trees. Seems like a lot of the citizens have evacuated north, it seems that your prediction might be off though." Her gaze flicked south. "Some of the trees are warning me of the clashing magic over the waters. They are approaching faster than time says."

Milos stilled. He focused on the magic swirling so far below, trying to parse everything else going on. He heard the Aqua Wraith's song and…he felt familiar surges of another powerful magic almost pressing against the Aqua Wraith's and overpowering it.

He suddenly felt a need to swear. "Kara, we need to go." He spun on his heels, shooting north. He needed to warn Rita and notify Alex and Suzuhah somehow.

It seemed the psychic was aware of their choice, if Rita's words were true. He wasn't sure how that group managed to get that crazy water Demon on their side, but if he was controlling the water to get the ships through faster, then they were in trouble.

Kara didn't hesitate to follow him as they shot up the stairs, almost two at a time. It wasn't long at all before they reached Rita, waving people through. He blinked, startled, as he saw a man and a woman standing at her side, helping coax people through. The two shop-keeps Rita befriended. They were helping those who seemed to be falling out of Alex's charmed song to convince them to go through. Well, that was a relief, though he supposed that meant that the group sent to the witches' district didn't have as much to do.

Rita's gaze flicked to them, and she blinked, surprised. "That was fast." She glanced between them, raising an eyebrow before turning back to Milos. "Ari and Leon took the lead, they said they would take the front to guide everyone, Trisha and her father said they would help me convince the stragglers, you alright?"

Milos nodded, straightening, having caught his breath from his sudden sprint. "I don't think we have that full hour."

The simple words caused Rita to still as people brushed past them, giving them only a brief glance before hurrying into the cavern entrance.

Trisha seemed to notice their tension, and stepped in front of them, taking over Rita's position.

"Shiesse," Rita muttered. "I should have…of COURSE they would realize we are trying to flee and try to push up the supposed timetable." She shook her head, gazing to Milos. "We don't have time to get anyone else's attention." She paused before seeming to think. "You are fast." She glanced toward him. "You can sense where the strongest Demons are. Let the council know they have to flee now."

Milos hesitated.

Rita, seeming to notice, rolled her eyes and shoved a finger on his chest. "Look, Milos, I don't have the ability to get to them quickly and Alex and Suzuhah are busy trying to convince everyone they can to flee. You are the only one who can get to them on time. They are probably already aware anyway, but having you, an Alertian, tell them it's time might get them to actually move." She paused. "Just avoid Maritus, one of the others can inform him."

Milos snorted, but let out a breath, debating.

"Go." Kara spoke softly. "I'll stay with Rita."

"I will as well." Trisha spoke up, her voice as gentle as before, potions were settled at her side, those blind eyes turning toward him, clearly aware of where he stood. "You need not worry about your friend and focus on the task at hand."

Milos observed the two of them for a moment before nodding, spinning on his heels and taking off down the steps. He focused on the magic swirling around, picking up trails, powerful ones.

With practiced ease, he honed in on the closest, Sechrondes. Barely with much thought, he sprang forward. Rita was right, as much as he held no desire to see them escape, he knew having the leaders of the sanctuary trapped or killed could be a blow they couldn't risk. The people were going to struggle to listen as it was, just like Artorius mentioned, having their leadership left behind without warning would just end badly.

It wasn't long before he found Sechrondes, who was helping some stragglers who were unable to flee quickly due to injury. She turned to him, clearly on a mission, her normally flirtatious movements now sharp and pointed. "Milos," she said simply, gaze flitting to him. "What brings you here?"

He came to a halt, tilting his head. "You might already be aware…"

Sechrondes turned to him, shaking her head. "I, and many of the others, have been busy. Alex's song helps, but he's still young, its influence is not absolute yet, though it is incredibly powerful." She paused. "What is it that I should be aware of?"

"They are coming, faster than believed." Milos spoke simply, causing the woman to stiffen. "They have a water Demon on their side, a powerful one similar to Alex."

Sechrondes' attention flicked to the water and her tail thrashed suddenly in a seeming realization. "I can feel it." Her gaze snapped back to Milos. "Time is short." She paused, a sense of sadness falling over her as she peered over the city. "So much work…gone so quickly." She let out a hiss before snapping her tail forward, almost using it to point. "I will speak with Maritus, he is to the west. Go east, I believe Eren is that way. Do not worry about us, we have our own means of escaping back into the southern lands. Some of us may even lead a few on a merry chase to take off some of the pressure. Stay safe, child." With that, she seemed to shift, the powerful snake-like tail shoving her forward.

He didn't know a Demon like her could move that fast, as she quickly slithered around the corner.

He shook his head, changing direction and following her words.

As he traveled, he came across those he commanded, telling them to retreat north. They nodded, accepting his words and following suit. He could feel the change of pressure in the air, almost like an incoming storm. However, looking around, it all almost seemed calm, an eerie stillness over everything as the city was practically a ghost town. He could hear Alex's voice starting to falter above as Suzuhah suddenly twisted, heading back north.

It wasn't long before he reached Eren, who didn't need a word, she simply nodded and pointed to the coast.

He turned, heading that way, the magic almost overwhelming in its strength. He came upon Valencia, Lillianna and the Aqua Wraith very quickly after, Lillianna's gaze flicked to him, a strange tiredness on her face.

Valencia glanced over and nodded, a pull at her lips indicating an attempted smile. "Thank you, Milos. I have nothing else to say to my son, but…keep him safe for me. Alright?" With that, she turned back to the ocean, seeming to concentrate on the waves once more.

He stepped forward, coming to a halt, unable to approach. He thought they were just standing there, but he could now feel it, almost like a powerful barrier. He peered forward, toward the crack where waves crashed relentlessly, shoving back and forth and then…the first bow of a ship pierced through, a powerful wave shoving it past, winds howled, but the sails were already pulled up, and Milos could see what appeared to be lines of Demons on either side of the ship, Demons he remembered seeing from the last island under HIS control.

"Is everyone evacuated?" Lillianna asked, her voice rough.

"As many as we could." Milos spoke evenly, though he was a bit surprised at how calm he was at that moment.

"Good." Her words were soft. "Then it is time for us to go south." Her expression turned pained, a strange sorrow over her words. "I can feel it, the strength of others like you and Alex. Demons and Humans…if only we worked together like the past, but…" She shook her head. "Go, hurry north. I will keep them at bay with Valencia and the Aqua Wraith as long as we can. I won't be able to break down the stone like Rita's vision dictates, but I hope that will still give you all enough time to escape." She peered over the ocean. "Milos, I know you are an Alertian, but remember, you are my nephew. You are an Alertian of the PAST, not of the cretin that abuses the name now. You are a true Alertian, remember that and help protect and lead the people that fled from here." Her gaze met his and he could almost feel the magic press over him. "Go."

He didn't realize he spun on his heels and left until after a minute of running.

The commanding voice…she had it as well. He hated it, but he found his muscles not listening to him, pushed along by Alex's diminishing song.

# Chapter Twenty-five

Rita stared over the city, tapping her foot as worry settled over her. Even the one vision she found was going all weird and she felt a sense of panic rising in. Was she too late? Had she taken too long to realize which path to take?

She looked over as Alex and Suzuhah landed, no one in Suzuhah's grip as her vision dictated. Lillianna was nowhere in sight and a strange girl stood at her side; hands clasped almost in prayer. Trisha and her father slipped away, having heard a commotion from their escape route.

She wasn't a Demon, but even she could feel the strong sense of fear and unease. A few stragglers hurried up the stairs, but Milos was nowhere in sight.

She swallowed, impatience and worry clouding her thoughts as Alex's head snapped to one side, his gaze firmly on the ocean beyond. "They are here." His voice was quiet.

The woman beside her simply nodded, hands clasping even tighter. A few others gathered around, weapons bristling. The woman told her not to worry about them, that they were there to help defend if anyone tried to follow, but Rita barely gave it much thought.

"Where is that lout," she hissed under her breath, ready to head down the stairs herself. Alex leaned against Suzuhah, catching his breath as he glanced at her, seeming about to respond when the sound of footsteps caught all their ears.

Rita's attention snapped to the stairs where the familiar gleam of red and gold met her gaze. Relief settled over her as Milos slid to a stop in front of them, sweat beading down his face as he caught his breath.

"We need to go," he said simply, hand on his knees.

Rita never saw him so out of breath before. She nodded and gestured. "Is Lillianna coming? We need her to close the path."

Milos shook his head as Alex hurried to his side, helping support him. Suzuhah switched out of Vulfulas form, gesturing. Rita clicked her tongue at his response. There was nothing they could do; they would just have to hope it was enough time to get away.

The group, along with a few stragglers, that strange girl and a few Demons that gathered around Milos, hurried into the cave, leaving the city behind. It seemed strange to Rita. After all the blood and fights in her visions, it seemed they were getting away somewhat unscathed.

She shook her head, hoping not to push their luck anymore. She would rather avoid all the bloodshed she saw. Both Milos and Alex were tired from running around, she and Suzuhah were probably the only ones at decent strength to do anything and that was NOT an encouraging thought.

They stepped into the cave, the embedded light stones glowing a soft blue as they hurried down the path. While the entrance seemed wide, the path itself was only wide enough for two or three people shoulder to shoulder and was low enough that if Milos reached up, he could probably touch the ceiling without much struggle. Not a good place to be in if they had to fight. No one said a word as they moved, and it wasn't long before they met up with the rest of the citizens. Rita hadn't realized there were so many until she came to a stop at the back of an incredibly large crowd of refugees. The cavern opened up to a much larger space, light stones specifically set into the walls to help guide the way.

This must have been the commotion Trisha heard. She couldn't see Ari and Leon, but she could see the path they must have taken, a much smaller tunnel entrance that only allowed two at a time if they squeezed. There was a sense of panic amongst those there as people tried not to stampede forward. Trisha and her father stood to either side of the tunnel, ushering people through one at a time. Rita looked around, surprised to see no other path. Was this really the only option? She was now grateful they started the evacuation as soon as they could.

"Milos, sir."

Rita turned to see a young man with a long fish-like tail turn to Milos. "We'll guard the entrance and notify you all if anyone is approaching. Let us know when the crowd has diminished enough for us to get through."

Milos hesitated before nodding. The young man straightened and gestured to some of the Demons before heading back the way the group came.

Rita blinked, completely surprised. "Sir?"

Milos just sighed and shrugged. Alex smiled at that, but didn't say a word.

Suzuhah, in male form, leaned against the wall, peering over the steadily moving, but slow shifting crowd. "This is going to take forever."

Milos nodded as Alex swallowed thickly.

"I guess I thought too soon." Rita spoke quietly.

If it was just a straight path they could run down, they could all escape, but having a large crowd of panicked people converging in a small path? It was a miracle, there were as few left as there were.

"Five minutes." Milos peered over the crowd, startling her. "This crowd would need about five minutes to get through. However, we can better defend once the last of them are through, since they will be at a disadvantage as well and if we can collapse that tunnel behind us..." He stared for a moment before his gaze flicked to Rita. "All we can do is wait."

"I hate waiting," Rita grumbled, but didn't argue, grip tight on her bag as she peered back the way they came. Did they even have that long?

She wasn't sure and found herself pacing back and forth, listening as the crowd slowly lessened. She could see a few in the back, looking around wildly, clearly trying hard not to panic and a few failing.

It was only about a minute or two, or maybe three later when Alex and Milos both stiffened, peering back down the path as Suzuhah suddenly pushed away from the wall. The young woman, whose name she still hadn't gotten, peered in, swallowing nervously.

A moment later, a scream that was promptly cut off echoed down the path.

Everything froze, the people, their breath, sound itself.

A second later, that barely held panic surged and the few people left to get through suddenly rushed toward the tunnel, pushing and shoving, shouts and cries echoed through the air as Milos swiftly tugged out his sword and Alex shifted, one leg back, a hint of fear on his face. Suzuhah looked around and cursed, shifting back next to Rita. It was clear the space was too small for him to shift to Vulfulas form. Footsteps echoed loudly off the passage as the young man, Artorius, she thought they called him, raced around the corner, calling out, only to still, stumbling.

Barely a second later, she saw why, as a blade was pulled from his back, revealing a young woman standing behind him. The young man stumbled, meeting Milos' eyes and mouthing 'run', before collapsing in a heap. The woman, hair cut raggedly with bloody tips and a reddish chain around her neck, tilted her head up. Sharp, familiar features stared back at them, green eyes glowing almost blue in the light of the surrounding stones. She stepped forward, kicking the young man aside, her gaze firmly on Milos. The same Milos who now stood frozen, sword extended between them as if both a weapon and a shield.

The sight of his stiffened yet trembling hands terrified her.

"Ah, big brother. It's so good to see you again." The voice that came out was the exact same as Rita's visions, an almost sultry and resonating tone that dripped with venom. "Of course, when I heard you were dragged north by some awful Demons, I just had to come up here myself." Her gaze flicked around the group, her expression seeming to light up at the sight. "And so many to bring up with us!" Her gaze settled back onto him as she snapped her blade down, blood splattering on the floor. "But dear brother…why is your pretty hair still so long? I get it, but you know what tradition dictates." She flicked her head in such a way as to show off the raggedly cut bloody tips.

The woman, though she seemed relaxed in her posture, was clearly anything but, even to Rita's gaze. Every muscle seemed tense and, even behind the smile, there was a strange cold malice. She mentioned big brother, but the woman was clearly only a few years younger.

"Serena, how did you…" Milos' voice shook just the tiniest bit.

"Get here? The same way you did. I just started the initiation a year early is all. I wasn't fond of teaming up with that half-Demon, but I will profess the usefulness, and I can always take care of him later."

She stepped forward, only stopping when Milos extended his blade forward, his hand shaking just enough for Rita to see, but clearly hidden as best as he could. The scrambling behind Rita barely reached her ears, which seemed strange, considering how much louder it should be, compared to the quiet conversation in front of her.

The woman, Serena, frowned slightly. "Milos, my dear big brother. You still underestimate me. All those times, every time, you never noticed me, never paid attention to me." She tilted her head, the blood on her hair scraping the bottom of her chin, staining it. "Why now? Why do you finally notice me? I came to find you, a year early. I always wanted to stay beside you and here you are." Her gaze drifted. "And now I see. So, did you get seduced by the Demons? You were warned."

Her gaze drifted to the young woman beside Rita, then to Rita herself before landing on Alex. Alex was tense, wings twitching, almost as if they were ready to flare outward, tail lashing as a fierce look of fear and anger crossed his face.

"Oh, are you the little thing whose voice we all heard from so far away? That Demon we had to work with would not stop talking about wanting to see you again. I can see why." Her gaze flicked back to Milos. "Of course, I can't let my big brother end up with a Demon, no matter how pretty the Demon might be, or how alluring his voice is. You, my dear brother, are too important for me to lose. Come home with me, don't worry, I'll protect you from our older brother, from Mother. It'll be just us."

Alex's expression turned to disgust and Rita almost felt the need to throw up at the words.

"Serena, don't make assumptions." Milos spoke carefully, gaze flitting to Artorius. Rita wasn't sure how Milos was staying so calm after hearing all of that, but her attention was swiftly diverted toward Artorius. Rita thought he was dead, but he shifted, just a bit, while Serena's gaze was on Milos.

Serena didn't even bat an eye as she flipped a dagger from her side, and down, piercing into Artorius, causing him to still.

Rita felt her entire body freeze, her blood chilling in her bones.

"She is not someone we can fight." Suzuhah spoke softly, just enough for Rita to hear, and even then, the smile grew wider as Serena's attention drifted to him.

"Why, thank you. I watched Milos so much; I learned from him and honed my skills even more. After all, he is my big brother, my precious older brother, but I won't let any more of my siblings perish if I can help it and he's so sensitive sometimes." She put a finger to her lips, a faint cold smile crossing her face. "He takes after Father in that way. But I don't mind. That's why I love him."

Rita found herself staring at Milos, her thoughts now on his family, the one he never talked about, even when Rita and Alex would constantly talk about theirs. He was always silent as the grave and now she was starting to wonder why and if she needed to have a word or five with his family. If Serena was any indication, she was starting to realize that Milos turned out strangely sane…and that was a worrying thought.

If they survived this.

"Who else is with you?" Milos spoke, swallowing thickly.

"Oh, that odd psychic who kept mentioning an annoying witch, that Demon and the Martinet guild, though, last I heard, they were struggling a little to get through because of some wraith or whatever. Don't know what happened to all of those powerful Demons though, they must have just abandoned everyone, fled back into the Underlands like parasites…or rats. Fitting for a Demon." She tilted her head to the side, hand dropping to her side. "Now, brother, why don't you come back with me to the Overlands. Our jobs are done, and we have more than enough heads to show to Mother. You will be safe; I will protect you from her and brother."

Rita could almost hear the clacking of teeth as she peered over her shoulder. Only a few more had to get through and then they could flee.

"I can't." Milos spoke. "I… "

"Right, seduced. Why don't I fix that for you?" She shot forward, faster than lightning racing off Suzuhah's fur.

Milos was just as fast, sword clanging loudly as he caught the tip with the side of his blade, entire body in front of a startled Alex. The young woman with the flower-like hair stiffened beside Rita, shocked.

"Go." Rita hissed. "Get the last of the people OUT."

She nodded, staring at Milos before she said, "Please, be careful!" With that, she spun on her heels and shot to the other side of the cavern, quickly breaking up the clog and helping to gesture the last few through, Trisha alongside her, shuddering and seeming to clearly sense just how dangerous the whole situation was.

Rita turned back just as Alex stumbled away, pulled sharply by

Suzuhah.

"Hm?" Serena tutted. "And there went another one, that female Demon." She seemed to meet Milos' eyes, pausing for a moment. "Your gaze is not one of someone who has been seduced, but I will not believe you are willingly in cahoots with the same creatures that destroyed our siblings so maliciously. You saw what they did to our brother."

With that, she sprang backward, kicking off the wall. Like a spring, she snapped forward, trying to swing from a different angle. Her sword, much thinner than Milos', was even faster and it seemed to take everything Milos had to catch the blade in time. He slid backward; the impact almost strong enough to be felt then it was just madness. Rita could barely keep track of the clash of blades and flash of clothing.

She felt a sharp wind from a wing flaring out and then a scream of pain as Alex grabbed her, one wing up around them, sliced through, blade inches from Rita's face. She heard a shout as Suzuhah snapped a dagger out, shoving it forward as the thin blade was suddenly pulled backward. Alex stumbled, blood dripping down his wing as pain flared over his face. Rita quickly grabbed out a potion, tossing it to him before digging into her bag. She glanced up, spotting the woman as the swords clashed once more and she used the momentum to flip gracefully over Milos, who spun on his heels, almost catching her legs, only to meet empty air as she pulled them up.

Rita, relieved to finally get the bottle she was after, grabbed it and flung.

To her relief, the woman slashed upward, cutting the pot in half with a quick swing, only to sputter as the liquid within spattered onto her. A moment later, she let out a scream of rage and pain as that sputtering turned to hissing. Milos, using that moment, swung forward.

She managed to block it, flipping back over and stumbling backward just as a group of Martinets and a strange-looking fellow hurried around the corner. "Mistress Serena!"

"Shut it," she snapped back, glare now on Rita. "All of these pests are getting in my way!"

"Alex," Milos barely could keep his breath in his throat, chest heaving from exertion. "Can you sing?"

"I'm not sure, but I might be able to stun them." Alex grimaced, having downed the bottle. Suzuhah was at his side, quickly trying to help with the stab wound.

"Good enough." Rita dug into her bag, pausing as her fingers grazed over one of the potions she made recently. It was a mistake, she accidentally finished it wrong, but found herself curious since it was, technically, complete.

When she showed it, all Trisha could say was it was a potent wave of some sort. Well, whatever. "Milos, get Alex and Suzuhah down the tunnel."

Milos didn't even dare turn his gaze away as the psychic threw something onto Serena, who howled for a moment before grabbing a towel and wiping furiously, the acid now gone, but the damage still left behind. "Well, I need to at least get my brother back. I will NOT let him stay in the hands of such wretches!"

The Martinets around her shuffled past, hurrying forward. Rita glanced back and let out a breath. "Go!"

At her word, she heard Alex draw in a breath as she darted toward the opening, Milos a step behind. Suzuhah tugged Alex through just as a piercing note echoed through the cavern, the stunning sound rattling the walls. Rita heard the footsteps and spun on her heels as she got through the opening, seeing Milos flash past her, gaze flitting to her in surprise. Her gaze met Serena and the psychic... just as the psychic's eyes widened. The Martinets were right at the entrance, stumbling back, hand to their ears as Alex' piercing cry caused them to stop. Rita grabbed the bottle and slammed it down.

She felt an arm grab her, startling her, just as the entire area started to shake. She found herself wrenched backward, almost flung half-way down the passage by the person holding her as an echoing BOOM ripped through the air.

"RUN!" Suzuhah shouted as Rita found herself clinging onto Milos, who shoved his sword into his sheath, pain crossing his face as he bounded over the ground, Alex stumbling ahead of him, pulled desperately along by Suzuhah.

A familiar echoing crash met Rita's ears, and she had to

acknowledge, she was WAY too used to hearing the sound of shattering stone behind her at this point. There was a curve ahead, a few stragglers gesturing them along, peering back in horror. She could feel the crash right behind her and she could only think just HOW powerful that potion was. She peered over Milos' shoulder and suddenly wished she hadn't as he burst forward, almost kicking off the side wall and sliding across the floor to their right…just as the last stone slammed into place behind them where they had just been standing.

The rumbling slowly came to a halt, everyone on the ground as they peered back, Rita's and Milos' feet inches from the rubble, dust covering them like a sheet.

"That could have gone better." Suzuhah's voice pulled everyone out of the moment of silence, and Rita found herself grateful, not only for the words, but that the potion seemed to work.

"Thanks, Milos." She spoke softly to the man who saved her life yet again.

"You are an idiot," he said simply, with no heat, as the young woman from before bent down, slowly pulling them to their feet, relief clear on her face.

Trisha helped steady her as she peered around at the group beside her, briefly noting the fallen rubble inches from her toes. The passageway was small, only allowing about two people to tightly fit shoulder to shoulder. Alex was a little in front of her, holding his wing which was somewhat curled around his body. The blood slowed, but it still looked pretty bad. Suzuhah quickly started patching it up.

"Well, what the heck was that?" Rita asked, gesturing toward the rubble, "Who WAS she? Like, I know she was your sister, I've seen her in visions, but that was…what?"

Milos shifted uncomfortably, and that was when Rita noticed it, the torn pieces of tunic on his arms, a nick on his cheek and another with a bit of blood leaking from his side.

She pulled from that thought, quickly burrowing into her bag, muttering to herself. "Well, here, drink this." She handed him a drink and peered toward the collapsed tunnel. "I can't help but wonder what happened to those Demons, did they actually get away like she said?"

"They escaped." Alex swallowed thickly. "They had to. Mom had to."

Rita wasn't sure if his words were more desperation or a willingness to believe they did and she didn't contradict him. None of them knew, so she was just going to hope they were fine. "Your mother is strong and fast; I have no doubt they got away." Rita smiled faintly toward Alex before gesturing. "Anyway, let's keep moving, we'll patch everyone up when we are away from the murderous psychopath and her goons."

"I can agree to THAT statement," Suzuhah piped up. "It seems the crowd has moved ahead, now that there isn't a blockage. I guess they were all stuck simply because of the small space, but it seems pretty level here."

Rita nodded before turning on her heels and heading down the path. Alex and Suzuhah were right in front of her with the new girl at her side and Milos only a few steps behind, gagging only slightly at the concoction she gave him earlier. Look, she had been trying to improve the taste, but there is only so much you can do when it has to be very precise on certain ingredients and timings.

She shook her head, taking a deep breath before turning to the girl. "I'm sorry, I just realized, I haven't gotten your name."

The woman glanced toward her, a vine of soft leaves falling over her shoulder like hair. "Kara. My name is Kara." She glanced toward Milos before turning back toward Rita. "I'm a Demon you freed from Raynout. I want to help make sure you all stay safe. It's nice to finally meet you, Rita."

"How—"

"We were a public spectacle for a while." Suzuhah shrugged, glancing over his shoulder.

Rita blushed, unable to argue. She cleared her throat. "Well then, thank you. I appreciate everyone's help in keeping these louts safe." Kara raised an eyebrow at her wording, but didn't say anything. Mostly because she suddenly stiffened, peering over her shoulder. She wasn't the only one. Pretty much everyone in their little group hesitated, as if hearing something. "Okay, everyone with a much better perception than me, what is it?"

"It sounds like they are trying to break through." Alex's words were rough, a little hoarse and tinged with panic. "And I think they might be making progress."

"You gotta be—shiesse." Rita cursed before gesturing. "Well, we aren't going to just sit here and wait for them, unless you want to." She gave a sharp look toward Milos. "Let's catch up with the rest and try to hurry them along as best as we can."

The group nodded and, soon enough, they found themselves moving once more. The light stones glowed brightly around them, giving a pseudo warmth to everything. The breeze that Rita felt up until this point was now turning more into a gentle gust every so often, not quite windy, but close.

It was something she hadn't felt in a while, not since Raynout and, on the one hand, she felt a strange giddiness, on the other, a strange sense of unease settled over her.

She didn't like it.

# Chapter Twenty-Six

Milos followed behind, his thoughts racing a mile a minute as they walked. There was no point in running, especially with how small the area was and how hurt some of them were, specifically Alex.

He shuddered, thoughts flicking back to Serena. He hadn't seen her in a while and now he was grateful. He hadn't really noticed when he was above, or maybe he tuned it out like so much else, but...

He shook his head, thoughts flicking to Artorius, trying so desperately to shift away, to survive, only to be slaughtered without remorse. Something he, as an Alertian, was supposed to be able to do.

He squeezed his eyes shut for a moment, using his hearing to not bump into anything for a short time as he tried to shove the memories away. Which Alertian did he want to be? The Alertian he was raised as? Or the Alertian that Lillianna spoke of?

And could he even BE that Alertian when he allowed those who agreed to work with him to die? Could he have saved them when he could barely save Alex and himself? It was Rita, in all her normal stupidity and ingenuity, that gave them the chance to escape. Rita was always underestimated, but, he had to acknowledge, it was only because of her they all even survived this long anyway.

He slowly opened his eyes, gazing on the people in front of him. Suzuhah pulling Alex along, trying to keep a light attitude, Alex holding his wing and glancing back over his shoulder to check on them. Rita peering ahead as always, looking toward something Milos never could see. It was strange. She called herself the least perceptive and yet he would say she was probably the most perceptive of their little group.

His thoughts wandered, no solid place to land or go, he could faintly hear the sound of digging even so far along, that ever-present reminder that they weren't quite safe yet. Then again, they were heading to the Overlands.

As vast as the Overlands felt when he was there before, he knew it wasn't exactly safe. However, it was probably safer than down here at this moment.

Yet, no matter what he did, his mind migrated back, back to the deaths at his hand. Maybe his sister was right, maybe he was sensitive, maybe that was why he was never able to do what he believed he needed to.

They were just Demons that fell, he shouldn't be upset at their demise and yet he was.

"Master." Ari's voice echoed in his head. "You gave them freedom, just like us, they decided to use it to follow you. Don't despair at their loss, for they made their choice and protected you and those important to you."

He barely suppressed a choked sound. Sure, those were his own thoughts, but it certainly sounded like something Ari would say.

He let out a breath, shaking the thought off. He wasn't going to have to worry about it again. There was no one left for him to lead, nor any reason for him to lead.

They would get these people to the Overlands then go their own way, just as they always had in the past.

He heard a sound ahead and peered forward to see they caught up with the back of the pack. It seemed the movement slowed and there were quiet murmurs of confusion from the group ahead of them. Kara moved to the front of their group as the rest of them glanced at each other in confusion.

"Um, what seems to be the issue?" Kara lightly poked a woman holding a small child.

The woman shrugged, peering ahead, the curling horns stark against her pale skin, even paler in the blue light of the surrounding stones. "Something about a perilous walking area. Not sure."

"Great." Rita threw her hands up at that before letting out a sigh. "Did no one check to maintain the only known evacuation area? I mean, it's really dumb if they didn't."

The horned woman glanced back with a faint frown. "No one thought we would actually have to use it and many would have fought, if not for that one." Her gaze shifted to Alex, who winced under her heavy look.

"If not for THAT one, you and your child would be dead right now, lady. Now shut it," Suzuhah snapped, annoyed.

The woman quickly shut up, peering ahead.

Milos wasn't surprised at the woman's reaction. He remembered feeling his own annoyance when Alex used his voice on Milos before, but Suzuhah had a very good point. They waited in quiet silence, a few of them occasionally peering back, expecting Serena to appear at any moment. Or more so, that was what Milos was expecting.

He doubted a collapsed tunnel would stop her for long. She was persistent and obsessive, if nothing else. He sighed. Father got the chance to name her, he remembered hearing, and he hoped she would have serenity and kindness like her name suggested.

Instead, she took more after that woman than her namesake. Milos wasn't surprised, but it still always led to awkward situations of people constantly assuming and then being surprised. There was a reason he never said her name and probably wouldn't have, if not for being startled by her appearance.

Rita held visions of her, but it was another thing to actually see his sister in person, standing in front of him in the Underlands, of all places.

Soon enough, the people started to clear enough for them to take in the situation.

Milos just shook his head as Rita cursed her usual strange words.

"I'm sorry...why is there a PIT in front of us?" Suzuhah's voice pitched upward in sheer annoyance and disbelief.

Kara just seemed to stare as Alex groaned.

In front of them was a long stretch of path that was missing. The only clear route was to one side where people were very carefully using a rope to traverse across the thin walkway, only large enough to sidle sideways. Two people held the rope firmly from either side to help people to hold on in case of slipping. It was wide enough that you couldn't hold on to the other side, but not enough to open wings for flyers to get past.

Milos could see a Demon on the wall below the path, clearly positioned to catch anyone who tipped over or slipped from the rope, their spider-like body clung on and, where the mandibles and head should be, was a beautiful woman with six eyes and silk-like hair. She was poised, moving along under each person before scurrying back to help with the next one. A Drivier, a half-woman, half-spider Demon, usually quite rare, due to their unique make-up. Their silk WAS supposed to be incredibly strong and, looking at the rope again, he realized it wasn't rope, it was a long piece of hardy silk.

The woman with the child gulped before settling herself to go. She grabbed the silk with one hand and held the child close to her chest with the other, taking a deep breath and carefully sidestepping across. The Drivier cooed softly, helping to calm the crying child in the woman's arms.

Milos was honestly surprised to see a Drivier down here. They were incredibly rare Demons, hunted for their silks and chitinous scaling until they were made practically extinct. He never thought he would see one or to see one risking their life to catch any who might fall.

"How did…? Elderly or disabled wouldn't have been able to cross that." Rita glanced over the path, peering over the edge. Clearly, it was a long drop, because she quickly pulled back.

The Demon holding one end must have heard her, because he spoke. "Fyra moved them across while the others that could walk, crossed that way." The man gestured to the spider woman below, her elegant features clear even in the dim light cast from the light stones scattered throughout the tunnel.

Demons kept surprising him. They were instinctual creatures and yet they seemed to sometimes hold more compassion than humans. It always left him flustered.

Soon enough, it was their turn. Kara started crossing, that same boldness as before not fading even now. Alex went next, holding tightly onto the Silk, wincing whenever his wing twisted or brushed the rocky wall behind him. Suzuhah and Rita followed right after. Suzuhah's Vulfulas form was too big for this small space and, even the Drivier's head was barely a few inches from the other wall.

Milos paused, peering over his shoulder as he felt something settle over him. "Go."

"But…" The Demon holding the rope went to argue and Milos shook his head. "I will be fine, cross now. I'll cover the rear."

"If you say so…" The man shook his head and holding the rope tautly, began crossing, pulling himself along and letting the rest dangle down, caught by the Drivier.

"Fyra, right?"

The Drivier peered toward him. Two of the eyes clearly focused on him while the rest kept an eye on the Demon on the path. "Yes," she hissed, the sound more like clicking. "You are the last. Is my assistance necessary?"

He shook his head, and she seemed to relax, clearly aware of who he was. "Then I shall go." With that, making sure the Demon got across, she scurried up and rejoined the group fleeing north. He could appreciate the lack of argument for what it was.

Rita, Alex and Suzuhah waited on the other side with Kara and Trisha ushering the last of the group forward, leaving only Milos on the far side. He nodded to himself and started crossing, hearing the footsteps starting to echo behind. Suzuhah stiffened before the young man called, "Are you kidding? You heard her and decided to stay behind? Are you an idiot?"

Milos ignored him, scooting along the edge. Halfway across, he heard the sound of scraping before, darting around the corner, slightly out of breath and definitely disheveled, was Serena. Their gazes met and her eyes widened as she narrowed in on the situation.

She pulled back in her stance, meeting his gaze fully as he found himself coming to a halt halfway across, feeling a bit of rock crumble under his toes as he stood there.

"Milos, why?" she asked simply, brandishing her sword. "Why won't you come home with me? You are heading to the Overlands anyway. Both of us know this. You aren't seduced by them, or under their control, so…"

"Sorry, Serena, but I can't."

He found the words slipping from his throat before he even noticed what he was saying. He couldn't and he didn't want to go back with her. He would deal with the repercussions of going to the Overlands alone. This wasn't safety, this was simply giving those fleeing a chance they wouldn't have down here.

It was prolonging their lives, which was good enough for him.

With that realization, he tugged the sword out, pointing it back at her. "Stop following us, Serena. You have what you want, you succeeded in your descent even though you are younger than any who has done this in the past. You survived, unlike our siblings, go back to Mother and Father."

"Not without you." She put one foot on the path, sword at her side. "When I found you were missing, I desired to come down even more, not to follow in some Alertian path, but to find you. My dear brother, why don't I take you to safety? Stay with us, stay with me and I will keep you safe. I will protect you in the way we weren't able to protect our siblings. Just like I said before. I need you, brother, I need you to notice me."

"Your siblings." The words came rough from his tongue as he shifted along, his harsh words strange with his sideways shifting across the thin path. "You and I both know they were never mine. And now I know why."

"I don't care if your mother was some courtesan, or some wh— "

"Don't." Milos felt himself snarling at her words.

"You are still from Father, you still lived with us, which still makes you my big brother...and I WILL bring you home." With that, she darted forward, steps light as she put one in front of the other, practically running up the path most had to slide sideways across.

Realizing with a mix of horror and panic, Milos twisted, slamming the sword down, shaking the path in the force of the blow before spinning on his heels, feeling himself slip only briefly before the other foot caught and he leapt forward. A surge of fear shot up his spine and he found his thoughts flailing. Maybe, if he started running like his sister, running, it would have been easier, but the twisting movement almost sent him over the edge and he heard a shout of surprise from beyond; however, he ignored it. He tugged his sword free, feeling bits and pieces of the path starting to collapse as he slammed a foot down behind him, using the same movement to leap forward.

The next bound had him landing oddly and he almost went sideways, he felt steel miss his side, inches from his back as he found himself leaping once more, almost racing across the path, even faster than his sister had gotten to him, his footsteps harsh every time he landed. He wasn't thinking as instinct, pure and unadulterated, flooded his mind. He needed to get away from her. Now. He needed to destroy the path so she couldn't follow them.

*Stay away from me.* He mentally cried, the mental barriers

crumbling in sheer momentary fear.

He heard a startled shout from behind, barely noticing as he felt something crash down hard behind him that didn't feel like his foot. A sharp pain shot up his spine at the same time as his foot…or no, that wasn't his foot, as SOMETHING slammed down behind him, propelling him forward with one last leap, the ground crumbling beneath his foot as he jumped. He skidded across the ground, caught by a pair of hands as he peered back to see the path destroyed and Serena staring at him, her sword embedded in the wall, the only thing keeping her up as the path below her crumbled. She swung backward, tugging the sword free as she managed to land on the safe piece of path behind her, her gaze never leaving Milos.

There was a strange expression on her face as he felt something brush against his arm, scaly and slightly cold before disappearing.

"You—" Her voice caught, her gaze flicking to where he felt something on his arm. "You've been tainted…that courtesan." Her gaze met his as horror settled over his body and he felt himself pale. Panic surged up his throat, his thoughts returned to him, that strange feeling he was so used to suppressing was now front and center. "You are a Demon, big brother."

His gaze snapped down to his arm where he saw the flare of a long, thick white tail, almost more reminiscent of the drega he encountered long ago, though that one was black. Slowly looking back, the darkness was now more illuminated, every detail shone with a clarity that wasn't there before.

Serena's stance, even from across the chasm now between them, was one of shock and a myriad of other emotions. Her gaze met his, the green and gold much more visible against the blue surroundings. "Brother, I guess I know what my next task is." She slowly sheathed her sword, not breaking eye contact. "I will find you again, just as I always have and this time you WILL be mine."

Her words echoed as footsteps settled behind her.

"Come on, let's go." Milos felt a tug on his right arm, then another on his left and he was suddenly pulled backward, stumbling, his mind still frozen. "Ignore the damn crazy psychopath. We need to go before she can get that chance to try to think of something stupid, like catching up." Rita's voice reached his ears loud and clear, and it took all his effort to break away from Serena's gaze, but not before something settled in his thoughts, a voice that was not his own, but was clear as day.

*'I didn't know Demons could be so pretty, my dear, sweet Milos.'*
He swallowed thickly as horrified realization settled over him.
Her mouth hadn't moved. She hadn't spoken a word.
Those were her thoughts…

# Chapter Twenty-Seven

Alex peered back, unable to hide the worry as Suzuhah and Rita pulled Milos away from the edge, the man visibly shaken and pale.

Alex couldn't blame him, unable to pull his own gaze away from the new additions. The long and thick white tail, the curling scales up the side of his face that were a myriad of whites and soft blues and around his neck. His ears shifted, fur-like and pulled back, more reminiscent of an animal than human. His eyes glowed brightly, the same blue as the light stones lining the walls. Horns, quite different from Alex's thick and curled ones, swept backward elegantly, a beautiful white. The features faded as Milos was pulled away and around the corner.

"So beautiful." Kara's voice reached Alex's ears.

The words snapped him out of it and he nodded, hurrying up to Milos, keeping his injured wing back. He reached up, startling him by putting his hands over the man's eyes. He felt the man recoil and heard Suzuhah and Rita yelp in surprise.

"Milos," he let a little of his song into his words, giving them a strange lilt. "We have to go. We need to get these people to safety. We will figure out how to deal with her later, we need you right now, just like always."

They continued, Alex stepping backward so as to stay in front of Milos, almost stumbling in the low darkness of the tunnel before Milos finally slumped. Alex slowly let go as Suzuhah peered over. Rita shook out her hands before crossing them over her chest, watching quietly.

Milos slowly opened his eyes, a strange fear in his expression that quickly returned to the normal stoic. "Right." The word came out clipped and a little hoarse. Alex could relate. "We need to go."

Rita let out a breath as Alex smiled. He nodded. "And we'll figure that out later." He spoke softly. "I'm sorry it came out when it did, but I think it honestly saved your life. The movements and jumps you made were…" Alex shook his head, mind flashing back to when the two were crossing, almost dancing in an area where most others had to slide precariously and slowly. Their steps were so light, almost unheard, if not for the crumbling and crashing of stones as the path was destroyed behind Milos. It was terrifying just to watch. He was grateful Milos survived.

"Also? What is with all the people so obsessed with Demons?" Rita spoke up as she started walking along, Milos only a step behind with Suzuhah at his side just in case he stopped again. She threw her hands up. "First, there is that Demon who was WAY too focused on Alex and now that sister of yours? Like, what is it?" She shook her head. "Even as a human, I don't understand."

"That's because you already have what they want." Kara's voice caused all of them to peer over. "You are willingly surrounded by powerful Demons who see you as family. Who will do anything to protect you."

Rita rolled her eyes and leaned forward. "And that's so difficult, how? I would do anything to protect them. It's what family DOES." She paused, seeming to realize what she said as red flared on her cheeks.

Alex may or may not have stumbled at the words, feeling his own face flush in surprise, he was trying to ignore it as he spun, staring at her.

She was distinctly not looking at him as she crossed her arms over her chest once more. "They are my family." She spoke simply. "Family isn't just blood, after all, and you don't have to force it. If they didn't want to be, then that would have been fine by me. I have my own path I can follow anyway, just like the rest of them. They decided to work with me. I decided to work with them. I don't see why that's so difficult to comprehend."

"You are certainly a strange one." Kara spoke softly. "So many try to force what they want onto others, it makes them feel more powerful, like they have some say or control over the situation. And yet you would be willing to give it up?"

"If it means they can follow their own paths and keep themselves safe? If they truly wanted to walk away, then that is their choice, not mine. God, how is that not obvious?" Rita shrugged and, at that, Alex had to turn away, the impact of the words settling over him.

Would she let them go even after having lost her own family?

He heard footsteps and a yelp. He peered back, startled to see Suzuhah hugging Rita tightly, startling the girl. He must have changed at one point, now that little girl as she hung on tightly. "Thank you, Rita, but don't say that again. I don't plan to leave you or the others any time soon. I don't want to lose those important to me again, you hear me?"

"That's not what I…ugh…" Rita lightly patted Suzuhah's back, her gaze moving hesitantly up to Alex and Milos. Alex found himself shifting forward, leaning against her, unable to hug like he might due to his wing, but she still got the point.

Milos was the most hesitant, his grip on the pieces of hair settled over his shoulder, peering ahead, clearly unsure. Suzuha put a finger to her lips before slipping away. She stepped behind Milos and, with a start, leapt onto his back, causing him to stumble forward in surprise. Rita let out a snort, as Alex chuckled softly, pulling him into their strange little half-hug.

Milos didn't resist, leaning into them in a moment of vulnerability they so rarely saw. It wasn't long before they pulled away as Rita gestured with her head. "Let's go, sappy time over." She was brushing her eyes furiously as she spun on her heels, moving ahead.

Kara's expression was so filled with warmth, Alex thought of his mother at that moment.

"That's good." Her voice was soft as she stared at Milos. "I'm glad."

With that, she followed Rita and, soon enough, their little band was on their way up the path. Wind started to pick up, pulling at them. It was strange; on the one hand, it seemed to push them away, on another, it tugged at them, almost begging them to step closer, to move along. The path slowly started to widen until, finally, they made it into a large cavern. Wind rattled through the tall stones high above, and, to one side, was light. Not the light of day stones or the light of the light stones. It was light from something Alex had never seen before. He saw the people standing around, a few standing in the tunnel, peering around the corner in quiet silence. Trisha and her father waited near the exit. The woman let out a sigh of relief upon noticing them approaching. A moment later, she and her father disappeared into the crowd, leaving them staring in silence.

The group exchanged looks before moving quietly through the crowd, now certain there was no chance of Serena or the Martinets following them.

Alex felt his wings flutter in excitement as he hurried down, the wind growing stronger, the smell a mix of storm and fresh air, a sweet smell that clung to him and drew him ever closer. They reached the tunnel where the people stepped aside, revealing Ari and Leon, staring in shock around the corner.

"Alex. Stop."

Milos' voice reached his ears, and he slid to a stop, peering back. Now that he was closer, he could hear the sound of wind from so close, howling, loud and clear. He was SO close. He wanted to ignore him, but something about Milos' voice stopped him.

The man stepped up to him, peering at the path in sudden understanding. "We are at the edge." He spoke softly. "Which means…" He pursed his lips and nodded. "Be prepared, Alex, you might not like what you see."

*Huh? What was Milos talking about?* He shook the thought off, watching as Milos walked forward, nodding to Ari and Leon, who let him pass, though with a hesitant nod in his direction. He stopped, peering around the corner before letting out a breath, even heard above the raging winds. "As I thought. Is there a path?"

"A small one, but it's dangerous." Leon spoke evenly.

"All of them have been."

Milos stepped forward around the corner and Alex shook his head. What was he talking about?

His mind flashed to the books in his grandfather's home, a few talking about a calamity that occurred a long time ago, but that was over two thousand years ago. He shook his head and hurried up to the two with Rita and Suzuha at his side. They spun around the corner and Alex froze.

Before him was Milos and beyond that…

Was a storm unlike anything he ever saw before. Light broke down through the wide opening where a bit of cliff extended out before he was met with a wall of wind and debris. He hesitantly stepped forward, a strange warmth brushing his skin, but his attention was glued to the roiling behemoth of a storm before him. Lightning crashed far within as winds howled like a raging beast. The very world in front of him, for as far as he could see, was just a tempestuous landscape of death. Far below, barely seen through the howling storm, was land, a wasteland of destroyed rock, sand and nothing.

"Welcome to the edge of the Overlands." Milos' voice was soft, barely heard over the wind. "The lands beyond are known only as the Fallen Cataclysm. Those storms have raged for millennia, can't you feel it? The powerful magic within the winds?"

Alex wanted to deny it, so desperately, but he could feel it. Magic, uncontrolled and ferocious.

"I'm sorry, this destruction has been going on for millennia?" Rita gestured out. "How has it not destroyed this place then?"

"No one knows." Milos shook his head. "I hoped to not see it for myself, but it would explain the vent here…and how no one found it previously." He turned to Alex and the group, the wind tugging at his hair, his entire body silhouetted in light. "The path we need to take is to the left. If we can get to above, we can get away from the Cataclysm and find refuge. If someone is caught by the storm, then they are gone. Do not try to save them or you will be killed as well." The words were stern.

"There is no saving those pulled in." Kara's voice reached their ears.

Alex didn't look back, just listened as she spoke. "There is nothing beyond those winds. Nothing lives beyond that destruction, for so far. It's so quiet."

Alex shuddered at the thought. The world felt so big in his books and now it felt so incredibly small. "That means the Overlands are the same size as the Underlands." Alex swallowed thickly. "And I was able to cross that in only a few weeks."

Milos simply nodded before heading toward the path. "Come, follow my lead, single file." With that, he started walking up the path carved into the side. Alex couldn't move, he didn't want to.

THIS was what he had to look forward to? THIS was the Overlands he dreamed of seeing?

Milos stopped before peering over his shoulder. "Alex. That's not the Overlands, that is a destroyed land, you have not seen what you are looking for yet." With that, he turned back on his heels and continued up.

Alex pursed his lips, peering straight up the cliff side. He wanted so badly to fly, to shoot straight up and see what he meant, but with his wing injured, he knew he couldn't. With a nod and strange resolution, he hurried after Milos, and soon, the others began to follow. He heard Ari and Leon call, telling everyone to move one at a time, that the path was safe.

Milos was stalwart, leading them up, his pace neither fast or slow, simply constant and Alex appreciated it.

He peered up, feeling that strange warmth. When he looked straight up, he could spot the edge of blue, but it was hard with the crash of lightning every so often, the wall of wind seeming to extend endlessly into the sky. He nodded to himself, determined. He was so close. He was grateful for Milos' warning.

The path continued up, switching back at one point, giving them more space away from the wall of wind and then, before long, Alex could see the top. Something green poked and curled over the side, almost like vines, and a faint smile crossed Milos' lips. Alex felt his steps pick up pace and by the time they reached the top, Alex was even with Milos.

He turned his head and froze, breath pulled out of his lungs at the sight in front of him.

Green extended to either side before being met by what looked like golden stalks of something that blew in a soft wind. He looked up and now he could see it, a beautiful blue sky, filled with softly drifting white that looked so much like cotton. An incredibly bright sphere of light beat down at him and he quickly had to look away.

"I wouldn't stare into the sun if I were you." Milos chuckled quietly as Alex turned his gaze back down, peering over the golden field swaying gently before him and, beyond that, he could see the beginning of what had to be homes and then, much farther, barely a speck in the distance, was what could only be a city, glowing brightly in the light, seen even from so far away.

The warmth felt heavenly after the ever-endless chill of the Underlands and, as he stepped forward, the ground beneath him felt almost soft and spongy. His gaze snapped down, his memories pulling up the name from the many books he read.

Grass…soil…

Rita wasn't far behind, and he could tell because she suddenly pulled in a breath as well before saying, "It's beautiful."

Milos pulled Alex forward, nodding toward the golden field in front of them. "This is one of our many farms. This one seems to be the wheat field to the north, not surprised." He stared over it, expression more relaxed than Alex was used to. "We should be safe, for now."

Alex reached forward, lightly brushing the stalks of wheat, a sense of awe and wonder settling over him.

He didn't dare look behind him.

It wasn't long before murmuring filled the area behind him as the refugees soon arrived up the path, their voices filled with a similar awe and wonder.

Alex felt himself smile as he heard footsteps before Ari and Leon joined them, their expressions brightening in delight.

"I finally made it." Alex felt that giddy delight settle through his veins as he peered toward the endless blue sky above. "The Overlands."

"There is a lot to do, but I think for now, we all need a moment to rest." Rita spoke up beside him, her words almost breathless. "All of us went through a lot to get here and I think now is the time for all of us to take a moment to breathe."

Alex found himself settling on the ground, leaning back on his hands, feeling the soft grass and earth below as he leaned back, eyes closed as the sunlight settled over him. He felt pressure on either side of him as two people leaned against him. He briefly opened his eyes to see Rita to one side, with Milos settling beside him on the other, not necessarily leaning, but there. He could hear the people behind him spreading out and settling down as well to rest.

However, for now, he was content. He felt safe in this place, even with Milos' warning. He felt a presence against his back and recognized it as Suzuha. He relaxed. As Rita said, they had a lot to do, but, in that moment, he found himself not caring.

Peering over the beautiful land before him, he felt comforted. He held onto the hope that his mom was safe, much like she had been before, and they were as well. They would find a way to get the refugees to safety, but, for now, he just wanted to rest with the small family he had around him.

The family he found and held so dear.

# About the Author

Julie Boglisch, author and artist, adores writing, artwork, tea and animals. Always surrounded by her two adorable fluffy cats, she finds herself at peace when being creative.

## *Demon's Song*
## Requiem of Stone Book One

Alex always wished to see the Overlands, a place of sunshine and freedom. However, as a slave in the far corners of the Underlands, it was all but a dream. That is, until he's framed for murder and is forced to flee during a demon attack.

Searching for the answers to why he was framed and seeking a chance at the fleeting freedom he's always dreamed about, he journeys to the capital, meeting friend and foe along the way. But the Underlands are both beautiful and dangerous. Having a demon hunter on his tail and a witch whose sole desire is to become the high Seer around him, he's in for quite the journey.

### Chapter One

Alex stared out over the crystal-clear water. Thin streams cascaded from the rocks to one side, falling into the pool that shone with the light from the moss. The rock felt scratchy against his bare feet and his hands were bruised from scrabbling up the steep slope that led to this little cave, but it was worth it. He breathed in the smell of the water and knelt down, delicately dipping one hand. He pulled his hand up, watching the water flow between his fingers.

Water such as this was such a rare thing to find in the Underlands, so pure and untainted. Of course, the rivers were clean, but this, this gentle sparkle and warm glow was just something else. He turned his head up to the ceiling where the moss glowed softly. He wondered if there was water like this in the Overlands? That mythical place of sunlight... Would he have a chance to go there someday? No... he knew. With every fiber of his being, he knew it was impossible. After all, he couldn't leave these lands...

Even so, he reached his hand up, touching the cool moss as his thoughts wavered. He wanted to see it, to see what it was like above the stone. Sunlight, blue skies, meadows...

Alex's hand dropped to his side as he toed the cold water with one foot. He loved the feel of the water on his skin, how it just flowed over in gentle waves, just like he imagined an ocean would. It helped calm his thoughts.

He sighed. For some reason today, it only made him feel a bit depressed. He shook his head before turning away from the spring. He glanced out the cave entrance and quietly cursed. The day stones were starting to wane. He needed to get home soon, or his mother would have his hide. He peered down the steep slope, trying to find a safe path down. After all, this was only his third or fourth time here. He never used the same path, so he didn't know the best way down. The cave was high up, hidden by the curve of the ceiling. He could clearly see one of the day stones, its brilliant yellow white light, beaming down, even as it slowly faded into the blue of the night stone right next to it. If he reached up, he could touch the top of the ceiling. That didn't mean much though, considering the ceiling curved downward, dipping starkly toward his spot.

It made sense. It was near the edge of the Underlands, after all, buried deep underground beneath the stone and earth. He shook his head and focused on finding a path safely down. To his relief, he managed to find the path he used to get up this time and scurried down, just barely avoiding sharp rocks. His skin was already scratched from the climb up and was only made worse as he barreled down the hill. In the distance, he could see his home, the owner of which was the Grand Duke of Liliay. Past that, he could see a road, which stretched to a town in the distance. Off to the other side was a river, the only indication of it being water, being the thin blue band seen against the stark gray.

The slope eased up until he was once more on flat land. He raced ahead, dodging through the tall rocky outgrowths that resembled a forest, something that existed on either side of the house, blocking it from intruders on all sides except from the town.

At least, that was what his mother called the rocky outgrowths, but she was told that by her mother so who knows?

He took a sharp corner around one particularly big outcropping and came upon a large, but squat home, being only about two stories. The dirt path stood on his right, weaving out of sight. He could almost see the set of gates, blocking the way in. He turned toward the home, hurrying up to the delicate entranceway. It held a front porch with wood double doors and wide windows, set with weak light stones. He could see Riviera working on the house, repairing parts of it that had rotted away and replacing what he couldn't fix with stone. He was standing on a stone ladder, the dual sides stopping it from pushing into the rotting wood. Alex slowed down, wincing as the pain from his sore feet was made known to him now that he was stopped.

"Yo, Alex. Good to see you back!" Riviera called down, as he continued hammering the board into place, his signifying wrist chain jangling with a steady clacking sound. It was thick and looked heavy.

"Watch what you're doing," Alex called up right as Riviera yelped, barely avoiding smashing the hammer into his hand.
He grinned sheepishly. "Well, yes... Anyway, better get inside. It's late."

"I know." Alex waved him off as he stepped up to the doorway, ignoring the white flowers decorating either side of the entrance, the only other form of life and the only flower that somehow managed to survive in the Underlands. He pushed the door open as slowly as possible, peering around the doorframe.

The inside was quiet. There was barely a light on in the house. He opened the door more and almost cried out as the Grand Duke of Liliay stepped from the shadow of the doorway with a 'boo.'

"Duke..."
The Duke frowned and Alex quickly adjusted his wording. "Grandpa!"

Alex placed a hand on his chest to catch his breath as the Grand Du...Grandpa gave a hearty laugh with great booming chuckles. He was fit for his age, but the wrinkles and liver spots were quite visible on his skin. Wispy white hair was partially slicked back and a wide smile with surprising white teeth shone as brightly as the pale skin of an Underlander.

His signifier, a delicately made earring shaped in the form of a pair of wings, swung gently from his right ear as he turned and flicked on the lights. It was pretty, the signifier his grandfather had. It was carved of the finest metals, completely unlike the clunky signifier of a slave like Riviera and himself. After all, the duke's signifier was part of the upper class, a sign he was of a higher caliber than those bound by wrist or sometimes neck chains made of cold harsh metal. He looked down at his wrists. He heard his grandfather step down the hallway and turned his head up.

Alex watched as the stones heated up like the rising of the day stones, slow yet sure, until they were glowing with a soft ruby color.

"Lad, that's what you get for worrying an old man and your poor mother. Don't you know what time it is?" he asked, quieting his chuckles into a knowing look as he turned to face Alex. Alex gave a sheepish grin as he shrugged, toeing the rug.

Grandpa sighed and shook his head before gesturing. "Well come on, son, come inside. Your mother's making dinner as we speak."

Alex groaned.

"Oh, don't be like that! You know she tries her best. Plus, if you got home before all day stones died for the day, you would have had a chance to make something yourself," Grandpa chided, his tone lighthearted. Alex sighed, mentally agreeing with the assessment. It was partially his fault for staying out so late. "Now hurry on into the kitchen, I will see you two when dinner's ready."

Alex nodded as Grandpa walked off. Alex watched him go. The foyer was now lit bright enough to showcase the splendid items of porcelain and jewels. A picture frame sat over a mantelpiece, front and center.

He recalled his mom and, vaguely, his dad both eyeing it oddly when he was growing up. He personally didn't mind the picture. It showed a knight holding the head of a grotesque creature in the sign of victory, sword gleaming in what Alex could only deduce was sunlight. Green could be seen as far as the eye could see in the picture and Alex always wondered if that was mostly what the Overlands consisted of, sunlight and green. What an amazing sight it must be...

He shook himself from his thoughts, trying to convince himself, as usual, that there was no way he would be able to go there, no matter how much he dreamed of it. He hurried to the left toward one of the two hallways. Traversing the long halls, he finally arrived in a room where the distinctive smell of burning came from. He winced before he opened the door and stepped inside.

Close to the stove was his mother, running around in a frenzy. Her frazzled expression was only amplified when smoke billowed out of the stove when she opened it.

Alex shook his head as his mother gave a quiet whine. He grabbed the nearby extinguisher and liberally spread the gunk that came out of it onto the fire. Slowly, it died, and he stopped, letting the last of it dribble to the floor as he sent his mom an exasperated look.

"Oh, hey, honey..." she said somewhat sheepishly, though confusion still sat on her face. "I could have sworn I set it right this time. Four hours and fifty minutes at one hundred and twenty-five degrees."

"Mom, did you check to see which was time and which was temperature?" Alex deadpanned.

His mother looked at him like he had multiple heads before she picked up a surprisingly unscathed box and looked at it. She pointed and said, "Yeah. It says right... here..."

She stopped before glancing guiltily at Alex. Alex resisted sighing as he gave his mother another deadpan expression. "Let me guess, you were supposed to set it at four hundred and fifty degrees for one hour and twenty-five minutes."

"Well, that's all in the past. I made some sandwiches earlier, and I only nicked myself a few times this time."

"Why...Mother...are you in the kitchen again?"

"Because Agatha called in sick, and you know how my lor..." She stopped before shaking her head and continuing, "Callen likes to make sure his people are okay. She's on bed rest until she feels better, and the others have other priorities."

Alex shook his head, wondering about that. The others would have come running to stop his mother from entering the kitchen. Alex stepped over to the cold storage. An ice stone sat in the corner, cooling the small cubby considerably. He looked around at the shelves before spotting the plate of sandwiches. He grabbed one after pulling off the paper wrapping and stepped out. He bit into it.

Damn. How was it she was so bad at the directions, but could make something taste so good?

"Hey, Alex, honey?"

"Hm?" He asked around a mouthful of sandwich.

He swallowed as he turned to his mother, who was already cleaning up the place.

Her black hair fell in sheets around her thin shoulders. The green dress she wore almost every day showed a petite figure. She had long fingers and wide brown eyes that seemed to look at everything with a type of naivete.

He knew his mother was nowhere near naive though, even as she turned, exposing the scar on her neck and the thin chains around her wrists. He shivered as he remembered one story she told him about her childhood, when she talked about it.

It happened long ago, before Alex was even born. Supposedly, she was seen as a rare specimen. Alex didn't ask why. Mother never explained, but that made it so she was often feared. In this particular instance, she'd just gotten through a... beating, as she phrased it.

Alex had a sinking suspicion she meant something else, but didn't interrupt as she continued to explain. It was around that time she met Father; they fell in love at first sight, but...fate was cruel. Father was promptly sold, punished for grabbing her affection and she was secluded, unable to even leave her room.

Thankfully, after that, the duke, who managed to buy Father not long after that initial exchange, found her and bought her off her original owner.

Still, all the things she left out...it sent chills up his spine. After, she insisted he knew how lucky they were to end up working here, under the Grand Duke. Alex glanced toward her wrists, watching the chains shift against her skin, scars crisscrossing thinly across her flesh, just like it did around her neck.

In comparison, his skin was practically unblemished. He knew from the conversations with the others, he was qualified as a slave, property of the duke. All he could recall was the duke caring for him like a parent would.

He pulled himself from his thoughts as his mother huffed and put her hands on her hips. "You weren't listening to me again, were you?"

"That depends," Alex replied, looking toward the stove.

His mother let out a long sigh and dropped her hands. "Alex..." She shook her head and looked him in the eye. "I heard that the Martinets are coming through soon, so please stay in the house, okay? You don't wear your signifying wrist chains anymore."

Alex glanced at his wrist, vaguely remembering the cold bite of the chains. He couldn't remember when they came off, but he knew he was still very young. It was only thanks to the Duke, he got them off, and his mother. For some reason his mother fought with a vicious tenacity to have him no longer wear them, even though he was given them by the Martinets of the time.

Once the Martinets left, the duke conceded very quickly, supposedly having wanted to do that anyway. Still, it meant he had to avoid Martinets like the plague.

Why did his mother insist on his being removed again? Part of him didn't mind, considering how harsh, clunky and overbearing they were. Still, he vaguely wondered where they were now.

His thoughts were quickly returned to the present when his mother continued, "Both the duke and you could end up in trouble. So, don't make it hard on him. The Capitol is already giving him a hard time for not trading in his old slaves for new ones. We don't want to make it worse."

Alex hesitated. He was one of the only ones that worked for the duke that didn't have the signifiers. For some reason, everyone else was so used to it, they felt weird without them. Alex couldn't fathom why.

Still, she took his silence as acceptance, relief clear in her voice as she thanked him. "Now get to bed, it's late."

"Yeah, yeah." Alex waved, muttering under his breath as he walked toward the doorway.

"And sorry about not having dinner ready for you. I need to bring what I can to the others."

Alex nodded, knowing how busy his mother was. Even with her botched cooking, she did have to feed the duke and the other slaves. He also knew the duke planned to meet them at dinner, but Alex doubted there would be enough food if he went, so he stuck with the sandwich. His mother sent him a kiss, which he promptly looked away from, before calling another good night. Alex let the door swing shut and climbed up the stairs, chewing on the last of his sandwich.

He would have to watch out for those Martinets. From the stories he heard from the older slaves, it wasn't pretty to be caught by them. In all honesty, he would be seen as free bait, considering he no longer held a chain tag.

Maybe he should stay in the house for the next few days...

He shook his head and stepped into his bedroom. It wasn't big by any stretch of the imagination, but it was cozy. A bed was set off against a small window with a stand next to it made of stone. On top of the stone side table was a simple, yet elegantly designed light stone. He wasn't sure what the history was behind the stone, since he was never able to go into school or anything. From what he'd gathered from the books in his grandfather's library, they were leftovers from the age of the demons, a race very similar to humans, long since thought to be extinct.

Alex gently touched the light stone, feeling it pulse slightly under his fingers. To him, they felt almost alive in a way that was different from the normal everyday stone that surrounded him and everyone else in the Underlands. He closed his eyes, feeling the slight pulsing of the light stone. He wondered what it was like above. What did a sky look like? The sea? He wasn't sure he could even imagine, what with being confined to the manor his whole life.

He knew he was luckier than many people. He couldn't deny the fact. Even so, it felt like he was just there, another person to live his life and die.

He didn't want that.

He opened his eyes and pulled his hand away from the light stone and turned to his bed. He fell onto it and curled into himself. It was a pipe dream, he knew. There was no escaping the Underlands, even more so for those seen as slaves.

Yes, he didn't have the mark, or the chains like he once did, but that didn't make a difference down here. Unless you were known, unless you were part of a family, an elite, then you were nothing more than a piece of property. His hand slammed into the bed, feeling the mattress give under his hit. After all, a signifier, the only indication of where you lay, was created upon birth. The only signifiers he ever had were chains with no meaning, something his mother threw away for him years ago, almost to the point where he couldn't even remember what they were. Yet he couldn't get a new set, even if he wanted to, after all, the census had him qualified as a slave, even now.

Why was he even thinking this? These thoughts never got him anywhere and only ever made him more upset.

Still, even though he knew how hopeless it was, he couldn't seem to give up, he would see the Overlands, just once. He let out a sigh and uncurled his fists. He would think on this tomorrow. He needed to get some sleep tonight, especially if the Martinets were coming. He'd need all the rest he could get.

# Other books by Julie Boglisch
at
Rogue Phoenix Press

## *Epidemic*
### The Elifer Chronicles Book One

It has been forty years since America closed its borders and separated from the world following the Vietnam War. In the ensuing years, the country has developed in incredible ways, or at least, that is what Maxwell and Karina, a set of twins from a community deep in the forests of New England, have been told all their lives. In a town surrounded by larger than life trees and crags, they didn't have a reason to believe otherwise.

That belief is put to the test when they find their house ransacked, their mother missing, and their only chance to live is outside of the barriers they've grown used to. Barriers... that they never realized existed.

## *Retrieval*
### The Elifer Chronicles Book One

Maxwell and Karina, twins who are the cure to a disease which is ravaging the country, find themselves journeying to the distant locale of Collern City in search of their missing mother. Meeting strange allies and dealing with dangerous enemies, they must learn to navigate the treacherous streets and discover more about what is going on behind the scenes in both the gated community and outside of it.

Meanwhile, their guardian and friend, Lex, struggles to deal with his family's desires. He finds himself caught between his own wish to flee his home, never to return. and the wish of his brother, Caym, who desperately wants him to stay.

www.ingramcontent.com/pod-product-compliance
Lightning Source LLC
Chambersburg PA
CBHW060351260626
47160CB00006B/2273